Fated to be Monsters

by

J. Von Tobel

Cover Art by *Teddi Black*

The Wild Rose Press, Inc.
PO Box 708
Adams Basin, NY 14410-0708
Visit us at www.thewildrosepress.com

Publishing History
First Edition, 2025
Trade Paperback ISBN 978-1-5092-5995-3
Digital ISBN 978-1-5092-5996-0

Published in the United States of America

Dedication

For everyone who is angry
and doesn't want to be.

Praise for J. Von Tobel

"…a magical adventure with lovable characters and a bold, page-turning plot. You won't regret buying this book. Von Tobel is a master of fantasy!"

-Joel Brigham, Brigham Editorial

"It has all the best of humor and dire stakes for characters who draw you into their struggles, hopes, and dreams from the very first page."

-Danielle & Vincent Morrone,
"The New Apprentice"

"Curse of Flame is an immersive, gripping fantasy. The world-building, character development, and magic systems are flawlessly portrayed and had me rooting for the characters from start to finish!"

-AA DaSilva, author of "Periphery"

Chapter One

They were too late. The smoke trails rising in the distance made that obvious. Anca was already beyond her authority, marching into another Nobil's territory to hunt a monster that wasn't her responsibility. She didn't cross this line for her legacy or the arrogant queen. Anca Sulia hoped that lives could be saved. Like many things in her life, it didn't work out that way.

The town of Pese was gutted. People emerged from their homes as Anca and her entourage of monster hunters rode into town. Flimsy thatch huts were abandoned or flattened in the madness. Ivy-wrapped brick homes, lit with dingy light bulbs from a past age, sheltered the scared, sleepless survivors. Small raindrops plinked against the rusty, aged metal roofs and darkened lamp posts.

Two other riders flanked her. Doia Marin, her avuncular advisor, was prickly as usual. The other was a leech in a man's body named Rezgal Chertse, representative of the queen.

"Wasted. The idiots. There's nothing of value left," Chertse said.

The stubby man curled his fingers tight around the reins of his horse and sniffed through his button nose. He adjusted the cream-colored hat on his head before flourishing his ledger of debts.

More villagers emerged from their homes as word

spread. Tense jaws and worried looks greeted her as she rode into town: a Nobil of a Hunting Household and hand of the throne. When Pese's hunting Nobil was not there to help, Pese was forced to defend itself. A hopeless option. That anyone survived was a small miracle.

"They didn't have a choice," Marin said in a low voice. "They've nothing but farm equipment. I haven't seen a single, damned iron sword or coilgun between them."

The fight torched their fields, eviscerating any chance of paying their yearly tithe. Now it was Anca's mess to clean up. There were casualties to count and agricultural shortfalls to assess. The Nobil who should have been here was too busy drinking himself blind at the capital. All the crown could be bothered to do was figure out how much food it was out and levy the debt on the survivors.

Despite the agonized throb in her chest, her features were emotionless. A well practiced ruse. Anca twisted the tawny braid of hair over her shoulder and turned her sharp chin toward the charred western end of town. It was razed to the ground, their plentiful fields gone with it. Cornstalks had gone up like matchsticks. Heads of lettuce were turned into blackened, flaky marbles. The fire had begun in town and spread farther than they anticipated.

Marin scratched at his fuzzy, red hair and wiped a few flecks of stray ash from his graying beard. He was dressed similar to herself: a black riding cloak sodden by the rain. The blue-dyed armor underneath was adorned with bones and fur tethers. The only difference between them was her ridiculous plume helmet. Seated with the crest of her family, it was expected of her station.

"Don't play to their excuses." Chertse snapped his head back to Marin. "There are ways to avoid a Shadow beast without putting your entire town to the flame. Reckless. Stupid. These low people surprise me more every day."

"People died. Try to show some respect."

Chertse brandished his ledger like a weapon.

"Do you know the consequences of this? We had to requisition food from the royal stores to cover losses from the blight in the south. The queen even had to cut corn from the banquet menu last month. They won't have fields to till and work. Flame bless, we don't even know how many people of working age died. Did they even kill the creature?"

"Quiet," Anca said.

Her green eyes did not tear away from the ruined homes to the west. A body slumped against one of the torched homes. His final emotion had been fear. The terrified grimace forever stuck on his waxy features. She looked away before she could imagine his last moments.

"Anca." Marin intoned his head but kept his eyes on the Nobil. "We need to proceed."

She pursed her lips. This was hardly her first compliance order, but it never sat right with her. Her grandparents, her parents, all of them had done this for decades now. Count the bodies, let the Rezgal set the debt, and leave them to rebuild. Flame help them if Chertse suspected unrest. Were that the case, she'd fulfill her other purpose: jailor.

Anca nodded and Chertse cackled.

"Let's remind them who is in charge." He gnashed his teeth into an ugly smile and rode back to where the townspeople gathered. Anca gestured toward the other ten hunters she brought with them.

"Marin, help Chertse with his assessments. You three," she pointed at the hunting guards nearest her, "start counting bodies."

Marin cleared his throat. "I'd rather you not leave, ma'am."

"I need to ensure the beast is dead. It wouldn't be the first to stand back up after appearing to have passed on."

"You have the authority to keep that maniac behaving. I don't."

She glanced at Chertse as he excoriated a few survivors for not bowing. Such loutish behavior was expected. At least he had not struck them, a sad thought. Anca refused to use such tactics, and it had left her an outcast among the order. No one else was bothered about where their wealth came from.

"That maniac is unfortunately in his rights to do what he wants here. Just keep the people in line. If they don't act out, he won't have a reason to."

Anca noticed large prints in the mud, similar to a bear in size and shape, crossing back over the many impressions left by fleeing townspeople. She dropped from her horse and stroked its mane as she left it. The tracks ran through the ruined west end of town. It was nothing but blackened wood supports and crumpled bodies. Some were crushed to a pulp under a behemoth paw and others ripped to gory shreds. Anca drew a great spear from her back. The fearsome weapon had no chance of killing the creature by itself, but it would buy her enough time to come up with a plan.

Broken glass and burned-out light bulbs mingled between blood and dirt. Clockwork tractors were shattered alongside chewed corpses. A convoluted engine of brass gears and wiry tubes, the mechanical wonder could haul four times what a horse could at twice the speed. Each was a treasure from before the Great War. It would be a grievous loss to any community

The tracks grew sloppy and labored. The pools of blood became more frequent until it was a river of dried black stains running through a fence and into a wooden hovel made of bundled reeds. The walls were wrenched open, and the beast laid over the shattered furniture inside. Sprawled on its belly, the creature finally died here.

It was fifteen feet long and ten feet high at the shoulder by Anca's guess. It looked like a bear at first glance. Its muscled limbs were sliced, stabbed, and burned. Its back feet had five toes, but its forepaws bore gnarled fingers. Each digit ended in an avian talon as long as her forearm. A pair of fangs and tusks crisscrossed from its short snout.

At a distance, it appeared dead. That was an easy mistake to make. She had seen too many Shadow beasts that learned the benefits of playing dead until its prey was within reach. Anca leveled the spear at its rib, one of its hearts likely a few inches within. Her arms tensed, feet slopping through the mud. A sharp breath drew past her lips and she held it, hesitating just outside of its reach.

Anca bent at the knees and listened for breath. A fly buzzed over her head and set down onto its open eye. She exhaled when the sodden, bloody heap did not rise to swipe at it. She rose from her squat and looped the strap of her great spear back over her shoulder. Moving its head back and forth, a large purple tongue slid out of its mouth.

For all the centuries they struggled against them, there was so much they did not know. Were they born in broods like any other animal or woven into existence, fully formed and hungry for violence? They were tinged with the elemental magic of Shadow. The enemy of everything that breathed.

Another rider approached from down the road. She knew the familiar pattern of Marin's pulse from a distance. Of course it was him. No one else in the entire Household would ignore a direct order aside from her oldest family friend.

Stubborn bastard, she thought.

He slowed next to the collapsed hovel as Anca removed a small bag from her belt.

"Sweet sunshine, that's a big one."

"I believe I told you to help the Rezgal." Anca did not turn to him. She ran her fingers through its fur, still sizing up the creature.

"It's taken care of. There's uh…" He looked back to the ruined village. "There's far fewer of them than we expected. We're still counting the bodies."

Anca ran the tip of her nail across one of its teeth and listened to the hollow scrape.

"They paid dearly to kill it. I'm not sure I would call this a victory though."

She opened its jaws wider and gripped one of the tusks. She wished she faced this creature sooner. Better her than the people of Pese. Maybe if she pursued it across Household borders. Maybe if she disregarded the rules of the order.

House Sulia was a dedicated Household. No one expected her to break the rules. Anca chewed on her lip as she stepped away from the creature.

"I spoke to Nobil Bire about this two weeks ago."

"Did you now?" Marin's tone was resigned, not surprised.

"I was tracking it when it slipped into Nobil Bire's territory. I knew it was more than just some Shadow wolf or razor owl."

"Did he listen?"

She chuckled with all the aggravation in her chest.

"Oh yeah, he sobered up straight away and saved the day. Didn't you see him?" Her features flattened as she scowled at Marin. "What do you think?"

"And once it slipped over the line," Marin mused.

"It was not my business any longer. Would you stop that? I don't need you reminding me."

Anca pulled out a silver box and a pack of matches. Runes were smithed into it and the metal held a dull warmth. Marin merely watched her work. She could predict what he would say next. It annoyed her so badly that her teeth ached.

"You think I should have pursued it anyway?"

Marin sniffed a wad of snot into his throat and spat it out.

"Do you think you should have?"

Anca nodded. "The town isn't coming back from this. So much for enforcing the queen's will. There won't be anything here in a year. They've lost at least thirty people to defend their home, and the crown is just worried how the crop yields will be affected."

"I would offer some cynicism, if I may." Marin leaned forward on his saddle, "This isn't our land and these aren't our people. If they've got an ax to grind with their Nobil, they can take it up with the queen. We aren't here to make their lives better. That was Bire's job."

That name again. Nobil Bire. A drunkard with a dozen bastards scattered across the country. There were plenty of Nobils that made her hate the legacy in her veins, but he might have been at the top of her list.

"He wasn't here. And what are the other Households going to do? Give him the far table at the next gathering?"

She made deep cuts across the creature: arteries, joints, lymph nodes, anything that would send the purifying fire through its body. It was easy to imagine the knife in Bire's chest.

"He owes us. That's something you can take right to the throne," Marin said.

"The queen can hang if this is justice."

Marin chuckled and glanced over his shoulder a bit too fast to be casual.

"We don't need to be antagonizing them and getting our food stocks rationed. We would do well to send Sir Chertse home with the impression that we all acted to the letter of the queen's expectations."

"There's got to be another way to do this, Marin. This isn't right. It's not even well intentioned."

"It's just the way things are. I don't like it either."

Anca blew out a frustrated breath as she uncorked the silver box. The oil glistened like a star-filled sky bound in a bottle. The fluid dripped down the creature's fur and worked into the deep slices across its body.

"Not going to give it to the villagers this time?" Marin asked.

The body had some use. Furs could be turned into clothing. Bones carved into tools. The flesh could be used as food, but you'd be hard pressed to find someone willing to take that risk on a Shadow beast. Though with how low food stocks were across the territories, maybe not.

The Households kept skulls of their kills as trophies. They were meant to commemorate the fallen who helped bring the beast down. If the town kept it, it might give them some courage. It could be a reminder that despite everything they lost, they prevailed where even a Nobil would struggle.

However, that might look like a reward. With Chertse eager to punish them for destroying their crops and losing young, strong laborers, it would not be permitted. At least not without punishment upon herself.

Anca glanced at the brands on the back of her hands. The scars had faded over the years, but she could still make out the royal seal they burned into her. Brands, she thought, brands of disloyalty. No one escapes their transgression.

"I've learned my lesson." She popped the cap back into the vessel. "Return to Chertse and tell him we've burned the beast. I'll follow soon."

"Understood, young Sulia."

"That's Nobil, old bastard." Anca smiled and flipped him off.

"And my title's Doia, not old bastard."

"Though you are one."

"Don't remind me." Marin winked and rode back through the ruined town.

Once he was out of sight, she drew her knife and went to the creature's head. She jammed her blade into the gums and pressed the tooth back. Anca grunted, but the knife ripped through flesh as the tooth came free. She cleaned it off and slipped the trophy into a pouch on her belt.

Maybe she could have it both ways.

Anca lit a match and tossed it onto the corpse. Green flames leaped up along its fur as unique minerals purged the remainder of Shadow's hold on the body. Its limbs wriggled and jaws snapped without thought. Black steam rose from the deep cuts in its skin and evaporated in the dim sunlight. The green fire turned red as the oils exhausted themselves. Anca climbed into the saddle and rode away from all of this death that could have been avoided.

The crowd still hung about. Rezgal Chertse looked over the shoulder of one of the scribes as the final records were checked. Chertse pointed his stubby finger at a detail with an eager flourish. Marin waited by the road with a few of her Hunting Guard.

Anca rode across the square to the remaining villagers and held the bloody fang up for all of them to see. She wanted to extol their bravery. Even though they lost loved ones, they could still memorialize their strength. However, she was expected to be cruel. She would have to conjure venom into her voice to not arouse suspicion from Chertse.

"This is a piece of the beast that trampled your lives. Merely a tooth, it is a reminder of your failure to the crown. My Household, the Household who tends your land, and the sun-blessed authority of Queen Astasia herself have been shamed by your actions. Because of you, people will starve this winter. Make no mistake."

Anca knitted her eyebrows in a scowl. Chertse's face was buried in his ledger alongside the scribe. The idiot would not be listening very closely.

"Keep this and remember it. For those you lost.

Those who fought and died here. Look at it. It's all you have. I have burned the rest."

She threw the tooth onto the ground in front of her. It landed on a dry patch of dirt where they would easily find it.

"Use it to remember your dead. Use it to remember how hard you fought."

Several of the townsfolk shared confused glances and muttered to each other. Some of them understood. Others were too scared to consider anything but their grief. Anca did not linger to see if they would all figure it out eventually. She rode over to Chertse.

"Do you have what you need? I would like to begin the journey back to my own lands."

Chertse grinned as the scribe made one final alteration to the long scroll of losses, damages, and debts.

"We do, Nobil Sulia. We can be ready to ride within the hour. Your Doia tells me the beast is dead. Is this true?"

"It has been burned with sanctified oils as the code calls for."

"Damn your codes, all I need is the yes. The queen's will has been enacted. I am satisfied. Queen Astasia will be pleased with these results and of your own behavior, Nobil Sulia."

Chertse grinned with wet lips. He was too pleased about the sorrow he inflicted. Anca forced a small smile and tried not to gag at the effort. She gave him a polite half-bow before riding over to Marin.

"Sun-blessed authority?" Marin asked under his breath.

"They will remember that beast for the rest of their lives."

"Inconvenienced the queen and the Households?"

"It wasn't a pleasant ride out here." Anca held his gaze and tried to not crack.

After a moment, Marin waggled his eyebrows. Unable to fight the chuckle in her chest, she looked away before she would smile. "They killed the damn thing. They deserve some kind of trophy."

"There it is," Marin groaned.

"Don't get on me about it after all that jeering back there."

"You're not even a little bit worried about more punishment? Do I need to remind you how long it took for those brands to heal?"

She was not afraid, not anymore. Anca would suffer again if it meant breaking this cycle. There were more towns out there exactly like Pese. Behind crumbling walls, equipped with rusty tools from a dead world, their people starved as the Nobils heaped praise on themselves.

This is not who she thought she would become. Anca was determined to reverse this suffering.

Chapter Two

The storm was blown out by brisk, northern winds that swept into the queen's country. It gave Anca and her riders just enough time to dry out their cloaks by the time they reached her homelands. The sun was high in the cloudless sky and Bastion Sulia could be seen from miles away. Sanuli spread out from the fortification like high weeds around a limbless tree. Farther out from it, farmlands sprouted from the fertile soil.

The majority of homes were made of aged timber or unevenly mortared brick. They mimicked the eccentric architecture of the capital: arching loops and ovular windows. A song rose from the open window of a tavern. The tune was giddy. It was certainly not about her.

Her legacy made their full adoration impossible to earn. Her grandfather executed dozens in his time. Her mother, paired with her father's keen tongue for politics, had brought even more rebellious towns to heel. It was no secret she had been taught to break morale alongside history, mathematics, and archery.

Anca did everything to shake that mantle. They were fed as best she could. They did not yearn for the upheaval of change. That was more than what she could say of others. She thought of Nobil Bire, the slick bastard. There would be a reckoning. She would ensure that.

Bastion Sulia consisted of three, five-sided towers of staggering heights. The roofs pointed like spikes up at the sky. She looked at the highest window of the tallest tower. It was open to cold winds that washed across the plains. She was certain Victor, her perpetual and unwilling fiancé, was composing flighty poetry or painting yet another landscape.

The bastion's stone doors slowly slid into the earth as metal gears drew them down. The words carved above the gates roughly translated to "You go no farther." It was a credo against invaders credited to her ancestors, the first to draw their blades against Shadow and its beasts. The truth was her family was paid first for their stubborn defense. There was no love lost between the Households and the throne, but that did not matter as long as the money flowed.

A horn blew as Anca and her company passed through the stone gates. Guards who had been left out of the company beat their chests and growled maxims in the old tongue of their land. On the other side of the parade ground, her fiancé walked out to greet her.

Victor Kisu's hair was styled in unchanging, pampered perfection. Blond and twirly where fashion said it should be. Voluminous to frame his sharp cheekbones. He favored the decadent clothing the courts were known for. Today, he wore a silky, light blue doublet with filigree lined shoulders and a high collar. His gray trousers seemed modest by comparison, but she knew they were made of the finest wool. Even when he did not put on airs, Victor made sure to have the best.

He had never been a hunter. Poetry, politics, fashion, and art critiques were his realms of combat. Their conversations were polite, but they had nothing in common. She dismounted and crossed the ground toward Victor.

"Anca, shall I call a feast?" Marin asked.

"No. See the horses to the stables and find out if anything happened while we were gone."

"But we have just returned from the field. It's customary."

Marin knew the traditions were important to all of the hunting guards. They should feel that their Nobil had faith in them and celebrated their work. On a better day, she could have swallowed it.

"We didn't do anything worth celebrating. Get to work."

Anca turned from her Doia and walked into Victor's arms, but did not return his embrace. It was important to him that people saw them hug and touch often. It made them appear to be in love, he said.

"As bad as you thought?" Victor asked.

"I need a bath."

"I think all of you do. Especially Marin."

They entered the bastion and followed the winding stairs, going from the first tower to the third, and upward to their chambers. The passages and rooms of the bastion were bare, but elegant. Humble by design and artisanal in craftsmanship. There were no gold fringes, experimental architecture, or exotic trophies as the aristocracy was known for. The walls were made of a light gray stone, accented by the occasional blue banner stitched with the navy seal of House Sulia. This was a Household bastion. It was no place for excess.

Anca hardly noted the servants as they passed by. Victor made some idle chatter, but she had no stomach for conversation. The more her thoughts dwelled on today, the more she could not escape the truth. She was a part of the problem no matter how she insisted she was somehow different.

The main table in their personal chambers was made of polished cedar. Servants carried in pots of stew and baskets of bread for dinner. A roaring hearth stood across from their four-poster bed. Above the flames, the leering, avian skull of her first kill was mounted on an oak placard.

In the corner of the room was her armory: a massive, wooden cabinet that towered over both of them. Her eye caught a sword tucked into the second row. The jeweled pommel glimmered back at her despite the thin layer of dust coating it. She rubbed it clean, bothered at the idea of any of her weapons going unused for so long.

It had been her mother's sword. That sword killed more beasts than Anca had hunted so far. It was the same sword pointed at the throats of hungry people. Anca slipped the great spear off of her back. It clanged to the floor and rolled to the foot of their bed.

Anca glanced at the far window. As she had predicted, his painting easel and brush set had been brought out. He captured the dull, green color of the lands and the pale light that the cold sun cast everything in. She conceded that he was talented, even if she did not care for landscape paintings.

"You're letting all the heat out the window."

"A small price to pay for artistic accuracy." He took a bite from a dinner roll and sized up his next brush stroke.

The smell of lavender drifted from their personal bathing chambers. As she did with her spear, she yanked the chainmail over her head and whipped it to the floor. Once past the doorway, Anca stripped off her loose, broad-lace shirt then her breeches. She flipped her undergarments against the wall as she approached the steaming tub ahead.

Usually bundled behind armor or corsets, it was a relief to let her curves be as they were. Her figure was lean, sculpted into shape by constant practice and a life in the field. Her rich diet gave her enough shape to fill out a dress, but she was glad to not have anything more than that. In the face of monsters that could break stone and crush bone, she needed to be fast.

The steam-shrouded bathing room was made of soapstone to hold warmth. Arched ceilings were built to cycle the warm air back down. She ran her hands through her oily hair and inhaled as her feet crossed the chilly floor. On the other side of the room, the door to a servant's quarters stood partly open.

She sank into the wooden tub, the water stinging her hips, waist, then shoulders as she sank into it. Surrounded by a white sheet for privacy, only a small gap remained for her to come and go. Despite the burn, it felt good to scrub between her fingers and toes. Lavender flowers floated across the bath water. Her favorite bloom, she crumbled one of the leaves and breathed deep.

Her hands flushed the steaming water through her hair and settled against the wooden side of the tub. How many people in Pese had taken a bath scented with lavender? Would they even recognize the scent?

She felt ill at the thought. This hot water was decadent. The flower petals were an indulgence. Anca fought the impulse to wrench the tub onto its side. Tears stung the corners of her eyes. She pounded her fist against the wood, grinding the flowers in her clenched hand against the weeping urge.

"Stop it," she chided herself.

A servant, dressed in simple black clothes, appeared with a small jug of steaming water and an armful of cloth. Anca let the crushed petals fall back into the water.

"Is the bath to your liking, ma'am?"

"Yes."

The servant was around ten years older than Anca. Her curly brown hair was streaked with gray and tucked into a square hat. Her hands were callused from work, but she was well fed by the softness of her cheeks. As much as Anca tried to recall her name, it eluded her. She once tried to know everyone who served in the bastion. The names were getting away from her since she became Nobil.

"I've brought you a towel and robe. We recently acquired some salts that make the water bubble if you'd like to try that."

The boons that this suffering and bloodshed afforded her.

"No. No, I don't need that. Just leave the towel and robe. It will be a short bath."

After a few minutes, she dried off and wrapped a warm robe around herself. She walked back into her bed chambers, a small trail of water left by her feet. Victor had closed the window and stoked the hearth. He sat at the table with an empty plate in front of him and a book in hand. She recognized it as a volume of poetry a cousin had written.

"Feel better?" he asked.

She sat on the bed. The door to her armory was closed, her spear and chainmail put away properly. Victor put a great deal of importance on appearances and honoring traditions. Even the ones that he still did not understand. To her, those weapons were fouled by her actions. To him, they were priceless relics to be shown off.

"Not yet."

"This was that trip the queen sent you on because Bire was busy, yes?"

She nodded before rolling her eyes. "Sure, he was busy. I was just there to tend to his errands. Making sure his tomatoes hadn't ripened too much."

Victor set the book down.

"Sorry, perhaps too casual of a term for what it was. This was another compliance order."

She hated hearing other people say it.

"It's fine. The people suffer, the village is broken, and Bire will go unpunished. The crown knows how much to overwork them in the future to make up the slack."

Victor walked over to the wide window that looked west. Far away, only visible in the clear light of day, was a distant, black mountain on the horizon. It was Bastion Nilor, capital and throne of Queen Astasia.

"Which ghoul did they send with you this time? Boris? Thiegs?"

"Chertse. I should've let Marin kill him and spare me the headache."

She joined Victor at the window. They stood next to each other straight-backed and pensive, more like business partners than lovers.

In the first months of their engagement, months before a fever would take both of her parents, they would stare out this window in each other's arms. He said it was romantic. She agreed even though she didn't see how standing in front of a drafty window was anything other than uncomfortable. She told herself that the discomfort with these overlong embraces would go away. It did not. Her guilt was assuaged when he admitted the same uneasiness.

"What luck," he said. "What is next for you?"

Her eyes settled on the shape of Bastion Nilor. It was the nexus of wealth and their brat of a queen sat at the peak. The city at its base, the squalor known as Thronetown, was the wretched refuse that clung to the monarchy's riches.

"Thought I would maybe get some venison for us," she said.

"I heard that we got a good batch from House Keller. Something about settling some nastiness between you and him. I'll have the servants bring it up. How do you like it cooked?"

"No, I mean to go out with a bow. Take a day just stalking a herd. Find the weak ones, the sick. Work out their patterns—"

"Anca."

"I've seen tracks in the eastern groves. Farmers have complained. Might just be better to remove the issue. It would really be in their interest."

"That's deranged."

He didn't understand. She did not thirst for blood or crave violence. The act of hunting, the tranquility and quiet, the focus, it was all a distraction. With no hope of saving villages like Pese, the best she could do was practice her craft.

"I take it the Shadow beast was already dead?"

"You should've seen it." Anca fumed as she shuffled to the hearth. "It was as big as I thought, but it's different to see something like that in person. He could have still handled it."

"But he didn't handle it."

Anca shook her head. "I don't know why I try. All of the households along the border have the worst Nobils. They weren't always this lazy, right? That isn't what I'll be in ten years?"

"You might be as wealthy as them. *We* might be, if we ever settle on a date for the wedding."

It had been four years since their wedding was called off. Her mother, Nobil Dolores Sulia, fell ill ten days before the ceremony. Her father fell ill two days after that. They both died the day after she and Victor were to be wed.

Their relationship was not strengthened by that suffering. At first, the wedding was delayed because of her grief. Then it was delayed because she was too busy as a newly-appointed Nobil. After that, Victor insisted on traveling with a friend for six months. He said it was to enjoy his final days as an unmarried man. When he returned, neither of them raised the matter of the wedding in a serious way.

"Maybe you could talk them into transferring Nobil Bire's land into mine?" Anca asked.

The food on the table was cooled, but she still loaded her plate high with loaves of apple bread, marinated white beans, and a bowl of rich, brown stew. A feast far greater than anything Pese will ever know again. The thought wormed into her head.

"Why would I know how to do that?" Victor asked.

"You know how to talk to them."

"You can banter with the court just fine if you ever cared to play the part."

It was true. She was acquainted with corsets,

dresses, foundation, eyeliner, lipstick, curtsies, bows, and which fork to use at the right time. These things had been necessary for a time. Truth be told, she enjoyed the ritual of it. She liked how she looked in a dress as much as a set of chainmail. Eyeliner was really just a kind of camouflage, same as war paint. It was hard to conjure that sort of enthusiasm these days.

Oh no, now there was a whole new world of expectations, she thought. Nobils weren't supposed to be pretty. The Hands of the Throne couldn't be pleasing.

"But you've been doing it since you were barely a man." Anca slid a chair out from the table. "Your mother is the most conniving, politicking, and accomplished woman I've ever seen. And she does it all in heels, remarkable. You've got all of her charm."

Victor pursed his lips and leaned against a post of their bed. The barb had slipped out despite her best intentions. She shrugged and swallowed a spoonful of stew.

"I meant that in a good way. Do you remember the absolute steal that she talked my parents into during our matrimonial bargaining? If my father hadn't liked you so much, they might've called the whole thing off at the first offer."

She did not think Victor was cruel like Bire. He wasn't a bad man, but he valued looks too much. He was terrified of losing an inch of prestige. When she sympathized with the poor, he quickly moved to more pleasant topics.

Anca sipped wine from her glass. It was fruity and too sweet, but she was ravenous. She wondered what the survivors at Pese were eating tonight. Radishes? Onions? None of their livestock survived. Perhaps they had some salted pork left?

"Anca?" Victor said.

She woke from her thoughts and swallowed a bite of food she had chewed for too long.

"Yes?"

He chuckled and refilled his glass of wine before leaning across the table and topping hers off. His blue eyes sparkled in the fire of the hearth. Victor's good looks had disarmed her at first. She considered herself lucky to be with one of the most handsome men in the court. Of course, she saw now what was beneath it.

"Talk to me," he said.

Anca fiddled with her plate. They had talked at length about her feelings and nothing changed. Nothing ever changed. Any hope of things improving were beginning to look as impossible as Victor learning how to shoot a bow.

"I don't want to do this," she said.

"Do what?"

"This bullshit."

Anca flipped her fork off the table.

"Helping the crown figure out the damages and not how we can prevent these attacks altogether. In the meantime, the people who are supposed to protect them are too busy with feasts and bragging rights. Ask me how long it has been since I hunted. And I mean really, hunted. Not a compliance order. Not stalking some elk for a lark. I mean in the shit with a snarling thing made of Shadow and piss and teeth and I'm the only person who can stop it from killing people. How long do you think?"

Victor leaned back in his chair and waved his left hand around as if weighing a bag of gold.

"Six months?"

"It's been a year. I tracked the beast of Pese for a week. I could have caught it if I tried harder."

"You worked plenty hard. I barely saw you. I almost thought about asking Marin to hold me at night in your stead."

Victor snorted at his own joke. It did not tickle her.

"I've gone soft. If I caught it, I could have saved them."

"Don't go there." He sat forward in his chair, but she was still too busy tracing the ceramic dishes to appreciate the gesture. Her feelings were fit to burst at the seams. If she allowed it, she would be screaming at Victor. He didn't deserve that. She wanted Noble Bire, that piece of trash who let his people die.

"You did what you could. You warned Bire and he made his decisions. It isn't your land. They aren't your people to protect."

"Why does everyone keep saying that?" It came out harsh, her voice boiling in the base of her chest. She tucked it away. This was not the time to go to pieces. "We're barely Nobils anymore. Just brutes who've grown used to comfort and power."

Victor pointed to the skull that hung over their fireplace.

"When our houses merge, you will be one of the best Nobils in the history of House Sulia. Eventually, our child will learn from you. And they will take up your charge because of the example you've set for them."

"Stars above," she said before she could suppress it.

The scant talk of marriage was backlit by other pressures. No one dared ask Anca directly, but they still bubbled at the edges of her court. She was two years past thirty now. Most women her age had two or three children at this point. Any that didn't were at least married. She felt the knot in her neck like a spring-loaded coilgun pointed at the back of her head.

Anca wanted a husband. She wanted to sire heirs for the line of Sulia. It wasn't Victor she wanted to do that with. However, her parents had blessed this union. Letting it go would feel like spitting on their legacy. The more she learned, the more she discovered that she did not love him. She believed the wedding would never happen.

"I know we aren't as close as we should be," he shifted in his chair and avoided looking at her, "but your line must continue in some way. You know that as well as I do. Even if I would rather be touring vineyards and painting. It wasn't my hope to be hobnobbing with people like Marin. It is expected."

"Expected by who?"

He sighed and sat back in his chair. "I was asked by Queen Astasia herself when the wedding will resume. Don't shoot the messenger, but she used the word 'spinster'."

Despite her young age, the queen manipulated the royal lines with the best of the biddies. Her mother was once the preeminent spinner of gossip and leverage. The daughter had learned well.

"She's worse than your family." Anca dropped her forehead into her hands. "The royal line is spoiled past usefulness. The Households are letting their power bleed away with every beast that breaks through our territories."

He cleared his throat and cast an eye toward the door, another uncomfortable shift in his seat.

"Do we have to talk about this?"

"When is the right time to talk about it then?"

Irritation boiled behind her forehead. Everything had to come at the right time and in the right manner. Of course, this meant he never wanted to talk about anything that would further his own discomfort.

"Think for a moment before you fly off the handle. We don't want to burn our bridges. We still have to live. What's a just world worth if everyone is worse off for it?" He tipped back another glass of fine wine.

She wanted to stick their people's suffering in his face. The Households too. They needed to remember what the world was like out there. This sort of change could only be pushed forward by the Elder Nobil of the order. For her, that was Nobil Keller. Only his seat had a hope of shifting the queen's standing on anything.

Proving herself as worthy to command the order would mean a grand service to the throne. She would need an achievement that no one could ignore. It would mean kowtowing and behaving like them, something she could not stomach. Only after all that manipulation would she have the chance to shift the balance.

"The Kellers, the Paegras, the Stancus, damn them to a wet grave."

"Let's not be hasty. I get nervous enough talking about this with you in our quarters. You aren't seriously considering taking this to Nobil Keller?"

There was the wedge that drove them apart. Maybe she unconsciously picked up on it within days. It took a few years to rise to the surface, but she could see it now in him as plain as that handsome grin plastered on his face.

"You can't have it all, Victor."

He waggled his finger. "I don't believe that for a second. Things always work out."

They always work out for you, she thought.

Armored boots walked down the hall. Her ears picked it up an entire minute before they reached their door. Victor was deaf to it with his normal, dull ears. Anca wondered what it was like to be so blind to your surroundings. A fist knocked on their door.

"Anca? It's Marin. A letter arrived while you were out." His voice was muffled behind the solid wood.

"It will have to wait," Victor said, "She's tired and needs some rest."

"It's urgent. It's from the queen."

Anca and Victor shared a look.

"And I just got comfortable." Anca sunk into her chair.

Her shoulders sagged, but Victor held out a hand.

"I can handle this."

Her lips mouthed the words "thank you" as she leaned back in the chair. She closed her eyes and listened to Victor walk toward the door. The door swung open on its heavy hinges.

"Your paintedness, good to see you. You look—" Marin searched for a word, but failed after several moments.

"Don't give yourself a migraine. I'd hate to see you embarrass yourself," Victor said.

Marin handed the letter to him. "Don't sprain your wrist. The paper's good quality."

"I'll try not to."

Victor closed the door on her Doia and ripped open the seal. Anca opened one eye. He pulled the letter from the envelope and read through it.

"Well? What's it this time?" she asked.

Her humor fell away as Victor's face hardened. Despite the untested, unstrained life of luxury he had known, he seemed to age in the few words he read.

"What is it?"

"It's a general summons. All Households are to gather at Bastion Nilor in three days. There's been a massacre. The village Moura under Nobil Stancu has been—" Victor read over a line on the paper two more times before speaking again.

"The entire village has been emptied. Wiped out."

"Raiders?" Anca asked.

"An animal did it. It left the bodies, killed the livestock, and took nothing of value."

Her heart pounded at the mere concept. Whenever a Household was ravaged by a Shadow beast, it was indisputably a great loss. They were never wholly wiped out though. No creature could ever hope to break a Household single handedly. Not since House Furloc. Not since her mother united the Households to burn out a canker in the heart of their order.

"House Stancu?"

"Decimated," Victor said. "The Nobil was at Bastion Nilor as a guest of the queen."

She leaped from her chair and flung open the armory. Disgust and mourning would have to come later. In a world of bounties, swagger, and machismo, a grand kill meant more than one-hundred compliance orders.

This was something greater. Something dreadful. Anca had never heard of such destruction caused by one beast. The throne would want blood and the Households would stumble over each other to earn its head. Whoever came out on top would be a hero of the land. A hero to the queen. How could they deny her a seat as Elder with this under her belt? She was halfway into her breeches when Victor yanked her away from the armory.

"What are you doing?"

She pulled herself out from the grasp of his fingers and snarled at him. "What I was meant to do: hunt. An entire village wiped out by a beast is unheard of. Unbelievable. What were we just talking about?"

"That is what you think of? People are dead, Anca."

"I can only think about the many lives beyond the village of Moura. Another uncaring Nobil. That bounty is the sort of prestige Keller can't say no to. It's enough to impress the lower Nobils into a vote on leadership."

"Just slow down, damn it." He reached his arms toward her again, but her glare kept him at bay. Victor's fingers wriggled as he pulled them into loose fists.

It was impossible for her to slow down. It was not in the nature of Nobils to debate and hesitate. It was that tendency that made them excellent attack dogs. However, her limbs ached and her eyes were heavy. Leaving now would not reflect well. For Queen Astasia, much like Victor, perception was everything. She dropped the chainmail from her hands. It irritated her to no end when Victor was right.

"We're leaving tomorrow," Anca said.

"Done. First thing in the morning. After breakfast, of course."

It was still a territory in shackles. It was still a kingdom where Victor would never let go of his plenty, even if it helped others. She wanted to cleanse her legacy, and he was too concerned with how it sounded when read aloud.

Chapter Three

Eugen Furloc could not decide if the queen's strategy chamber was parody or achievement. Maps of every realm, covered with tiny colored cubes, were spread across a table made of rare blue timber. Hooded scribes disgorged voluminous reports and tactics to the young queen herself. It was a nexus of strategy full of people who had never seen a battlefield or ended a life with their own two hands.

Not everyone in the room was so inexperienced though. Eugen did not inherit the title of Queen's Executioner. He earned it.

Buzzing glass tubes colored the room with off-yellow light. Beyond, vast round windows, looping arches, and precarious designs, the palace gleamed in the low light of the day. Hideously colorful curtains were drawn partly open. Another storm would soon blow in. A chief scribe and three of his apprentices labored over scrolls long enough to be bed sheets. While the apprentices wrote, the chief scribe reported.

"Did you arrange these maps yourself?" Queen Astasia asked.

The chief scribe browsed the map before conferring with an apprentice.

"With my assistants, yes."

Astasia loomed over the table spanning maps, her features too sullen for such a young person. She was barely two decades old, but still carried her crown with all the dread that her mother conjured before her. Beauty was too casual of a word to describe her.

The young monarch cultivated a physical majesty. Graceful, elegant, smooth, she attempted a look of perfection. She labored to appear indelible. It was just a façade. Eugen knew that she was heartless beneath her preening perfection. She kept some of her closest connections fooled, plied with money and favors. The real Astasia always bubbled to the surface eventually.

Her crown, made of white gold and capped with gems and diamonds, nestled into her tangle of auburn hair. Her gown lacked the usual high-backed collar and trail of royalty. She measured a distance near their southern border with a compass, drawing a small line with a pencil in her other hand.

Eugen continued to pamper his blade with an oiled cloth. The curved greatsword was almost as tall as him. The hilt was fashioned like the jaws of a reptilian beast. They were called Sarlats before his ancestors hunted them to extinction. At the thought, cinders flecked from the orange gem seated in the pommel of his sword.

All gone now, just like his household.

He pulled a pouch from his pocket, small enough to fit in the palm of his hand, and breathed deep from the herbs within. Minty and cold, it suffocated the building rage. The little bag of calming remedy was almost as important as the magical Focus set in his sword.

Without this substance, he would be no better than his berserker forebears. Any chance at redemption he might win in the throne's service would be forfeit. The throne took a chance on the last Furloc. He was younger than Astasia when he entered their service. Now thirty-five, Eugen had served for over a decade as their bag man. When people needed killing, they sent their monster.

"Our territory extends to the eighty mile mark from the northern point of Lake Piet," the queen clarified.

"Indeed, that is what these records say. I could look again, of course—"

"Then why does this show them ending three miles short of it?"

The scribe coughed, but it might have been two or three thoughts running into each other. Eugen let his Othersight settle on the man. A gift of his Nobil bloodline, all of them possessed it. To Eugen's eyes, green lines raced from the scribe's heart, out to his limbs, and back in. He had seen similar reactions in people moments before their execution.

"We must have pulled an outdated map. I promise that we did our due diligence. Whoever filled out these scrolls must have been misinformed, not my staff," the scribe explained.

Astasia set her compass and pencil aside. Her crystal blue stare was as sharp as a dagger.

"Have it corrected. Would you have me send loyal women and men miles off course? If we lost anything by a clerical error, of all things—"

"Absolutely not, my queen. This is a contained mistake. I will fix it."

He bowed and snapped his fingers at the nearby apprentices. The group left as quickly as they could, fumbling to carry their scrolls as they walked past. Eugen's gaze lingered on the throbbing vein in the scribe's neck.

Prey. The urge to give chase built in his legs, feet

tensing against his will. The magic in his veins pushed the thought forward. Eugen breathed from the bag of herbs again. The queen rubbed her temples with one hand and removed the crown with the other.

"I apologize, Eugen. It was not my intention to keep you waiting."

About damn time, he thought.

"No offense taken. Your duties are more important." He set the blade down and crossed to the strategy table. "A killer, rather, a general might make for better counsel."

"My generals don't need to see these grand designs. They might get ideas. The scribes are too incoherent in the ways of war to know what they are telling me."

"And you think this will win the day?"

She gave him an annoyed glare that was reserved for close allies, not her subjects. He was quite familiar with it.

"It will buy time. Time for when we can fight on equal footing."

A time when we can hack and rip. The thoughts pushed to the surface, instigated by the burning magic in his blood. It beat like a second heart, words coming to mind between the thump-thump of his pulse. He tried to smile, but he might have looked deranged. Instead, he swallowed and nodded.

"Dreadful news from the north." She pressed on with the briefing. "House Stancu has been hollowed out. Moura is a ghost town now."

"I saw the summons." He sat down at the table.

"Nobil Stancu was here when it happened. So far from her own territory, it is tantamount to desertion."

She was here at your invitation. Your wine and

maids readily offered, he thought.

"It was so careless," he said.

"A brushfire war in the south wasn't enough, I guess. The threat from the north never ceases and now we are squeezed from both sides to bleed like an orange."

Astasia reached for a nearby bottle of wine and filled a glass. Eugen would not remind her that she started this border skirmish. Reminding her of truths was not useful. All his bridges had burned in the fire that consumed his family. Everyone else saw him as a fiend who delighted in bloodshed and misery. They called him unhinged.

Queen's Executioner was the only position he could manage with such a horrid reputation. The royal family needed a brute to put down the worst of the crown's enemies. Anywhere else in the kingdom, he was certain to have his throat cut in his sleep. He was a bedtime horror story come to life. They all skittered from him when he came close and spit when he was a suitable distance away.

"Without Stancu, our territory has essentially shrunk by that much." Her finger tapped the north-westerly edge of the map.

Let those prideful bastards adapt. Bulwark of the north my ass, he thought. The Households were the reason why he was despised and alone. It was unlikely that debt of vengeance would ever be paid. Not by him at least.

"The Households have great wealth and manpower to spare. They can help Stancu recover," he said in a small voice.

"It's not just her. House Bire is weak. House Sulia had to assess the damage to Pese. Another village ravaged."

"Another killer? Was it the same that ripped Moura up by the hind end?"

"Pardon?" Astasia pursed her lips and blinked.

Eugen shook his head. These slips happened at times, usually not in front of the queen. He was used to giving orders and killing whoever needed to die. Such language was not tolerated in her presence. Eugen understood it was a way to put themselves above their subjects. It gave him a headache.

"Excuse my tongue. Was it the same beast that attacked Moura?"

The queen watched him a moment longer before she answered.

"No. That incident is an alarming exception. The Households are reluctant to help each other. They are more like rivals rather than the allies they once were."

"So Bire and Stancu will fester?"

She shook her head, each movement curated for effect. "Once I told them that their taxable people and fields had been eviscerated, they pulled themselves from their debauchery long enough to accept my deal."

Pin them to the wall. Take everything from them.

"What sort of deal?" Eugen asked.

"I bought them out. A large sum of Royal Talons for their lands. Including their bastions, their hunting guard, and their people."

"And they accepted?"

"Without hesitation. At the next convening of the Households, Houses Bire and Stancu will be dissolved and their territories added into my direct rule."

Eugen leaned back in his chair. He smiled because he wanted to. Astasia walked around the table, circling out of Eugen's eye line. He could still hear her pulse and smell her skin, lilacs and rose water. He could put a knife through her ear without looking if he wanted to.

"Despite these gains, we still have a problem. The cause for all this turnover."

The True Fucker. The quarry of a lifetime.

"The Beast." Eugen's heartbeat quickened. The gem on his sword began to glow once again, a single ash flaking from it. He had been an executioner of people for too long. Trained by the Nobils of his family, he had been on the cusp of joining their hunts.

Then the Households decided they were out of control. Eugen knew his family had been too wild to save. He had seen the butchery left in their wake. He was only alive because he had not yet indulged the apoplectic tantrums of his lineage.

"As much as I would love to bleed the Nobils, a roaming threat that can empty a village overnight is not acceptable. I intend to call an expedition into the north to find and kill the monster."

"And you would have the Households do it?"

"It is their right. They contain the darkness in the north. They keep their territories and the taxation levied from the lands. Who else would I go to?"

She laid a hand on his shoulder, her delicate fingers drawing a line along his black vest. It was not affection. Eugen recognized the taunt, the subtle implication that she owned him. He took a deep breath and reached for the small pouch in his pocket, but he did not need it yet.

"It is their right." He forced the words out of his lips.

"Oh, you're sweating Eugen."

She wiped a bead of moisture from his head, and he jerked away from her touch. She chuckled and walked to the other side of the too long table. Eugen could not help but watch the Life circulate in her neck. He thought of all the ways he could end her. The fire in his blood never knew peace. It only wanted to indulge in violence and then seek more.

"Don't be so hurt. My Executioner will ensure justice is done."

"What do you need from me?"

She reached the other side and sat in a chair that was both taller and grander than his.

"These are extraordinary times. The throne must answer alongside the Nobils. When the questing Household is nominated, I will require that the throne aid them. We will open our armories and your hunters."

The royal contingent would need a leader. Eugen did not dare to hope.

"A commander of the royal army would be a wise choice."

Astasia groaned. "Stop your groveling. I am sending you."

His anger dimmed as if a bucket of water had been thrown onto it. Three and a half decades of struggle across his life and he had never had such a chance. No, he thought, it was still impossible. She was dangling this just to torture him.

"The bastards will squirm. They won't accept. They'll moan and invoke my exile."

"Let them." She smiled with a mouthful of perfect teeth and raised her chin.

Eugen went around the table and knelt. "They won't go, not with me by their side."

"They can and they will. At least some of them. What will they do? Allow the beast to carve a swathe through lands that they expressly own and are charged with?"

Eugen shook his head and grinned. "Thank you."

"In addition to protecting the Nobil and their Household." Astasia's eyes went to the door. "We must make sure that this thing is not what I think it might be."

Eugen looked up at her and the excitement drained from him. Her raised eyebrow confirmed it. It should not be possible. Cold fear clutched his heart. No, it could not have been. That dark secret was destroyed, burned to ash. How many times had Astasia assured him that his role in that plot was at an end?

She promised you, he thought. What good are words if a monarch's vow is useless? The possibility made his anger rise to life, throbbing in his veins as heat streaked up the back of his neck.

"You told me it was buried. You looked me straight in the eye and told me it was gone."

"Silence."

"I told you I wanted it dead. It's dangerous, you figured out as much. What other lies did you spin for me?"

"And if you say anything, I'll tell them all it was your idea. Your blood. Your magic. I will gladly kick the chair from under your feet when they string you up by the neck." Her lips twisted with anger, and she stood over him.

He dragged his eyes back to the ground. What was he thinking? No one else had ever held him in such confidence as Astasia. He could not turn against her.

"Remember yourself, Furloc. Son of murderers and monsters. The Households wanted you to die. Do you remember that? My family saved you. How dare you even raise the idea of betraying me. Who do you think they'll believe? Hmm? Do your fucking job, the one thing I ask of you."

She shoved his shoulder, barely making him shift where he knelt. A feeling crept up his spine, like a loathsome bug crawling over him. It was so wrong, but he told himself that this was normal. She was a queen. Rulers had their own set of rules. He was a servant. He would serve because Astasia was right. Who would believe that he wanted no part of this?

"They are my plans, my orders to make. You follow them, Eugen. Understand me? With a word, I would have your bloodline ended for good."

Eugen reached for the pouch of calming herbs and breathed deep from it. He was closer to violence than he liked. That it was aimed at the one person keeping him alive was too dangerous.

She lied to me, he thought. It was supposed to be gone. That mistake had been destroyed and his role in it forever erased. If it was still alive, if she had lied about this, what else had she not told him? The snake. The haughty brat.

"I'm sorry, my queen." He spoke slowly, holding back the rage inside with all of his might. "I would never betray your trust. I was merely surprised. I ask for your forgiveness."

Astasia tutted her lips and raised his chin up to face her. The venomous glare had melted away into a saccharine smile. He traced the panicked flows of blood through her veins. She was scared, but the queen was too practiced to ever show it.

"You're confused. It's your role to kill, not think. Now get to work."

He rose from his crouch and hurried over to where

his sword waited for him. Scooping it up, he did not look up at the gorgeous curtains or the excellent paintings. All of this silver and gold, it could never be his world. This was a place of heroes.

Eugen cradled the sword close to his chest, the warm glow of his magical Focus warm against him. The Blood Flame was his only real friend. Without it, he would be no use to the crown. If he ever stopped being the monster that she wanted, what would he be?

If he led the Nobils against this beast, he could prove himself their superior. Eugen would shove his talent in their indolent faces and remind them what a real Nobil looked like. That was the way out from under her thumb, the only way out of this life as a skulking killer. He would have to beat the Nobils at their own game.

Chapter Four

The walls of Thronetown were gray, weary guardians. Long slicks of black grime traced from spouts and leaky pipes, directing water away from the top of the walls. Eerie, orange lights burned in the interior halls of the structure, like glowing eyes of a titanic beast.

Gaps along the walls revealed shining gatling-barrels of coilguns, spring loaded weapons that could put a steel rod through a set of plate armor. Weapons of a glorious, lost age, each one was a relic and nearly irreplaceable.

Cold, exhausted fields surrounded the fortress. Gaping wounds in the earth, quarries in search of anything useful, crushed downward with jagged edges. The remains of broken homes were barely noticeable beneath the layers of dirt and dust that covered them.

Behind the walls, pointed roofs were shoved together like disordered rows of crops in a filthy field. The town was squeezed between the outer walls and the shore behind it. The discoloration that stained the walls was worse within. Rickety houses with shingle roofs leaned against each other as though they might fall over. Wires ran like black spiderwebs along the avenues to bring power to the overworked, dingy light bulbs.

Nestled at the heart of this labyrinth was Bastion Nilor, seat of Queen Astasia. The ivory walls were capped with expressions of grandiose architecture and colossal illustrations of their history. It towered above all the poor, a reminder of the grand wealth they would never achieve.

It made Anca nauseous. They would be treated to the finest food and drinks. The silk bedsheets sourced from a secluded, secret farm. Every utensil was honest silver. An orchestra chamber carried music across the upper floors through a series of pipes. There were banquet halls upon smoking lounges upon warm wading pools and there was a throne at the top of it all.

Altogether, it was the greatest accumulation of wealth in the settled world.

Anca raised her cloak against the downpour. Her company was made up of herself and five other riders. Two of them were Marin and Victor. They moved like a greater creature through a crowded forest. People on the street silently scurried aside when they spotted the soaked banner of House Sulia. She doubted they knew which Household they were in this gloom, but they knew to move quickly.

Down a narrow side street, a flood of voices rose over the patter of rain. A cramped street market had turned into a brawl. A city guard, topped with a horned helmet, ripped a sign from the hands of a protestor. The people wore red sashes over their faces. The rain made them look more like bloody wounds. Behind them, not turning from the threat of violence, more people hoisted signs that read "how long will we starve?" or "eat the rich." Several guards ran past Anca and down the alley, blasting a whistle as they drew clubs or small shields.

It was worse since she was last here. Winter was closing in, the harvest nearly finished, and people were figuring out how hungry this season would be. As long as the Households were in lock step with the queen, they would have no choice but to hope for a brief winter.

They reached the ivory walls of the palace and more horned guards emerged from shelters. They carried pikes which ended in viscous looking hooks. Behind them was another figure. She wore a blue robe, her long, graying hair hung below her deep hood, but the rest of her cloak was held around her like a coat. The figure raised a golden rod from inside the folds of clothing, no longer than her forearm. It glowed blue and the rain overhead stopped.

The rain drops veered left and right as though they were breaking on a glass dome. Anca suspected the queen's mages would be present. Even though her Othersight was tantamount to magic, the work of mages was foreign to her.

"Please, remove your hoods. You all look as if you came from the sea," the mage said in a cheery voice.

Anca pulled hers off and the rest of them followed. Victor shook his hair and slicked it back with his hands. Marin's curls were wetted back and looked brown under the cloudy skies.

"Thank you, we appreciate the cover," Victor said.

"Even the skies kneel at the whims of Queen Astasia," the mage replied. "Identify your Household."

"I am Nobil Anca Sulia of House Sulia. We answer the summons sent by her majesty, Queen Astasia Stratra of Margecei."

The mage and the horn-helmeted guards bowed.

"Ah, the fiercest of many arrives as the storm bares its teeth at us. What a credit that the skies should herald your arrival."

The mage rose from her bow and removed her hood.

The whisper of wrinkles around her eyes and full cheeks reminded Anca of Victor's mother. She wore a different earring in each ear. In her left was a small totem of a fish and a hawk. In her right was a green gem set in rose gold.

"I am Costea Gradi, Mage Superior."

Costea waved behind her and the gates groaned as the titan gears shifted the colossal door. Beyond was a cavernous room lit by rows of buzzing, bright tubes. As they entered, Costea lowered her magical Focus and the downpour resumed.

Victor shook the water from his traveling cloak. He put his hair back into place and attended to the minor details of his clothing that had been abused by the ride. Anca rolled her eyes at the fuss he made over his looks.

"Appearances are always important, dear. Maybe you should attend to yourself. You're the one who brought swords and shields into a place of finery and dresses."

"This isn't going to go how you think it will, Victor." Anca pulled a scimitar from her horse and buckled the scabbard onto her belt. "We can use weapons in place of trophies or recent kills."

"It's a dick measuring contest: the highest and purest form of intimidation." Marin hauled a bag full of armor over his shoulder.

"I admittedly do not know how the Households hold court, but I know a thing or two about attending a function with monarchy present. I'm not as lost as you think."

True, they grew up in different worlds, but they had matured in the same careless hierarchy. She ground her teeth at this refrain. He reminded her of what they were instead of what they could be.

"I've attended these before. Including the ones you've been at," she said.

"Not since we've been engaged." He cocked a fist against his hip and raised an eyebrow. His tone was too acrid to be curious. "Tell me, dearest. What do you usually win from these gatherings? What blood have you taken from the stone?"

Anca was the runt of the Households. In addition to being one of two women amongst them, she was a relatively new addition. Her place was to behave and agree with what the senior members wanted.

"I have not asked for much," she admitted.

"And you want the honor of hunting this thing for House Sulia when all eleven Households also want it? No, you need candor. You need wit. You need someone who knows this sort of prey. A hunter of the courts. The game trails are different here and you need to know when one is old or if it's been used recently. You need an aristocrat." Victor ruffled the hems of his shirt again and looked up at the high domed ceiling above them.

"I'm always surprised by your ability to go on and on about a thing," Marin said. He took Victor's wet cloak and then Anca's. Marin shook them out over Victor's tailor-made boots.

"There's a bit more to hunting than pate and parties."

"They have more in common, my pugnacious comrade. I'll show you that by the end of this. It will all work out."

Costea approached them, flanked by a pair of servants in high collared green tunics. Anca was grateful for anything to stop Victor from talking. The moods he got into in the company of high society were unbearable.

The Mage Superior let her robe hang free as she no longer contended with the cold, damp weather. She wore a puffy sleeved white dress beneath. Her lemon-yellow hair was coaxed into roiling curls.

"I would like to formally welcome you into the queen's graces," Costea said. "Bastion Nilor will be your home for the next two days. My assistants have details on the locations of your lodgings. The hallways can be confusing to those unfamiliar with them. Between the old defensive layouts and the newer accommodations for artistry, I must refresh myself on their layout at times."

Her saccharine tone echoed off the ceilings above.

"I would also ask that during your time with us that you stay within the bastion grounds. Everything you could ever desire is at your fingertips within these walls. Books? The grand library has been hailed as one of the most complete collections of literature, second only to the Archive Primeval in Naelan. Do you crave food or drink? Our cooks are some of the finest in the known lands."

Marin raised his hand and spoke before Costea could acknowledge him. "I think I can pick out my own mead. I'll not trust the teenager in a tunic." He jerked his thumb at a nearby servant.

Costea grinned and crossed her arms, her nose wrinkling in delight.

"I am sure Doia Marin of House Sulia knows more than this servant here. But the question is would he know more than our master brewer? He has served the family for decades and has come into possession of some of the highest quality and rare brews. Could you trust the sense of such an individual?"

"Master brewer?" Marin arched an eyebrow.

"He's a friend of my family," Victor added. "He also likes to bake when not occupied with royal duties."

"I don't think that is hardly going to sway him," Anca muttered.

"No, no," Marin waggled a finger, "your man does have a divining tongue for wine. I'll take my chances with your brewer, mage."

Costea led the group out of the stables and into the winding hallways of the bastion. The walls were covered in portraits and busts of kings, queens, mages, and other supporters of the crown. Chandeliers made of polished silver were adorned with pearls and diamonds, more noisy bulbs in place of candles. Stained glass windows colored the gloomy city in brilliant hues. It was almost enough to wipe away the squalor she saw on the way in.

"Mage Gradi, where is that grand library you mentioned?"

Costea tapped one of her servants on the shoulder and gestured toward Anca. "Please show the Nobil the way. They will attend to your needs when you arrive."

"Take this to our room, will you?" Anca handed her pack to Victor before she followed the servant down the hall.

"What are you doing?" Victor asked.

"Reading about the climate near Moura. I need to know what this thing might eat, glens it might be hiding in. Refresh myself on the other Nobil's proclivities."

Victor made a small sound of protest that died in his throat as she disappeared around the corner. She walked at a pace that the servant struggled to match. The portraits of past Nobils were a reminder that their legacy was hers. The work she did might be recorded in some similar way. Were there Nobils, known for their cruelty, who had struggled as she had?

The servants that tailed her remained silent as they walked. Perhaps they could feel her irritation or they were intimidated by seeing a Nobil in the flesh. They reserved themselves to a small gesture left then right then right again.

A wooden door, twice her height, beckoned at the end of this twisting hallway. The hall was lined with sculptures of royalty she could not recall. The door opened on shiny hinges and a flurry of similarly dressed servants scurried out of it like cockroaches through a hole in the wall.

Though their pace was only a vague hurry, she could tell they were running from something. The pounding, green light in their veins tipped her off to their fear. They cleared a path from the door as quickly as they appeared and the elegant shine of jewels bloomed under the lights.

Queen Astasia strode forward, her silver gown augmented with golden filigree. Her hair was tied up in a simple bun, but her rose gold earrings were stacked with enough gems to be exquisite paperweights. She flipped through a dusty tome in her hands, eyes focused on the fading text on the pages. Behind her, another servant carried five more similar books.

The queen might have walked right past Anca if not for the few servants who stopped dead in their tracks to bow. The three who stopped were knocked over by the few behind them. Curses and groans filled the hallway and Astasia pulled herself from the book. A flash of alarm crossed her delicate features before she muted them a moment later.

"Nobil Sulia, I hardly expected you. You made it just fine? Even through this rain?"

"It wasn't a long trek."

The queen's eyes narrowed, likely noting the lack of exaltation from the Nobil.

"And so soon after your recent compliance?"

"When the crown calls, we answer. It's expected of us. Speaking of that, I wanted you to know that—"

"And your fiancé, Victor? He made it in? He's so charming. Most of the other Nobil's spouses are so glum or serious or tense. Victor brightens up every conversation I have with him. You better put a ring on him or I might venture to steal him for myself."

Anca fought the urge to grind her teeth. It shouldn't surprise her that Astasia didn't care what happened to Pese. The real shock was if she asked about it without prompting. This brat couldn't be bothered to merely listen to what Anca had to say. Whether it was intentionally malicious or the queen was really that unconcerned wasn't clear.

Astasia rubbed her chin and took in Anca's outfit. Still in her riding leathers and blue cloak, she was soaked all the way through. Her hair was a gnarled mess of brown. The queen's eyes searched her for something else.

"It is still two days until the convening. Why so early?"

Anca gave a small bow. She kept it as close to a nod as expectation would allow. The queen did not look like a revolting parasite, but Anca wasn't fooled. Their interactions were always brief and to the point. Anca accomplished her orders to the letter, but her decorum left something to be desired. Victor wanted her to speak kindly with the young queen, but Anca would not. It was enough to obey. She did not need to grovel.

"Your majesty. You know me, I'm punctual. I'm not one to wait around as our people are slaughtered like cattle. Like your other guests."

"Guests?"

Astasia almost laughed and searched Anca's face for what she meant. Anca knew the queen was not dumb. Looking into those icy blue eyes, Anca found the driving impulse behind that word: How does this relate to me?

It didn't make Anca angry. She was sad to see her worst assumptions proven right. Astasia was so careless that she barely remembered the two Nobils within the walls of her palace.

"Bire and Stancu," Anca said. "They've been out of the field for weeks. From what I've heard, they've been reveling in the riches you ply them with. Like you almost want us to seem weak."

Astasia's thin smile broke for the slightest moment before twisting into a coy smirk. Every move of her lips, her cheeks, and her eyes was as practiced as Anca's sword arm.

"Dear, I think ply is a bit strong. Don't you think I'm right?" Her voice purred. Scarlet lips pulled back in a vicious grin.

"You don't deny it?" Anca growled.

"I entertain many of my subjects within these artisanal walls. Why should I turn them away? I trust them to uphold their charges and if they don't, well I know you can't say no. What are we without these bonds, my servant? You look so tired, when was the last time you had someone pamper you? Please tell me that pretty little boy toy of yours is treating you right. I know how men can get. When they linger in the shadow of strong women like you and me. Maybe you should lighten up."

Anca's teeth ground together. An acid taste rose in the back of her throat as her knuckles went white from clenched fists. The world tilted.

Don't roll your eyes. Don't laugh. Don't shake her until she passes out, Anca thought.

The idea that they were the same made her want to heave out her guts on this perfect, exquisite rug. Anca's parents clung to the throne's laws and ideals. She was raised to serve them without question. However, her parent's zeal was not resolute. The reticence was plain in their eyes even as they sentenced hundreds to hard labor.

When she questioned them, which was often, they were never mad at her. They were frightened for their daughter. They had allowed themselves to become monsters, and train their daughter as one, for fear of the larger one that sat on the throne. This preening, beautiful monster in front of her.

Anca had waited too long. As she kept her bile down, moments passed and Astasia's smile grew deeper as the Nobil squirmed.

"You are keeping him satisfied, right?"

Anca choked as a practiced response failed to come out properly. Something else came out instead.

"That's hardly your business."

Astasia giggled and stepped closer to Anca. She was a bit shorter than the Nobil, but not at that moment. Anca felt as though the queen towered over her like the walls around Thronetown.

"I'm your queen. Everything's my business, sweetie."

Blissfully, Astasia had grown bored with this and pushed past Anca. Her dainty, exposed shoulder plowed into hers and Anca let herself step out of the way. She could knock the monarch over with the slightest push. It was horribly tempting. All it would take was to dig in her heel and let the pampered woman crash into her. She swallowed and let the impulse go.

"Do make yourself comfortable," Astasia said as she passed. "Walking around with a stick up your ass has to be uncomfortable."

The procession of servants moved past Anca as quietly as they could. The two that had escorted Anca followed their monarch back down the twisting hallways. After a few short moments, she was alone before the grand doors to the library.

Breathe in, she thought.

Her eyes closed and she turned toward the library. Breathe out. She blew out a furious breath. The warm candlelight of the library flickered beyond, full of the knowledge she wanted. Anca turned her thoughts toward what she needed: topography, climate, local fauna, caves, rivers, streams.

Anything that would distract her from that horrible thing in the shining dress.

Chapter Five

Two long days after they arrived, the convening began. Anca could not help but grin as she strode toward the Hall of Feasts. It felt good to wear the colors and iconography of her ancestors.

A loose cloth wrap covered her torso but left her arms exposed, if not for the coat of dark fur that hung from her right shoulder. Fangs and bones dangled from a low hanging, hemp necklace. Her hair was spun back into a bun with dull, ceremonial knives stuck in.

Victor walked slightly behind and adjusted his furred shoulder sash. These events were unlike the corseted, high-collared affairs he was used to. When she revealed what was expected, he nearly fainted. The sash ran down into a long, black cape that fluttered only a few inches above the ground. An iron pauldron on his left shoulder was attached by a strap that ran across his shirtless chest. His hair was slicked back and teased to curl out at the nape of his neck, the one flourish that Anca could not deny him.

Marin's ginger mustache was twisted into coils. He carried the imposing banner of House Sulia in his hands, but it came nowhere close to the ceiling of the long hallway. Ornate decorations and gilded bulbs lined the walls. Horned royal guards stood to their left and right in three sets with coilguns hitched to their shoulders.

At the end of the hall, a royal servant wore a

horrifically tight silk outfit. His hair had the loud volume and meticulous styling typical of royal fashion. He bowed to them as they neared and pushed the wooden doors open. Violins, fiddles, gruff laughter, and the smell of food poured through.

"House Sulia arrives," the servant announced.

The voices within dimmed and they shuffled from their seats. She set her hand on the hilt of her scimitar and stepped inside.

The Hall of Feasts was made of dark gray stone that was polished to a shine. On sunny days, the walls were like mirrors. Long banners hung from the ceiling over two long tables that ran down either side of the room. Each had at least a dozen high backed chairs placed next to them. A variety of pork, fruit, chicken, mushrooms, potatoes, sauces, and more were carted around from table to table. A hearth, tall enough for a royal bred horse to march into, burned at the far end of the room.

In front of the hearth and between the two tables, Queen Astasia presided over the gathering. Her silver dress sparkled with diamonds and gems studded into the shoulders. Her long hair tumbled down, past her plunging neckline, and into her lap as a long braid. Tribal bone tassels were braided into the curls of hair, a tribute to her guests. An empty seat waited next to her.

Ten of the Households had already arrived and taken seats at each table. In this temple to excess and finery, they were splotches of flesh, metal, and fur. They stank of deep wilderness and sweat. The Nobils clamped their hands over their hearts and spoke as one.

"Set down your bow and rest your head! Tomorrow, we hunt and you may be found dead!"

"Anca!" An enormous man called with a vigorous

whoop and waved her over.

Nobil Maciter, a family friend, was like an older brother in the order. Just as annoying and teasing as a sibling, he failed to understand how broken the world was. He thought that usurping the throne would only cause more misery. It would take more than a few deaths to shift his stubborn bulk.

Some of the other households clapped and hooted before sitting down. She only counted eight of the feathered, Nobil caps: the vibrantly dressed House Margest, the oily, grimly clad House Paegra, the top-knotted House Carlut, and the regal, medaled House Keller among others.

Anca stiffened as she caught sight of Nobils Bire and Stancu.

The disgraced Nobils had their own table. Piles of food, even more than was provided to the other Nobils, were heaped on platters in front of them. They drank from deep cups that were topped off after every sip. Extra candles had been brought around them like they were trophies or guests of note. Bire had a maid under his left arm and his right hand clutched a leg of lamb. His hair was barely tamed, washed not that long ago. Anca could still smell the soap from across the room.

Stancu had her own scantily clad woman next to her, kissing her fingers as she fed herself grapes. Her blond hair had grown much longer since Anca had last seen her. Stancu's nervous, strained jaw line and bloodshot eyes had been cured, her shoulders loose as she laughed alongside Bire.

Marin set their standard in its place, took his seat, and immediately went to work on a basket of honeyed rolls.

Nobil Maciter glanced over with a grin. "Old age hasn't taken your appetite it seems, aye?"

"I'm as sharp as the day I was born," Marin said through a mouthful of bread.

"Yeah, being so far from the border will make you plenty soft and hungry."

Maciter's Household attendants howled.

"It's alright, Marin," Anca said, "Don't be offended. Being stuck in a border Household will make anyone envious of fine living."

"Fine living?" Maciter asked.

"Indeed. We have these things called baths. You smell like you could use one."

The table roared with laughter and Nobil Calin Maciter came to her. His hair was dyed with bright colors and trimmed into a clean mohawk, like the rest of his hunting guard. His armor was made of dense plates of steel that were interconnected by rods of iron. Axes and hammers as large as adolescent children were their weapon of choice. As hunters and loggers, it seemed a prudent arsenal.

Maciter held his arms wide and hollered at her. "C'mere wee Anca, let me take a look at you."

"Now, now I won't have you accusing me of being a wee Doia to a wee Nobil," Marin said before swallowing down some roasted potatoes.

"Everything is wee to these great, blundering oafs." Anca conjured the best smile she could manage. She liked Nobil Maciter. He was one of the only other Nobils who was decent to his people.

She met his hug and clapped him on the back. "I can handle myself, Maciter. I am not wee."

"Course you are, but I wouldn't dream of crossing

you in a sparring pit. You're too fast and small. I wouldn't be able to catch ya'."

Anca let the barb pass by and tilted her head across the chamber toward Bire and Stancu.

"Maybe if you were a bit thinner and a bit younger. You see that?" she asked.

He turned and stared at Bire and Stancu for a moment too long.

"Them two? Aye." His joyful features collapsed.

They were not pigs to Anca. Pigs had value. You killed and cleaned the animal when the time was right. You were grateful to a pig for its contribution. No, these two were like wounded rabbits set to lure a hungry wolf. They were bait. Bait for what though?

"You know why they're living big when their people are dead and dying?"

"I know as much as you, Anca. Was Pese as bad as they said?"

"Worse. They won't last the winter. Come this time next year they will be carting away the survivors and we'll only ever hear about how inconvenienced the queen was."

"Shhh." Maciter pressed a pudgy finger to his lips and glanced at the head table where Astasia sat. "Don't be profaning the throne. Much less in her own house."

"Doesn't change that those two over there belong in stockades. Where are their banners? Their Doias? Their armor?"

"I think we'll find out soon." Maciter clapped a large hand over her shoulder and winked.

Anca settled in her chair and noticed the bearded Nobil Keller looking at her from across the room. He was as old as her father would be by now, hair white like a foggy morning. His beard rolled down to a chest covered with medals and icons. His left eye, long lost in a hunt, had been patched over with skin and sunken into his skull. He nodded to her and she returned the gesture, trying her best not to grimace at his injury.

"Stancu and Bire seem to be having a good time," Victor said between bites of seasoned pork.

"So much for mourning," Marin added.

"No banners or relics. They aren't in armor." Anca chewed on her lip. "I hoped the queen would have punished them for breaking the code. Protecting the north is the entire reason for all of this."

Anca swallowed a bite of pan-fried river fish. She found herself looking back at the errant Nobils. It was like a bad rash forming on her brain. Though this was what she imagined they had been up to, it was far more frustrating to see it play out. She wanted to hear Keller call them out or Maciter make a joke at their expense. There had to be some sign that they were being punished. Where was it?

A nasty, metal squeak came from her plate as her knife ground against the dish. She cut right through a piece of bread, forgetting herself as she pondered all the ways she would punish them.

"It's almost like their Households aren't here." Victor sized the two up, absorbing every detail he could.

"No, Victor. They're right there," Marin said.

"I was illustrating a point."

"Well, where's your pencil if you're illustrating?" Marin could not hide his grin as he took another bite of potato.

"You did that one on purpose."

"Marin, stop it," Anca said.

"Yes ma'am. It's just a little ribbing."

Victor leered at Marin a moment longer before speaking again.

"It's tradition to have all of this barbaric pomp and itchy circumstance, yes?" Victor scratched at the fur cloak again. "Maybe there is nothing to bring because they are not here like we are here? Maybe there is no Household to represent?"

"Flame, were I that lucky," Anca groaned.

Nobil Keller stood up from his table and cleared his throat.

"Your majesty, thank you again for hosting us, but we have filled our stomachs and drank ourselves to the edge of sobriety. Without stimulation, I am certain to be fast asleep. We should begin these proceedings."

Astasia flowered her fingers in a grandiose gesture.

"Shall we not wait a while longer? Only ten of the eleven Households are present."

"Eight of the eleven are assembled," Nobil Paegra rasped, draped in soft, gray robes adorned with corvid skulls. "I don't know what you can call Bire and Stancu."

Quiet chuckles shook both tables. Bire and Stancu clinked their cups together.

"To be without Households has been far more pleasant than to be with them," Bire said.

Anca could not take another moment of this nonsense. Keller was upset. So was the sullen Paegra. It was a game of the queen's design and she was tired of not knowing the rules.

"Explain yourselves," Anca growled.

Bire slurped down the last of his wine before answering. "I thought the women bore the children. I don't know what you're doing in armor."

"Nobil Stancu is a woman, but you toast her and insult me?"

"Don't pull me into your feud," Stancu replied. "I am done with those long nights and terrifying ordeals. Give me a warm bed and a full plate instead."

Bire nodded his head toward Stancu.

"She can have her women all she likes. As long as she makes an heir or gets out of the business."

Stancu withered in her seat and shoveled another handful of grapes into her mouth. Anca was not sure if she was more hurt by being in league with a lout like Bire or by having her dishonor aired before the rest of them.

"Stancu's weakness and Bire's ego. Maybe you two should shack up? Together you might make children worthy of cleaning my boots," Anca said.

Bire shoved the maid off his arm and sneered. He began to conjure a response when Queen Astasia raised her hands.

"Peace, Nobil Sulia. The matter is no longer a Household concern. After the devastation at Pese and the tragedy of Moura, both Households were compromised. To ensure the safety of their surviving wards, they have both agreed to a period of reconstruction under direct stewardship."

For all the indignity Anca had carried, the mental arguments she had practiced, they were not willing to defend their own behavior. They were worms. They were the lazy and delinquent fools she had thought them to be. Anca knew Bire was that bad. Stancu's surrender stung.

"You were supposed to protect them," Anca hissed at the other woman.

"I don't have it in me."

The maid next to Stancu seemed insistent on

calming the failed Nobil, like she might wake from a dream if she was not bathed in pleasures. Stancu raised her right hand: four scarred stumps where her fingers should have been.

"This happened to me when I was ten. I lost my brother at twelve and my mother at thirteen. I couldn't sleep. I still have nightmares about the hunts. Which are going away now that I'm behind these sturdy walls. They say I was born for this, but I've never felt it. You have to understand," she pleaded.

Anca was angry at her cowardice, but hated that she recognized it. It was hard to be a Nobil. To be a woman and a Nobil was something more. It bothered her because it sounded too familiar.

"I'll weep for your family as I weep for the families you were supposed to protect," Anca said.

"Shut your mouth!" Stancu shook as if she might fall over, "Do you think we all had such good families and peaceful lands? Do you know what it is like to guard a border territory? Do you know what it means to go to sleep with nightmares lingering outside of your window?"

Stancu shook. With a crazed look in her eyes, Anca knew that pushing further wouldn't bring anything but suffering. She looked away.

"Same for you Bire? Scared of the dark?"

"You have no idea what you're on about." Bire took another bite from a leg of lamb.

"I had to bury your dead. Care to know how many of your people are left?"

Bire pointed his empty cup at her like a sword and staggered on his feet.

"Heavy weighs the crown, heiress. You'll figure that

out eventually when you are done gallivanting around other Nobil's territories. Save the nagging for your eternal fiancé and let him knock you up already."

Anca set a foot onto the table and reached for the sword at her hip. Victor grabbed her arm. She let him pull her back as several other Nobils rose to get in her way.

"Not here, dear," Victor whispered.

She balled her hand into a fist, but resisted the urge to punch him. He called her dear whenever he disapproved of something. It burned like a collar. The syllables made her wince.

"Control yourself, Nobil Sulia," Keller said.

"Control? You see their behavior and I am the one who's acting out?"

Keller ignored her and turned to the queen. "This is all assembly talk. We haven't convened."

"Apparently, we have two Households that need to be dissolved," Maciter muttered.

The great doors of the hall swung open again and a man in black leather armor entered. Taller than her by a head, his hair was shaved short. A small beard and mustache framed the vicious frown plastered on his face. Even through his armor, Anca saw the flex of his muscles. All six feet of his frame swiveled to take in the gallery of scowls.

Anca nearly flinched at the first thud of his heart in her ears. It beat hard like a clockwork engine, but did not flutter with panic or fear. The resolute pulse in his chest reflected the look of disdain he hurled back at them. The sweat on his rippling body exuded a smell that overwhelmed her senses. He was a hunter bare of any pretension. Her skin prickled as her own pulse rose with an unrecognizable thrill. She had only ever heard the stories. Never had she been in the presence of the Executioner.

In one hand was a furled, muddy banner. The other hoisted a curved greatsword over his shoulder. Eugen Furloc strode into the center of the room before saying.

"We have one more Household to bury."

Chapter Six

"What is this dog doing here?"

Nobil Keller gnashed his teeth with every word. Every other Household slammed angry palms onto their tables, called for his expulsion, or spat death threats. Anca watched with pursed lips, a wary hand on her sword. She knew all of the rumors about Eugen Furloc. A part of her wanted to finish the job her mother started, but another hoped the creature would ignore her.

He was a villain. A monster. Though she had never seen him fight, the stories about his actions traveled wide. Where he and his company of hunters went, death followed. The Nobils at least had good roots. They once protected people. Eugen Furloc worked in the arts of murder and assassination. Spared from execution, he became the vilest collaborator with the throne. Eugen was everything she feared that she might become.

"The line of Furloc is exiled. He cannot be allowed into these proceedings, your majesty," Marin croaked.

"You are correct. House Furloc is long dead and dissolved." Astasia rose from her chair. Anca knew the queen had just made her first move of her little game. "Eugen joins us as a guest and as master of the Queen's Company."

"Queen's Company?" Victor asked.

"The queen's own hunters," Anca whispered under the rancor. "Not as good as us, but a far sight better than royal regulars."

Astasia gestured to Eugen with an open palm. "What do you have for us?"

Eugen unfurled the soiled cloth. It was hard to discern the polished bronze under the dirt and blood that stained it. The fabric was torn and singed on either end. Anca's stomach soured when she recognized the emblems.

"House Varcop is dead. Obliterated at the hands of the Beast of Moura."

The cloud of anger above the room drained in a flash. Anca felt panic fill them all up as it did herself. All of their majesty and traditions, their haughty positions and wealth reflected in this soiled battle standard. They could meet the same end.

It frightened her so badly that she questioned her desire to pursue this terror. She assumed by the sudden silence in the room, she was not the only one. The quiet only lasted for a moment before the storm clouds opened again.

"Impossible!"

"Another Household dead?"

"That makes three. Three! We've never lost that many before, have we?"

Eugen spoke again.

"They went without warning or note. It was only a fluke that I found out. I asked the few who remained at their bastion, your highness. Nobil Varcop believed they would benefit from being the first."

Astasia leaned forward in her chair.

"The first?"

Eugen licked his lips and fumbled through with words as he spoke.

"The first to kill the Beast of Moura. If they could kill it and bring in the carcass before the others could even muster, Varcop imagined he would be rewarded."

"Bravado," Maciter scoffed. "That bastard never played well with others."

Anca stood from her chair and raised her voice across the chamber.

"We have to begin the assembly."

"You speak out of turn, Nobil Sulia," Keller barked. "We cannot allow this rabid cur to linger. Only the Elder Nobil may call for assem—"

Astasia scarcely raised her hand toward a trio of nearby attendants as Keller went on. A bell tolled above their heads, the loud gong of the titan bell shook their table and silenced the room. Keller deepened into a further shade of red.

"He is not deserving of this place, but we cannot wait any longer. Bylaws be damned," Anca said.

A few flakes of cinder lighted from the blade on Eugen's shoulder and his lips twisted with hideous gratitude. His eyes were deep like a lightless forest. She wondered if he had forgotten how to accept goodwill.

Eugen dropped the banner on the ground and stepped around it. He sat at the seat next to Queen Astasia and a servant brought him a plate of food. He tore into a link of sausage and kicked one leg up onto the table.

"Your majesty," Keller tried once more. "With all the respect I can conjure, this is a grand offense for our order. It violates the very backbone of our agreement with the throne. None of us are safe while that thing remains among us."

"Eugen has served my family as Executioner for

years now. True enough, the Heretical Flame burns in his veins. My mages have revealed ways to control his temper. House Furloc was a mistake that needed to be purged. As the last of his line, he has made great strides to correct that record. He is on a long leash, but a sturdy one." Astasia wove her fingers together.

Keller traded glances with the other Nobils around the chamber and sat in his chair.

"Blasphemy."

"Noted." Astasia gestured for the others to sit. Anca followed the queen's motion and leaned back into her chair. She could not remove an eye from the black-clad murderer and his thunderous pulse.

"We are all devastated to hear the news of House Varcop's destruction," Astasia said. "This is a crisis the likes of which we haven't seen in twenty years. First, I would like to commend House Sulia. Its Nobil showed great loyalty to the throne and the Contract of Households by aiding when Noble Bire was, um, indisposed."

Unphased, Bire took a long drink of wine.

A vein throbbed in the side of Anca's head. This meeting was torture from the start and the real misery was about to begin. Victor would fuss and titter at anything besides pristine politeness. She was far beyond illusions. Anca raised her voice, careful to keep a respectful tone.

"I would like to commend the people of Pese. It is no small thing to stand against all the nightmares that Shadow can conjure. They faced desolation, your majesty. It was not plain rebellion. It was survival."

The queen's jaw tightened.

"Does House Sulia question the queen's judgment

in this matter?" Nobil Paegra asked from across the room, unclear if he supported or judged her.

"I merely want to remind you all that the real villain of Pese sits before us. House Sulia follows the royal decrees to the letter and that same respect has not been shown by House Bire. I demand that he be punished."

Victor uneasily whispered something under his breath. Queen Astasia uncrossed her fingers and rolled her tongue inside her jaw.

"I spoke to Nobil Bire when I learned of his violation. He agreed to give his lands over to royal authority for a period of ten years so that it might be rebuilt. During this time, Bire is a private citizen of the kingdom."

Between their family fortunes and the payout, it would be a holiday. Not an internment. Anca considered pushing for flogging. However, she was not a child. She knew that was not how the world worked.

"If they are no longer Nobils of Households, why were they here?" Nobil Margest asked.

"This is their last duty. After business has been concluded, they will leave with me so that the Households may speak of internal matters for the remainder of the convening," Astasia said.

Anca thought of the tired, hungry faces in the burning village of Pese. She doubted they would feel at ease to be under a new taskmaster's lash. They would not see any gain from their bravery. The village would die. That was the end of it.

"Then that takes us to our next item of business." Maciter pointed a finger at Eugen. "That wretch you have at your table."

Eugen made a show of ripping meat from a cut of

pork.

"His presence is related to our primary reason for meeting: the Beast," the queen said.

Anca hissed under her breath. "Here we go."

"Two Households have been destroyed by this creature. Even on a war footing, Varcop was unable to best it. The Households cannot make the same mistake as them and march with only the strength you possess." She set a hand on her breast as if she brought charity. "You need my aid."

"The north is ours," Keller snarled. "All the blood that has been shed is on our hands. No royal citizen has yet to fall to the Beast of Moura."

"And how long until they do?" Maciter asked. "Even two Households banning together is risky. If my hunters do not hold back the wights in the northern woods, they'd spread into every nearby territory."

"I intend to help you stop it before this becomes a royal matter. We must answer as a united people," Astasia said.

Anca almost laughed at the irony of this royal snake asking for them to play nice.

"And what do you have to offer?" Keller asked.

Astasia sat up in her chair, perhaps trying to project strength.

"Eugen suggested that it will stay in the north for the next few weeks. You have one chance of killing it or it will flee into the wilderness. I offer you the royal armory, our larders, and reinforcement."

"Reinforcements?" Keller drawled.

"We need to send a message that we are all in lock step. To that end, any aid provided by myself will require you to hunt alongside the Queen's Company and the

Queen's Executioner."

The outrage came as quickly as the words left her mouth. Paegra threw his hands into the air. Maciter flung a plate of food at a far wall. Even Marin rose and kicked over his chair. They howled and jeered with equal furor.

Anca's stomach snarled at the idea of serving alongside this traitor to the Households. However, the opportunity was clear. The other Nobil's tantrum would do nothing to shift the queen's requirement. To answer her demands would cross a line between Household and Throne, a truly loyal action that none could miss. This would certainly be a great service to the throne. An I-O-U for the ages.

Could she bear it? It made sense, but the idea bore a stink so bad she could taste it. Anca could swallow her disgust and work alongside someone like Paegra or even Stancu, but Eugen was a different beast. It was not just the vile magic that throbbed under his skin. There was a history between them, even though they had never been in the same room before. It was Anca's family who led the charge against House Furloc. Her family was directly responsible for the extinction of Eugen's bloodline.

The knot in her stomach graduated to nausea. This was the only way, she told herself. You can keep the mutt on its leash. Shade, maybe keep him at the end of your sword. Once the job's done, once the Beast is dead, she could dispense with them all. Even if she had to lie, she would ensure they did not get a drop of honor.

Now she just had to agree to this poisonous deal. Anca wasn't sure she could live with that sort of compromise. Even if it was for the right reasons.

"You ask too much," Keller snapped.

"If royal assistance is tied to Furloc's presence you

can forget it. None of us will budge." Maciter crashed back down in his seat.

"Never in a century," Nobil Margest said before spitting again for good measure.

As the Nobils and the queen argued, Marin leaned over to Anca.

"What are you thinking?"

Victor rasped under his breath before she could answer.

"It's damn risky. That's what I think. Too risky."

It would require more than she could have possibly imagined. To hold back such bile might kill her if Eugen didn't. This would not merely require playing a doting Nobil to the royal court. Playing the part could make her a pariah with the other Households. Not that they were chummy to begin with.

Despite all of this, the possibility was still there. Anca pressed her hands against her mouth.

"I haven't said no yet."

Victor pulled his chair closer to her. "Don't be impulsive. Are you actually considering this?"

Anca looked back to the outraged court. What did she care if these Nobils disdained her? Stuck to their thrones like moss on a tree, was it possible that their indolence would stop them from doing anything at all? The queen was the one who makes the laws. She was the one who could punish Bire all the worse if Anca could catch her ear.

Victor drove his finger into the table. "Eugen may be a willing servant of the throne, but he is a tool. I cannot think of anyone whose company is more toxic to embrace. Don't let your emotions get in the way."

Marin balled his hand on the table, a murderous look

in his eyes. "It's the Nobil's decision, prick."

"Stay out of this, Doia."

"Watch your tone with me. I may only be a Doia, but everyone in that bastion of yours answers to me."

Victor settled in his chair. The panic was barely contained behind his eyes.

"I'm sorry, but this is outlandish. Can you imagine a Household riding with Furloc? The Household so bloody they had to be put down? Disgrace. Scandal. Your family was the one to do it. Have you considered that?"

Anger crept up her neck and heat followed. Only the distracted eyes of the court kept her seated. She knew Victor would defer any action she suggested, but how could he refuse her with this opportunity at their fingertips? They were barely friends, but she expected more from him.

"This is my chance, Victor. Have you realized that? Did you even listen to what I said after I came back?"

"And how will you afford it all without the Household's favor? I will not be a pauper because of your damn sentiment."

Perhaps he wasn't as good as she imagined him to be. The fearful glitter in his eyes, like gold coins, laid bare the last of her illusions. Even when he winced, realizing he had gone too far, it could not erase the knowledge of what lay beneath that well-meaning, pampered face.

"I'm sorry. I shouldn't have spoken to you that way."

She looked away from him as Eugen stood from the head table. Nobils recoiled in their seats. He opened the palms of his hands and spoke through his bared teeth.

The gem in his dreadful sword sizzled.

"House Furloc is dead. Nothing's changing that. I am just a servant of the queen. Your decisions and punishments…" He fell quiet. His hand waved back and forth as if deliberating with himself. "They still stand. I will never be a Nobil."

"You don't deserve to be breathing. That madness in your veins can't be trusted," Maciter said.

"It makes me stronger than you."

His dark eyes snapped to the mohawked man near Anca's seat. A shiver ran down her spine.

"It makes you a beast," Maciter said.

Eugen snarled and Anca thought that he would lunge across the table.

"My family were never beasts!"

A shower of cinders burst from his sword. The Nobils in attendance recoiled in their seats and the Doia from House Paegra drew her knife. Wiggling his fingers toward the weapon, Eugen instead pulled out a small leather pouch from his pocket and breathed from it. The sparks from his weapon quieted and then ceased.

"Still a wild dog." Marin shook his head. "How many graves were buried before they figured out that you all had become monsters?"

Her eyes drifted to the scars on the backs of her hands. Would there be Nobils fifty years from now with the same scars? Would there even be Nobils or would their order have collapsed under its own divisions? Keller would never change. Neither would Maciter for all his good intentions. They would ensure that the queen's power was sustained and their own wealth with it.

Would her children carry these same scars?

She stood from her chair and stared down Astasia's icy glare. Anca tried to push Eugen out of her mind. He was just a tool. A means to an end.

"House Sulia accepts. We will join the Queen's Company to hunt this Beast."

Her voice echoed across the chamber as every other voice stopped to listen. A quiet groan of annoyance squeezed from Keller's mouth. Victor quietly fumed, his face turning crimson. Eugen slapped his knee and cackled.

"Seriously? You?"

"I can see the importance of this moment. That you can't see it confirms that you're even less of a hunter than I thought. Regardless of that, if this is what the queen demands then I will meet it."

Eugen's smile leached from his face and he pressed the bag of herbs to his nose. A pulsing vein trailed down to his wide shoulders. The hair stood up on the back of her neck. It was the same feeling she had around a Shadow beast. She felt like prey.

"Anca, what are you doing?" Maciter whispered.

"Doing my damn job. What about you?"

The queen rubbed her hands across her table and beamed.

"I accept this pledge. House Sulia will be given four days to muster strength and gather supplies."

"Your parents would not have stood for this."

Keller's voice carried the tone of profanity. His mood had gone from nasty to angry over the course of the gathering. Now he looked at Anca as if she were a monster to be hunted. The Elder Nobil, the same one she hoped to unseat, judged her actions. If this pissed off Keller, it had to be the right decision.

"Do you remember them well?" Anca asked. "They would not dawdle while people died. We are servants to the throne and the throne has offered a boon. I am not yours to command."

Keller shook his head. "Unthinkable—"

"We find those terms acceptable, your highness," Anca interrupted Keller. "I request you keep our payment for the bounty. It is my wish that you use it to help rebuild the village of Pese."

"Granted." The queen gestured for Eugen, Bire, and Stancu to follow her as she stood. "I will take my leave. The chamber is the Households' for any business they deem fit to discuss. Please eat and drink to your heart's content. You are all my guests. Anca, please come by the throne room when you are done here."

The queen walked by, the two ex-Nobils and Eugen following behind her. Eugen watched Anca. As he passed close to her, he gave a small bow. This close to him, a prickling sensation ran over her skin. There was a vile heat about him, as if his entire body thrummed with fire. His brown eyes glanced up at her and she detected something sincere in their darkness.

"Thank you, Nobil Sulia," he said in a hushed voice.

Anca gripped the steak knife next to her plate. With the queen still watching, Anca nodded to him, every fiber of her being screaming against it. It was as if her very bones refused. She knew to do it. She had to.

Get the job done, work around the bastard, and get rid of him and his ilk at the right time. This glory would be hers, all hers. She was not going to let some craven monster like Eugen profit from her hard work. This was her chance, not his.

Chapter Seven

All those cowards shivered when he passed by. Even his new ally of convenience, Anca Sulia, was ready to gut him. He did not miss her hand twist around the knife next to her dinner plate. What he said was no lie. Eugen was thankful for this chance. That someone, anyone, would swallow these terms to protect their people was a pleasant surprise. He believed that these Nobils were so complacent that such slaughter would not move them.

Eugen made a habit of staying informed on the various Nobils. Nobil Keller feared the queen more than any Shadow beast. Nobil Paegra was itching for old man Keller to die so he could make a play for his seat. Nobils Margest and Grotor had been having a secret affair for the last two years.

Anca was not so complacent or assuming. She knew her lands and regularly patrolled them. She took an active hand in neighboring Households. Her brevity did not make any friends, but he admired that. If a Household's people were rebellious, but had not crossed the line to violence, they called upon Anca. The Executioner was reserved for the worst cases. It had made House Sulia notable. Not just because they helped purge his ancestors.

She was risking all of that legacy to sign on with Eugen. He could not imagine the scathing criticism she would endure without the queen present. Would there even be anything to discuss further? She would get to know what it was like to be an exile, to be a Furloc. Eugen hoped that the lesson would not go unnoticed. Anca was only a few years younger than himself. Still young enough to question things.

They would not strip her title. He doubted they would move to weaken House Sulia while three other Households were dead or dissolved. They needed all the help they could get. It would be scorn and gossip then. Let her feel that burning hate, the cindering pulse in your veins when everything turns against you, he thought. Her lips pulled back in a hideous grin. Those sparkling green eyes filled with revulsion. It would not be Eugen she hated anymore.

"Eugen." Astasia's chiding voice tore him from his thoughts. "You're flaking again."

He looked where his sword leaned against the table. Cinders blistered from it and settled into an ashy pile at the tip of the blade. The elegant green rug, crisscrossed with patterns of black and white, dulled to a featureless gray.

The throne room was twice as wide and long as the Hall of Feasts. Large, stained-glass windows, each of them a masterpiece, lined the ceiling. Silver fringed lamps hung in a line above the blue runner. Skulls of dead beasts mounted along the walls were dwarfed by a massive trophy above the throne itself. Multi-lobed, reptilian eye sockets leered above fangs as large as broadswords. The bones had been polished and cleaned, yellowing with age in only the farthest corners.

The throne was made of marbled black stone. Jewels were set into each of the four steps that rose to the royal seat. It was flanked by smaller chairs, like the high-backed chairs of the gathering. Closer to them was a long table alongside the left side of the chamber. Lit by the rainbow shine of the stained glass, papers and maps were laid neatly on it.

Astasia had taken the tribal knots and bones out of her hair. Her near-platinum curls allowed to run down her back, she still wore the silvered gown. Barely in the shadows of the room, a battalion of servants waited for the smallest request.

"Apologies."

He moved toward the blade and cupped his hands to scoop up the ashes.

"No, no. That isn't your place."

Astasia snapped her fingers and jerked her hand toward the mess. One of the cadre of servants who lined the room broke from their silence and hurried as though compelled by a scalding prod.

"I can help."

"Don't you consider it. You know your place. They know theirs."

They feverishly scooped the ashes into a bucket while two others prepared a broom and soapy water. When they took a moment too long in their cleaning, Astasia hissed and rolled her eyes.

"Hurry up or I'll have you all replaced."

None of them looked away from their work. They frantically finished cleaning the spot and disappeared into the shadows around the room as the grand doors at the end of the hall opened.

"A moment later and I'd have to have them branded. I won't be made to look messy in front of the competition."

Astasia checked her dress and plastered the usual,

fake smile across her face.

"The Nobils are not competition, my queen," he corrected.

She rolled her eyes and gestured toward the door.

Mage Superior Costea stepped through and swept her arm in a revealing motion. On the other side of the door, Anca stood with her chin slightly raised. Marin and Victor followed behind, the fiancé's face twisting from a scowl into a smile as fake as Astasia's.

"Nobil Sulia and her companions, your majesty."

Eugen groaned. "No need for formalities, Costea. We just saw them."

The trio crossed the grand hall. Victor was quick to wrap his hands together and give a small bow.

"Honored, your majesty. We're all honored by this place and your gracious pleasure, from my toes to my brow."

Anca subtly bit her lip, her eyelids flickering. Astasia beckoned to the Nobil, who took her hand before bowing. It was an automatic response, something baked into the Nobil's heads. He was prepared for the glad handing smiles they always had. She bowed and bent her back into a straight line pointed at the monarch's hand as expected. Predictable.

With her face toward the floor, her lip curled. Her teeth bared in disgust. Her eyes lifted to the silver flats that peeked out from Astasia's flowing gown. Anca's eyes were a light green, like the glow of sunlight through a canopy. They gleamed like steel sharpened over a grudge. There was a smoldering flame beneath all of that conditioned servitude. Ready to catch fire if given too much fuel.

Her eyes flicked to him. Their gaze met for the

briefest moment before he pulled himself away.

"Thank you. Bastion Nilor proves to be a grand host once again," Anca said.

"Really, I should be thanking you." Astasia beckoned for the Nobil to rise.

Anca's eyebrow raised as she straightened her back. "For what?"

"The Households have been intractably difficult for years. They second guess everything I say and lay provisions on every request. They don't trust me. Unthinkable. When have I ever been duplicitous?"

"That plainly isn't true," Victor spoke up. "It's a symbiotic relationship. They need you as much as you need them. However, the Households pride themselves on their autonomy. Without that, what claim would they have to their lands?"

Astasia laughed. It was a stilted, haughty sound that was more akin to fascination.

"His face is as handsome as his words. He certainly knows how to dress up an ugly truth."

Anca tilted her head, her jaw muscle tensing. It would have been cute if he didn't know just how lethal she was. She was one of the few that actively hunted. Those nerves were practiced. He wondered how long he could match her in a duel. Life force rushed from her chest and up her neck. She was losing her patience.

"He has many talents. But, with all due respect, we aren't here to discuss Victor's better traits. There's a monster to hunt."

Eugen nodded his head. There's the Nobil he had heard stories about. Someone willing to get in the thick of it.

"Damn right," he said.

As the others walked over to the table, Victor stepped out ahead of Anca.

"Executioner, show us what you've got so far."

The pompous prick rubbed his hands together, but his heart raced as he met Eugen's eye. The Flame bled violence into his thoughts. He imagined snapping Victor's spine like a toothpick. Anca reached forward and grabbed Victor's shoulder. She gently turned him toward herself.

"I need you to get the others ready to ride. I want us to depart before sundown."

Victor gave a wheezing chuckle. "Anca, I feel like I should be present. This is important."

"It is important. You've done your part, let me do mine. Can you gather the others?"

He raised his hand toward Astasia and looked for some intervention. The queen watched with a small flicker of entertainment in her eyes. She always enjoyed seeing people twist against each other. Eugen had seen her spin various aristocrats against each other with gossip she planted months in advance.

The silence lasted three moments too long, the pain of it sending a flicker of heat up Eugen's neck. The idiot did not quite realize how useless he was. Victor opened his mouth, then smiled instead.

"Of course. I'm told that I must prepare for our departure. My queen, Mage Superior." Victor bowed to them before leaving.

The couple gave each other a look as he passed by. The cold steel look flickered in her eyes again. He brushed his hair back with a flip of irritation and stalked down the long, glorious hall. Victor looked up to the glories around them with envy in his eyes before disappearing past the imposing throne room door. Anca did not watch him go. She looked over the maps and notes spread across the table. Eugen inclined for her to look at a specific point on the map.

"I was near Moura when I found Varcop's bodies. The creature's tracks suggest a solitary beast. Very mobile. Perhaps nine feet long. Carnivorous, but not every kill is for food. It left many bodies behind."

"Is it possible it only defends itself? It might be retaliating if it isn't killing for food," Anca said.

Eugen shook his head after a moment. An observation he had not considered. She was smart. Add it to the tally of surprises, he thought.

"Doubtful, but we'll know more once we get there and have a look around. I've already drafted a list of items to be included in the Queen's Company inventory."

"What about dogs?" Marin asked.

"Dogs?" Astasia perked her head up from whatever thought had occupied her.

"A pack of dogs could sniff it out. Send it up a tree," Marin said. "Not terribly effective with Shadow beasts. If it's only a little bigger than a person, then it might be intimidated by a dozen hounds."

"We won't be bringing any," Eugen said.

"I'm guessing Varcop had dogs?" Anca smirked and arched an eyebrow. Her smile was too bright for such a killer.

"It didn't help them. We'll need tools to constrain its movement: net traps, flares, bolas. I've also requested a few variations of snares. If we can cripple it, killing it will be easier."

Anca traced the game paths that wound through the

northern territories. As her eyes went to the manifest of requested equipment, Eugen became aware of a raised pulse in the room.

It was low and steady. A heartbeat used to a drip feed of stress. It was behind Anca, a handful of steps from the table. Doia Marin watched him, arms crossed. His hand dangled near the hilt of his sword.

He had almost forgotten. Anca's clarity and focus drove those lingering reminders from him. It was only a few moments, but he couldn't remember the last time he had been regarded as human. The red headed man to his left was there to bring those thoughts right back.

"I do not bite, Doia," Eugen said.

Marin let his palm fully settle on the pommel of his blade.

"That's not what I've heard."

Heat flared up Eugen's spine. His fingers trembled as power crept into his hands. Cinders flaked from his sword as the lure of rage began to ring in his ears. He could show the Doia how his steel could bite. These Nobils waltzed into the heart of their authority, in front of their monarch, and still carried such disrespect. It was intolerable. Bruising Marin would be a little lesson to his Nobil.

"You haven't seen what I'm capable of."

The queen cleared her throat. "Please, focus and continue."

Eugen tore his eyes away from Marin. He glanced at Astasia and hoped for her venomous glare to be settled on Marin. Instead, he found her glowering at himself.

Of course, he thought. Remember yourself. He was truly lesser than them in the eyes of the world. In the eyes of his queen. Even if he was better than nearly all of them. He struggled to focus as he went back to the map in front of him.

"The uh, weather. Weather in the area is rainy, like here. Easier to track if…" Eugen blinked and shook his head before continuing. He rambled as he talked. Drifting from point to point. Marin bristled in the corner of his eye. Eugen's blood itched to spill the hot, red violence that gave him power.

Anca stabbed a finger at the swampy terrain near the borders of their land. Focused on the job ahead of her. At least she had more restraint than those beneath her.

"The marshes on the borders of the Lost Lands are hard to navigate. Camping will be difficult. We will need a few clockwork wagons."

Eugen's jaw tightened and he nodded slowly.

"I was getting there."

"You're moving too slow for me."

"We would gladly spare two of our rigs. Not our best of course. Those are needed in the south," the queen said. "As for other arms, we will not need your support. I thought it might be the other way around."

Anca raised her eyebrows and shifted onto her other foot.

"You might be too used to fighting people. Your equipment will be ill-suited to pursuing beasts."

"You'd think that, wouldn't you?" Eugen muttered.

"Calm yourself," the queen said.

He reached for the bag of herbs at his hip. The lights around the room grew brighter, his breath quickening. I'm not helpless, he thought. I can control this. Anca shifted her full attention back to him. He had the briefest impulse to step away from her.

"I don't need an out-of-practice Nobil who's never

been in the field telling me how to conduct my hunt." Anca clamped her hands behind her back. "This is my hunt, not yours."

He shouldn't have been surprised. She was a Nobil, just like the rest. Anca knew to focus on the hunt, but that didn't mean she thought any better of him. It still hit him like a hammer. Eugen fought the urge to bite back, to curse and howl. He had to play nice.

"Yes. I would be honored to serve under one of such ambition." He pushed the words out of his mouth, each syllable more unwilling than the next.

"Keep it that way," she snapped. "Remember that your prey is usually in stockades."

"You would do better to speak to him kindly. He is your ally in this matter, not an opposing hunter," the queen said.

"I am treating him kindly."

Marin grinned. No doubt, he despised the queen as much as Eugen did.

"We are tolerating his presence. I would remind you that every Household, mine included, sees Eugen as a canker. His legacy is a blood stain and perhaps the darkest mark on our history since the Lost Lands became so. His research is welcome, so are the hunters under his command. I will not be told to make amends with this spawn of slaughter."

Eugen could see the anger wriggling in Astasia's eyes. He guessed that no one had spoken to her like that in years. Maybe her entire life. How desperate was she, he wondered. Anca was a wise hunter and knew when she could bully a larger predator into compliance.

Can you afford to scold her? Show your cards, little queen, he thought.

Astasia remained silent as she chewed over her words. She then slowly nodded, her eyes closing with solemn purpose.

"I understand."

That was all he had earned. It felt colder than any winter he had seen. What had he bargained for then? Years of fighting, no, years of murder. That's what he had done for Astasia and her parents before her. It was not even enough to bring this truant Nobil in line. He was nothing to the Households. Eugen realized he might be less to her.

"We will plan to meet at Bastion Ochepti in four days. Eugen, can you and yours make it in time?" Anca asked.

"I can handle my own muster," Eugen said through his teeth.

"See that you do."

Anca turned from them after giving a small bow toward the queen. Chestnut brown hair curled after her like a great cat's tail following the creature into the brush. Marin cocked a curly eyebrow and bobbed his head as he followed Anca out. Each clicking boot step inflamed the rage beating in his heart. Every one of them was a challenge, echoing like laughter against the stony arches above.

Eugen thought it would be easier once the grand doors closed behind them, but he stewed. Boiling, he crumpled a parchment under his fingers. He would prove her wrong. This hunt would remind them that Eugen Furloc was not a carrion-gnawing mutt. They would be made to understand. The Nobils, even Anca, needed to be embarrassed at their own game.

Chapter Eight

In all Anca's life, she had never seen such a tremor of gossip pass through the otherwise somber Household. She was feared by many for the compliance orders. Gossip was scant and always hard to find. Perhaps it was this wrinkle in an otherwise indelible reputation, that set the hunting guards' tongues loose and the villagers yearning for details. Hunters gossiped to their servants, who told stories to their families at night. Within two days, everyone in Sanuli had heard the story.

Anca Sulia would hunt the Beast of Moura alongside Eugen Furloc.

By the third day, it had begun to change the way often-repeated stories did. Some said that she was being blackmailed by the throne to do it. Clearly, their Nobil was hiding something if she could be forced to take such a blasphemous order. Another version said it was her own free will and had she spat in Nobil Keller's face. One man, a fast-talking, glory hound named Cezar, had added that House Sulia had been dissolved and Anca was trying to hide her shame. He was thrown into a nearby pond.

She had already looked over the topography of Moura, the local fauna, former population, known game trails, and caverns. Her arrows were re-feathered, her crossbow cleaned and reassembled, her coil-spear tuned, daggers sharpened, and scimitar polished.

As the Household prepared to ride out, Marin was weighed down with ledgers and barrels. It was his job to ensure they rode out with everything they needed. It was her job to prepare for the killing to come.

The only thing left was to forget tradition and help Marin load boxes for the journey ahead. This business took her to the armory of Bastion Sulia. The studded iron door was heavier than most livestock. It was warm in the winters and cool in the summers. During her younger years, when grunt work was forced onto her as a test, she had dozed away hours down there. It was a place of comfort. It held memories of days when her dreams were brighter. She gripped the worn copper latch and pushed the heavy door open.

"Damn thing."

A hunting guard stumbled to his knees as he chased after a bundle of arrows. His amber hair was barely visible as he ducked under a table after the lost item. His shoulders bumped into the low table as he climbed under it. She dimly recognized him. A new member of their order, he had been with them for just over a year. The new hunter had yet to see the field.

What a hunt to be your first, she thought. Very few were being left to guard their bastion. A young person like this would be valuable in the days to come: compliant, eager to prove themselves, and quick to recover from injury.

"How's the tally?" she asked.

"Almost finished. Damn twine broke again. Did you ever hear if we need to bring a dog leash for Furloc?"

The man chuckled at his joke. She was not sure he had seen who entered the room before he went scrambling after the ammunition.

"I don't believe we will," she said.

Anca crossed behind him to a set of crates. Wool jackets would be a valuable asset against the coming cold. Autumn was nearly over and they would be riding into the face of winter.

"That is assuming that we are meeting with House Furloc or Queen's Company. Whatever they are calling it these days. Flame knows it's about as clear as dishwater and the Nobil is just as opaque."

Anca was never privy to gossip these days. Everything was spoken in hushed tones behind her back. He must have assumed she was one of the other women in the Household. She decided to play coy for now.

"Then the Nobil ought to have a good reason for it."

Her tone must have given her away. The man froze in place as his fingers grabbed the loose bundle of arrows. He swiftly turned on his toes and his eyes went wide. He stood, almost falling over as he did, and quickly bowed.

"Nobil Sulia, I apologize."

"Relax. There'll be enough bowing and title-calling when we're in the field. Spare me a little for now." She opened the lid of the crate she sought and made a tally of coats in their stock.

"I thought Marin would be handling equipment tallies," the young hunter asked.

"Doia Marin is otherwise occupied. I thought I could lend a hand rather than twiddle my thumbs."

Anca leaned her elbows on the table between them.

"Well, it is an honor to work alongside my Nobil."

There were very few times she could get those under her to be honest. Letting this one wriggle away would be a missed opportunity.

"They say I'm unclear, do they?"

He swallowed. He was visibly trembling as the words finally came out of his mouth.

"Is it true? What we've heard about House Furloc?"

Anca was hoping to keep this under control. It was foolish. She saw that now. Maybe her hunters could have kept their bile and suspicions to themselves with another Household of ill repute. They did not even have the whole story. Only the oldest hunters would remember.

Better that he knows, she thought. Anca exhaled and ran a hand through her hair. She knew the story well. That didn't mean she relished telling it.

"Their specialty was Flame magic, but not the kind we all know. They took the fire into their veins. Just a bit. Not enough to burn themselves out."

"And they didn't die from it?" Doru asked.

"It's a dangerous practice and plenty did burn out, but not enough. It made them stronger than an ox, faster than a hawk, and ferocious as a starved wolf. It turned them into monsters. All they wanted was blood. People, livestock, entire villages. They were a plague by the end."

She barely remembered those days. The details were told to her in stories that passed the royal censors. What she remembered most was the look on her parents face before they went out to end it. They held her longer than they ever had, tears in their eyes as if they already lost her.

"My mother led the coalition against them. It took three entire Households and the royal army to do it. Eugen is the last of them."

Doru scratched at the table idly. He spoke with reverence that would be fitting at a funeral.

"I've never heard these stories."

"Astasia's mother was afraid of what might happen if the story was confirmed. Things are already too tense."

"And we will be pursuing this beast alongside them?" He pulled his lips into his mouth.

It was bold to pursue this line of questioning. Most of her other hunters would have clammed up by now.

"Yes. We will be pursuing the Beast with the aid of Queen's Company and the Executioner."

"And we are still recognized by the other Households?"

"What?"

"It's another stupid rumor. But still, there was worry that our lands might be forfeit."

Anca clicked her tongue. "The other Households are not happy about this, but we are not disbanded."

His terrified eyes broke with a smile and he slapped his thigh. "That's a relief."

"Doru, isn't it? I do my best to remember all my hunting guards, but your name is slipping my mind." His name had come to her once he smiled. Among many dour, hardened veterans, his optimism was notable.

"Indeed, Doru Clagza. I was tapped to join the expedition."

"Glad to have you. You must've caught Marin's eye. Only a year and he chose you to come along. The elders of our company are not easy to impress."

"I know it. My friend Vali served under your mother as well. Older than my own da. He likes to remind me what is right and wrong. He's gruff, but I think he's pleased."

Anca's gaze drifted to the corner of the room. Vali Groia was a veteran of veterans. He began his service under her grandfather and rose close to Doia for decades. He never made the effort to claim the title. So set in his ways, he would never have the flexibility that the role required. He was alongside her parents when House Furloc was destroyed. Anca could not imagine the distrust her actions might have fostered.

"I'm sure he isn't too happy about this Eugen business."

The tremors of dissent were just gossip for now. Anca knew rebellion though, she had seen enough in her compliance orders. It always started in the smallest places. You could never tell what the match would be.

Some towns could bear atrocities and tyranny for decades without a quiver of resistance, only to rise up when some ethereal trigger had been tripped. Others would roil the moment that butter prices rose too high. Sunali had been placid for nearly a century. Anca's stomach turned to think of that streak breaking under her rule.

"You know, Nobil Sulia, I meant what I said. There's no shame in this."

His eyes were warm, his tall stature bent to seem less intimidating.

"House Keller and the others beg to differ," she grunted.

"Let the old codgers grouse. You've made it clear to us, ma'am. This isn't a royal court where favors are the currency of the day. We're here to help the people. They need help now. Even if it means we have to work with erstwhile allies."

She chuckled. "That's a nice way to say a family of mass murderers."

"I don't know the Executioner, but isn't he just a

shine older than you? He would've been a young man when the House was purged. For all we know, maybe his hands are clean?"

"And that would excuse the Flame magic? The brutal repression?"

"I'd like to think we all deserve a second chance. We are not the stories told about us. Might be time to put down the ax. It's been ground enough."

It was refreshing to hear out loud. When thoughts were allowed to linger for too long, they filled the air like gnats. She had heard nothing but buzzing for days.

"Are you sure you're a hunting guard? You sound more like a poet or a philosopher."

Doru snickered and shoved his hands into his pockets.

"I come from the same breed as your fiancé. Had my fair share of literature courses as a boy before shipping off to fight monsters. You're not the only one with expectations from a bloodline."

The mention of Victor soured her thoughts. One problem at a time, she reminded herself. He would be dealt with soon. The way he behaved at the convening was a bridge too far. She brought her mind back to Doru.

"It suits you. Finish up here and report to Doia Marin. We're leaving soon."

"Yes, ma'am."

Doru grabbed the bundles of arrows and went back to counting and wrapping. She double checked her count of coats quickly and went for the armory door.

"One more thing," Doru said. "Is the Furloc business a secret? Best way to kill a rumor is to air out the truth."

Anca tapped her fingers on the door handle for a

moment. What did she have to fear? If the truth was out there already, it might only mutate into something worse without confirmation.

"Go ahead and share it. Like you said, no shame in turning over a new leaf."

"As you command."

Chapter Nine

The colors were raised. The banners of House Sulia
flew over the train of twenty riders who left through the
legendary stone gates. The family's ancient credo carved
into the arch above them, they looked every bit like the
stories described them. Just as the convening of
Households was a tradition with pomp, so was the ride
out for a new hunt.

Their armor was polished to a shine. Deep blue
cloaks flapped in the mid-morning sun. After leaving the
village of Sunali, they were on their own. Resupply
would be an unsure prospect. Two clockwork wagons
ground forward on shiny, brass wheels.

She did not need to look back to know Victor
watched from their high window. He would rather be
caught dead before going beyond the walls of a mansion
or a bastion. Regardless, that wasn't why his sulking
gaze traced their route down the road.

He had slipped a yellow velvet tassel out of his
pocket and put it into her palm. "Put this in your hair.
I'm told it's a common tradition amongst those who ride
to battle."

It would be good to fiddle with during quiet times.
It was played out, expected, not entirely deep, and would
give her away in the deep brush if she wore it. Anca
swallowed, her throat suddenly dry as she searched for
the right words. This conversation was unavoidable.

"Why do we keep playing these games? Gestures. Gifts. It's all for show and neither of us really care about what it's trying to fake. You made that much clear at the convening."

Worry pinched his brow.

"We will be wed someday, dear. Someday when we both feel the time is right. After this, perhaps. Imagine the prestige you would carry as Elder Nobil. Does it come with tithes? Taxes?"

"I can't do this anymore, Victor."

It leaped from her lips as if another second in her head would make her scream.. Anca could not tolerate him anymore, now knowing what he really was.

"You don't mean that," he said.

A trickle of moisture beaded on his forehead. A harried pulse raced up his neck traced in the green of her Othersight. So close to him, the hammering in his chest nearly deafened her. Anca knew what a panicked pulse sounded like.

"I've wanted to say this for a while. If you really wanted to get married, there have been opportunities. You aren't the only guilty one here. I didn't seize on them either. Because…" She took a deep breath. "Because I don't love you. I'm not sure I even like you. And deep down you don't want to marry me either."

He shook his head.

"No. I can't go home after four years without a wife. Not without something to show for the fucking time I've spent in this rock."

She scowled, her arms crossing as his resistance crumbled with every successive breath. "You said it a few days ago. You'd rather be touring vineyards and painting pretty pictures. I'm just giving you what you want."

He stammered, shoulders high around his ears. His eyes did not search her for pity. They skittered across the ground as if imagining his next steps.

Anca almost pitied him. Almost. Had he reacted like this to the massacre at Pese, to her proposal at the convening, to anything that mattered to her, she would have gladly taken that stupid ribbon. After tolerating several more of his gasping breaths, she gestured to the tower's gates.

"Take your time packing. I understand making arrangements will take some time. Don't be here when I return or I will make our broken engagement a public affair no one will miss."

Victor ran his fingers through his hair, shaking his head with a fraying energy. His eyes darted to the few hunters who watched them say goodbye.

"Anca," he whispered with a harsh voice, "what will they think?"

She pulled the engagement band from her side pocket. Pulling it off that morning felt like lifting a yoke from her shoulders. Anca shoved it into his hand.

"Goodbye, Victor."

He did not move as she climbed on her horse and rode out to her waiting hunters. An uneven rasp left his lips as she trotted away, but she did not stop to see if he recovered his nerve. Victor must have judged it better to keep those words to himself. Passing under the phrase "You go no farther" once again, the endless plain seemed wider and brighter than it had in years.

Anca led from the head of the caravan, Marin and Doru close behind. She wore the feathered cap of Nobils, but the rest of her outfit was the well-worn armor and cloth that she was used to. A dark blue cape flapped over a layer of chainmail. Her spiked gauntlets were fortified with plates of impenetrable Warden Tree lumber.

They traveled west for a few hours until they reached a juncture. The western road was well paved and ended at Thronetown. The other road, covered by crumbled flagstone, went northwest. Anca pointed to this second road, her whistle rising over the panting horses. A murmur over the clacking of hooves acknowledged her order and the caravan turned with her. A twisted, aging wreck of a wagon sat by the roadside. The bed was torn to pieces. The metal banding rusted to disintegration. Anca knew it was just the first of such reminders.

"Stars above." Doru looked down the long, dilapidated road ahead.

The gray, withered plains were littered with the dead memories of Households. Low, wrecked ruins of walls and rusted shields barely escaped the earth that dragged them ever downward. Half-buried catapults and the merest bones of scorched camps spread across the endless landscape of carnage.

A little farther and the rusting ruin was replaced with a sea of tarnished ivory. Gargantuan rib cages of monsters bulged from the dirt like trees. Flowers sprouting at their bases. Skulls sunk into the earth after centuries, only parts of their once fearsome jaws visible above the ground. There was more armor here. This time you could spy bits of gnawed bones within them. Left undisturbed by both the crown and the Households, Anca thought of it as a memorial.

"Don't be somber," Marin said to Doru. "You'd be lucky to meet the Fated Death of our ancestors."

Fated Death was what waited for all hunters. The profession was not without risk, indeed hunters usually died in every hunt. Nobils denied that they felt fear, but she knew just how human they were. For some, like Stancu, it was the bloody, screaming, painful end that kept them awake at night. If Fated Death waited for her at the end of this road, with this much at stake, it would be the cruelest fate she could imagine.

She had spat in the face of House Keller, questioned the queen's judgment, in her own throne room no less, and now had a chance to make things right. Turning back was not an option. Anca broke from her thoughts and put her horse back to a fast canter.

Down the road, the bones became more brittle and the wreckage more rusted. Their flags had blown away, the wind making a mockery of such unshakeable defenses. This far out from the capital, people did not have easy access to brick, stone, or even cob. Bones would have to suffice.

They entered the territory of House Paegra that afternoon. A twin-peaked bastion that flew gray flags, it lorded over a town that clutched to the side of a far riverbank. Homes pressed tightly toward the shore as though they had grown from the reeds. A Household known for its skill at tracking and stealth, they must have seen Anca coming.

Along the roadside, they had raised foreboding black flags. Illustrated worms crawled from the eyes of a red skull, its jaws hung open in an endless scream. These banners clustered around the main turn off into the Household's bastion. There was no time for a detour, even if it would make her feel better to pay back the ill will. They would bear this insult on the chin.

"Lovely to see they regard our hunt so highly," Marin grunted.

"That's the mark of Death Magic," Doru said, "Are they mages?"

Anca would not give Nobil Paegra an inch of satisfaction. Even if it would satisfy that beat-red, angry part of her that wanted to rip down their flags. She kept her features neutral as she said.

"That is the mark of Death, but it has another meaning."

Doru let his fingers run through the worn, ragged fabric of the banners as they passed by. "They wish death on us?"

"They don't wish for it." Marin said. "They expect it. That's the Funeral Flag. It's only flown when a Nobil dies. You don't see it on their bastions, do yah?"

A handful of Paegra hunting guards stood nearby. Their helmets were forged to look like hawks, the beaks sharpened so carefully that they could kill with them. Before Anca passed by them, one lifted the front of their helmet and spit onto the middle of the road.

"Hey!" Marin rose in his saddle, fingers reaching for his ax. "You wanna bring your lily-hided Nobil down here? You're going to need it when I—"

"Stop!"

Anca cast a harsh glance toward Marin, who quickly sat back into his saddle. She did not slow her horse and none of her company dared to break rank with her.

Even if she succeeded in this endeavor, what sort of welcome would she receive from the others? Anca imagined a magical passing of the order, everyone begrudgingly obeying the new way of things. She was the resistance. The rabble-rouser. Such a convulsion might shake apart the foundations of their trust. Paegra, at least, would need to be brought to heel.

They left House Paegra behind and reached the farthest limits of the kingdom as the sun tilted toward the horizon. The last dying rays of the day flashed on the stony side of a distant tower. Anca recognized the shape of Bastion Ochepti by its silhouette alone.

It was merely a watch tower despite the title of bastion. It had no wall, no moat, and no way to survive a siege. It was too new to know the rage that once filled the countryside with nameless graves. Though it technically belonged to House Paegra, it flew the royal flag. It was a lonesome thing, a single tower built against the untamed wild that spread out in front of it. Tonight, it would have company to spare.

Her Othersight showed twenty beating hearts in the camp. She smelled wine and the stink of tired horses. The Queen's Company had beat them to the muster grounds. Anca chuckled back her irritation. Eugen must have urged them into a frenzy of preparation to already be camped.

At the edges of the camp, the green pulses of Life flashed to an end as grass and weeds were ripped from their roots. A ridge of stone walls broke upward from the earth. Three gaps around the perimeter were left open, but these were flanked by bonfires and coil gun-wielding guards. Earth Magic was a rare thing, the grumpiest and least accommodating of the elements.

"A mage? They brought a damn mage with them?" Marin stammered.

Anca waved a cautious hand toward him. "It's probably just the one. No reason to get nervous."

"They could have warned us. Our people aren't

happy to be working alongside Eugen to begin with. Now they have to tolerate a witch as well?"

It was an unexpected complication, but likely only the first of many. Anca had met enough mages to know they were as varied as anybody. However, it did little to erase the universal suspicion. Those that commanded the elements were a reminder of why their world was so broken in the first place.

"Wasn't enough for them to tear everything up with their war. They had to linger," Marin muttered.

Doru could not take his eyes from the tents and fire set around the lonesome tower.

"Aren't they just people? How do we know this one is so bad?"

Marin poked Doru's chest, nearly falling out of his saddle to make his point.

"Because it's Eugen's mage. Think of the kind of person who would serve that rabid dog. After that, understand that they could kill us all and we'd be hard pressed to stop them."

"Too late to turn back. Keep your opinions under your hat, Marin," Anca said.

Anca and Marin dismounted not far from Eugen's camp. Members of the Queen's Company wore black, studded leather armor and shining chainmail. Anca's eyes caught the hulking shape of their leader amongst them. By the flash of his eyes in the sunlight, she knew his Othersight had seen her as well. Without the prying eyes and heavy obligation of the crown, she was wary of how Eugen might behave.

He wore the same black armor and chainmail, but was augmented with an oversized pauldron that covered his neck and upper-right arm. The bulge of his biceps flickered in the flames. A vein throbbed under skin marred by a dozen nicks and diminutive scars. His body was undeniably impressive. The terrifying sword was missing, though Anca suspected it was nearby.

"Welcome to the border. I'm told its new for you all," Eugen said.

Anca would never admit it, but it was true. Past the line of bonfires set by the bastion, there was not a light to be seen in the Lost Lands. The setting sun showed the stretches of untamed forest and swampland. She had never set foot there over her time as a Nobil.

Eugen lifted his chin toward them.

"My guards have prepared you all food. Eat up while it's warm."

Marin hawked a wad of filth in his throat, but swallowed it back when Anca shot him another glare.

"We brought our own food. No need for yours, dog."

Anca had not been looking forward to this next part. If she was anything other than a loyal servant, it could compromise how Eugen would report back to the monarch. At the same time, she would have to keep him at arm's length or risk alienating her own hunters. She was accustomed to difficult situations. However, she preferred the ones you could solve with a knife.

"Glad to see you ride fast. I was afraid that your tarnished pedigree would keep you rusty," Anca said.

Eugen smiled. Snide and tight.

"I assumed your ego would keep you from arriving on time."

One of Eugen's hunters gathered a few bowls and went about spooning out the soup. Anca could smell chicken, potatoes, and carrots. Her stomach answered with a growl.

"As I said, we have our own supplies," Marin said.

Eugen cocked an eyebrow. "We prepared a meal for your entire company. If you do not join in, it will be wasted."

"It would be rude to turn away a warm meal." Anca nodded her head, an unstated order.

Marin groaned and accepted a bowl after Anca took her own.

"It's appreciated. We will be tending to our own camp," Anca said.

"Don't let me keep you." The Executioner dug into his meal without another word.

They led their horses to the temporary stables. The hair on her neck prickled as she felt the Executioner's eyes on her. She would prefer to keep him within sight as well. There was a strange restlessness whenever he was close, like a herd of sheep when they smell a wolf.

Marin poked at the soup as if it might sting him.

"It is probably poison. Don't you think so?"

Anca took her first spoonful. Her eyelids drifted closed at the twist of flavor along her tongue. She snapped them open and turned to Marin.

"There is only a modest chance. I've seen you eat worse."

"That isn't funny."

Anca clapped her hand over his shoulder.

"Leave the anger for the Beast. You will earn your chance to vent it soon."

Chapter Ten

To reduce their footprint, the two companies agreed to share campsites. Only a handful of the campfires had any sense of camaraderie. Most were occupied with the unwelcome duty of getting to know each other. Anca and Marin chose one such site, a sign of solidarity with their hunters.

"Can you imagine me making chit chat with a bunch of royal snobs? Forget it, won't have a thing to say to them. Best that I eat dinner and go to sleep before my mouth says something I'll regret later." The Doia lugged a weathered rucksack over his shoulder and swung his other hand like a scorned child.

"I'm not asking you to share a bunk with Eugen. These people might hate him as much as you do," Anca said.

"I doubt that."

A young, lone woman sat near their campfire with a weathered book in her hands, a notebook at her side, and square reading glasses perched on her nose. She wore black, studded leather like Eugen, but had set her chainmail aside for the night. A necklace with a yellow gem dangled from her neck, twinkling in the sparks of the campfire. Her olive eyes did not hold a shred of interest as they approached.

"Where's the fourth?" Anca asked.

"Sleeping." She looked back down to her book. "It

was a long journey from the bastion and he is more of an early bird than a night owl."

Marin set his bag down next to the campfire. "Figured you all to be more pigeons than owls."

The woman threw him a look that would have broken skin if he were any closer.

"Big talk for someone we're supposed to be playing nice with."

"I'm thrice your age and twice the hunter," Marin grunted.

Anca held up her hands and smiled for the both of them.

"Let's try this. My name is Anca, my curmudgeonly companion—"

Marin snorted.

"—is Doia Marin. As you could guess, we're both with House Sulia."

Straightening her back, she conjured the smallest smile she could. Even the title of Nobil did little to change her tune. She flipped a page and looked at Anca: repugnance masked with an arched eyebrow. The woman could impart disrespect without speaking a word.

Anca liked this one.

"Craita. Pleased to meet you both."

Craita set down her book, a volume of regional history, and went to finish her dinner as they did. The veil of night felt as if it might smother the stars. Anca looked up at the looming watchtower. In one of the tallest windows, two people looked down at the camp. They clutched the windowsill as if something might happen below.

"What are they so afraid of?" Marin asked.

Craita scooped another bite from her almost empty

bowl.

"They are afraid for us. They're scared of the dark like everyone else."

"Right," Anca said. "They're just not used to seeing us in our element."

"No Shadow beast is squirrely enough to attack a camp of forty or so hunting guards. We're safe. Besides, we've got a mage in our company."

Marin leered at Craita.

Before she could ask, Anca took a second look at the yellow gem around Craita's neck. The jewel was unmistakably a magical Focus. A Focus was always a valuable keepsake. They all looked different, but had a tendency to be precious stones. Anca imagined mages to be dreadful, grand figures. Old men with long beards and hooded women came to mind.

"You're the mage?"

Craita rolled her eyes after meeting Marin's stare.

"You're sharp for a geezer," Craita said.

"Just keep one eye open, Anca," Marin muttered. "No telling what she's capable of."

"Your odor might be the most dangerous thing here. I can control myself. Can you say the same?"

"I certainly can't say that for that mongrel you call a master."

Marin worked on the last bites of his stew. Anca smacked Marin's knee, but he gave no apology.

"It's not personal. He was a part of House Sulia when, well, you know."

"Monster," Marin said under his breath.

"Only to some," Craita replied.

Marin shook his head and let it go.

An angry voice bellowed across the camp. Marin's

sentiment must have been catching. She recognized the wispy voice of Vali, the elder hunter she had been worried about. Predictably, he was furious.

"Well, that was how we did it. We didn't quibble over right and wrong or kowtow to special requests. We enforced the law to the letter. No more, no less. And now Anca wants us to help a couple of stooges like you all. She wants us to work alongside the last memory of the monsters her family nearly exterminated!"

Others turned from their own meals to watch Vali's tantrum. Aware of the glares from Queen's Company and the mixed reception among her hunters, Anca dropped her bowl and sprinted from their camp. Vali's voice was not quite a roar, but it could be heard a few fires from them. She had to stop this quarreling, but did not want to draw even more attention.

The rumors were boiling over. The same discontent she worried about was on full display. Hopefully, no one had taken it personally yet. An old fogey like Vali could at least be satiated for a time. There was one person she was particularly concerned about.

Her heart dropped when she spotted him in the shadows just behind Vali's campfire. At first, she thought it might have been a wolf that somehow snuck into their camp. Tall, shaved head, broad chested, it could not have been him, right? What were the odds that he would be there at the worst moment? It was only when a Queen's Company hunter bent a knee that she realized it was just as she feared.

"Vali, stop it," Doru said, sitting at the same campfire.

"Quiet. You don't know any better, boy. I'll have it known that Eugen Furloc is a heartless, feckless, brainless villain who should be worm food like the rest of his family."

"Is that so?" Eugen growled.

The Executioner had ditched his armor for a loose woolen shirt and trousers. He slurped from the soup bowl in his hands. Anca sprinted toward the fire. Hunters dove out of the way of this sprinting shadow that cut through the camp. Crossing over to them, the conversation came back to her sharp ears.

"I bet you would love to put a blade through my throat. With the way you talk about Nobil Sulia, I can't imagine how much you despise me," Eugen said.

Vali did not flinch.

"I'd do it now if it were proper."

Eugen took another step toward the Sulia hunter, now within range to land a punch. "I could make it proper. Isn't that an old tradition? Every beast needs its bait."

"A bloodbaiting? Fine, I'll gladly lure the Beast with your stain."

She elbowed through the small crowd and pointed at Vali. "Step back!"

"No ma'am." The tenacious veteran was frothing at the mouth. He tied his white hair back into a bun, expecting a brawl there at the campfire. "It's bad enough to tolerate a mage hunting alongside us. But allowing this fiend in our midst, even giving him the chance to hunt again. It's beyond the pale."

She glanced at Eugen, expecting to find him drawing a dagger or winding up for a sucker punch. The bastard was smirking. The chestnut glow of his eyes almost seemed amused to goad the veteran further.

"I am your Nobil and you will not speak this way to

me."

Vali stamped his boot. "You broke my trust when you made this decision for all of us."

He drew a dagger from his belt and turned back to Eugen. "Your presence here is a mark against all of us. Blood for bait, paid by an unworthy hunter."

Anca was helpless to stop this. She doubted even Marin could change Vali's decision. Loyal and furious, he was too far gone to think about changing his tune. Eugen casually tossed his bowl onto the ground and looked at Anca. The fire lit those deep brown eyes, the lightless forest of his eyes glaring back at her. The twitch of his lips brought a flash of pity to his face. It was gone before she could consider it.

Despite how he antagonized Vali, he seemed to not relish what was coming. Was this all to prove himself? Anca suspected that this was the first step to earning some sort of respect from hunters of a Household. If she was right, then he was a fool. Bloodshed would not win that for him. Not with her hunters.

"A Fated Death given by your fellow." Eugen recited the old code. "Does House Sulia wish to rescind this challenge?"

Anca pushed her fist against her mouth. This bastard, she thought. He was giving her the chance to humble herself before him.

"I do not," Vali said.

"The question is not for you," Eugen's gaze did not turn from her. "Does House Sulia rescind?"

If she sheltered Vali like some mother bear, it would do nothing to quiet the unrest. Vali would learn nothing and those like him might be emboldened. Reason would not sway them, there was too much blood in the water.

Every older hunter itched to finish the line of Furloc for good.

Anca never believed in violence as a teaching tool. Now with the two companies watching her, with Eugen waiting for her decision, she winced to see her principle crumble. This hideous lesson would have to be learned.

"House Sulia accepts. Vali Groia will fight."

Doru's mouth dropped open, looking between Anca and his friend. A crackle of gossiping whispers erupted around them as Vali nodded to her.

"Thank you, ma'am. I'll do this for both of us."

Doru crossed to Anca's side, his fingers almost reaching up to shake her. He reeled back as she glared. She would not tolerate much lip from the young hunter. Even one that Marin favored.

"What are you doing? You know this is useless bloodshed."

"What do you want me to do? Maim him? Ask him to apologize?"

Her voice carried the heat she could not throw at Vali or Eugen.

"So you're going to just let him die?"

Anca glanced at Eugen. He had retreated through the crowd, a group of his hunters fluttering behind him like flies.

"I never said that."

She pushed back through the watching crowd. Anca would not allow a single hunter of hers to die needlessly. The ritual had been invoked and there was no turning from it without dishonor. Vali would take his lumps.

Chapter Eleven

The entire camp stirred as the story spread with feverish haste. So many believed this was the reckoning due ever since the queen put forward the Executioner as her champion. Once Anca took on this ludicrous quest, blood would be spilled. It was just a question of when.

A handful of tents were taken down. Campfires were quickly cleared off. In their place, a circle of torches glowed, twenty paces across from one side to the other. Across from them, Eugen only wore the large pauldron at his shoulder and black trousers. Shirtless, he smeared a cyan paste across his neck, chest, and arms from the pouch on his hip. Craita stood nearby, watching with a focused scowl.

The crowd parted as Anca and Marin found Vali. Doru was trying to talk some sense into him. The veteran hunter sharpened his dual short swords, nodding his head to arguments he would ignore. Marin ran his fingers through his curly hair, almost pulling at the roots.

"I'll commend you for taking a shot at this bastard. So I'll be delicate. This is the dumbest, cockiest, half-sure move you've ever made and I'm embarrassed to see it."

Vali waggled his finger at him. "I've heard enough of that and I don't need anymore. I've made up my mind."

Marin cocked a wild eyebrow and stepped back.

"Oh good. Glad there's still room for reasonable discussion."

Anca stepped forward, her hands clenched together. "I can't talk you out of this, can I?"

The old man shook his head and straightened his back.

"Sorry ma'am. This is bigger than just me. If Eugen comes back with us, it would be a black mark on our Household for decades."

"Only if we give a damn what the Households think," she said.

Doru choked out a small, surprised sound. This was talk that sounded awfully close to treason. It came from a Nobil no less. It was risky to raise the curtain on the larger idea, but it might be the last thing to budge him. Vali had known her parents and her grandparents. If he was loyal to anything, he was loyal to the Household. She hoped it would be enough.

"I don't want to hear it." Vali drew his second sword. "If the Households mean nothing to you, then we're farther apart then I suspected."

Anca bit her lip and swallowed whatever plea she had planned to trot out next. There was no avoiding this. The only thing left to do was to help him win. If Eugen was going to use this as a chance to embarrass House Sulia, then Vali needed every advantage he could get.

"I wish you luck, Vali Groia." She scratched a spot on her head, covering her face with her arm. "Eugen favors his right knee. Work his left as best as you can."

The veteran smiled and bowed to her as she walked away. At least he's got a fighting chance, she thought. Marin walked into the middle of the circle and raised his hands to quiet the crowd.

"Listen up! This is a bloodbaiting. Things born of Shadow are drawn to our blood like moths to a flame. Not very useful these days, but here we are. Observing the old ways. Neither can leave the circle. Nor can they leave until one has surrendered or is dead. Ready?"

Vali clanged his swords together. Eugen raised his greatsword, flakes of ash spiraling from the orange gem.

"Begin!" Marin stepped out of the circle.

At the signal, Eugen's Focus flared like a match. Cinders burst and shimmering light grew in the veins of his right hand. He heaved his sword forward as he charged ahead. Vali caught the greatsword with both blades and knocked it aside. Eugen adjusted his footing and brought the weapon up like a shield to catch a trio of strikes from Vali. Shifting one step back, he swung the sword over his head and back toward his target. Vali ducked and slashed Eugen's left side.

A trickle of blood flicked onto the ground and the side plate of Eugen's armor fell free. Anca's voice leaped in her throat as the rest of House Sulia roared with life. She thought it would feel better to see Eugen bleed. Instead, she worried that neither one would accept surrender.

When Eugen winced at the pain, she squirmed.

He was far too human still. She might have been a killer of beasts, but she had never killed a person before. When she looked back at Vali, there was a flash of anxiety in his eyes. It was drowned with a snarl, but Anca saw it all the same. If they were here to save people, why would she wish for anyone's death? Even Eugen.

The old man was quick on his feet. That big, damn blade of Eugen's could rip Vali in half with a single swing, but he would have to hit him first. For a moment, she had reason to hope the veteran would survive. The next moment, the entire camp saw why the old hunters feared House Furloc.

Eugen's breath grew ragged and uneven, like a man who had been running for hours. Pressing his hand against the wound, a dim glow rose in his eyes that drowned any suggestion of humanity. His Focus blazed. Bright as a torch, heat shimmered around it as light shot up along the veins in his arm. His entire body seized. His skin flushed. Slamming his blade into the earth, he catapulted his body forward.

Vali rolled away as the juggernaut crashed into the ground where he had been. Eugen kicked Vali in the chest and sent him onto his back. The gap in speed was closing. The Executioner could swing the blade as if it were half its weight now. He leaped twice as far as he could before. He was a whirlwind of rage, his weapon trenching deep gouges into the earth wherever he went.

Eugen leaped up and swung his sword down toward Vali, but the old man rolled at the last minute. He came to a knee as the grass and soil erupted beneath the berserker. Eugen's arm bulged to remove the sword from the ground, but Vali struck toward Eugen's unarmored side. She traced the edge with her Othersight as it plunged into his heart. The Executioner's face twisted.

Most of the Sulia hunting guards cheered at the fatal stroke. Anca remained silent. She never wanted this. That anyone died was a needless loss. Vali would live. Eugen would die. It seemed impossible even a minute ago. Across the fight, she caught sight of Craita. She watched the death blow hit her master in the side, but did not shout in dismay. She did not gnash her teeth, curse, or even flinch.

It made sense as Eugen grabbed Vali's sword arm.

The gem in Eugen's sword burst with flickering flame, cinders burning wisps of smoke at his feet. His veins pulsed and muscles bunched as a low groan crawled from the Executioner's throat. His fingers locked around Vali's arm, stopping him from removing the blade stuck into his side. The cheers from House Sulia died.

Eugen snapped his torso around and sent Vali flying head over heels to the far edge of the circle. A gout of blood spurted from Eugen's side as he removed the weapon and launched it like a javelin. The blade pinned Vali's shoulder to the ground, the old man's scream rending the air. His hands weakly grabbed at the hilt and tried to yank it free. Eugen strode over to his prey, the supposedly fatal wound no longer bleeding.

"Enough!" Anca shouted from the side of the circle.

He didn't stop. Eugen was a predator and his prey was bleeding.

"You should be dead. Your heart, I got your heart," Vali sputtered.

"Eugen, stop!"

Veins pulsed under his skin, red creeping into the whites of his eyes. He hefted the sword up to bring down a killing blow. This was the end of it. There was no time to hope Eugen would make the right decision.

Anca crossed the circle in only a few bounds and brought her sword up to catch the flaming blade. Their swords rang like a bell as she caught Eugen's tremendous swing. The blow pushed her back, but her heels ground into the moist earth under her feet. She gritted her teeth against the shake in her arms.

"I said enough! Blood's been drawn. You win."

The mania in Eugen's eyes glittered. It was a hungry light that Anca had seen in wolves. He leaned his weight onto the sword and she slid a few inches back. That move put him dangerously out of balance. She was certain he would not expect the counter.

"To the death," he rasped between his teeth, gums red as blood. The rattle in his throat was not his own. It was like Flame itself spoke to her. "Do you shelter all of your weakling pups?"

Doru took one step into the ring, but Anca snarled her lip and sent him back into the crowd. She adjusted her stance and shifted the blades. It looked as though her guard would break and topple over, but Anca had faced her fair share of beasts that outweighed her. A slight twist of her blade and a sidestep sent his killing strike, long delayed, crashing into the dirt. Another flick of movement and her blade's edge pressed against his throat.

"It's done, Eugen. You know we are better than this."

The killing light in his eyes weakened, the dim glow faded. His deep brown eyes bloomed again, the whites emerging from the red veins that threatened to swallow it all. A small piece of Eugen emerged from the monster. He shook his head as though it were swarmed with gnats.

"Better?" he muttered.

"Hunt with me. That's why you're here."

After a moment, he nodded.

"I'm better than this."

He grabbed a pouch on his hip and sucked down a gulp of air. His fingers slipped from his blade, still driven into the ground. Anca's gaze did not leave Eugen, but she motioned for them to take Vali away.

Doru was the first to break the line and other members of House Sulia followed. One of them pulled the sword from Vali's shoulder, the old man trying to hide the agony he felt. Doru helped him stand and carefully sheltered his friend's wounded shoulder. Even the slightest movement made the old man wince and howl. It was likely broken.

"He should be dead," Vali babbled.

"Come on friend," Doru said. "Let's lie you down."

The Executioner should be dead. She traced the blade with her Othersight to the pumping, throbbing center of the man. Vali had not missed. Yet here the Executioner stood healthy and alive. She had no idea what she had seen.

Anca still needed to defuse this rabid animal. The fire was fading from his veins, his voice evening out, but he still followed the wounded Vali with a wolf's attention. Eugen paced in circles, breathing deep from the pouch. The wound in his side had already sealed.

"Are we done here?" Anca asked.

If this was what Flame magic could do within Eugen's veins, she was not so certain her Doia was wrong to fear it. It consumed whatever existed of the discerning man she met at the palace. Almost as sharp a hunter as herself, she wondered how he could stomach disappearing into all that anger.

Eugen drank in the night air with gulping breaths before putting the pouch away and wiping away a bead of sweat from his shaved head.

"You are right, Nobil Sulia. Blood is blood."

She kept her sword raised, not ready to trust him.

"Your Nobil spared him," Eugen said to the remaining members of House Sulia. "Any other challengers might not receive the same mercy."

"They will always have my protection."

His pacing stopped, his brow wrinkling with interest.

"You would protect them even when they speak so ill of you?"

"Always. No one is beyond a second chance."

Anca felt as though she towered over him, despite him having close to five inches on her. He shrank back. Something knocked loose in the Executioner and his determined ferocity slackened. His restless eyes searched her face for something before he yanked his sword from the dirt.

"You're full of surprises, Nobil Sulia." He rounded to face his own hunters. "We're done here. Go back to your camps."

Anca's shoulders fell. Sliding her sword back into its scabbard, she watched the shirtless monster stalk back to his camp with several of his own following. His last few words to her made her wonder.

Did he seriously think she would let people die for sport? He must have thought she was thankless and fickle. His experience with other Nobils was surely one of relentless hatred. It was not a far leap that he thought she was slavishly devoted to money and power.

Maybe there was more to this monster that she had been taught to fear? Just as there was more to her. It seemed obvious that there was always another side of things. She was ashamed to admit that it never occurred to her that Eugen might also be deeper than a thoughtless bastard.

"That was a dumb move. But the right one."

Marin waited for her at the edge of the torches, arms

crossed. A few other hunters began resettling their tents and building campfires.

"Might've pissed off the big guy though. This fall in line with your plan?"

She strolled next to him as they meandered back toward their tents. Protecting Vali was pure instinct. He mentored her in sword fighting for a year. Everyone in the Household knew Vali. If the oldest of them all was mistreated, they might worry about themselves.

"No, but it will work out for us. Eugen seemed to respect my actions. Confused maybe, but respectful. Did he seriously think I'd just let my own die?"

"That brute is a few eggs short of a dozen. I wouldn't assume he understands anything except violence."

"He's coarse and direct, but he isn't dumb. That fire in his veins clouds his mind. I wonder if he really does have a handle on it."

"Don't try to understand the cur. Just keep it at arm's length. You're liable to be bit."

Eugen was made of knots. She could understand being wrapped up in your grudges, isolated with your own thoughts. Cooperation might have been easier if she gave them a chance to defy the prejudice she carried. After all, wasn't shaking off the old ways at the heart of her motives?

Chapter Twelve

When dawn's first light fell on Bastion Ochepti, they were already five miles from it. By mid-morning, they reached the ravaged town of Moura. The occasional songbird flitted between brown and orange leaves, but Eugen could not perceive deer, coyotes, rabbits, or anything else on the frosted ground. They were not dead. He would have noticed the traces of bodies or scented their decay on the wind. The wildlife was scared.

He chewed over the night before as the town's gates came into view. Anca risked her own life to save a rude, nasty, old codger who disrespected her in front of the camp. It was egregious behavior. Any other Household would have him in irons. At best.

Yet the white-haired irritant walked free, albeit with a sling around his left arm. Anca did not fit the callous enemy he had prepared for. Exceptional as a hunter, he assumed she was as morally bankrupt as any of them. Eugen had read her very wrong. After last night, he suspected that he wasn't the only one realizing some things about someone else.

Be better, she said.

Better was giving a damn. It meant rising above that cynical assumption that everything was shit and no one would help. Being better would mean exposing himself to others. Vulnerability. The concept scared him more than death.

121

Eugen rose from his thoughts as they neared the end of the road. Moura's gates were locked from within. The smeared bloodstains on the battlements were a grisly teaser of what was to come.

"I'll hop over the wall and scout ahead."

Anca stepped forward, but he shot his hand out in front of her. Colliding with him, she rested her fingers on his forearm for a moment. The hair on his neck prickled. Like hackles rising on a dog, he was used to the angry sensation that followed when people laid hands on him. Though his shoulders bunched, the Blood Flame did not rise as expected.

Sending her in first was a bad idea. If she died in some stupid accident, there would be no hunting down this beast. No glory. No future. As much as he would love to see a Nobil fall face-first into their own arrogance, she was too important to risk.

"If you get caught alone, you'd be isolated. Let's just knock down the doors. Won't take more than a few minutes."

Anca pulled her hand from his arm and snarled. "This is my hunt. I can handle myself."

"Five minutes. I promise I won't stop you from blundering ahead after this."

She stared him down, the risk and reward weighing behind her eyes.

Marin cleared his throat. "The mongrel's got a point for once."

Anca gave him an annoyed look before stepping back.

"Fine. We'll do it your way this time."

Eugen's shoulders eased with tension that gathered beyond his notice.

One of the clockwork wagons was put into overdrive and a large ram attached to it. The gates crashed open on tarnished hinges and a putrid, reeking breeze washed over them. Many gagged, but Eugen and Anca accepted the stench. There was far too much to learn. The fetid wind was a mix of copper and sickening rot. All sorts of decay and death buoyed each other into a stomach-turning potpourri. Within these repulsive fumes, he could tell there were new dead mixed with old. The killing didn't stop the night that the Beast came here.

A dry, deep red smudge ran from the center of the road and off into the trees nearby. Farther ahead, Eugen could already see the glimmers of green Life clinging to the corpses as the cycle of decay took its course. The Nobils rode into town alongside each other, supernatural senses pricked for snapping twigs or a growl from the underbrush.

Eugen slowed in front of a house made of bone bracing and cob walls. A small wooden shed in the back had been torn to pieces and collapsed on top of some animal. A mule, he guessed. His eyes went to the uneven, wooden planks that made a fence around the house. Candle lanterns were smashed and the door caved in. A streak of blood ran out of it and around the side of the home.

In the middle of the road, not far from the home, was something that was once a person. Marin and the other hunting guards passed by the grisly scene, but the Nobils hopped off their mounts.

"Everyone stay close, don't wander far."

She leaned close to the body, her delicate neck strained over the reeking mess.

"Something of interest?" Eugen asked.

"It's still here." She flashed a dismissive look at him. "You didn't notice? It gorged itself on the dead and then waited for more. The only way to explain the missing fauna around here is a lingering predator. To its perspective, this whole land is a smorgasbord with nothing that can contest it."

Now that she spelled it out, it was obvious. Master tracker indeed, he thought. A tiny, envious part of him wriggled. He could not be bested so quickly. At least no one else heard it.

"So certain?"

Anca ignored him and focused on the body. Their limbs were wrenched from their sockets, behavior unlike an animal. However, the cuts and bite marks could not be anything except claws and teeth.

If he let her take the lead, she would have the whole thing figured out by lunch time. He let his Othersight stray toward the tracks ripped into the ground. Glittering highlights coursed along bumps and marks that the creature had pounded into the dirt.

Four fingered hands rested on either side of the body while it ate. Deeper prints, made by strong legs, leaped from a great distance and stopped nearby. It was close to eight feet in length, lanky, and quadrupedal, but it could stand if needed. Eugen pieced its trail together from the tracks.

"We're at the end of its trail. Not the start."

Anca looked away from the body and to the creature's prints. They went into the foliage and moved off toward the center of town. Her face wrinkled as she put together the same sequence of events. He knew the challenge was coming before she spoke.

"Show me."

He paced alongside the impressions, unwilling to admit how good it felt to work alongside an equal.

"It's backward. It approached this kill from the center of town before fanning out to the houses nearby. Those tracks skirt behind that hovel and up the road."

Anca looked to the street ahead to where he lost the green, glimmering trail. She made a small noise in her throat that might have been a snicker.

"I'm impressed."

"You'd be surprised. If you didn't swallow every lie about me, you might learn a thing or two," he said.

"I'm just surprised there is a brain beneath all that muscle."

He could not keep the scoff back. The last thing he expected her to care about was anyone's looks. Though if she actually cared, her features did not betray it.

"Believe it or not, a person can be two things," he answered.

Anca tied her hair back before climbing onto her mount. The brown horse canted away from him as she spoke.

"True. After all, you are both a sarcastic ass and thoughtless."

"And you're presumptive and cocky."

He climbed onto his horse and gave it a small urge to catch up with Anca. She turned on her saddle to flash him a scowl. Eugen gave her a snide grin in return, allowing a sliver of his teeth to peek through.

"And you're slowing me down." She motioned for him to speed up. "Come on, we've got work to do."

The long, bloody street led to a town square. The few business fronts were empty like the rest of town, though perhaps not as grotesque. The well's bucket was unwound and knocked against the stone lip in the breeze. Leafless, gray branches scratched at the thatch roofs. It was the only sound that the dead town dared to make. Guards who peeked into houses quickly recoiled or solemnly muttered prayers to Flame.

"You've got to be shitting me."

Marin stared at a body left in the high branches of a tree. They would need to fell it to recover the corpse. Doru shuddered, seeming small inside of his winter coat and armor.

Eugen barely recognized the horror around him. He distantly worried whether he had grown used to it or was too focused on the hunt ahead. Looking over the grotesque, terrified faces, he thought it might be best to focus on the hunt.

He crouched next to the body of a former Stancu Hunting Guard. Eugen ignored the condition of the body and instead slid the sword from the corpse's grasp. The blade was stained by a crackled, black paste. Anca watched quietly behind him. Once lifted into direct sunlight, the paste hissed quietly. The last bits of moisture wicked away with a bit of smoke.

"Is that what I think it is?" Marin asked.

"Shadow lingers in its veins. Find that stock of Night Bane flares and see they are distributed to everyone," Anca said.

"You mean everyone-everyone?"

Marin's eyes bounced to the Executioner and back to his Nobil. Anca nodded to her Doia.

"We wouldn't have those flares without them. Distribute to Queen's Company as well."

"I was afraid you meant that."

Marin rode toward the clockwork wagons. Doru

ogled the cracked, smoking splatter and leaned his weight onto the spear in his hands. As he craned over Eugen's shoulder, the Executioner swatted him away.

"Keep your distance."

"What does that mean for us? Night Bane?" Doru asked.

Eugen dropped the sword on the ground and Anca kicked it away from them.

"Night Bane flares are a mixture of phosphorus, fluorite, and silver. Magically fused by mages. Burns like sunlight. Shadow beasts can't tolerate it," Anca said.

"Shouldn't we have those out all the time then?"

Eugen laughed. These young hunters were almost as clueless as royal regulars.

"Too expensive and they burn too fast. It's not a light source. It's a weapon. You're lucky the queen gave up a portion of her stock."

Doru nodded his head, recognition barely registering on his pale face. He swallowed after a moment and settled a hand against his hip.

"Well, thanks. I certainly appreciate the extra firepower. Grateful even."

Eugen cocked his head. Where did this whelp get off toying with sarcasm? Right to his face, no less. The hair on his neck bristled as he balled his hand into a fist, until the snide smirk never came. Doru beamed at him with earnest appreciation. Flame, Eugen thought. The dumb bastard is being honest.

"Umm, of course."

Eugen's body felt overly stiff. If he wasn't going to curse or threaten, how was he supposed to express himself? Being confronted with generosity was as strange as the prickles along his arm that Anca's touch had brought. Smiling? Yes, smiling was ordinary in this situation. Eugen smiled, but immediately felt that he was showing far too many teeth. Doru's face turned into a confused frown and he shifted where he stood.

"It's called a compliment, Eugen," Anca interrupted. "Don't be worried, Doru. He isn't used to nice things. Go help Marin move the bodies. We have work to do yet."

Doru bowed and went off to find the Doia. Eugen cocked an eyebrow toward Anca. He was uncertain what more business they could have with each other. Not that he minded being around her. Her focus eased him. For a change, he did not feel like the only predator in the flock.

"What did you have in mind?"

Anca gestured toward the end of the bloody, body-strewn road. Bastion Stancu, hollowed out of life and light, leered over the ruined town with empty eyes.

"We need to inspect the bastion. It's work for Nobils. Not new hunters like Doru."

They walked toward the bastion with hurried steps. Crunching along the shoddy, gravel road. A word lingered in his ear. She said they were Nobils. Plural. It was a quiet recognition of his talent, whether she meant it or not. He considered asking her why she had said that.

Keep it under your hat, he thought. If she realized her error, she'd remind him how useless he was.

Eugen looked over at her, certain she would be looking at him with a disgusted glare. Anca barely noticed him next to her. Her eyes went from corpse to corpse, a sliver of red building in the corners of her eyes. Her angry steps told him it was not pure sorrow.

"Don't look at them," he said.

Anca shook her head as if pulled from a trance.

"What?"

"Don't linger. If you think of the dead for too long, they'll pull your spirit down with them. This isn't the time for mourning."

He recognized that somber look. Eugen wore that face in his early years as Executioner. Defiant villagers who murdered town guards and set grain silos alight begged for their lives with innocent zeal. Of course, they were innocent in a way. They did not wake up and decide to spread chaos. Hunger pushed them to light the match. Desperation put the knife in their hand. Eugen condemned them, as the job demanded.

It made him want to lie in bed until starvation took him. Those early kills made him wonder if he had truly escaped his family's legacy. Maybe it would be better to die with a clean conscience? To do what was right would mean forsaking the last person who gave the Furloc name any purpose. Eugen would die a pauper and his family unredeemed if he did what was expected.

"I guess I can't expect sympathy from you," Anca muttered.

"It isn't that. You care too much. It's your only weakness."

She chuckled, shallow and sad.

"Is that what you think? I've got plenty of weak points. Sometimes it feels like I've got nothing but soft spots." Anca screwed up her face and shook her head. "Water and Flame, why am I talking to you about this? Never mind."

"You're not weak. In fact..." Eugen hesitated.

He knew she would just call him stupid or a mongrel or something else that he had heard a thousand times. Why was he trying to sympathize with her? Because he recognized that same sort of desperate anger? The light in her eyes was the same he felt whenever the queen cut rations to the Households or sent another division of conscripted soldiers into the southern meat grinder.

No, I should just stop talking, he thought.

Eugen was certain he had made the right call until Anca cleared her throat. To his surprise, she waited for him to speak. Her head bobbled back and forth with an agitated wiggle.

"In fact, what? I'm just cocky? Spoiled? Naïve?"

His armor felt itchy, the sun too bright. It would have been better to let her sulk in that despair. That way he could avoid exposing himself this way.

"In fact, you're stronger than the rest of them."

The words poured out.

"They're all hollow, shameless bastards that won't lift a finger unless their wealth or prestige is challenged. The things I've heard them say about you. You went out to Bire's mess and cleaned it up because you wanted to. Compliance order my foot. You would've gone just to make sure that creature was dead. With maybe the possible exception of Maciter, you're the only one worth half a damn."

Anca stared at him like he was wearing a fish for a hat. He said too much. Why was his heart pounding so fast? She would certainly see his elevated pulse. Eugen hated this feeling. It was worse than any insult and barb.

"Not that I'd say any of that to them."

"No." Her voice lacked the edge. Anca looked at the gravel underfoot and then off to the tree line. "That was a fine thing to say."

Her thoughts were elsewhere. Eugen could not begin to guess the struggles in her own life. Between that thorn of a fiancé, the Households hounding her, and everything else in this damned world, maybe she did need to hear that. If he could bring a little light to someone's world and not have them throw it right back into his face, he could enjoy that.

Of course, he couldn't pass up a chance to piss off a Nobil.

"It's called a compliment."

Her head snapped around to him with a frown, but he didn't miss the tiniest laugh in her throat.

"You did not just say that."

Eugen grinned and looked to the tower ahead of them. Humor was a dim concept to him. No reason to push it, he thought. Even as the silence grew between them, he felt a strange pull to say something else. Fear kept his lips locked together.

The bastion was a lone tower with a wooden gate. It was left ajar. The bronze-colored flag flapped limply in the cold breeze. Ivy wrapped up around it as if the stone had thrust from the earth and nature tried to pull it back down. Eugen scented blood inside. Lots of it.

Anca slipped into the door, Eugen close behind. He was so preoccupied on whether to say more that he failed to prepare for the smell. All the lights were extinguished and only the pale rays of light from occasional windows lit the horrible scene inside. Turning into the entry hall, Anca lit an oil lantern and turned the amber light around the room.

These people died in the dark. They wore night gowns and linen clothing. Some had weapons, but only the commonly used things they would have on hand. Some had the luck of finding daggers and hunting knives before the Beast found them.

"Bleeding, rotting Death," Eugen said through his shirt, part of the cloth drawn over his nose.

He recognized hunting guards among the dead. Veterans of a dozen or more hunts were killed without any sign that they wounded the creature. Amid the smears of dark red and the buzzing thrum of flies, there was not a single drip of the Beast's own black blood.

They took a narrow staircase that wound up to the second floor. Sunlight brightened this hallway, but heavy curtains kept it dim. The story here was the same as below and the stench was no better. A long hallway stretched back to the far side of the tower. At the top of the stairs, an open door led to an abattoir that used to be a bedroom. A locked, wide window was covered by cream colored curtains.

"We should open that window. Air this place out if we can and see if we can't get some more light," she said.

Eugen took a step toward the bedroom door, but ground to a halt. A low growl rose from the far end of the hallway. His fingers reached for the sword across his back, a flicker of light coming to it. This hall was lifeless beyond the traces of rot. Speckles of flies and fungi dimly clung to the bodies and the walls. He was not the tracker that Anca was, but no creature could get the drop on him.

The end of the hall was empty, barren of visible life. Despite that, Eugen still heard the rumble of a rattling, deep breath. It was like the darkness itself breathed. A void of darkness crouched ahead of them. Its snout was pointed to the ground. Eugen blinked, unsure of what he saw. Shadow sometimes moved in strange ways, but it never coalesced into a physical form.

"Anca, do you see—"

"Yes," her shaky voice answered.

Before Eugen could think of their next move, the darkness lifted its head. Blood red eyes stared back at them. He recognized those eyes. He once believed he never would see them again. It made the blood freeze in his veins as his own bad dream stared back at him.

The Beast of Moura rose from its haunches and jaws opened with a wet pop. Anca flung the lantern at the ground in front of them. Oil gushed from the smashed glass and ignited into a barrier of fire. Its claws flashed over the flame as it rose between them, close enough to hear the killing strike whistle past his ears.

The light filled the hallway, but the living shadow reeled backward. It never came close enough to see. Eugen squinted against the light, sword raised, but failed to catch a trace of the thing that had been mere inches from them moments before.

The second heart beat a drum in his head. Time to kill. Time to hunt. Time to right the wrongs. Heat radiated from his Focus and into his veins. A wall of fire separated him from his prey, but the Blood Flame insisted he dive through it. Go, it whispered in his ear. Eugen drew his blade and prepared to plunge into the burning hallway ahead.

He choked as his shirt pulled around his throat. Anca snatched him by the collar and hauled him backward with all her strength. Caught off guard, the killing instinct stumbled as he nearly dropped his sword.

No, we must hunt, the Flame said.

As he tottered backward, Eugen's eyes scanned across the fire. The Beast was gone. It had turned tail and fled. He gnashed his teeth, pulling against Anca's grip as she dragged him farther from the spreading blaze.

"You'll burn, you idiot!"

His belt twitched as Anca yanked the pouch of herbs from him. She jammed it toward his nose. Icy, chilling, familiar scent. His vision wobbled and swayed as his rage quieted. While the Flame within settled, the fires around them only grew. Drapes caught in the blaze and rugs went up like matchwood.

Anca yanked on his arm and he followed, her swift steps racing down the stairs. They sped over the rotting corpses and out of the hollow shell that was once House Stancu. Stumbling out of the front door, Eugen leaned on his knees and gasped for air.

The creature's talons came too close. All his preparation and they had been caught flat footed. Behind the flare of anger, it put a chill down his spine. If it heard them a little sooner, the entire hunt could be over right now and two more Nobils would be added to its tally.

A window shattered on the other side of the tower and something dashed into the thick canopy. It was not just some manifestation of Shadow. It breathed, it thought, it hunted. Trees and brush thrashed as it disappeared into the forest.

Smoke billowed out of the second floor as Marin and other hunting guards came running from the village.

"Are you alright? Where is it?" His voice was hoarse. By the pounding of his veins, Eugen could tell that the Doia sprinted here.

"It slipped away. It almost got the drop on us," Anca said.

Marin slowed as he neared them, confusion adding to his snarl. "On you?"

"Othersight can't trace it."

"And it's fast." Eugen still tried to even his

breathing. "It cleared the entire other side of the tower and vanished into the brush."

"Do you think it'll run?" Marin asked.

Anca shook her head.

"Not with all of us here. It thinks we are easy prey. We'll correct that perception tonight."

She looked up to the smoking tower, licks of fire now poking from the higher windows.

"A fitting end," Eugen muttered, a small chuckle in his voice. "They get a funeral pyre all the same. Kindled by their own Household."

He expected her to correct him or to reverently watch the tower go up, but Eugen found Anca staring at him instead. Her face was placid like a mountainside, unmoving and resolute. Whatever judgment she had for him today, she kept to herself. Her eyes turned to the tower above.

"Let it burn. We can't stop it anyway."

With her profile framed by the raging fire, smoke wafting through the air, he found something beautiful in her. In that moment, he truly saw the formidable woman who had made the Households quake before her.

Chapter Thirteen

Tents were raised, food was cooked, and defenses set in place. Anca's extravagant tent was near the center of camp, only a few over from Eugen's. Anca yearned for the chance to undo the braid that pulled on her scalp. It had been nearly fourteen hours since she removed her armor. She would have to smother the urge of creature comforts for a while longer. There was still work to be done.

She stood alongside Eugen's mage on a small hill that overlooked the town. Craita, dressed in the somber black of Queen's Company, held the Focus in hand and kept her eyes closed. Her fingers traced through the dirt like she caressed a sleeping child. She was communing with Earth. The Nobil and the mage had been at this for hours. The sun had not fully set, but they did not have much longer left.

For all of their work, Craita had only been able to raise three stone walls and one of them was out of place. Anca spluttered her lips and shifted on her feet.

"I thought you were good at this."

They needed to set the pitfalls and barriers in specific places to match the plan. There was no other option than to have Anca supervise this process. When she mentioned it to Eugen, assuming he would butt in, he answered with a wry grin.

"Craita's one of my best. She can keep you in line

in my stead."

The mage clenched her jaw and hissed as though she was moving the ground herself. The earth rumbled and Anca took a half-step back. Without the chirp of birds or squirrels in the brush, the grinding sound of moving stone was unsettling.

"I *am* good at this. It isn't easy." Craita did not open her eyes.

Anca never meddled with magic beyond the Othersight. There was not a practice of mages within the Households, especially after House Furloc was purged. Margecei kept them at arm's length, but their benefits could not be denied. They could heal crop blights, save ships from sinking, and fight with the power of entire armies. She could appreciate why they were so feared. An angry mage, or even one who had not mastered the gift, was a loose cannon.

On the north side of their camp, trees shook and windows shattered in an abandoned shop. Splinters erupted from the walls and a plume of dust burst from it as the entire building broke in half. Nearby hunting guards stumbled away. A stony wall wrenched up from the ground. It settled and stopped when it came seven feet out of the ground.

"Shit." Craita gasped for air and collapsed onto her elbows. "Stupid, stony bastard. Why did I do that?"

Perhaps she was being too harsh, Anca thought. It had taken her years to master Othersight. She could not comprehend literally moving the ground beneath her feet.

"At least you got close. It isn't like anyone was going to shop there anytime soon."

"I'm better than this. We're taught to be better than

this," Craita grumbled as she began to stand. Anca offered her a hand, which Craita accepted with an uncertain glare. Craita snatched a flask of water from the ground and took a deep drink.

"I need a break. Working with the Earth is taxing. It's almost awake though."

"Awake?" Anca laughed a little. The idea of Old Sleepy Earth snoozing beneath their feet was supposed to be a simplified parody, not an accurate description.

"It's not as fluid or forgiving as the others. It doesn't want anything to do with us. We're just mold growing on it as far as it cares. This whole hunting business, wars between Flame and Shadow, is just noisy children making a mess."

"It sounds grumpy."

Craita chuckled. "You've no idea."

The mage was close to twenty-five years of age. She was sure on her feet and the coilgun on her back was polished to a gleam. Though they had spent very little time together, Craita's demeanor seemed at home in House Sulia.

"Mage is a hard job," Anca said. "And you decided to be a hunter too. Did you decide that risking your life in just one way was too tame?"

"I didn't have much of a choice."

Her answer was automatic. Sharpened like a blade, her grimace was the same sort that Anca allowed herself in private moments with Victor.

"I was orphaned young and drafted at fourteen. Service made me who I am today, service to Eugen. Service to the queen. At least I have a home with them. I didn't find out about my gift until I was training with the company."

"You're lucky. I can't think of any other place that would appreciate a mage in their ranks. The others would kick you out or worse."

Craita quietly simmered before she answered.

"Is that what you'd do?"

The contempt was obvious. It was an assertion that Craita was already convinced of. Anca could imagine the lies that Eugen filled their heads with. Even the strongest of minds could not endure an unrelenting lie.

"I wouldn't. Won't say that I am thrilled about having a mage among us, but you seem to have a good head on your shoulders. I know most of the fields in Sunali are tended by a few Life mages. What could the harm be?"

Craita's gloomy smile emerged again and she rubbed the back of her neck. She had something on her mind that she was not comfortable with. Anca could tell before she spoke.

"The other night, I was just doing what everyone else said to do. I think it isn't news to you that we don't see eye to eye. Eugen told us not to get too close. I'm not the friendliest person around, but we might have prodded your hunter too hard. Vali was his name?"

"It was bound to happen one way or the other. I just wish that it didn't happen quite like that," Anca said.

"I guess I'm saying that I'm sorry for blowing you off last night. It was unbecoming of me in the presence of a Nobil. In the presence of anyone, really."

This expedition was full of surprises. Anca thought herself too observant, too highly positioned, to fall for needless grudges. She knew the lies of the throne when she saw them. That was quickly proving false.

Was she still so willing to burn them? She imagined

discarding these royal servants once she was done with them. They were still serving the queen. How could they deserve anything better than her own Household?

"We are losing daylight," Anca reminded Craita. "Think you're up to trying again?"

"I think so."

The mage took a knee and worked her fingers through the dirt. Her Focus glowed a dim yellow light, brighter than anything before, and a small tremor began under their feet.

"Come on, you codger," Craita whispered.

Dust shot up from the ground and the earth cracked. Around the perimeter of the camp, more stone barricades rose in places safely outside of buildings and tents. Other sections collapsed into the earth, pits to be filled with spikes and loose rocks.

"There you go. Was that so hard?" she cooed.

Craita opened her eyes and looked over her work. She even managed a chuckle from behind her scowl. The work needed just a little bit more, a few pits widened or camp entrances closed off.

"What else do you need, Nobil Sulia?"

****

Building the trap was a tortured process. House Sulia and Queen's Company disagreed on everything from rope knots to euphemisms. Craita's stone works were festooned with camouflage and intricate snares. Their cooking fires had been snuffed and only the perimeter of blazing torches remained.

The town square, formerly open and plain, was surrounded by two layers of walls. The outside was much higher and plunged down into a low trough over twenty feet deep. The inner wall was just tall enough to take cover behind. Past those fortifications was an open area for their tents.

A single stone pathway carved through the defenses. Should they need to flee quickly, this would be the only avenue of escape. To ensure it was not an easy entrance for the Beast, three gatling coilguns had been set up within. A dozen torches and distance markers turned it into a shooting gallery. The solid, iron ammunition would punch through just about anything that came in their sights.

The plan was simple: lure the beast over the walls and into the low trough. Sticky tar had been dumped onto the rocks and spikes in addition to nets and snares. If it did not capture the Beast by itself, the Company's coilguns were loaded with tethering ropes. Once a rod pierced its skin, they would be able to hold it back. Anca doubted one person could do this, but three or four would be enough to limit the creature's movement. Once it was trapped in the gutter and covered in sap, they could kill the creature with ease.

Anca and Eugen knelt at the center of the radial trap. They wore full hunting regalia: green paint smeared across their faces, masking oils dripped down their necks, weapons sharpened, and two Night Bane flares on their belts. Their hunters took concealed positions in low holes or against the trunks of trees. A few walked around the perimeter with torches, obvious like the bait they were.

Beyond the walls, the night shimmered with the green glow of Life. It was a useful backdrop. When the Beast showed up, the empty space in her sight would be a dead giveaway.

"This is too much," Eugen muttered. "It's too

obvious."

"It's an animal," Anca replied.

"You know that isn't true. It basks in death. It left its trophies all over the place. We should be out there." Eugen motioned to the single camp exit and the wild woods beyond.

A primal part of her agreed. This felt like a war zone: garrisoned and planned to the final detail. It was wrong. This was not the hunt Anca had in mind, but what choice did she have? They had to be cautious. Others had tried the normal way of doing things and that ended in a massacre.

She wouldn't mind plunging into the woods alongside him. What a pair they would make, she wondered. Her tracking and accuracy combined with his matchless ferocity.

"If we could, how would you proceed?" she asked.

Bent down on one knee, his eyes looked black under the moonlight. Only the red shimmer of fire brought out the warm brown in his pupils. A low rumble rose from his chest, either a chuckle or a growl.

"It moves faster than us and likely can see in the dark. Stalking doesn't make much sense. You're not off the mark to set up a trap. It's good instincts. Just too grand."

"Your mage was the one to carve this from the earth."

"Craita is a talent. I won't do with you besmirching my protege. This was the plan, but now it feels like something is off. I don't like walls. They remind me too much of a prison."

Anca had no idea what his life was like before the monarchy inducted him. After House Furloc was destroyed, the few survivors were held in dungeons across the Households. They all met various deaths, most of them suspicious. Eugen was the only one to find any kind of salvation. Though his life barely seemed like freedom. She never spent time in any kind of cell, but she knew what it was like to be trapped.

"Any experience with those?" she asked.

He looked over at her with a mean grimace. Taking a breath to speak, he pulled the snide remark back. He let the breath go into the frigid air. It was like he carried a great weight on his shoulders, his neck low beneath the strain. His silence carried volumes.

"I'm sorry you had to go through whatever happened. It wasn't me, but it was my family. I'll admit that it's weighing on me. I mean, you had to be young. I would suspect too young to share the heritage of your Household."

He turned away as if to hide something. His Focus was quiet as a grave. Anca's face heated with embarrassment. She chided herself for thinking he would want to speak with her about anything beyond the hunt. "I shouldn't have said anything."

"I don't blame you." Eugen barely shifted. "My family were monsters. I have no illusions about that. Keller, Margest, all the older ones were there. They're culpable. Not the younger generation. Not you."

He blew another steamy breath into the chill night.

"The truth is, I don't have any good reasons to dislike you. All of this bad blood is because of others. You're smart. A talented hunter. Loyal. Kind to your people. It's been a relief to have a hunting partner who isn't so concerned with hogging all the glory."

Anca wanted to know more about the vast wound he

nursed. If she learned more about it, it might help knit hers as well. She also had a bleeding injury in her heart, a pain that had been there for decades.

She told herself this was how everyone felt. Surely, they all carried around pain and disappointment. They all mourned who they could be if things were not so bleak. The court was full of blustery wealth, the queen only cared for her legacy, and everyone caught in between were pawns. At best, they shrugged off the state of things as unavoidable. Eugen was the only person who swallowed his pain like she had. Anca cleared her throat.

"I never wanted to be a Nobil. I didn't want to rule anyone. I loved the banquets, the gowns, the wealth. After a while, you can't ignore the vast cruelty in it. We built our wealth on towns like this. When they dared to ask for something better, all we cared to do was put a boot on their neck."

Eugen craned his neck back to her, one eye allowed to watch her speak.

"I've always told myself that we can be better than this. That has to be true. There is no way our entire society can be so morally bankrupt. This cannot be who I am, even though it is what my mother and father wanted more than anything else."

"Better," he muttered.

Eugen said nothing for a long moment. She waited, her own repeated words lingering in her head. When he spoke, it was with a delicate tone.

"I know something about being raised with a destiny in mind. Aching against it. Hating it. When the chance comes to change things, we have to take it. Right?"

Before she could answer, the sparks of Life in the distance parted for a black shape in the tree line. It crept forward on all fours directly in front of the main path. With no concept of a coilgun, it was blind to how vulnerable it was.

"Eugen."

In the corner of her eye, Eugen's Focus flared to life. It glowed like a torch.

"I see it."

They moved toward the edge of camp with silent steps. It was a speed only mastered by Nobils, to cover distances with the slightest sound. The two arrived at the gate as the Beast of Moura lingered at the edge of the darkness. Its snout crept close enough to catch the light of the torches. The rest of its body was masked by the night, moonlight only showing the barest contours.

Gatling coilguns were cocked by the operators as they drew a bead on the creature. The nearest marker was so close to the Beast. Just a few steps farther would put it in range. Too soon, and there was no guarantee they would land a hit.

"What are you waiting for? Kill it!" Eugen shouted.

Clanging metal deafened everyone near the gate as a storm of steel rods filled the space between them. The pointed tips ripped into the ground and whistled around the Beast as it spun backward into the night.

"Damn it, Eugen!"

Her words fell on deaf ears. The fire tapered off as Eugen barreled past them. The gem of his sword trailed ash as he thundered into the forest. She ground her teeth and followed after him. It was a stupid move. One Nobil was already dead to this Beast and she didn't want Eugen added to the list.

Deep down, she loved not having any choice but to run headlong into the brush.

"Stay here. Be ready if it circles back."

She sprinted into the night, past the flickering torches, and into the midnight forest beyond.

Chapter Fourteen

The night whispered in her ears like a bashful wretch. Vulgar obscenities mixed with half-truths and pleading babbles. Not every dark space put the voices in her ear. It was only in hideous, haunted places that Shadow seemed intent on speaking. The scoured village of Moura, still festering with its dead, was one such place. She was told that listening would allow Shadow the first foothold on your heart.

Eugen's rampage trampled off into the dark of the forest. She kept pace, but still trailed a distance. She traced him by the pulsing beat of his heart and the glimmer of Life that coursed through his veins. As the forest grew deeper around them, his green glow mixed with the other auras.

The forest canopy swallowed everything in shades of black and blue. Only the occasional glimmer of pale moonlight gave any direction. Anca drew on the senses blessed by her Nobil blood. She reached down to the grass beneath her. Past the whisper of night in her ear, she felt for tremors of footsteps. They were barely noticeable. Nothing more than a pinprick of sensation, but to Anca it was clear as a dinner bell.

Eugen's thunderous steps went north, but were bending west. The Executioner had forgotten all of his lessons in stealth. The Blood Flame must be pulsing at near full strength. At least it was loose against the Beast now and not each other.

She tried to detect the other set of steps. The four paws of the Beast would be quieter, but they would fall like a chain of impressions rather than the cascading boom of Eugen's. She opened her mind to the west and hoped to find the rattling vibrations on her fingers.

Nothing. Eugen tore off with nothing ahead of him. Was his rage so great that he was truly blind? That meant she also did not know where it was. Her breath shortened with panic and she opened her perception all around her.

She heard it before she felt it. A slight change in the breeze was the only warning. Leathery wings plummeted down toward her. It held its breath as it cut straight through the air like an arrow. Anca rolled into a patch of mud as the Beast dug its talons where she had just been. She blindly drew her sword and brought it up to catch the swift slice of its claws. Steel rang against bone and the black shape barreled into her. It threw her back and she angled her sword to pierce it as it came to her. A classic trick any dumb animal would fall for.

Her sword sliced into it as the Beast charged, but it did not flinch or scream. Her sword had gone through it, but not drawn any blood. She did not even feel it catch against its flesh. It was like the Beast was made of pure Shadow. It was on top of her, hissing and biting. Its fangs snapped close to her ear as she shoved against its bulk.

She would not die like this. Anca desperately repeated that in her mind. The hunt was botched. Anca could have let Eugen run off to his death. It would be one less complication. Whatever goodness he had in him would disappear into the night and the entire hunt would be hers to command. That was the kind of thinking her parents had fostered.

Never interrupt your foes when they falter. Better that they die on their own sword than yours. It would fulfill her fate.

"No," she managed to force out.

It lifted into the air on black wings. Flat on her back, there was no chance to dodge the next blow. Anca's window was only a moment wide. The wrong move would be her death. Without confidence in her sword, she reached for another weapon. Her fingers slipped to one of the Night Bane Flares and cracked the cap open.

Heat bloomed in a bright, white flash that filled up the night. The Beast shrieked and beat its wings higher. Through the flash, she saw Shadow wriggling at this purifying light. The Beast turned in the air and flew out of sight.

She gasped for air and lifted the flare above her. The shadows shrieked away, slithering into the sheltered boughs nearby. Coated in mud and bleeding, she couldn't feel the pain yet. Time crept by after the rush of near death. Her scimitar whipped forward against another onslaught, but it never came.

All was still except the hiss of the flare. It would only last a few seconds longer. There was no Eugen. No help. This was not a hunt. Her thoughts were only of surviving through the next few minutes. Every tactic and strategy she had memorized was useless if she couldn't stab the damn thing. Shadow beasts were always supposed to bleed.

The bright light in her hand faded and she dropped the charred stub into the muck. The quiet forest chattered with the voices of Shadow, whispering every doubt and fear she ever had. Blade held towards the quiet forest, Anca's breath fogged in the frigid air. She did not dare move from her spot. Minutes passed. The chirrup of crickets rose from a nearby log. In the distance, another sound reached her.

It was a clear ringing sound somewhere south of her. She recognized it as an alarm bell from camp. They had an arsenal of weapons that would do nothing to their quarry.

Anca forgot all ideas of stealth and ran as fast as her legs could carry her. The allure of a visceral hunt among the trees and bushes smothered tactical instinct. Her sword slashed through low branches, ditching her mud-soaked cape when a branch ripped it from her. Through the next line of trees, a blazing, orange light consumed the camp.

Haphazard pins of brilliant, silver light flared among the tents only to burn out seconds later. Dead hunters, sliced and burned, laid past the entrance. Her stomach turned as she counted the bodies. It was a massacre. The earth trembled and a section of wall blew apart. Chunks of rock blasted across the forest. From the cracked rock, a crowd of hunters hustled through the new exit.

She entered the camp and found the intimidating coilguns abandoned. Their ammunition was completely spent into the ground. A loud voice bellowed over the flames and Craita rose from the ground on a pillar of stone. Her yellow Focus glowed as she forced waves of dirt onto the raging fires. It would not put out the flames quickly, but it might save some of their supplies.

"Craita!" Anca shouted, "Where is it?"

The mage looked away from her work long enough to point to the other side of camp.

"It went that way. Drive it off and I will come once these flames are doused."

Sword in hand, Anca checked the last Night Bane flare strapped to her belt and ran through the chaos toward her quarry. Tents burned up like matchsticks, guards staggering from them in flames. Others came with buckets of water or heavy cloth to stamp it out, but many failed. Anca rounded a corner of tents and the world was consumed in a burst of blinding light.

All sound disappeared into an imperceptible ringing. Her feet left the ground as something slammed into her from behind. A shockwave threw her to the ground. For a brief moment, everything went black.

Anca's ears rang and the world faded to gray, her Othersight completely disabled. She tasted blood and dirt as she stood back up. Knees weak, she gritted against the weakness that tried to drag her back down. One of the clockwork wagons sizzled with shining, silver. Its metal frame was blackened, the delicate machinery warped and twisted. Scalding hot cinders scattered over more tents and the flame spread. She cursed under her breath when she recognized that the burning wagon held most of their flares.

Ahead of her, at the edge of the fire, Marin stood in the middle of the ruined camp. He had a shield on one arm and a broken sword in the other. He saw Anca and relief eased his terrified eyes. Her heart dropped as she saw a dark figure emerge behind him.

"Get down!"

At her warning, Marin spun just in time to meet the coming attack. The Beast crashed into his shield and knocked him to the side. Anca crossed the ground between them moments afterward. She brought her sword down on the creature and drew no blood. It reared back on its hind legs and lowered its fang-studded jaw.

It was nearly nine feet tall with skin as black as tar. Even in the fire light, she saw a coat of black mist weave around its body. Horns rose from its head and turned into a row of spikes that ran down its spine. It moved like water, coiling and smooth. Its short snout ended in nasal slits which drank in her scent. A mouth of fangs, only slightly lighter in shade than its skin, dripped with fresh gore. Its frame was muscle and bone. For how gaunt it appeared, she thought it should be dead. The drip of saliva from its mouth confirmed that it was very alive. Its blood red eyes opened wide as it took in this new target. A long tail whipped behind it as it lunged for Anca.

She dodged the creature's swipe and rolled to preempt the next. Claws studded into the ground. She brought her sword up as she rose to her knees. Its claws caught on her sword. She slid her blade to shrug the blow and stabbed into a scab on its shoulder. Blood spurted from the wound and it howled.

It lifted away from her and hissed, wings fanning the flames nearby. Its red eyes went to Marin as he crawled back to his feet. It dove toward the Doia, but he threw a handful of dirt into the Beast's face. It coughed and snorted before retreating again.

"Go! Get out of here," she said to Marin.

"You need help."

"You look worse than me, old man."

One of the Beast's wings swung back into a burning tent and the wispy, shadow-coating evaporated. Its skin scalded and it flexed the wing wide in pain. Anca flipped the grip on her sword and threw it. The point punctured straight through the thin webbing.

Marin scrabbled off to the side as Anca drew her last

dagger. The Beast threw itself at her and she barely dodged one of its cruel hooks. The other paw caught her leg and left a long cut on her thigh. She slid to where her sword lay on the ground.

A loud shout came from her right. The colossal, armored shape charged headlong in. Eugen crashed into its ribs and threw the Beast away. Veins pulsed in his neck and orange light traced up his veins. His skin was bare of the cyan paste, the measure forgotten in the rush. His cindering sword buried into the ground as the creature stepped to the side. Anca took advantage and popped the Night Bane flare from her pocket.

The small, silver flame clawed back the few shadows around them. The dark weave that protected the rest of the creature shivered and drew back. Its flesh exposed and vulnerable, it leaped onto a nearby crate and flapped its wings, but only managed to glide over their heads before crashing into the earth.

Eugen spun around, his blade swinging within inches of Anca, and pounded toward it with a barbaric scream. The two had the creature on the defensive, but Anca found it hard to deliver a killing blow. Eugen swung where he liked to with a maniac's strength, whether it would block Anca's movement or not.

She growled in frustration and swung in toward the Beast's leg. A strike that would certainly maim the creature for good, it never landed. Eugen lunged forward and her pierce went through his lower leg.

The creature took advantage of the break in tempo. It jumped onto the nearby stone wall and swiftly climbed to the top. It lifted with what strength it had and escaped into the forest beyond.

Cold panic flushed through her. They had it, it was

right here without anywhere to run. The chance had vanished right in front of them. Anca prepared to run as Eugen turned to face her. That mad, hungry light glittered in his pupils. Red consumed the whites of his eyes. There was not a single whisper of Eugen left inside. The Executioner roared at her.

"Eugen, we have to catch it!"

Spittle flew from his lips. Bloodshot veins pulsed, his flesh a shade of ruddy red that matched the color of blood. His mouth was an open, snarling maw. The curved greatsword rose upward in a killing pose.

This was the monster she was warned of.

Marin sprinted from where he had been hiding with a flaming club. The Doia kicked Eugen's knee and it bent to the side with an agonizing crack. Marin brought the club down. The wood broke in half on his skull, barely phasing the berserker. His hand shot out to Marin's throat. The Executioner's arm flexed as he began to crush the life from Marin, the old man pounding on his arm.

Anca stabbed through his sword-bearing arm, the tip punching clean through. She twisted the blade and his fingers dropped the sword as broken bone ruptured through his skin. Eugen threw Marin into her, retracting the blade as she fell.

Sword in hand, she would behead him if she got the chance. Frighteningly, she was not sure that would actually kill him. The Executioner roared again and flexed his hands. His body was wearing down, this much damage should have killed him already.

"Don't try it!" she shouted.

The bones in his broken arm snapped back into place of their own accord. Muscles pulled underneath his skin, his body seething with unnatural strength. The guttural sound of his voice carried through the camp as he dragged his foot through the dust like a bull. He was gone, too lost in the lust for blood to remember why they were here.

"Are you an animal? What did we say about being better than what we are!"

The Executioner took one step forward, fingers snapping at the air in front of him, and then ground to a halt. He shook and screamed, his body seizing as though muscle and bone disagreed. The light in his eyes dimmed to a warm glow, a hint of brown emerging. She readied her blade.

"We can fix things and you're throwing that away. Don't make me do it, Eugen."

He snapped his neck back and forth, but his feet remained still. One hand grabbed the other and pulled himself backward a step.

"Don't be like them. Stay with me!"

Marin watched from behind her with terror in his eyes. He looked between Anca and the Executioner as though it were an act of magic.

"Still—here! Still!"

The only words that Eugen could conjure amid his rage. He took two steps forward and threw his face into the dirt. His murderous will was spent on the earth, fingers clawing at the ground. He balled his hand and brought it down over and over, grunting and screaming.

Anca watched his pace of strikes slow. His sword, flaking with ash, began to dim. Deep breaths flexed his barrel-like chest, slowing into a gasping rhythm. With her sword in hand, she took a step toward him.

"Are you mad?" Marin whispered.

Her arm was ready. She eyed the angle that would behead him. This beast, this thing in Eugen's skin, might snap back to violence at any moment. If he so much as gave her a bad look, she would kill him.

Anca took a breath, raised her sword, and stepped next to Eugen. His fists loosened. Eugen reached forward with a flushed, mottled hand, and rested it on the toe of her boot. His breathing settled with a deep exhale and he brought his eyes up to her, bloodshot and brimming with shame. The orange light faded from his brown pupils. His lips tightened and he shook his head.

"Here… I'm still here."

Chapter Fifteen

He remembered running after the creature.
Darkness. Frustration.
Fire.
Pain.
And then Anca. Out of the mist, like the first morning ray through the night.

His world ached. The cooling embers of the camp were a shade of bloody red. Tan canvas tents seemed pink behind his bloodshot eyes. Had his armor always been so heavy? He groaned as he tried to stretch his left arm, the tendons not wanting to extend.

Existence was pain.

Most of his wounds healed into thick scabs. Pale, scar tissue ran along his left arm where the bone pulled itself back together. A brace of cloth was wrapped from his shoulder to the elbow. He winced and rolled his bloodshot eyes. His skin was mottled with painful, red splotches.

"What happened?" Anca asked.

The only place left for them was Eugen's tent. The single bed was austere, with sheets of plain, wool cloth. A small case, lined with satin, laid next to his bed for the dreaded greatsword. Several jars of his calming paste sat on a table next to maps and lists of supplies.

Marin cleared his throat and spoke with a harsh, thin voice.

"This moron charged headlong out of the perimeter and you followed. It was quiet for a few minutes. I was gathering some hunters to go after you when the Beast returned."

"Over the walls?" she asked.

"No. Right through the damned front door. If it knocked, we still wouldn't have been ready." Marin shook his head. "Arrows, coilguns, spears, it didn't care. It seemed afraid of Flame, but none of us thought to set it on fire. Not that we could. It was too fast."

Craita attended to Eugen's wounds, applying stinging paste on the deeper cuts before wrapping them in clean cloth.

"Deep breaths," Craita murmured. "Your body overworked itself. I read a book on Flame magic once. It said your condition isn't unlike heat stroke. However, an archivist of Naelan claimed that you physically cannot die. So who knows what might have happened."

"Oh joy." Eugen winced as she cleaned another wound.

Craita fidgeted and glanced at the other two people in the room. Anca eyed Eugen like a wild animal. The mage did not know how the fight ended. Just that Nobil had fought Nobil in the wake of the attack. He had betrayed them.

"What started the fire?" Eugen asked.

Marin glanced at him, his lip curling, and then returned his gaze to Anca.

"Someone must have knocked over a torch or rightly tried to set it on fire. I don't know. We've never seen anything like this."

Anca drew in a sharp breath as she shifted on her stool.

"We hurt it though. If you burn off that coating, it bleeds like anything else. It's some sort of Shadow magic."

"Shadow has only created monsters. The beasts can't wield it," Craita countered.

"I'm telling you what I saw. Night Bane flares completely removed any protection. I cut one of its wings to shreds. It won't be flying for a while."

"Good," Eugen said before falling into a coughing fit.

"And then you tried to kill her," Marin interrupted.

Anca and Marin came out only slightly better than he had. Her hands were blistered and the long slash on her leg was bandaged. Anca did not hide the dagger she clutched in her left hand. She leaned onto her knees and her neck sagged from exhaustion. The furious look in her eyes told him that she had not decided to let him live yet.

Looking at her burned him worse than any flame could. It was all his fault.

Anca nearly died because of him. He almost killed her and he did not remember any of it. She was not the only one who suffered. Purple and red bruises bloomed around Marin's neck. When he spoke, it sounded like there was a wad of gravel in his throat.

He winced as if Craita had jabbed one of his wounds. Acid burned in his joints as his body tried to conjure more power. His form might be able to fight through the pain, but his spirit was shattered.

What could he do? What could he say to even begin to make up for this? They were warned about Eugen and still took the chance. Anca wanted the same thing as him. This was a chance Eugen did not deserve and he almost threw it away.

"How are we supposed to trust you after this?" Anca asked.

His skin flushed at her scathing tone. It was the damn Blood Flame, he thought. Though it twisted him into a beast of a man, he could not resist the power. Eugen would be dead without it. What use would he have to a world that despised him if he could not be their monster? The queen would not have him if he could not accomplish the quiet, clandestine things she needed out of the Nobil's eyes.

Eugen had to prove that nothing had changed, even as everything was irreparably different.

"I am still dedicated to the hunt. Our losses are great, but we can still prove them all wrong. You're here because you aren't them. You want change. You want to prove the other Households are fools." Pain rolled back into Eugen like a wave. He gripped his knee and spoke between his teeth. "Don't lie. I know I'm right."

Anca glanced at Craita, but found the Queen's Company mage as confused as herself.

"I thought you were supposed to be my handler? A minder from the throne. That flimsy excuse about supplies was never the real reason, was it?"

Anca was half-right. There was a deeper reason, a secret that could never surface. If he pulled this off, it would never have to. His deepest crime could remain buried.

"Astasia thinks so. At first, I was prepared to be that."

"I don't believe him for a second," Marin muttered.

Eugen tried to stand, but his wounds brought him back down with a wince. Every muscle pulled tight, like they were trying to tie themselves into knots. He took a deep breath and tried to think of something calming. Anca's eyes flashed in his mind.

"Believe me, Doia. I'm on your side. Do you think I like being treated like this? My name is a curse. My bloodline is a stain. I thought if I could beat a Nobil at their own game, prove that I am better than the best of you, it would pull the wool from your eyes."

It was a petty thought. His wound seemed so obvious now. Eugen lived his life assuming things of the Nobils as they assumed things about him. He never questioned it. Astasia's lies were sweet as honey.

"And what does the queen gain by showing me up?" Anca asked.

"Keller has hated her family for years. A friendly Household on top would let her bully the Nobils into obedience, given enough time."

"I'll remind you that it was the queen's wine and pleasantries that occupied Bire and Stancu. The queen chose to weaken us. After everything we've done. Flame, they requested my mother lead the charge against your kin. Are we so inconvenient to your little schemes?"

"Her schemes. And please," Eugen gingerly sat forward on his stool, "I don't give a damn about what your family did to mine. Last I checked, aren't you the most feared enforcer of the queen's will after me? You say you aren't your parents. Prove it."

That pissed her off. Anca's predatory cool vanished with a snarl of her teeth. Good, he thought. He wanted her to be plain with him.

"I could have let you die tonight and hunted that damn thing on my own. Magic or not, I can kill you. I still might."

"I don't doubt it. You're twice the hunter I could be

and that's why you should trust me. I need you more than you need me. Even if you spare me, I'd still be the same hated beast that they say I am. You'd still be House Sulia. Still brave. Still proud."

Eugen stumbled from his stool and kneeled before her. It wasn't intentional, but he didn't correct himself. It would take a vow of loyalty to gain their trust again.

Anca's breath caught as he did. He growled against the ache as his bruised knees crashed into the dirt. His eyes settled on the ground in front of her, like when he had vowed to serve Astasia and the throne. No matter the cost.

"I blinked. I lost myself in a way that I swore to never do again. You brought me back, Nobil Sulia. I've never done that before. When I find myself ablaze, I can't be stopped unless I run out of steam. Everything is murder. All I see is red, but I saw you."

His voice cracked and Eugen looked up at her. He wanted to be trusted. He had to hope that she understood that need.

"Stay back from her," Marin growled.

"I didn't have my calming herbs with me. For so long, it was the only way I could live in my skin. I don't know how or why, but you helped me pull it back. This purpose, this chance, must be true if it can pull the Flame in me backwards. I'm not going to let that go".

Her features did not flinch. Only the searching look in her eyes told him that she was considering it.

"Let's show those bastards and that brat on the throne what it looks like when we move beyond these grudges. I'm tired of keeping us rich at the cost of the innocent. I'm tired of being told what my fate is. I'm tired of being hated."

Craita and Marin watched them knowing that the slightest move would send them down a path that they could not turn from. Anca blew out a long breath, her face finally twisting from anger. There was contempt, but something muted her raw ferocity. Eugen thought he saw a flash of amusement before she rolled her eyes.

"Get up."

He slowly rose, stumbling forward as his right calf seized up. Craita moved to help him, but he held up his palm. It felt important to do this on his own. Meeting Anca's gaze, he found her lips bunched in thought. Arms crossed and her chin raised, she was ready to render her verdict.

"You let the Beast get away. Marin tells me what is left of our companies are ready to draw swords against each other at first light. If you want my forgiveness, you have to make this right."

"You're not seriously trusting him?" Marin hesitated on his feet as if he considered yanking Anca out of the tent. "He'll bite you as soon as shake your hand."

"Eugen is right. All of the Households would cheer if we turned on each other. Keller would be proven right. Bire and Stancu would keep the non-punishment and live it up. I wouldn't get my chance to right these wrongs." Her voice fell as her eyes settled on him again, a small warmth softening them. "Neither would he."

All the pain in his flame-ridden body seemed so small now. His heart might have risen out of his chest. After a lifetime of damnation, the chance to make up for his wrongs was a stronger fuel than the Blood Flame itself.

"I will take responsibility for my actions," Eugen

said.

"I need you to make sure no blood is shed between our people. Get our remaining supplies cataloged and find me in the morning. We need to figure out our next course of action."

"Action?" Marin asked, a delirious cackle in his voice. "Anca, we barely have anyone left. Most of our supplies are burned up. Who knows where the Beast has gotten off to."

"Probably to finish us off tomorrow night," Craita added.

Anca beckoned them all to Eugen's table and found Moura on the map. She drew a line westward with her finger.

"It's wounded. Shelter will be its chief concern. It will want to heal and hunt again."

"How can you know that?" Craita slipped on a pair of glasses from a pouch at her hip.

"It's never been hurt before. Everything that came before was easy pickings, but we made it bleed. Its hunting grounds are occupied. The Beast will be looking for a home. Wherever it came from."

She indicated the coast to the north and the marshy grasslands to the south.

"It isn't aquatic, so seaside habitation is out," Anca continued. "It can't survive in sunlight so the marshes are no good to it. The only choice is to go west." Her finger led across the bogs and marshes to their west and to the deep, forgotten woods beyond.

"Teragva," Eugen purred.

No, he had to find a way to keep her away.

"That far west?" Marin asked. "What could possibly be out there for it? It's full of beasties just as bad as itself.

No easy pickings at all."

"It will know how to evade its own kind, but that isn't our only problem." Eugen pointed at a small dot on the map, the name "Teragva" written next to it. "There's a tribe of people called the Trigvan. Survivors of the Great War that the Nobils abandoned to Shadow. They've existed on this land for centuries and they hate us worse than the Shadow beasts. We'll be walking into a fight."

"Wait. I've heard about them." Craita went into her pack for one of her notebooks. "Scavengers, but they tinker. Absolutely brilliant engineers if the stories are true. It's a shame they don't have any real manufacturing. Everything they have is scraped together from the past. The throne's been trying to learn more about them for years. Not that they'd ever trust us."

"Maybe we should wait for the Beast to return. We can prepare and rearm, we'll be ready." Eugen looked away from the map.

It was the absolute wrong plan of action. Limping back home would likely bring another Nobil amongst them. Anca might even be replaced in favor of Keller or Paegra or some other egotistical, glory hound. He would certainly be sent home. She wouldn't get the kill. Instead, it would be another trophy for the Households to brag about and declare their rightful place on top of the world.

Eugen swallowed and tapped a finger against his leg. She would notice his pulse rising. Stay calm, he thought. There were ways to keep them from finding out. There had to be.

"We must pursue it, no matter how far it runs," Anca said. "What if it breeds and we are fighting five or more of these things come spring? What if it strikes somewhere else? It could elude us altogether and massacre farms for years if it wants to."

"Too risky to let it go now." Marin traced the old roads and trails they would need to follow. "Not going to be terribly fun getting there either."

Eugen's lips moved to speak, but the words stewed inside. Anca knew the right action and there would be no swaying her. Even if he tried to argue further, he would be peddling obvious lies. It would draw more attention if he pressed the issue.

"That doesn't help us with the Trigvan. They will treat us as invaders and they might have coilguns. Perhaps even gear-walkers," Craita said.

"What if we gave them a common enemy?" Anca suggested.

"Like a beastie they can't deal with?" Marin's wily eyebrow rose.

"We'll have to buy them out," Eugen grunted. "They aren't much for charity."

"We'll figure it out. Marin, Craita, get some sleep and then figure out how many hunters we have left. It's a long journey ahead."

Anca gestured for Marin to follow her as she left the tent. Eugen stepped away from the table, but his eyes followed her. Even battered and tired, his heart beat a little faster when she was in the room. He recognized that bleeding center in him as tenderness. Maybe it was his grievous injuries. Maybe it was how Anca saw him as an ally and not a dog on a leash. Eugen knew it was dangerous.

Putting it out of his mind would be best. Keeping her angry at him would ensure they would get to the end of this without complications. He could have her trust and kill the Beast. They would ride back heroes and maybe he would get that shot at a new start.

Maybe a new start with her.

He winced at the thought. True, her eyes made something inside of him weaken. Her smirk drove him wild. She was beautiful, but that didn't matter. It was an insipid emotion that he had no time for. This was the edge of the world, not a courting banquet. He leaned onto a chair and tore his eyes away as she reached the lip of the tent. His resolve failed at the last second.

"Goodnight, Anca."

Eugen had used her name, not Nobil Sulia. Flame, what was he thinking? He gritted his teeth. He could have kicked a stool in frustration. At the very least, he could hope for her to help smother that small, needy part of his soul. As he berated himself, his ears stayed perked for her voice. She had not yet left the tent. After a long moment, she answered.

"Goodnight."

It was a kindness to not breeze out of the tent without another word. He deserved death and he knew it. The plan had not changed, but it felt like they had lost the map. As Craita finished bandaging his last few wounds and left the tent, he realized how joyful he felt.

Goodnight.

He was a repentant wretch to her. However, he was not beyond forgiveness. Maybe she saw the Eugen behind the Blood Flame, the man that he wished he could be someday.

The night was not over. There were hunters to make peace with and supplies to inventory. Eugen had to fulfill his obligation to the camp, to the hunt, and to Anca. Wincing from his injuries as he pulled his armor back on, he still could not fight the small grin that crept onto his face.

Chapter Sixteen

Anca gasped and rose from the warm sheets of her bed. Her heart raced. A heat coursed through her that she couldn't explain. It wasn't fear. She didn't want to acknowledge what it felt like. Sweat beaded from her hairline, but after a moment she found that her forehead wasn't the only thing that was damp.

She cradled her forehead as the previous night came back to her: the Beast, blood, Eugen.

She dreamed about a meal in front of the hearth in her bedroom. Eugen sat across from her. He lounged with a cup of wine in his hands. She said something to him, what had it been? It was something like a joke. He laughed and said something back to her. He looked at her, eyes glowing with adoration. Eugen leaned toward her.

Anca shook her head. Weird dreams always haunted her after close calls with death. That had to be the explanation for it. Rubbing the sleep from her eyes, she pushed the dream out of her head. Marin would have a heart attack if she told him about it. She decided it was fine for her thoughts to wander. It wasn't like she hadn't looked at Eugen's muscles. Any good looking man would tempt her the same way.

Not many of them could understand her as he did.

Flame and Water, stop it, she thought. Anca decided to get out of bed before her thoughts wandered into stranger places.

It was still early, the splash of dawn's midnight blue barely noticeable. The smell of eggs, toasted bread, and cheese rose from outside. She did not wake up to the sounds of hunters spilling each other's blood. Eugen must have been busy last night.

The cramped tent she slept in was a joke compared to what she had prior. Anca climbed out of bed and rubbed the last bits of exhaustion from her eyes. Her senses pricked to life. She smelled the dew on the moors outside and the mist in the air. The aches from last night woke with her and she leaned against the tent pole. Away from Marin and Eugen, she allowed herself a pained gasp as she put weight onto the wounded leg. It would not slow her down, but would need a bit more medicine.

She slipped out of her sweat-soaked clothes and dumped a small bucket of ice-cold water over her head. Anca hissed and washed under her arms and down her legs, taking a moment to rub healing herbs into the cut. Even with this frigid water, it felt like paradise to scrub the grime from her body.

There was celebration in an uncomfortable shower. The feeling of washing away dried sweat was a tribute to hard work. It was a reminder of how far they had come, but also of how much farther they had to go. Victor laughed when she explained that to him. Used to his courts and parties, exertion annoyed him.

She imagined Eugen could appreciate it. He struggled through enough shit in his life to appreciate a small relief. Anca toweled off and put on a change of trousers and an undershirt. Her chainmail needed cleaning before it could be used and the scimitar required sharpening.

"Are you awake?" Marin stuck his curly, red hair through the tent flap. Full green bruises covered his neck, but his voice had improved to a low growl.

"When do I ever sleep for long?"

Her Doia brought a plate of fried quail eggs and buttered bread alongside a bundle of parchment.

"I've got breakfast for you. I've already eaten."

"Who let them cook? We should still be on dry rations."

"I did." Marin groaned as he sat down. He pushed the plate in front of her and pulled a fork from his pocket. "After last night, everyone could use a warm meal."

She did not know how many died last night. Truthfully, she did not want to hear. More slaughter. More pain. More suffering at the hands of the Nobils and their Households.

"How many are left?"

Marin hesitated before he answered. "Half. Most of the dead are House Sulia."

"Half?"

"Bodies have been gathered for a funeral pyre. We will have to make time for that before we leave."

"Of course."

"Names have been noted for memorials when we get back home."

Marin tapped his fingers on the roll of parchment, his eyes roaming everywhere except to her. She knew him like family, right down to his tells.

"Something on your mind?"

His silence was swollen with smothered thoughts. Marin half-glanced at her, the gears churning in his head obvious on his face.

"Were you serious when you agreed to go along

171

with Eugen? You might have been tired. We were both injured—"

"I was serious. It's my order."

Marin's teeth ground together. His tension slid away a moment later as he leaned back on his stool. With an exasperated sound, he opened his palms before slapping them on his legs.

"What is this, Anca?"

She had not figured it out herself yet. The redemption of House Furloc was not in the plan. She would have sooner damned them before giving any sort of mercy. That her mother's daughter would be the one to work alongside the last heir of Furloc was ludicrous.

Not in a hundred years would she expect Eugen to be more of a kindred soul to her than Marin. He was a victim as much as the people of Moura and Pese. He had no hand in the chaos that swallowed his life, but the transgression of his family was paid down regardless.

None of this helped Anca come up with an explanation.

"We can't turn a blind eye to them anymore. I thought they would be corrupt and careless like their monarch."

"They are," Marin quietly thumped the table with his fist, "I've been in the order far longer than you. Trust me when I say they can all hang."

"Have you considered you're too close to it?"

"What?"

"Marin, you were there when they obliterated Eugen's family."

"House Furloc," Marin corrected.

"It was a family, damn it. His life was destroyed. You let the boy live, but told him he was a monster. Of course that is what he ended up as."

"Your parents rightfully sheltered you from the damage they caused. It's in his blood. The line of Furloc will always create monsters and no one can change that."

"There is a man underneath all of that rage. We both saw it last night. If he would just let go of that damned magic. Will we deny him a second chance? He's never had a first chance to prove himself as something else."

The Doia stood and pinched the bridge of his nose. "I can't believe this."

"Why is he any different from me? He deserves a chance to prove himself."

"Because he tried to kill us, Anca. Don't you remember or are you conveniently forgetting that detail?"

"And I didn't save us. He stopped."

"He's a maniac."

"He's a victim and doesn't know any better. All he knows is how to survive and that means doing what he has to. When you all turned your backs to him, Eugen did the only thing he knew to do."

Marin frequently disagreed with her. It was good to have someone who saw your weak spots before anyone else. His advice had shaped her family's decisions for decades. Maybe that was why it hurt to argue like this. Agreeing would have been easier. She would feel safe if she had his support. The easy way was not the right thing to do this time. She would just be damning more people to the cycle she wanted to break.

"You're not going to budge, are you?" he asked.

"Have I ever?"

Her smile felt sad. Marin mustered a chuckle and sat down again.

"Anca, I'm not your father—"

"You're family, Marin. Of course you are. That's why I need you on my side."

The old man set his hand on hers and squeezed. A memory crossed her mind. He had bundled her in a throw blanket during a winter festival. Her parents were holding court and someone had to mind her. He told her crass anecdotes about all the artfully styled servants of the court. None of them were true, but they made her laugh.

"You're not the hunter your parents wanted, but I know they'd be proud. In their own way."

"So you'll play along?" Anca kept the kind smile on her face, but her heart felt like it might seize up if he walked away.

Marin kicked the table leg and groaned.

"I think this is a bad idea, but it's your idea. I can't say no."

She could have collapsed from relief. Instead, she squeezed his hand back and nodded.

"Thank you."

****

Marin didn't exaggerate. They had lost half of their company. Most of the cold weather clothing and a quarter of the food stuff were consumed by the fire. The worst blow beyond the lost lives was their stock of Night Bane flares. Now critical to the hunt, they only had eleven left.

Every single rider among them was ready to leave. The companies reorganized along battle lines. They didn't even share breakfast. The warm meal was refused by many under the royal flag. To his credit, Eugen gave a deep bow to Anca as she rode to the head of the assembled riders. She repressed last night's dream.

"Listen up," he bellowed. "I know what you've all heard and it's true. I lost myself to my rage in ways that I'm not proud of. Nobil Sulia had every right to kill me, but she didn't. She has not wavered from our purpose and neither should any of you."

She trotted her horse toward the disorganized mob of riders. The small divide between the two groups might as well have been a mile. She saw the anger in the eyes of her own and the suspicion in the others. Doru sat on his horse toward the back row. Vali was not amongst the living. She had never been one for speeches, but she would try.

"We all lost people last night. We lost hope. We lost trust. You lost your trust in Eugen and myself. It is our charge to keep you safe even as you risk your lives in our name. I'm sorry for that. I did not understand the nature of our quarry because this is unlike anything we've hunted before. Whatever twist of magic shit this monster onto our doorstep, it is insidious and cunning."

Eugen shifted his footing, eyes not tearing away from their hunters.

"You're angry and have decided that the other is to blame. Eugen for turning on us, me for wounding him. I'm commanding you to do something that will hurt. Put it aside. Your true enemy is out there. Not me, not Eugen, not Doia Marin, not mage Craita. The Beast undid all of those tenuous bonds that kept us civil. We cannot let it pick apart our spirit. Hunters will not be bested by Beasts. Are you going to let it win?"

That put a stir in them. If they wouldn't get along, she would make them compete against each other.

"Last night wasn't without a win. We wounded our

quarry and now it will run and hide. The Lost Lands are where it likely came from and we will chase it to its lair. Supplies will be tight and the road will be long. But that changes nothing, we are hunters. We will not waver until we mount this monster's skull above our mantle!"

Doia Marin and Eugen shouted and thumped their chests, each hunter following them. Backs were straighter, eyes wider, and pulses beat harder. She conjured some kind of courage into them. Hopefully, it might hold.

Their dead hunters and the people of Moura were burned. Together, they met the same honored end. They waited until the large wood pyre, coated in flammable oils, was fully ablaze. She watched the green fire lick out from the first bodies and travel across and up the funeral mound. None of them kicked or fidgeted as Shadow would make them. At least their bodies would know a peaceful end. Untainted by the darkness that swallowed this town.

****

They hardly stopped to rest for the next three days. The caravan set a fast pace that their horses matched without hesitation. Anca worried that the strenuous ride would exacerbate tensions, but each company was eager to outperform the other. No one wanted to be the first one to be seen as weaker or slower. Even when they did stop to rest, concern for the horses were noted before their own needs.

These lands were wild. The ruins and bones common around the kingdom were nowhere to be found. Wild trees sprouted high and fallen timbers were consumed by seas of shrubs. Ivy draped over entire groves like a shroud.

Vast wetlands stretched out in a near featureless ocean of tall grass. Eerie, leafless trees rose from them like towers in a city. Their weathered, pale bark were like bones amid the thrumming life of the waters below. In the exposed roots peeking above the water line, rats coursed through the burrows and holes that dotted the loose soil.

They had to pick their trails carefully. The water was freezing cold and the muck was deep enough to swallow people whole. Their path turned into a meandering trail, straight as a wet noodle. Horses treaded along slowly. The surviving clockwork wagon ground through the mud without slowing. All of it was quiet except for the songs of birds safely roosted in the tops of trees. It was serene at first glance. Anca knew better than to trust that notion. These were lands that Shadow had dominated for centuries.

Craita was unconcerned for the sanctity of this land. Her magic ripped stone walls from the ground far higher than anything could hope to jump over. She was exhausted after each display of power. Her hunters did not trust the mage, but appreciated the security that her abilities provided. Anca was glad to see Doru give her another portion of food after a particularly demanding effort.

Eugen kept his distance from Anca as they rode. His zeal to be at the front of the convoy faded and he lurked out of her eye line. He was quick to settle arguments between the companies and give the slow riders some urgency. Through it all, he ensured that it was her command and not his own that was kept. She wasn't sure if he was just licking his wounds or had actually been cowed. By the way he avoided her gaze, tearing his face away when she looked toward him, she suspected the latter.

She was annoyed to find that she wanted him to look at her.

Nights were sleepless for many. In their own lands, they were predators and the Shadow beasts were the prey. Cramped inside stony defenses through the nights, Anca felt sympathy for mice, rabbits, and every other prey animal that spent their lives holding their breath.

These temporary forts left nothing to chance. No way in, but no way out either. They stoked their fires high and burned more oil than they should. The hostility between households was forgotten at sunset. Tents were set up closely together on this rough, shrub-choked ground.

Anca's Othersight traced stalking shapes through the stone barricades. They passed in herds and packs. Four legs, two legs, tails, and teeth. The faint tinge of green that ran through their veins was polluted with stretches of darkness. Things born of Shadow hardly glowed as brightly as something born entirely of Life.

Anca sat outside of her tent, crossbow in hand and two Night Bane Flares on her belt. Marin lingered nearby to keep her company. He claimed his concern was for herself, despite the elevated pulse she watched in his veins. At the squealing, snapping sound of something dying, he took a loaded coilgun and went to bed.

Eugen paced around the perimeter for hours. For the most part, he watched silently. He goaded things if they came too close to the wall, pulling his lips back and pounding the ground. At first, she thought he might be losing himself again. When she warned him, his rage vanished with an easy smile.

"Just scaring them away. If they think there's a bigger predator within, they won't be tempted to enter."

Eugen was smeared with cyan calming herbs as he did this. Anca watched him apply it every sunset. He slathered calming herbs from his sharp jawline, down his neck and onto the muscular arms that hefted the greatsword on his shoulder.

The first time had been by accident, but she sought it out the following evenings. He kneeled outside of his tent, blade set on the ground, head intoned in reverence. It had a mystic element to it, blending close to the mage's entreaties to the elements. She told herself it was due to her curiosity in magic that she watched. Anca wrote off the idea that she was interested in how his muscles worked through the air. Or how his pants pulled tight when he kneeled.

It was getting harder to resist the impulses by the third night. She made an effort to stay away from his herb ritual, but still caught the first few moments. Maybe it was because she hadn't been laid in a while, but Eugen began to bring a soothing thrill to her evenings.

That realization worried her to no end. So she focused on her crossbow, her sword, and her armor. Disassembled, cleaned, polished, and reassembled. Even though it occupied her thoughts, her hearing was still focused on Eugen's heavy steps around the perimeter wall.

She imagined what he might feel like under her fingers. His smooth skin was dotted with smaller scars that refused to fully heal. Anca imagined they were like small knots on a tall tree. Where else did he have scars? Under his well-worn trousers, would she find more scars on his calves? His thighs? She tore her eyes away from him, not liking the heat she felt between her legs.

"Careful. You're not the scariest thing in these woods," Anca warned him as he passed nearby.

Eugen swaggered away from his path and leaned against his sword.

"You might get what you want though," he said.

She flicked the string of her crossbow, not missing the irony of what she might want. What was she thinking? She didn't want him. Yes, Eugen was attractive by conventional standards. It was human nature to look at pretty things. She couldn't help it.

"Everyone is sleeping or frightened. We're not used to being mice."

"Hasn't stopped you from watching me."

Her heart skipped. She thought of explanations for her twilight peeking. Something contrarian and a little mean might work, but what could she even say? It was getting harder to fling insults at Eugen these days.

He jerked a finger to the stone walls.

"When you watch me walk the perimeter. You're hoping I'll get in trouble and you'll be forced to help."

She exhaled and gave him a weak smile. Of course. There was no other time she watched him. She would be damned sure that no one got any ideas about her interests. It was impossible. Not even worth considering.

Beyond the walls, her Othersight drew a shape in the green light. A wolf-like creature rose onto its hind legs as it tried to scent them. Eugen leaned down to her, watching the same creature. He smelled smoky. Maybe just a bit of orange or was that lemon? And savory like a bundle of herbs behind it all. He smelled like raw, bleeding life.

"Why not? We could climb the wall. Shade, we

could get Craita to open it. You and I slip out and stretch our legs."

Beating hearts and sweaty brows, gasping for breath as they chased something through the woods. Entwined fingers, a chance to cut loose and forget the stress for even a few minutes. She was not proud of the thought.

"Huh, yeah. Remember how that went last time? Even if we did, our duty is to our hunters first."

"They want us to be killers and treat us as such. We'd just be giving them what they want. What's the harm in indulgence? We're just playing house with all this court nonsense."

"What sort of future would we have then? Trust the queen will spontaneously give up her grip on power? Make the Households behave so you and I can have some sort of life in a kinder world?"

Eugen walked to the other side of the campfire.

"So, you don't mind me hanging around?"

She could not fight her grin. "You're not the worst company I've had."

His mouth fell open, but he snapped it closed. He buried the tip of his sword into the ground and sat down across from her.

"I think that's the first time I've heard anyone be chummy with me."

"How does it feel?"

He thought it over for a moment, nodding when he decided on the right word.

"Easy."

Eugen could have been anyone as he lounged there. Devoid of that Flame in his blood, there was not even a suggestion of monstrosity. Her dream came to mind, Eugen lounging in her home. What would he be like completely removed from temptation? She knew nothing about him beyond the suffering.

"So, what do Executioners do for fun?"

He cocked his head at her.

"Fun? I'm not sure you've seen my day-to-day, but fun doesn't fall into it very often."

"Surely you're not working all the time though."

His small grin grew wide and he draped an arm over his knee. He sputtered his lips as he thought. "Shade, let's see. Mostly we shop for the little black hoods."

"Shut up."

"Seriously, it's just as cutthroat as the royal fashions. Lots of trends to keep up with." He laughed as he finished the thought.

"Fine, wrong question. What does Eugen, dreaded Executioner of the queen, do for fun?"

The title clouded his smile. She regretted mentioning it. If he brought up compliance orders, she would not be able to keep up any sort of good humor either.

"Can't say that much at all. It's a dour business and there's a reputation to uphold. The queen's bag man can't be personable. Besides, you Household Nobils have made certain that I'm not welcome."

He pulled back into his shell by a degree.

"That's why we're here though. We both know how cruel they can be. Neither of us want that. Stick with me Eugen and trust. If we can kill this thing and bring it back, those bastards won't be able to deny us. With you in the queen's ear and my voice in the Households, who knows what we can do."

His eyes flickered across the space behind her. "Assuming she'll even listen."

"We'll work something out. Astasia isn't the only person who understands leverage."

They talked about small things: food, their shared dislike of winter, and other topics between something and nothing. Anca hardly noticed two hours pass as they chatted. During that time, barely a glimpse of anger passed through him. The sword lay quiet in the ground and Eugen didn't look at it once. She couldn't figure him out, but friend was starting to sound like the correct description.

****

The next day, fog swallowed them whole and their caravans piled in close to one another. Anca steered them along the Beast's trail. It fled west as they thought it would. Without the benefit of wings, it was forced to go on foot and glide from scant hills down into lowlands. Any other tracker would have no hope of following. The effort pushed Anca to the edge of her ability. She fumed knowing that Nobil Paegra would be perfectly suited to this. That frustration became her fuel as she followed the scarcest trail through the swamp.

The mist finally broke as they reached the far end of the wetlands. Barren trees drifted out of the fog like pale corpses. Each one was harvested for everything except the twisted, barren trunks. Some jagged ax cuts were left decades ago and others were no older than a few months. The entire forest was wan and dying. Many were already dried husks. The horizon was bent and gnarled like the bare bristles of an overused brush.

Trinkets dangled from stakes on long lengths of twine. All of them were rusted scraps of metal barely useful for any other purpose. The newer ones still had a dull glean of iron or silver. The oldest were chewed to pieces by the wind. Anca lifted one in her hand. They looked like people, effigies with arms and legs, but were augmented with horns and teeth.

"What beast carves totems of itself?" Marin asked.

"People." Craita smiled and batted at the totems. "These people have lived beyond the safety of the throne for centuries. Griel's 'History of the Great War' suggests that they have a strong oral tradition. They tell legends of strength without reliance on magic. They believe using elemental power attracts Shadow."

Marin let a totem drop from his hand. "They're not wrong there."

"What about the claws and teeth?" Eugen asked.

"Shadow magic. Perhaps the mark of the Wild Eye," Craita guessed.

Service to Shadow would leave you twisted into something new. Not human, not animal, but a half-way nightmare that only knew malice. Their children would not bear the entire curse, but just an echo of their wild forms. Eyes of bright orange, yellow, violet, these colors were hallmarks of the Wild Eye. It was a sign that Shadow inhabited a part of you.

It was not enough by itself to warrant arrest. However, people feared Shadow magic above all others and even the slightest suggestion could stoke paranoid fantasies. To be Wild Eyed was to be suspected of wrongdoing in every light.

Eugen drew away from the nearest icon.

"It would make sense," Marin said, "Looks like they've worn out all the firewood they can. You spend too long in the dark, Shadow will find you."

"Do you know how common it is for people to be slightly changed by Shadow? Those stuck in dim assembly shops and warehouses all day only to go home at night?" Anca asked.

"These aren't loyal citizens. About as far from that as you can get." Eugen looked between the desiccated trees.

Marin ripped a totem off a stake and tossed it at the ground. "How long you say they've been beyond our reach? Three hundred years? Lots of time to get familiar with the voices in the shade."

"Enough of that," Anca said. "The plan doesn't change. If they talk, we talk. If they want to fight, we go from there."

Past groves of barren trunks, a deep tree line formed on the horizon. They were as tall as the highest towers in Margecei. Their canopies were laced with dark purple leaves and bark colored a deep brown. Thirty feet across at the smallest, each one was a titan rooted into the earth. Even being at the edge of it, the staggering heights threatened to swallow them in shade. A single road, beaten by crude wheels and massive paws, slithered into the darkened woods.

"Warden trees, the border of Teragva," Craita said, a note of awe and respect in her voice. She quickly opened her notebook and scratched down a note.

"You say that like it's their land," Marin grunted.

"It's the point that they'll start shooting at you. Does that match your definition?"

"It's an earned suspicion." Anca turned her Othersight toward the forest interior.

She barely made out the trace of Life in these trees and soil. She suspected Shadow had infested everything. Even the trees thrummed with it. A shape moved beyond them. Armored, taller than any of them, large shuffling paws, and a mouthful of dense, dark green roots. She turned to the rest of the company that stretched out behind them.

"Two ranks, stay close. Don't fall behind."

The companies of Sulia and Queen's Company crossed the line of trees and entered the hungry lands of the Trigvan.

Chapter Seventeen

The forest interior reminded him of a home burned down to the braces and joists. The Warden trees looked black under the thick canopy, its murk shading the riders on the overgrown trail. Deep, rumbling groans echoed from farther in the wood. What sounded like a low whistle would deepen in pitch and rattle their teeth before fading to nothing. The wet aromas of wetlands and flowers were long gone. The near freezing breeze made their eyes water.

Eugen knew better than to assume that this place was lifeless. Black squirrels skittered down trees with a mouthful of food and disappeared into ground burrows. Birds sang far overhead before settling into nests wreathed with red thorns. He saw a lumbering beast grazing nearby. Its back was covered by a hard shell and a turtle-like mouth ripped whole shrubs from the earth. It stomped its simian knuckles, watching them as they passed by. They weaved around another tree and slowed.

At first, he was not sure what to make of the hulk of gears that blocked the road. He recognized a version of the majesty's war machines. It was an ancient clockwork walker that only the capital possessed. It was not new or polished. Scavenged and made to walk on parts that were as old as some of these trees. Six figures followed alongside it on foot.

Its metal was tarnished, rust polished away where they could. Four legs, each one a different color, walked forward with grinding sparks popping from the joints at uneven turns. They supported a platform made of wood. A pilot feverishly managed many levers and triggers.

Two more stood on the platform, but they tended to a turret-mounted coilgun. A large, wooden stake was placed in the chamber. Two spouts, forged like lion's faces, sat on the front edge of the platform.

Craita's horse trotted in front of them and she raised her hands, palms wide. She spoke in an ancient dialect. Bits and pieces were recognizable, but were scrambled beyond any meaning. One of the Trigvan stepped forward, this one wearing a large cape of dark blue feathers, and answered in the same language. Craita nodded and gestured to Anca and Eugen.

"*Noili ai gospaila,*" she said.

Their clothing was a hodge-podge of fur, feather, and scrap metal. Their disfigured metal masks were an old style that was meant to look like one of the ancient kings. They carried weapons that would have been masterwork back home. Their handles were bound with newer leather or bundles of twine.

"Descendants of old hunters, you are unwanted guests in this land."

The blue-feathered figure spoke with a deep woman's voice. Anca gave a small bow. It was considerate, but Eugen kept his arms crossed and chin raised. He knew these locals. They were honorable and straight forward, but they despised outsiders with every fiber of their being. He could not decide if bowing would boost their standing or indicate weakness.

"I would ask that you consider your safety before age old grudges. I am Nobil Anca Sulia, this is Eugen Furloc of the Queen's Company."

"We have turned your kind back before. Your bloodline does not scare us. Stories say you are brave because of what you fight. We face such monsters every day. You are not remarkable or impressive."

Marin scoffed and settled his wrist on the pommel of his ax. "Oh, you didn't get the letter? You could just move, you know. We would help, but we're too busy defending our own borders and finding a meal."

The figure leveled her spear toward Marin. Their hunters raised coilguns and crossbows, but the blue clad figure did not flinch.

"Do not speak to me of need with your fat cheeks."

"Bold words for a dirt monger," Marin goaded.

Eugen couldn't fight a small snicker. Anca shot him a cross look before facing the Trigvan again. Diplomacy might be best. As much as he loved to see Marin nettled and frustrated, this was not helping.

The figure gestured to the walking machine behind her. Its pilots spun wheels and snapped levers free of tension. A gurgling sound preceded streams of fire that arced into the air and singed the dense trees around them. Their horses peeled backward and neighed. Marin fell from his horse. Eugen's mount did not budge beyond shifting on its hooves, its rider wincing.

Of course, he had seen this before. Not that Anca and Marin needed to know that.

Red in the face, Marin climbed onto his mount again.

"We are getting off on the wrong foot," Anca said.

The figure chuckled under her mask.

"Liars. Damned liars. Damned mages," Marin cursed. "They've got magic. True Flame even."

"We do not plead to the elements like you do," the blue figure said. "Flame and Life have forsaken us and we ask nothing of them. Shadow stalks us day and night. We only believe in what we can build."

Anca uncurled her lip and put on an easy smile for the Trigvan.

"We've tracked a beast to your lands. It's a killer. Faster and deadlier than any we've seen. It has eaten entire villages. Even your clockwork weapons won't help you. I'm guessing you don't have the numbers to hunt it down yourself. Never mind in a forest filled with even more nightmares."

The figure said nothing. Behind the glinting metal mask, Eugen could barely see a pair of very human eyes staring back at them. It was an impressive war mask, but it did not hide their vulnerability. Only the mention of the monster had calmed her rhetoric. She cared about her people first and foremost.

"We won't be a burden on you. We have our own food. All we seek is a camping ground to conduct this hunt. I don't ask anything of your people beyond the chance to help each other."

The figure rubbed her chin.

"It is probably hungry and will seek another meal soon," Anca added.

She had the Trigvan on the ropes, hitting the same weakness Eugen noticed. For all of her charms and goodness, Anca was too used to the courts. A wriggle of annoyance pulsed in the side of his head, a flicker of Blood Flame. It was time to expedite this.

"And we can supplement you for your patience," Eugen said. "We have supplies to spare: weapons, clothing, food."

The last word gave the blue figure pause, her hand stopping on her chin. Her eyes went to the covered wagon far in the back of their column. Anca shot Eugen another sharp look.

"That's a lie and you know it. We barely have enough food for the return journey," she whispered.

Eugen did not look away from the Trigvan woman.

"These people only know hunger. You won't get anywhere with appeals to conscience and cooperation."

Whatever deliberations the figure made behind her mask were settled. She straightened up and said something to her fellows in their language before addressing Anca and Eugen.

"There is a plot of land near us where you may set up your camp. We lost two of ours to your Beast yesterday. If you provide us with some of your supplies, then we might work together. For a time."

Anca bowed to her. "Thank you. Lead the way."

She gestured for their caravan to follow the Trigvan. Now in motion, Eugen noticed movement in the trees. The gloom of Shadow had masked the pulse of a dozen other Trigvan hiding to either side of them. They lowered their shabby bows and joined the others as they led them to their home.

When Eugen first heard of this place, it was described as a village. Seeing it himself, he was reminded of a fortress. Three stories tall, the walls were made of slipshod metal and wood. The grain of the lumber changed color from plank to plank. Warped metal showed the mark of the hammers that bent it flat. All along the exterior, spikes were set into the walls and clusters of vines and barbs were mounted along the tops of the walls.

Blackened torches, burned for too long and slathered in a tarry oil, poked up from within the walls like leering heads. Glowing mushrooms were cultivated around the perimeter. The main gate was the remains of a cage door. Presumably meant to hold a beast of great size, it was bolted into place with twisted skewers of metal. All the Trigvan at the walls wore the same deformed masks. The figure who led them here removed her helmet as they stopped in front of the scavenged entrance.

"You can call me Zahrea. I speak for my people."

She was old enough to be Eugen's mother, maybe a bit older even. It was hard to tell. A life of stress, hunger, and violence could age you in strange ways. Straightening her gray locks, he saw that her right ear was missing, scar tissue around it suggesting how it was lost. Her Wilded, electric blue eyes did not betray a hint of emotion beyond contempt.

"Are there more villages nearby?" Craita asked, curiosity bursting from her. She had her notebook and scribing tool in hand.

"Perhaps. We have not heard from others since the last harvest season. We had close friends nearby until their village burned down two months ago. What remains sits on the only open ground aside from our home. It will be where you and yours will stay."

"Where is it?" Anca asked.

"Not far. My people here will guide you to it. Descendants of the old hunters, you come with me. We must discuss the price of your presence. The mage cannot enter."

Craita made a small, annoyed sound, first looking to Eugen and then to Anca for some sign of permission. Eugen liked the mage. After all, he had allowed her to remain in the company after her talents emerged. This was not the time to push the already frigid relations here. Eugen shook his head and gestured for her to leave. Anca dismounted and turned to Marin.

"Take our horses with you and begin setting up camp. Focus on our defenses first. We can figure supper out later. Craita, you go with them."

She huffed and leaned forward in her saddle.

"But it's the first contact we've had in centuries. Someone should document this. I've been keeping records and researching things like this for years. It's an opportunity we can't pass up on."

The executioner raised an eyebrow and waited for Anca's answer as he climbed out of his saddle.

"It is rude to ignore our host's request. I appreciate your interest, but we can make time for documentation later."

"But—"

"Craita. It's not happening and you're keeping us," Eugen said.

Zahrea's mouth bent into a small smile for the first time since they met. She clearly enjoyed seeing these outsiders squabble.

"He's right. Though I wouldn't have said it as directly. I will need your advice in the coming days, but not now," Anca said.

Craita gathered the reins in her hands and fumed. "At least we all haven't lost our manners." She trotted away after the rest of their riders, grumbling too loudly to be to herself.

"A bit harsh," Anca said to Eugen.

"Her determination isn't easily batted aside. We'd be explaining why for another five minutes and get the same result. She'll make a good Doia someday. Once she's learned patience."

Zahrea said a word to someone on the other side of

the gate and the metal door slid up.

"Join me. I can show you how we have survived in your absence."

Eugen could see why they were known as scavengers before anything else. Their homes consisted of the same materials as their walls, though perhaps shabbier. Small portions of food sizzled in blackened pans in a nearby open kitchen. A dozen people cooked over the same roaring bonfire and a line of others stood behind them, their own food and cooking plates in hand. In the center of the fort, a large skylight let pale daylight down into the dim hallways and rooms.

They all regarded Anca and Eugen with the same cold suspicion as Zahrea. Wild eyes, each one a different shade of brilliant colors, watched them. Their thin bodies were nothing but tight cords and bones. Only the scowling elderly, few and far between, held a moderate weight. Families ate dinner together in small quarters set apart by steel walls and cloth doors. They chewed on bugs, mushrooms, and roots. Some had the delicacy of being glazed with sugar or seasoned with a red spice.

These were people under siege. An endless pressure hounded them day and night. Children ran around the rings of metal and wooden floors with wild shouts and cries. He wondered how much longer their dreams would last. What age were they told of what lay beyond their walls and the terrible difficulty of the life ahead? Even though they were free from the throne, they suffered like everyone else.

"Seems cramped," Eugen said.

"It is tight. We cannot push our walls any farther out, so we must moderate our population. This isn't difficult. The forest has an endless hunger for human flesh."

"Couldn't you just settle where the other village was? Rebuild it?"

Zahrea was hailed by two men. Each could not have been older than seventeen and wore the same plain clothes as everyone else. They asked her several questions, clearly indicating their guests as the focus of the query. She waved them off, her tone ringing of impatience.

Eugen recognized them. They helped haul supplies to a location in the middle of the forest. He paid them well, but promised more work in the future. That work had never shown up after he learned the truth of what he was helping the queen with. He was relieved when they left with only annoyed stares burning into him.

"The other village found itself in the middle of a migration path. The larger beasts don't care what is in the way, including walls. They left the people untouched, but the things that followed them did not."

Another four-legged, clockwork walker paced down the street. Masked Trigvan managed a cargo of bundled goods and scarce lumber.

"We have no great treasure. No secret power or trick. You've seen that now." Zahrea spun, an arm extended to the homes and people around. "No magic. No wealth from the old kingdoms. We are builders, but we still need food."

"Of course. As Eugen said, we are willing to share a portion of our supplies as payment for our stay here," Anca said.

Zahrea nodded her head impatiently.

"Yes, we've discussed that. Something else has become obvious to me by the size of your company. You can only stay on our lands for four days."

"What?" The tip of Eugen's sword sank into the ground at his feet.

That trickle of annoyance threatened to become a stream. Eugen was accustomed to letting his Blood Flame flow freely. Now he felt a certain repugnance at the warmth building in his veins. He never felt shame for embracing this power.

The last time he had slipped, it nearly cost him everything. Eugen was a part of a team now, the other half of a whole. The calming herbs were synched to his belt. He swore to himself it wouldn't get as bad as last time.

No, there was no way to be sure. Eugen didn't want to lose control, even if it might fill him with power. Things he once thought of as familiar now felt foreign. He sucked in air and gripped the handle of his blade. You are in control, he told himself. You are better than this.

Four days might be enough to accomplish their mission, but such a rushed time frame was no way to conduct a hunt of this scale. They would need to settle their camp, learn the lay of the land, and track the Beast's movements. All of that before they killed the creature. Assuming their next attempt would be successful.

"The land cannot sustain both of our tribes. Food is scarce and you will doubtlessly hunt for meals while you are here. I would ask you to resist such an impulse, but I doubt your discipline."

Anca joined her hands together. Her eyes burned into Zahrea, despite her polite tone of voice. "You don't seem to understand the severity of this. This monster does not care about loyalties or timetables. It might not present itself to us within that window. Once we leave, your people will be just as exposed."

"You clearly know how to handle yourselves, but you are not ready for this," Eugen added.

"Is that so? The two hunters that live in the lands of Flame have come to lecture me on how to live among beasts? I will not accept the advice of one who takes Flame into his veins and makes a beast of himself."

"I'm not a beast."

His rage was like a worn shoe, so easy to slip into. The allure was hard to resist. Especially as Zahrea goaded the weakest part of him. Eugen bit his lip and tried to think of other things. His mind went to early days in the north country, before his family was purged. There was nothing after. Pain, exile, shame, hate, fear.

No, there was one other thing. Her green eyes reflecting in the fire, her lips pursed in that cocky grin. The curve of her neck, running down to the glimpse of her bosom, and the few buckles he could easily work off. Heat rose inside of him, but did not fill him with anger. His heart pounded as his throat suddenly felt dry. It was the same sort of power that would let him shrug off a fatal wound, but full of life and light.

Anca raised her hand before Eugen could say anything else. He leaned off his sword's handle and found himself watching the pulse of Life in her hand. As she spoke, he followed the flicker of green down her wrist, across her arm, and over the shoulder he imagined to be delicate under her armor.

"This creature does not hunt for food. It keeps trophies and kills because it can. This is unlike any beast you or I have seen."

Zahrea's cool manner cracked with a twitch of consideration. She looked at Eugen briefly before rubbing her chin. He pulled himself from his brief distraction. For the second time in Anca's company, the Blood Flame did not seem so impossible to control.

"And why did you not kill it?" she asked.

"We tried. Its hide can only be pierced after it is scoured with fire. It is covered in some strange weave of Shadow magic."

"An unusual threat, but nothing we cannot handle. Four days. On the fifth you will be treated as trespassers. Go. We have nothing else to discuss."

Zahrea waved them away.

"You're making a mistake." His choice of words had to be careful. The elder and himself exchanged words before. Their understanding was to never speak of it again.

"You have a history of betrayal and convenient alliances. Don't let this prejudice cloud your thinking. I know what that can be like and it doesn't do any good for us."

Zahrea's eyebrows raised, amused with Eugen. She knew what sort of fury boiled beneath. All the same, she was not intimidated. As much as Eugen meant it, he knew what he said would be seen as hollow.

"You do not scare me, Flame Eater. Your family were craven monsters who fostered flawed pups. Honorless warriors. Shed that clothing and go join your kind in the woods."

A spark of cinder shot from his Focus. The old hatreds were too strong. It aggravated him, sending the vein in his neck pumping like a dying worm. He reached for his bag of herbs.

Anca grabbed Eugen by the shoulder and pulled him away. She gave Zahrea a quick nod and marched back toward the gates with the somewhat cooperating Eugen in her hand. He ripped his arm from Anca's grip and matched her pace.

Zahrea's words remained in his head. Without her snarling in his face, they slowly dimmed. He fastened his sword over his shoulder as they exited the town gates.

"I can handle myself."

"I'm perfectly aware. I've seen what it looks like when you do."

The steel gate slammed shut behind them. Silent Trigvan watched them, weapons just in hand. Eugen eyed them, the last bit of rage snarling his lips.

"Enough of these deals. Everyone we meet has conditions and ego. Isn't it enough to have a quarry?"

"No." Anca rolled her eyes. "Even cooperation has to be weighed and measured."

"Four shitting days? It will take us the rest of today just to set up camp. Three days really. That's what we have."

They were so close now. Every barrier in his way felt like it might make the inevitable kill all the more gratifying.

"I think we can do it. We will need to move fast, maybe try to cut some corners," Anca said.

He couldn't tear his eyes away from her, gears clicking behind her eyes. That bright fire still lingered in his chest. It was new and strange, a variation of his usual Blood Flame that felt more like a purifying river than a grimy gutter of emotion. Despite his best efforts to focus on the job ahead, there was a simmering heat in his chest that wouldn't go away.

"What did you have in mind?"

"I won't know for sure until I see the camp. If this

place still has walls, we can send out scouting parties as soon as tomorrow morning."

It was not far to the ruined village, but a walk was in order. The trees did not completely blot out the sun along the road. No hideous creatures stalked them. There was just an eerie silence. An entire ecosystem built around not being noticed or being too vicious to be challenged.

"Wish we hadn't sent the horses back," she grumbled.

"At least we get to stretch out our legs. You'll just have to put up with me for a bit longer."

Anca grinned and he braced for a snarky quip. It would be easier for him to keep his emotions in check if she kept her distance. However, it didn't come. She instead regarded the forest around them, a small mist of rain opening overhead.

Her hesitancy shrank every day. In the last four days, his slip-up had only seemed to deepen the bond between them. At least, he thought it did. Prior to the fire, vulnerability had terrified him. It still did, but he saw that there was no other way to be better. No other way to win their trust after what he had done.

She said nothing for a long moment. He did not miss the way her pulse increased.

Don't even consider it, he warned himself.

The needing ache, the hot quiver that set his pulse racing, was something that could not, would not, be tolerated. Knowing this, Eugen strolled next to Anca, ready to walk that line. Despite his assurance there was nothing there, he had a feeling that she was ready to walk it too.

Chapter Eighteen

"My aunt showed me how to draw the fire into my veins. My uncle taught me to swing a blade. Thirteen years old. Just a year before they would teach me to hunt."

Anca listened as they crossed the field that surrounded the camp. It drizzled, but they took their time. Eugen did not seem to care, only occasionally wiping the top of his shaved head.

"And your parents?"

A look passed over his face.

"Busy on the front most of the time. They loved me and my siblings, but the Flame is…demanding. I understand that now. When I was a child, I couldn't imagine what they were going through. I'm not sure they could come home." He swallowed. "Near the end."

Siblings. Parents. Eugen had a family once. All snatched away by her own loving parents. His entire life burned down and she owned it in a way. He did not rise in fury at the memory. Those brown eyes looked unswervingly ahead. She glanced at the orange gem on his sword when she could. It remained lightless.

Her mind lingered on those words: the end. It was difficult to look over what had transpired since and not think of it as the beginning.

"I don't remember much of it," Anca said. "Everyone seemed worried. They tried to hide most of it from me. When my mother rode off, there was none of the fanfare that accompanied most hunts. I remember asking her if she was going to a funeral. In a way, I guess she was."

Eugen looked over the blades of grass and daisies under foot before smashing them with his boots.

"You can't know what it's like." His voice trembled as he spoke. He ruminated on his words, choosing each one how a farmer might pick over a bushel of apples. "It isn't just strength. It fills you with resolve. No fear or doubt. Anyone who scares you is just a target. No matter how low you feel or how hard the times are, it blinds the pain. You can forget for a time. I can be more than just Eugen. With it, I'm the Executioner. That's a far sight better than a reviled orphan who everyone would prefer to see hanged."

He spoke of it like it was a lifeline. To her, it sounded like an anchor. It dragged him down. So used to the way people treated him, he had no hope. Since the immolation of House Furloc, his life was nothing but a scrap to survive. That magic wasn't a plague to him. The Flame made him the monster he was believed to be. Without it, he was remorseful, clear, funny even.

She hoped that he saw it the same way as she did: a curse to be broken. That was the kind of Eugen she could hunt alongside. If he had no interest in losing it, where did that leave her?

"Could you let it go?" she asked. "They say you're a monster because of your name, but they are really afraid of that magic."

Some kind of burrow interrupted his path, no larger than a gopher's. Eugen took a long step and hesitated before he answered.

"I don't think I can. I've considered it, but what use would I be then?"

"Have you ever heard of the other half of our job? The whole leading part?"

"Assuming anyone would trust me enough outside of Queen's Company."

Anca tried to lean into his eye line, but found him almost avoiding her gaze.

"There's always a way to change expectations. Things come and go. They don't stay the same forever. At least, I hope that's how things are."

He nodded. "You and Victor are already living proof that things can change."

Anca's stomach knotted at the mention of her former fiancé. It wasn't guilt, but rather the thrill of what could be in its place. She told herself it was merely how fresh it was. The thoughts she had about Eugen, that urge to lean into his chest and drink in his scent, could not be acknowledged.

"Thank you, but we are no longer associated. There were differences that were too much to make up for." Her words came out a bit faster than she liked.

His head turned toward her and snapped back in a single heartbeat. Eugen's pulse rose by the slightest degree. If she had not become so familiar with the beat, Anca would have missed it. She tried to push the thought out of her head: he wants you too.

"I'm sorry to hear that. You two made a good match."

She snorted. "Bullshit. That's polite, but you know better."

He gave an uncommitted shrug, lips pursed with the rumors he doubtlessly heard.

"Come on," she continued. "Four years after the wedding was supposed to happen. We were only getting farther apart. It's for the best, really. He can chase whatever he wants."

Eugen did not look at her as he said, "And you can chase what you want."

"Yes. I suppose that is something I can do."

She intended to say more. Her instincts urged her to blather on about whatever crossed her mind. Anything to fill the air that felt closer with every step they took.

"I appreciated that he was another outsider in the Households. I suppose you're right, though. It's a good thing. Victor seemed polite, but he wasn't right for you. He looked at you like you were a prize. You deserve better."

Her heart leaped into her throat. She had faced monsters twice her size and been tortured by the throne itself. Confirmation that Eugen thought of her in any romantic terms set her trembling. If he knew what was a bad match for Anca, then surely he had opinions about the good matches.

"You think you know me well enough to say that?"

Eugen clicked his tongue. For a moment, she saw that infuriating impulse to clam up cross his face.

"You have too much fire in you."

Her parent's marriage had its challenges. They worked at it, like all courtships that last. Above all else, they had sparks. They had fire. She knew what it looked like when two people saw one another as they truly were. She glanced at Eugen, instinctively licking her lips.

There was a flame here and it wasn't his magic.

Eugen came to a halt next to the crumbled gate and charred walls. She barely recognized the broken barrier next to them as he loomed closer. Blue wildflowers stood at the edges of the snarled ruin of a town. Small raindrops built a hush that muted all sound beyond their gaze. Tucked behind one of the side walls, no one would see if she made a rash decision.

"I'm sure he kept you comfortable. You stuck up for him at the convening."

She imagined it looked that way. Lunging from the table, not aware of the chokehold on her wrist that he held. Without knowing what Victor said afterward.

"You were so keen to piss off the court I didn't think you saw that."

His voice rumbled in his broad chest. "Of course. I couldn't look away from you."

His gaze settled on her lips, the tension between them pulling taught like twisted bed sheets. Anca had kept her desires pushed down so far, ignored for so long, that now it threatened to undo her entire being.

They had been watched this entire time, whether it was Marin or a hunter or the Trigvan. Everyone wondered how long until the two came to blows. How soon would the broiling hatred between the Nobils finally burst? The previous fight was a teaser. That was the rumor.

He took a deep breath, his tongue pushing against the corner of his mouth. Eugen's eyes traced along her neck and down to her chest. She was only scarcely aware of how she took a step toward him and stretched out her fingers.

"I need someone I understand," she said.

Every loose thought was pressed out of her mind as his fingers ran up her arm. He leaned closer, his warmth bringing color to her cheeks.

"There are so few who can. You're remarkable, Anca."

His voice growled over her name. Her skin tingled along her back and up her neck. She leaned toward him as his grip went to her upper arm. Anca imagined his lips a handful of times. Take it, she thought. He's right here.

Eyes closed, she felt his breath on her skin and then his lips on hers. It was the slightest touch, but the sensation sparked across her body.

Heat flushed her face, toes pulling tight inside of her boots. It felt like the world shifted under her feet at the merest touch.

Before she leaned deeper in, before he could bring his hands along the nape of her neck, the hunt came screaming across her mind.

The two companies.

The whole damn kingdom.

Marin.

She pulled away.

"I don't think—" Anca gasped for breath.

What did she almost do? Her body wanted to twist back toward him, the heat between her thighs pulsing up her spine in a rippling ache. She still wanted it worse than her next breath, but there was an entire camp behind them. If anyone saw this, there was no telling what might happen. Eugen stepped away and cuffed his mouth. His Focus glowed with a dull light.

"It's reckless for us to even think about that," he said.

He was as flustered as she was. Eugen shook his head and flexed his fingers as if fighting an urge to pull her back into his arms. His eyes traced over the azure blooms at their feet before trailing up her legs and staring at the small of her back.

"But that felt right? Didn't it?"

Anca looked across the rows of trees on the other side of the field. No Trigvan. No tardy hunters. Only the distant brown birds witnessed their moment of weakness.

"It felt right to me," he said.

Eugen waited for her answer. He would not be set aside and teased. When the Executioner wanted something, he pursued it with everything he had. She wondered if his pursuit of her would be any different now that there was blood in the water.

Despite the danger of this horrible, alluring idea, she could not deny the thrill.

It felt right. She felt it right between her legs. If there was any doubt what was between them, she could not lie to herself anymore.

Anca cleared her throat and nodded.

"No matter how it feels, it can't happen. Not here."

She checked the scimitar on her hip and turned to face him. His fingers dangled free along his side, as if they had not moved since she let go. Anca could not help but look over his face, his neck, his chest. She imagined him naked, pressed against her headboard. Straddling him, stiff and inside of her while she rode the intimidating man into submission.

The thought made her suck in another breath.

"Stars above," she muttered.

Eugen bit his lip and shook his head, slapping a palm against his temple. She wondered if he was trying to get rid of the same fantasies. She was relieved to see reluctant agreement on his face when he looked back at her.

"You're right. Shade and rot, you're right." He kicked the flowers at his feet. "I don't know what I was thinking. Who would have ever thought that we—"

"Stop. If you say it out loud, that makes it real."

She wouldn't be able to fight this urge if it was real. Eugen leaned on the imposing sword and drew in a deep breath. The fire in his Focus faded and he glowered over the wildflowers.

"And we can't compromise this chance." His deep voice was nearly a whisper. "If we fail, neither of us gets what we want."

What she really wanted, or maybe what she needed, was standing right there. Anca would have laughed in any other mood. She gave him a final nod and left their small nook on the side of the wall.

"We've been gone too long. Let's assess the camp. Get reports from our hunters. It's a big day tomorrow."

Eugen followed shortly after. Her sharp ears followed his footfalls across the grounds and away from her until they mingled with the busy footsteps of others. She didn't dare to give him another look. The tremor in her hands weakened, but she knew it might roar back to life if goaded.

The drizzle turned into a downpour the moment they walked into the broken remains of the town. It once had corn, pens for livestock, communal living spaces, and a square that she suspected was used for dancing, of all things. The corn had been eaten by wild animals, the livestock driven into the wild, the walls breached, and the dancing square overgrown.

Nature had slowly come back. Like the other village, the trees parted over top of it and allowed the sun and the rain to come down as it pleased. This ruin had only one floor, much smaller than the other village of Trigvan. The grass was dark and coarse, the shrubs spotted with twisting, red thorns, but it looked more like home than anywhere else in this forest.

Anca tied down the last rope supporting her narrow tent and pulled her hood higher over her head. The last few rays of sun disappeared behind a storm cloud the same hue as the shadows in the tree line.

The two companies' divisions were written into the design of the camp now. Two blocks of tents faced each other, separated by a wider pathway. They shared food only because they had to. After Craita helped repair the walls with stone slabs and torches were lit, they pulled back into their own worlds.

Anca went to House Sulia's kitchen tent. Almost as large as a house, oil lanterns cast them in warm amber tones. It was a welcome change of pace from the frigid rain and pale light outside. It reminded her of the shared hall back home. Dinners were communal, brought out on large plates for people to spread between themselves. This led to friendship, collusion, and bonds they would need in the field. Surrounded by memories of their dead, in a land far from home, it was a small comfort.

Marin and Doru sat near a few other Sulia hunters. They nodded to her and Marin pushed a plate of food to her. It was meager: a slice of dried pork, a boiled potato, and a cob of corn. Anca knew this would be normal for some time longer. Worse, she imagined the Trigvan might ask for their sugars and the last casks of wine they had on hand. She had almost forgotten about these mortal threats entirely.

After what just happened, she wanted a mountain of food and drink to distract her. There was no reason for them to suspect. No possible way that anyone here could know what almost happened. As she cut up the small, lukewarm meal, her mind drifted back to it over and over. She imagined what more might have transpired.

"The town is secure enough. It looks like someone tried to fortify after the people left. We should be ready by nightfall," Marin said between bites of food.

"What did the Trigvan have to say?" Doru leaned in closer to hear her answer.

Anca shook her head as she swallowed a bite. "Nothing good. We've got four days to kill this thing."

"Four days?" Doru sputtered.

"Or what? They'll kick us out?" Marin asked.

"Four? Days?" Doru repeated. "I mean today's almost over. That's three days."

"I can count." Anca quickly swallowed a mouthful of potato. "After such time, they will consider us intruders. Something about the land can't sustain both of us. Zahrea's right, but I don't like it."

Doru fiddled with his potatoes. "That's quite a bit to unpack."

Marin drew his ax and dropped it on the table.

"What about Eugen? Is he out of our hair yet? We're here now, that means we can keep the babysitters here while we get to work."

Eugen's fingers twisted in her hair. The roaring smell of him wrapped around her. His broad chest, packed with muscle as her fingers ran across it.

"I was hoping to use some of Eugen's teams to scout. There is a lot of woods out there and Sulia alone doesn't have the bodies to cover it all," Anca said.

Marin slumped over his weapon, deflated.

"Shit. Was hoping to be done with that band of

misfits. Having to treat with the savages is embarrassing enough."

"Are you so sure they are?" Doru asked. "I saw those clockwork weapons, same as you. That is delicate, complicated stuff. They might be smarter than us. At least they've got the better inventors."

"Zahrea is keen to protect her people and doesn't trust us. She isn't dumb though." Anca tapped the side of a plate with her fork. "How much fuel do we have to spare?"

Doru finished his food and pushed the plate away from himself.

"Starving might be the larger issue," Marin said. "The Trigvan had their demands ready to go. They don't want weapons or money. Butter, meat, cheese, fruits. Anything these lands can't give them. I think we can give up to a third of our remaining supplies. We will have to forage on the way back."

He sat forward in his chair again, hands tented under his chin. "Have we ruled out telling them to pound sand?

"Yes," Anca deadpanned. "We need their cooperation. With our numbers, we can't hunt the Beast and fight the Trigvan. We don't have a choice."

She listened to their worries and gripes for a bit longer before leaving them. The remainder of the day was slow. Weapons were cataloged and food was rationed. The Trigvan came for their supplies a few hours after the company settled in. They certainly took their fill: a full half of their cheese and a good portion of dried meat. They seemed keen on beef. With no pastures, they had never tasted it.

Anca's tent was near the farthest back wall of the camp. She gave up on anything befitting her position and dwelled in a common tent that the others used. Her cot was wrapped with scratchy, white sheets and a straw-stuffed pillow. At least it would be warm against the chilly night that swept down on them. A single oil lantern hung above her head. Gilded and stamped with her Nobil seal, it was the only thing from her commander's tent that survived the fire.

Calling it cramped would be generous. There was no space for officer gatherings and just barely enough for her to move around comfortably. Their planning would have to be done in the kitchen tent or with Queen's Company. Eugen still had his command tent and map table.

She tried to not think about him. Thankfully, he had not crossed her path. Despite the lists of names and inventory, preparing for the scouting expeditions tomorrow, and ensuring they would not be ransacked in the middle of the night, he still bubbled to the surface.

Pursuing him would be a bad idea, but it did not erase the tingling possibility.

Pulling off her leather armor and unstrapping the scimitar from her belt, she imagined his fingers undoing the buttons. Anca closed her eyes and indulged. Her fingers traced down her arm and unhooked her belt. She shivered, a cold breeze whipping through the tent.

It was agony. Her training prepared her for all sorts of suffering. A mentor dislocated her finger on purpose so she would know how to reset it. She had broken bones, been poisoned, and cut all over. She knew how to handle those pains.

There was no balm for the jittering shake in her stomach. Alcohol might help, but they did not have enough of that to justify drinking at a time like this.

Drowning her emotions in booze would have been a worse idea on reflection. Anca would have to be on the top of her game tomorrow.

Her thoughts wandered for too long. The subtle sound of the tent flap opening behind her was entirely missed. The intruder took a step closer and a blade of dried grass crunched under a foot.

Her eyes opened and she spun toward the sound. Fist forward, her other hand went for her dagger. The cloaked man caught the punch, but her knee drove into his chest and sent him onto his back. Anca raised the knife as his hood fell back.

Eugen gave a wheezing laugh as the blade pressed against his neck. She made a small sound that would have been a shout if she allowed it. Her lips clamped shut and she looked to the front flap of her tent. They were alone.

Breathless, she laid on top of him.

"What are you doing?"

She loosened her grip and pushed her fingers across his chest. Anca tried to adjust, but only managed to press her hips into his. The sensation set her skin on fire. The urge between her thighs simmered and she couldn't resist grinding against him again. It wasn't a conscious move, something closer to animal instinct.

Anca flushed as her lips parted with a small gasp. She was on him, pressed against the warmth of his body.

On top of him.

All of the agony she felt moments before liquified into a puddle of need. There would be no playing aloof now. His hand slid up her leg. Her fingers drew down to meet his. Eugen's eyes burned with hunger.

"You said 'not here' earlier. How about here?"

She pulled his hand across the inside of her leg. Her eyes roamed over his body and imagined what was beneath his flimsy shirt.

"It would get it out of our heads. Relieve some stress," she said.

Anca dropped the knife and leaned closer to him. He drew his fingers along her neck, hips rolling into hers. Sparks lit down her body, aware of every inch of contact between them.

"Fixation isn't healthy for anyone," he whispered.

Anca fell on him as her last bit of doubt shattered, their lips locking. Her skin tingled with waves of heat, just as the first time they kissed. Her mouth pressed against his soft lips in a moment of disbelief. Neither one moved from that first touch, but the peace did not last. A carnal impulse rose. His tongue ran along hers before retreating to the press of her own. He growled as they writhed on the ground, her tawny hair falling around his shoulders.

The calloused pads of his hands clutched at her like she was the only thing keeping him alive. All of the strength that she lusted after twisted around her. She claimed him, pressing against his rising length, drinking in the taste of him. Each movement was a fevered, desperate pang of need bursting from him and she clawed onto him with equal ferocity.

Anca would not leave the crush of his arms for anything in all of the world.

Eugen's hand slid to her ass, pressing her against him. His other hand tangled in her hair. She moaned as his lips moved to her neck, his mouth worshiping the curve of her throat. The citrusy, smoldering smell of him flooded her senses.

Anca rose and suffocated the lantern above her bed, her other hand still wound around his fingers. In the darkness of the cramped tent, just large enough for them, Eugen pulled her to the scratchy, white sheets. Entwined on the too-small-bed, she fell into his arms and the devouring need in his eyes.

"You're so fucking beautiful." He growled as he pulled on her shirt.

She yanked up at the collar and threw it aside before moving to the binds wrapped around her chest. Her fingers hitched into the familiar, soft fabric. His hands met hers as the wrap fell away.

Eugen stilled. His lips parted as he drank in the sight of her.

Anca burned at his gaze.

His lust raked over her naked breasts and toned waist. Barely visible in the scant moonlight, but the glow in his eyes told her what he felt. A profound peace stilled them, aware of the line that had been crossed. There would be no going back now.

She would not stand to go back.

His rough, warm hands cupped her chest, his lips went back to her neck. Anca grabbed his chin and brought his mouth to hers. Straddling him, it did not seem so impossible to fuck him senseless now.

She slipped the notches on his belt. Buttons snapped from his shirt, one pinging off of the metal tent pole. They fought a giggle, aware that any stray sound could ruin everything. Anca pressed her hand against his mouth, the other one ripping his shirt upward.

The hem of his shirt went up and up and her jaw dropped when the solid, muscled mass of his torso did not quit. She had seen him shirtless a dozen times, but it was different with him so alluringly close. The possibility of feeling every bump and hollow of him brought a lurid ferocity to her breath.

"Quiet," he whispered.

Waiting a moment longer was too much. She purred as her fingers ran down his body. Hard as rock to look at, but soft and smooth under her fingers. Only the occasional bundle of scar tissue interrupted her caress.

Just this glimpse was not enough. Her face heated as she imagined more.

She needed all of him. He was the morsel she craved, the only water to slake her thirst. He crept into her heart, her blood, her mind in ways that she barely recognized until this moment. Her fingers shook as her hands traced down his pecs, across the cobblestone road of his abs, and yanked on the buttons that kept his pants around his hips.

She set her eyes on his rigid length and took a long, hollow breath. Everything that he was or wasn't barely mattered as she devoured the sight of him. Eugen did not let her gawk as she had allowed him to.

With his pants discarded, his lips twisted with hers. His body cradled her, fingers following the curve of her hips, her waist, her breasts. The crush of him around her could rip her to pieces, but she only felt safe in his hands. By the way he stroked her, kissed her, looked at her, she knew all of that ferocity was toothless. There was nothing in his arsenal for her to fear.

There would be time to memorize every piece of him. She needed more.

The fire in her chest swallowed her whole. It bloomed between her legs worse than it had when she watched him in the evening. Worse than when they first kissed. There was only one man she wanted and the huntress would not be denied.

"Fuck me," she demanded.

He slowed as his hands gripped the waist of her pants. A low growl crept up his throat, eyes closed. Anca rose up on an elbow, searching his features for a sign of hesitancy. All she found was a war coiling the features of his face. His chin whipped to the side, as if the sight of her would push him over the edge.

"My shame would be yours. You will be judged by who I am."

She shook her head. "I want you."

His hand thumped against the mattress, lips twisting in agitation. Those deep brown eyes, the ones that glittered with a hunger for her, stayed closed. She ached to see them again. All of this muscle, the pure amount of man on display, and the only thing she wanted right now was his eyes.

If she wasn't so desperate for his touch, she would have laughed at herself.

"I will only tear you down," he said. "We both know what they think of me. I've wanted this for days. For weeks if I'm being honest, but it isn't worth a thing if I hurt you. I couldn't bear to do that. Not again."

If he intended to pull away from her, his body betrayed him. Hot breath blew down her neck as he huffed pure lust from his lungs. Her fingers cupped his jaw, and she kissed him again.

"Enough. I don't need you to tell me what my legacy is or what it could be. I damn well know. I want you, Eugen. I want all of your pain and all of your power. I've wanted you from the moment I saw you, even if I didn't know it. Don't deny me now. I'll die on this bed if I can't have you tonight."

Anca pressed her forehead against his and Eugen's eyes opened. The sea of desire behind them, held back by the flimsiest restraint, sent her heart skittering. It was the same look when the Flame coursed through him, but the mania was replaced with something pure and starving.

"Now fuck me," she whispered.

With a hard push, she moved his hands down her hips and her pants went with them. He growled and pressed her against the bed. Anca writhed under his grasp, the crushing strength of him brought to bear. Something broke within him and now everything was bent toward appeasing her.

She growled into his ear as his considerable hardness pressed into her hip. His right hand traced her breasts, then down to her abs, and farther down until his fingers slipped into her undergarments. Sparks flared up her body as he rubbed and teased. They stayed like this for either seconds or hours, Anca couldn't tell.

"I couldn't stay away."

"I didn't—want you to," she said in between gasps. "What I said in the field—"

He kissed her, his tongue draining the words from her mouth with a caress. His thumb worked over her wet, burning need while another finger slipped inside of her. She almost wailed, squirming beneath him.

She allowed him to ravish her, her hands splayed to the side as he kissed her collarbone and roamed to her breasts. His beard scratched against her skin, but warm lips soothed every itch that it gave. Another burst of fire arched up her back.

"I wouldn't expect anything less from you." He

kissed her shoulder then brought his lips to her ear. "You're smart. Fierce as anyone I know. Now let go. Out there, you own me. But when we're on this bed, you're mine."

She ogled his naked body as he kissed over her freckled skin. Veins pulsed in his neck, powered by the thundering heartbeat that pounded in her ears. His naked, toned ass, the muscles of his back, his chest, it was all she could do to not wrap herself around him.

Anca boiled, the urge inside her not able to wait much longer. His fingers drove her higher and higher, like a building storm between her legs that spilled into her stomach. Each stroke made it harder to resist the moan in her throat. She needed more if she wanted to come apart in his arms.

Eugen caught her eye. A raised eyebrow from him was met with a quick nod from her. He slid her undergarments down and off, bringing his body along hers. She angled her toes and wriggled the last bit of her clothing down her long legs until they dangled off of her left foot.

"Are you sure?" Eugen cupped the back of her neck.

"I'm more sure about this than anything right now."

Anca wrapped her fingers around his length and pulled him toward her entrance. She saw the dam break in his eyes as he eased into her.

Eugen was done fighting this urge. He pressed into her with a quiet groan. She gasped, her lungs full of chilled night air, toes tensing. Her eyes rolled in her head at the delicious stretch of him pushing farther in.

The noisome need quieted. Finally.

They broke from the moment of ecstasy when he thrust and sent them into a slow frenzy of motion. Her hands scratched at his back as she pressed herself deeper against the itchy pillows, her mouth open in a quiet gasp. She clamped her hand over his mouth again, fighting her own voice.

They quickened. Moving her hips around the throbbing pleasure inside, days of lust drifted through her mind. The tumult of sensation pushed her closer to the edge. She no longer heard the breath in his lungs or the ring of crickets far in the field. Their heartbeats pulsed together, each one crashing into the other. His movement settled at a steady pace that built the heat in her higher than she thought possible.

Until it boiled over.

Anca turned her face and bit the pillow, pressing it into her mouth with a hand. She gasped, body frozen as tremors passed from her hips and up her back. The only thing beside the rattling release in her head was the desperate effort to stay quiet.

The waves of fire streaking through her veins calmed. When she opened her eyes, she found Eugen beaming down at her with glowing satisfaction. Her eyes went from the sharp angles of his face to the crushing dominance of his body.

She wasn't done with him. By the way he felt inside of her, neither was he.

Eugen said nothing. He merely leaned down and kissed her neck, his trim beard pressing along her shoulder. Her desire rose again with every second that passed, that last perfect moment harder to focus on as she thought about the next one she wanted.

"More," Anca growled into his ear.

She grabbed the back of his neck and pushed his shoulder. One leg wrapped around his knee and the other braced them as she flipped him onto his side. Eugen's surprise faded in an instant and his arm shot out to control the move. The twinge of discomfort from rolling while wrapped together was worth the satisfaction of putting Eugen onto his back.

"I'll never have enough of you," he answered.

They adjusted so that Eugen was mostly on the bed, The sheen of sweat along his body catching the moonlight through the vent at the top of the tent. Anca leaned back and ground herself deeper onto him. The gyration sent him snarling for breath. His teeth flashed as he rolled his hips into hers, sending a wave of lightning through her very core. Eugen's hands traveled up her waist.

She was his. He was hers.

Whichever way it was, he was real and beneath her.

Conspiracies and failing hunts fell away. All that mattered was the crackling thunder between her legs. Slow and quiet, his movement was measured as if he might spin out of control in moments. She intended to push him over that edge as many times as she could before the sun rose. Her passion ready to burst, she bucked her hips and bit her lip to smother the moan in her throat.

In the darkness of the small tent, Anca went after something she chose for herself.

Chapter Nineteen

Eugen's fingers traced the faded brands on the back of her hands. Resting on his chest, she had no idea how much time had passed. It could have been half an hour. Maybe dawn was dangerously close. It didn't matter. The throb of his heartbeat swallowed her world.

She did not know what would come next. By Eugen's silence, neither did he. Basking in each other's warmth, the cool air tickling their skin, she felt the uncertain trepidation between them. she savored the shivers that ran through her legs and up her body. The eruption of their desires had nearly burst the tent at its seams.

"I can't stay." Eugen kissed the top of her head.

"I know."

She wished he could stay. Though Anca was a leader and a dreaded hunter, that did not stop the pang of want that coiled around her. Anca hated the girlish thrum in her chest that wanted to hold him here. She wanted to tie him up in the locks of her hair. His presence, be it his smell or his voice, eased the wrinkle of stress in the back of her head.

"Can you make it back quietly?" She ran a finger along his chest, memorizing the feel of him.

"I think so. You're the only hunter here who could catch me out."

It was all she wanted: to speak without the restraints

of expectation twisting her every word into a tortured half-truth. Although she did not know where Eugen fit into all of this, or even what this was between them, he deserved that freedom as well.

He climbed out of bed and gathered his clothes. She admired every curve and hollow of his body as he dressed. Disappointed as he slipped his undergarments on, she grabbed the soft undershirt and wool pants she originally meant to sleep in. It was not wise to sleep nude in the wild.

As she slid her arms through her shirt and turned to face him, she found him watching her. His breathing came strong and loud, a vein bulging in the side of his neck. Eugen pursed his lips and reached for his belt.

"We can't let on anything. At the muster tomorrow, I will turn my back on you. I will seem cold." His even tone assured the distant worry that he would fall to pieces come morning. His Focus might be cindering elsewhere, but here he was calm.

He took her hand, palms tracing over her arm.

"But I want to tell you that this was everything I thought it would be."

Her other hand cupped his and she fought the impulse to tear his clothes off again. The smile on her lips couldn't be fought. It was beyond what she expected. The twist of their bodies against each other, his strength against her, and the moments when he relented and she pressed him against the sheets.

Anca shivered.

"Go. Before I pull you back to bed." Anca did not let go of his hand as she said it.

He grinned and leaned closer.

"Is that an invitation?"

"We'll both need some stress relief after today. Maybe we will hold a council in your tent next time?"

"Only if you can be quiet enough. My hunters won't make it easy."

"Then I'll have to climb you like a tree the moment I get to you."

Eugen slid his hand alongside her face and pulled his lips to her. She ran her hands along his arms and tried to commit his citrusy, smokey scent to memory alongside his body.

He finally pulled away and slid through the back flap of the tent. There was certainly a risk of him being detected. His Nobil blood granted him advantages that any other hunter would struggle to match. Eugen was right. She might be the only hunter who could beat him.

Anca slid back into bed with no idea if she could sleep. She grinned, the happy kind she had not allowed since passing notes back and forth with boys. The scent of him on her sheets drew her into a deep sleep. There were no dreams that night.

She did not slumber for long. Whether it was the lasting exhilaration of her tryst or the stress of the coming day, she woke just as the songbirds began their morning rituals. The graveyard shift of sentinels swapped with the morning shift. Armor clanked and snide remarks passed back and forth.

Their secret must be safe.

Out of bed and onto her feet, she went to gather some water to clean herself. The fires burned low, but their large bonfires held the light. Dressed in tan slack clothing and a winter coat, no one recognized her. Anyone close enough to see her face was sleeping or trying to coax a few more minutes of shut eye. Marin would be by to wake the Sulia side of camp soon. His bell would certainly wake Queen's Company as well.

She drained water from a large keg into a bucket. The water would be nearly freezing, no way around it. Frost formed on the patches of grass within the camp. Flitting snowflakes caught the final rays of moonlight, soon to wisp away under the warm sun. Anca bathed quickly, brushed her teeth, and dried herself before the frigid air got to her.

Dawn broke and all twenty-odd surviving hunters gathered in the ruined shell of the town. Anca wore a dark green cloak, her favorite for deep woods hunting. Her usual armor sat over warm, dark brown cloth that would keep the chill from her bones. The early morning snow turned into rain. It fell at an even rate, just enough to annoy her.

Craita stood next to Eugen, both in their polished chainmail and black armor. He did not give Anca a glance as she walked to the assembly, but she could not help but linger on him. He had trimmed his beard into sharp lines. Head freshly shaved so close that he was nearly bald. As she looked away, she caught a glimpse from the corner of his eye. The smallest crack of a smile twisted his lips.

The mass of hunters ahead of her were separated by House. All of them were dressed head-to-toe in flexible armors and swabbed in war paint. Decorum was called for in such a gathering, but the dirty looks they exchanged were impossible to miss.

"Everyone, listen up!" Marin shouted over the rain. The many, smaller conversations trickled off and Anca stepped in front of the combined crowd.

"Hunters, be glad. It's time."

They couldn't hide the simmering energy under their irritation. Even with their grudges, their breath came in hot heaves and weapons were twisted in anxious grips. They were dying for this chance.

"We've gone farther than any Household has in years. Some would be tempted to call that a success, but I know that isn't enough for any of you. None of us know these lands particularly well, so we're going to scout it. Group up by four. That should be enough for three groups and a rear guard to hold the town."

Eugen cleared his throat. "Nobil Sulia, may I suggest something?"

His eyes met hers. A flash of last night crossed her mind, but she suffocated it before color rose to her cheeks. Eugen straightened his back and waited for permission to continue.

"Go on." A curated note of caution in her voice.

"An idea has been brought to me by one of yours. In the spirit of camaraderie, why don't we mix our households? I doubt we could do it any other way."

"Bull's balls," Marin said.

"Would it be so terrible, Doia? Or do you think your smell will drive my hunters away?"

A chuckle ran through the crowd and Marin glanced across them. His gaze settled on Doru.

"You well-intentioned, sun beam of an idiot. You went over my head, you pugnacious, little—"

"Hunter Doru. Explain." Anca interrupted her Doia, who stewed without speaking another word.

The young hunter pulled back his hood and crossed his hands. He winced as he looked at Marin and then turned to Anca. She had not anticipated any good will from the combined company. However, if it came from anyone, Doru would be her first guess.

"Things have been tense, Nobil Sulia. If this hunt is really about moving past old grudges, we should embody that idea. I'm not asking for us to sing songs and hold hands. I would be glad to have a few coilguns backing us up. We are scouting out one of the darkest, Shadow-tainted forests in all of the world, after all."

Marin choked on a dozen words at once, his face deepening to a shade of red that almost matched his hair. He clearly did not know what to do with Doru when he was being reasonable.

"We don't share doctrines. We don't know their calls or signals. I don't like them."

Marin's observations were correct. However, this disdain between the companies needed mending.

"An excellent idea, Guard Doru. Form into teams of four: two Sulia and two Queen's Company. Don't make us do it for you. Remember that the forest out there is a lot meaner than anyone in this camp."

The crowd in front of her groaned and gritted their teeth. They drifted together to form teams. Anca was happy to see the difficulties begin to fade as their instincts took over. Both Houses were trained in separate styles, but not enough to suppress that killer backbone.

"You expect me to cooperate with them?" Marin's anger had not dimmed after the order was given.

"You can always stay behind and guard the camp," she offered with a bright voice.

He looked between her and Eugen, still watching them from the other side of the square, and chewed on his lip.

"I will be far away from him here. No need to play nice."

"And you were never very good at being stealthy. What with the red hair and everything."

Anca chuckled and Marin raised a finger in her face.

"Watch your tone or there won't be any hot soup when you return." His grimace broke into a small, worried smile. "Get back safe, alright?"

Anca slapped his elbow before walking away. She needed a group and recognized one House Sulia member who was outnumbered. Doru spoke to a pair of Queen's Company hunters: Craita and a blond man. He loomed over the Sulia hunter, a necklace of teeth dangling from his neck. Anca listened in as she approached them.

"Glad to see a member of Queen's Company that realizes that they need actual hunters," Doru said.

"Don't assume you are a master here," the blond man said. "We may not be used to hunting Beasts, but we can track just fine."

"I hoped we could all look out for each other," Anca said as she entered their circle.

Craita and the other man gave a small bow as she entered. By the pulse in their veins, she knew they feared any punishment she might levy. Perhaps not as much as Eugen's wrath, but close.

"I know Craita and Doru. You seem tenacious enough," she directed at the unknown Queen's Company hunter.

"My name is Matei. I've served under Eugen for nearly seven years and am proud to fight alongside a Nobil such as yourself."

If he was lying, he hid it well.

"We're on foot today. We'll go on a north-westerly path," Anca said.

"What bird calls do you use?" Craita asked.

Doru raised his fingers as he listed.

"Field Pigeons, Eastern Sawbeaks—"

"We use the Eastern Soimbird. It's common in the capital. Everyone knows it," Matei added.

"We don't." Doru scratched at the back of his head.

"Soimbird is similar enough to a saw beak," Anca offered. "Maybe you can show us? We don't need to be quiet until we hit the tree line."

The group headed for the gates and continued to hash out details. From what Anca could hear, every other group was having similar discussions. The three groups of hunters fanned out toward the shadowed forest.

She found him in the crowd. The glint of a greatsword stuck out from the Sulia hunters he was paired with.

Eugen nodded with recognition as something was explained to him. He was focused on what was being relayed, but broke from it. His stony demeanor did not change save for a wrinkle of an eye. It was all he could allow and everything she wanted to see.

Moments like these were usually filled with anxiety. The fear that she would never return, the last time she spoke to someone, or everything she had left undone. Fated Death waited for them all. Today, Anca was certain she would see him again. They drew farther apart, but her ears followed the thud of his heart until it became too faint.

The four hunters slowed at the edge of the canopy. Beneath the purple leafed boughs, the darkness seemed to suffocate any kind of light. Only a dim remainder of the sun slipped through in pale, cold rays. Doru dug his boot into a bit of exposed ground.

"Awfully soft soil. Burrowers maybe?"

"Flame help us if there are," Matei muttered.

They were all scared. She heard it in their voices. She saw it in the green light that beat in their veins. There was a tightness in her chest as well. Things that should have scared her merely incensed her. It was passed down, one Nobil to the next.

She had no illusions about that emotion: it was fear. Her body merely did something useful with it. The deep shadows of the forest hid creatures they could scarcely imagine and many they already knew. They were no longer apex predators.

"We've done this before," Anca said.

She dared to pat Matei on the shoulder, a move that tightened the grip on his coilgun.

"What? Navigate a forest of Shadow beasts, warped by Shadow itself for hundreds of years, in pursuit of the most dangerous creature the throne has ever seen?" Matei asked.

"The first part at least," Doru said.

Matei snickered. "You're an optimistic lot."

Anca drew her sword and raised her voice.

"Silence from here on out. Soimbird calls if you see something. Diamond pattern, ten pace spread. One of you two lead."

Craita volunteered before Doru could raise his hand.

"I'll do it. Doru couldn't find his way out of a burlap bag."

The Sulia hunter briefly pouted, but they dove into the brush before he could think of a comeback.

Anca spread out and crept along behind them. Her hunting backbone kicked in, avoiding twigs and watching the spaces between tree trunks. Ears were perked to the slightest sound. The smell of the deep forest washed over her as they stepped inside: mold, moisture, wood, blood, and bone.

Chapter Twenty

This quiet world came in hues of black and emerald. The wide, branchless warden tree trunks obscured any sight lines further than a few dozen feet. Even if they could find a stretch of uninterrupted ground, Shadow hung like mist. The inhuman intelligence behind it swirled against the dim light of day, threatening to spring out of darkened hollows the moment that the light died. Anca guessed that it was guiding its creations toward them. Every passing hour was a hazard.

Craita was busy checking for tracks or game trails. Anca was on the right of their formation, Doru to her left, and Matei was behind the three of them. They moved in near perfect silence.

There was a lurking noise that remained at the edges of perception. At first, she slowed and whistled a bird call to the group. A quick hand signal to them, inquired on the sound, but received no recognition. She stayed there for another moment before signaling to continue.

She heard it again minutes later. Low and deep. It was so faint that she wondered if it was someone's stomach gurgling. Anca carried on without note to the others, but listened for it again. It came again sooner this time and she recognized it immediately.

Eugen's heartbeat was out there somewhere. If she could hear it, he was close. She wondered if they both took a similar path or if he was shadowing her. She trusted him to give her space.

He was not cloying like Victor was in their early days. Eugen wanted to kill the creature as much as she did. She expected him to fight her every step of the way to be the one to claim it. It crossed her mind that he did not follow to protect her. She was the better tracker. What better way to ensure he knows when the creature is found?

A bird call came from Craita who crept near the base of a towering trunk. Anca hurried to her side and the mage nodded to a spot at her feet. Glimmering motes of Othersight picked out the faint impressions from the thin soil.

"Tracks. Not the kind we were looking for," Craita whispered.

Doru settled in next to Craita and Matei shouldered his coil gun, checking the area around them.

"Lumbira?" Doru asked.

"No. Human."

Anca ran her fingers along the dirt, indicating the barest imprint of a boot heel. More of them led deeper into the forest.

"How many?"

"Three individuals, at least." Anca said. "These might be a few months old. Four at most."

"So what?" Matei looked away from his vigil. "I'm sure the Trigvan are all over these woods."

Anca rolled her eyes. The claim that they could track seemed to be thinner than expected.

"These have steel-plated boots, treaded bottoms, and a heavy impression when they were left. They were wearing armor."

Matei looked away from the Nobil, rising as if to

leave. "The Trigvan wear armor."

Craita shook her head and flipped through her small notebook. Anca looked closer at the print. They were machined recently and well kept. She had seen this impression before. The realization drew her stomach into a nauseous knot.

Craita found the entry in her notebook and tripped over her words as she spoke.

"The Trigvan wear armor, but all of their shoes are old leather patchwork and sandals. I don't even think they could have scavenged a pair like that. These soles are standard issue for royal militia and regulars."

"Same as the ones you're wearing," Anca said.

This was not two tracks mixing or an imprint too vague to determine. Glittering in green light, the evidence was plain as the shine off Matei's coilgun.

"Did anyone else from Queen's Company come up here recently?" Doru asked.

Matei slowly shook his head, eyes now locked on the faint track. His pulse quickened.

"Eugen is as much a stranger to these lands as all of you."

"Then why are these tracks here?" Anca stabbed a finger toward the ground.

He shrugged, his voice rising in a way that did not fit innocence.

"I don't know, maybe some damn trader wandered too far and was chased into the woods by the locals."

"No one comes this far out." Craita's eyes went over the tracks and rested on Anca. "Only way we find out who they were is to follow them. Don't you think so?"

Matei glowered at the back of her head, his hand flexing around the grip of his weapon. He pointed back the way they came.

"We're losing daylight and we haven't found any tracks of the Beast yet. This is a wild goose chase. We'll just find an old set of bones, you watch."

The earth quivered, just barely a tickle under Anca's foot. Her head turned toward the sound as Craita's head perked up to it. Her Focus took on a dim, yellow glow. Through the misty veil, they both felt it. This was not Eugen's heartbeat. Though it was just as faint.

"Did you hear that?" Craita asked.

Anca felt the next thump under her feet. The one after rumbled in her ear. They were impact tremors. The group moved to the other side of the trunk. Anca loaded a bolt into her crossbow and focused the sights on the murk.

A creeping shape moved forward from the darkness. Its long, horn-covered legs strode into view first. Silent as a tiger in the brush, it reminded her of the hunting spiders back home. This horrific reminder stood two stories tall. The dark brown chitin was covered in barbs and moss. Its chelicera clacked and drooled beneath several tri-lobed eyes that swiveled around the forest. It came to a halt and grunted with a deep, rattling sound.

They might be able to kill it with just the four of them, but it would be risky. Hunting parties of ten were common for a creature this size. Through the hissing breath of the creature, she heard the faint murmur of Eugen's heart. The beat was faster now. He could hear her own pulse speeding up.

"It's scenting us," Anca whispered. "We move south. There's another group of hunters nearby."

"How do you know that?" Doru asked.

"Trust me. Quietly, move now."

Anca led them between massive trunks and broke sight lines whenever they could. They were gaining ground from it, but the damn thing had their scent. Whenever she looked back, its titanic, hairy legs crunched the ground where they had been minutes before.

Eugen's heartbeat was clear now. Thudding harder, he was worried. He could certainly hear hers at this point. They weren't further than a fifth of a mile away. The creature's pounding steps drew closer. With two Nobils and six veteran hunters, it might be disappointed to find what it was looking for.

Anca turned past a large trunk and the flash of steel caught her eye. Sixty feet from them, Eugen and his group hurried between thin shrubs. Her breath caught in her chest, relief flushing over her to have him within sight.

Matei and the others caught up with her. The Queen's Company hunter stepped ahead of Anca in a hurried walk and waved to his master.

"Mammoth hunting spider, not far behind—"

They all stumbled as the ground shifted beneath their feet. Soil spilled down into a chasm as the earth split open under Matei. He screamed and fired. The iron bolt flew from the barrel and lodged itself into a nearby tree. From the upheaval, a screeching, keening sound burst from the dirt as he tumbled backward. A wriggling, pale worm with pincers and hooked arms bit into its prey's leg. Eugen shouted as the creature dragged Matei down with it.

"Matei!"

Craita lunged forward and speared the midsection of the creature. Its armor cracked and pulpy yellow goo burst from it. Matei drew a knife and plunged it into its maw. Its pincers came loose, but a spray of sizzling fluid arced overhead and splattered across his features.

Smoke bloomed from his face and he scraped at his eyes, flesh and skin coming away on his hand. He screamed and the smell of burning flesh quickly followed.

Anca looked up from the nightmarish pit in front of her and saw the earth cracking across the space between them. Eugen's sword was in hand, Focus spurting ash as he gasped for breath. Light arced up his veins as he took one step forward. The ground split open between them and a nest of Burrowers broke from the loose soil.

"Anca!" He roared across the ground and heaved his sword forward.

The first insect split in two at his strike, but the second bit into his left arm. Eugen bellowed, slid his sword over his shoulders, and separated the creature's head from its body. An arc of acid spattered over the metal pauldron on his right shoulder. The squirming horde between them only grew in size.

Anca clambered to her feet. The pounding shake of the ground reminded her of the behemoth spider. It would be on them in moments.

Everything in her screamed to go after Eugen. Her heart burned against her ribs, as if it could guide her across the deepening chasm. However, the calculating part of herself knew the truth. It was suicide to reach him.

"Anca, run! I will find you!" Eugen roared across the growing wall of insects. The hunters in his group fought a retreat, one of them pulling on Eugen's collar to guide him backward.

"We have to go!" Craita grabbed Anca's wrist and

pulled her away.

Another pale worm erupted from the sinkhole and latched onto Matei's body. It disappeared into the loose soil and her feet came to life. She ran alongside Craita and Doru to the north, away from Eugen. The enormous hunting spider smashed pale worms as they emerged, but the lightless eyes focused on the hunters. It clacked its chelicerae and howled, revealing a mouth of saw-shaped teeth within.

There was nowhere to hide. The hills were slight, smooth, and without a bit of noticeable shrubbery. Anca looked for a hand hold or a hollow, something to climb these trees with. They were bare, the lowest branches wrenched off by hungry creatures long ago. The pounding behind them grew louder. The spider ran faster than they could ever hope to.

Out of the corner of her eye, the ground rose into an unnatural hill. She told herself that it was not in the shape of a toppled fort. Looking closer, brick and stone peeked out beneath piles of earth and vine.

"Over there," she said between breaths.

The spider's rapid pace closed behind them. Doru drew his ax with one hand and prepared a parchment-wrapped ball in the other. He threw it at the creature's eyes, the contents exploding in a flash of light and a loud snap as it collided.

The creature stumbled and he took advantage. Doru slashed at one of its leg joints and orange-ichor spewed from the wound. It instinctively lunged down with one of its fangs, but Doru stepped aside.

Anca swiveled on her heel, aimed, and fired within a breath. The broad-headed bolt lodged into one of its red eyes. Doru worked toward its back legs, cutting where he could and dodging any blow that swung toward him. He shouted Sulia war cries as he did, grinning in the flow of battle.

Craita fired her coilspear and the upper half of the shot lodged itself in the creature's jaw. A long metal wire connected the handle of the spear to the disconnected tip, leashing the creature to Craita. As it roared in pain, she opened a cross of spikes on the back of the spear and sunk it into the ground.

Half blind, the spider tried to climb the nearest tree. The spear tip in its mouth held and it was yanked back to the ground, legs scrambling to catch itself. The earth erupted around it and a clutch of wriggling nightmares latched their pincers and legs onto the fallen behemoth.

The earth bulged as more of the burrowing worms emerged. Doru ran back toward Anca, but a worm burst from the ground at his feet and catapulted upward. He brought his ax into its head and ducked. Acid arced overhead and he rolled past the wiggling carcass, wrenching the blade out as he passed.

The earth glimmered green in Anca's eyes. They were so close to the surface. She could see the horrid things just beneath the soil. She could see what Doru didn't. He was surrounded.

"Run!"

Doru noticed the earth warp with their movements and took a heavy step forward. The blade of his ax sizzled with acid, nothing left but a chunked butt of metal and the wooden haft. He looked at Anca, hope shining in his eyes. She felt the trust that he had in her. He truly believed that she would keep him safe, no matter the danger.

Maybe that errant thought slowed him a step too

much.

The ground gave way beneath his next step and he fell face first into the dirt. His back went rigid as he snapped back to life and tried to fight his way free. He screamed, his voice high and wobbling with fear. The loose dirt and leaves writhed around him like a stormy sea.

Anca loaded a bolt and fired at the next creature that emerged from the earth. The force tore it in half as the next one broke from the ground in front of Doru. She never saw the final look in his eyes, only the carapaced back of the monster as its jaws snapped shut over Doru's face. A small bloody scream gurgled from him before he was pulled below.

She fired another shot at the last glimpse of the hideous worm, but the bolt stuck into the dirt as her target vanished from sight. Anca roared and loaded another shot. There was at least one more worm chewing on his leg, pulling her friend farther under the ground.

I won't let you go. I won't let my own die like this.

A low scream rose in her throat as she fired. A yank at her shoulder sent the bolt flying into the forest. Craita pulled the Nobil back to her senses, almost dragging her through the woods.

"Get to the mound!" Craita shouted in her ear.

Anca stumbled as she fought the urge to go back for Doru. He was a young hunter condemned to a dark, horrible death. Far from their quarry, Fated Death seemed too hollow and quick to be honorable.

Vali died a veteran after a long life. Doru's story had barely begun.

Snapping pincers and soft, fleshy bodies emerged from the earth. She reacted with the only thing to keep so many at bay. Anca ripped the cap off a Night Bane flare. It flashed to life and the wave of hideous things screeched. The nearest ones caught fire as the brilliant light covered their retreat.

Anca dangled the flare behind them as they ran. The worms kept their distance, but pursued with hungry determination. Up close to the mound, she saw it was some kind of fortress. It had completely fallen onto its side, the foundations sunken into soft, tunneled ground. They were running up the face of the ruined fort when her flare died.

The creatures squirmed along the stonework, unable to burrow through the old structure. Thick burs and hooks dangled off their body, looking for anything to dig through. A single, black eye sat above the snapping pincers. Their hooked claws barely supported their weight above ground.

Anca did not wait to see how fast they moved on the surface. They both dove through a window in the slanted side of the bastion. Anca bounced on the ground and rolled. She drew up to her knee and aimed at the window. Craita raised a dagger, ready to throw it at whatever pursued them.

Keening cries echoed through the forest, but no wriggling monsters followed. After a few moments, they both collapsed against the wall behind them. They gasped with hoarse throats, Anca repressing a low sob in her voice.

He trusted you, she thought. Doru was dead because of you. He joined Vali and dozens of others. Dead because of her crusade.

She sniffed away the guilt. There was no time to mourn, not yet.

With the tilted angle of the fortress, they stood on what was once a wall, the ceiling behind them. Their landing destroyed the already tattered remnants of a faded tapestry. Craita lifted her toward the crumbling hallway ahead.

"Where are we?"

A sigil was imprinted on what had been the floor, now the wall in front of them. It repeated along the halls. The twisting, curved lines formed a veil with wispy edges. The symbol was crafted with patient artistry. It was as old as clockwork machines and powered lights. She usually saw it scrawled with tar or chalk in alleys. This symbol was banned in all of Margecei.

The mark of Shadow: the seal of their ancient enemy.

"Nowhere good."

Craita lowered her torch. "Look."

In the layers of dust that covered the walls and floor, Anca saw the footprints. She leaned down to them, holding her breath to not disturb it: treaded soles, armor plated.

"Craita, I need you to be honest," Anca whispered.

"There's nothing to hide."

Blood was splattered across Craita's face. Bits of her armor sizzled with acid, likely the leftovers of Matei. Anca looked at herself and smelled the same acrid odor. She wiped a layer of loose soil from her leather armor. She wondered if there were bits of Doru all over her.

Maybe there were dissolving bits of Eugen all over the forest floor. Whatever role he had to play in this strange trail was not entirely front and center yet. Her legs burned, her wrists ached, and she wasn't sure her heart could stand to lose Doru and Eugen in one day.

She shut it out. If they stopped to think, they would collapse for hours. Anca took a step down the hallway and gestured to the tracks. Forward momentum was their only savior, but she could not escape the thought of Craita's knife at her back.

"Either we risk the Burrowers again or we get some answers. Those are royal issue boots?"

Craita nodded.

"So you know what that might mean?" Anca asked.

The mage glowered at her as she lifted her torch higher.

"I'll form my own conclusions. I know my people. I trust my company."

Her bravado did not match that nervous look on her face.

Chapter Twenty-One

The eerily preserved beauty was marred by carpets of dust and mite-eaten fabrics. Its gradual collapse into the earth wrecked the higher levels, but much of the lower floors were still whole. Anca stepped lightly and kept her voice low. She could not imagine a worse fate than to be buried under a bastion no one knew about.

Not even a whisper of light leaked down here. There were no small cracks that went to the surface. It stank of mold and dirt. Stale air made each breath feel like it was pulled from the pages of a forgotten book. Shadows moved strangely down here. They slowly peeled back from their light like a creeping fungus, fighting it longer than they should have. Maybe Shadow had grown too familiar with this place.

With their torches overhead, breath held against the smothering silence of the ruin, they had said nothing over the course of an hour. The trail of footsteps took them deeper into the bastion. After so much time spent staring at these tracks, her mind lingered on their details. These were royal boots, not some scavenged, Trigvan footwear.

Matei had been certain it was not Queen's Company. As a senior member of Eugen's company, he had plenty of reasons to lie.

More importantly, Anca was certain that Craita knew something. The mage had been amiable throughout the journey. So focused on history and learning, why would she clam up at such a tantalizing mystery? The obvious answer was that she was afraid of the solution.

At the top of it all was Eugen. His earnestness bordered on offensive at times, but it was refreshing compared to the lying smiles she was raised around. Nonetheless, he might be lying to her as well. Even after everything that happened. What could Eugen have been looking for down here? Anca cleared her throat and looked at Craita.

"We're kind of close by now, right? Acquaintances at least?"

Craita did not look away from the receding shadows in front of them. "I guess."

"So, you would tell me if Queen's Company has been out here before."

Craita glared at Anca. Her standing as a Nobil might have spared a harsher answer.

"We're not traitors."

"I didn't say that."

"You didn't need to. No, we've never been out this far before. As far as I know."

As much as she knew. More likely, as much as they've told her.

"Is there a chance others in your company have?"

Craita began to speak, but snapped her mouth closed. Clearing her throat, her tone was as flat as pressed linen. "There are things kept between Households. Surely, you've got some things you'd rather keep to yourself."

There were some things she was keeping back. Eugen might have been looped into their grand purpose, but everyone else still believed this to be just a hunt.

Secrecy had its price, so she decided to pay it.

"I hate the order. The queen, the Households, all of it. The whole damn kingdom is falling apart."

"Not much of a surprise there," Craita muttered.

"I want to change it. That's why we're out here. If we can kill this thing, it'll be enough glory and attention to push Keller aside."

The mage gave her a look before focusing on the darkness ahead of them.

"That's quite bold. Why are you telling me this?"

"Well, I shared something with you. Now you don't have to feel bad about sharing something with me."

Craita shook her head. "I can't."

She said no more, but Anca saw the struggle in her eyes.

"I don't think Eugen is a monster." Anca sucked in another breath. This admission was harder than she expected. "In fact, I think he might be more earnest than most people I deal with."

Craita missed a step, the scuff of her boot echoing down these empty passages. That seemed to crack the dam. The fissures were plain in the tortured curl of the mage's lip.

"You should hear how he talks about you."

"What?"

"It's not even really a compliment," Craita cautioned. "But you know him. The whole kingdom thinks he is a foul thing. It's rare he finds allies. Especially one willing to spit in the face of the other Households."

Anca flushed with relief. The idea of Eugen airing their back-and-forth to his company terrified her as much as the Beast. Not that she was ashamed of what she did, at least she thought. So little time had passed since they had slept together. They were more than friends, certainly. The right word still evaded her. It felt good and it had been her choice. That was enough for now.

"You're not bad either. Mages have a reputation, but I've found you to be nothing but helpful. If not a little bookish."

Craita tilted her head to the side. "Someone has to be. No one would remember all of those damn Nobils if there weren't people like me to write it down."

They both snickered in the silence of this oppressive tomb. Craita resumed her careful steps down the dingy hallway.

"The Queen's Company aren't just mercenaries at her majesty's disposal. We handle things the throne doesn't want the wider world to know about."

"Felt like I knew that already," Anca muttered.

"Did you know the Shadow cults in the Lost Lands were made by us?"

Anca always suspected it, but those were wild accusations to make. She would have welcomed this gossip any other time. More evidence of the crown's wrongdoing would be fuel for her cause, but there was a fly in the tea now. Before they found this palace, she was so certain they were all worth redeeming. Eugen chief among them.

The last few hours had shaken her resolve.

"I thought they were just rumors," Craita continued. "Stories handed down between recruits in the company. The royal family has been interested in Shadow beasts for centuries. If they found some shared weakness, they wouldn't need the Households."

"And teaching outsiders witch magic was their first

answer?" Anca asked.

"This was centuries ago, at least it's supposed to be. It got out of hand and the tribes of the Lost Lands decided to use that power against the throne."

Anca lowered her torch to the symbols of Shadow that still ran along the floor. "So this place was built by the crown?"

"Presumably, but look at it. This is ancient even by our standards. I was sure the whole story was bullshit until we fell into it."

"And they don't do it anymore? Eugen isn't helping Shadow cultists and taking clandestine trips far north of the border?"

Craita's words stumbled. "No, I don't think so. No."

Their light revealed a wide doorway free of fallen stone. Beyond it was a ballroom. Decadent chandeliers were smashed and removed from where they were once anchored to the ceiling, now the left side wall to them. At the faintest edge of their lights, there was a camp. Anca raised her torch and allowed her Othersight to roam over it.

"That doesn't look old."

There was no life down here except for mushrooms and vines. A pair of empty beds were left unmade. A filthy pot hung over a cold, unlit campfire. Parchment and notes sat on a table underneath a canvas roof.

A large table dominated the tent. Made of a solid, stone slab, it reeked of blood. It was stained with dark red smears, long dry. An array of grisly tools was heaped on a small side table. She winced at the variety of blades, hand drills, and clasps. It looked like a nightmarish surgeon's chambers. A nearby bucket full of bones and withered flesh promised that it was once a busy operation.

At the edge of the camp were four sets of thick chains that ran out into the darkened side of the chamber. Each link was as thick as her arm and made of quality metal. Anca noted the royal smith's impression on them. Cautiously, they followed these chains from where they were bolted to the floor and into the shadow ahead.

Anca threw her torch across the room and it landed on a pile of chewed bones. The long chains ran to a handful of white circles, each one spaced five feet from the other. Claw marks were scratched into the stone floor. Dozens of the frantic impressions surrounded the space, like an enormous rat had been caught in a trap. Craita ran her hands over the white circles. They were not chalk, but painted divots with runes carved along them.

"It's a prison."

Anca took a step back. "Magic?"

"Earth magic."

Craita closed her eyes and whispered. Her necklace glowed with dull, amber motes of light. Nothing happened for a long moment before she spoke again, this time louder.

"Please, show us what they made."

She remained still, only a small tremor answering her efforts. Her shoulders sagged with a gasp before swallowing down more musty air. Craita winced, closing her eyes as hard as she could.

"Listen to me. Show us what lays here."

The ground rumbled and the indentations pulled apart. Slabs rose from the divots with a teeth-chattering rattle. Smoother than any stone worker could have cut, they slid above and around the central circle. Gaps in the walls dragged the chain higher. A single hole, just large enough to peer into, could look into the cell once the stone walls settled against each other.

Each wall was composed of six inches of solid rock. The slabs interlocked, stopping any one piece from being shoved aside. It formed a multi-layered prison cell of stone. Slits on the walls allowed the insertion of various tools. Craita glanced back at the camp, following the chains.

"No torches here, but plenty over there. Whoever was held here was exposed to Shadow intentionally. Deep Shadow too. It would have warped them within weeks. Judging by the bones, they were well fed."

Anca grimaced. So close to this cell, the stench called to memories of blood and fire. The scent was familiar. "Are we so sure they were keeping a person here?"

There was an unsettling familiarity to the air here. The chains, the walls, all of that was new, but the scent reminded her of Moura. The merest suggestion was terrible to consider. Heart rending to believe. Anca assumed this Beast was created by Shadow naturally, like all other beasts. That did not explain why this creature seemed so infused with magic. Almost like it was intentionally designed. Her stomach soured as she arrived at a sickening thought.

"This is only a few years old. The stone cell wasn't built into the original bastion. A mage made this, someone who knew their disciplines. Maybe it's a holding cell?" Craita asked.

"This far out? Why would they drag a prisoner into this terrible place just to lock them up? They've got plenty of room to do that at Thronetown."

Anca picked up the chains. The shackles at the end were shattered.

"Someone makes a cell built to expose something to the purest form of Shadow. Suddenly, we have a Shadow beast unlike anything we've ever seen. We find all of this in a bastion that the throne never told us about, run by people who aren't supposed to be here, in a region the crown isn't supposed to be active in."

"We just need to think this over." Craita's voice was frayed. She was trying to convince herself as much as Anca.

"It isn't crazy. I know you see that."

Craita grabbed her Focus and laid her palm against the stone floor.

"Please hide this."

The stone hurriedly slammed into the ground with enough force to shake dust from the ceiling. Craita's whole world was caving in. It occurred to Anca that her emotions might do more than move these prison walls. The worrying crackle of pebbles falling from a wall made her heart thunder.

Scaring a mage was a bad idea. Anca's grip on her sword tightened. It didn't have to come to that yet, but she would not let this mage accidentally bury them both. Anca could move fast, but she was not sure it would be fast enough.

Craita held up her hand, stopping Anca from coming closer. She took a steadying breath and gave one last look at the camp that her Household had built and the trail of boots that they doubtlessly left.

"I'm fine. We need to sort this out with Eugen."

Anca breathed a small sigh of relief and followed Craita as she hurried out of the chamber. They climbed back out of the ballroom and followed the passage further into the bastion. Backtracking would bring them to the Burrowers.

Anca thought she was hallucinating at the first sliver of light. A nearby room was filled with the glare of the setting sun. Above it, a shaft ran upward through the shattered stone bricks. Vines crept down along large nooks in the wall, perfect to climb.

"Better than nothing. At least if there's nothing good on the other side of this, we could go back and try our luck again," Craita said.

Going into the forest at night was a poor idea. Besides, she needed more time with Craita. She needed the truth and there was more to tell. If her worries were borne out, if Eugen was responsible for this creature and its slaughter, Anca needed a plan.

Her heart was bursting with nasty, sweaty, raging fear. If this were true, she didn't want to think about what would have to happen next. Eugen could not be allowed back alive. It twisted her guts to think it, her own emotion still so unsettled about the two of them.

It was the desire to know more that kept Anca from lashing out.

"We should camp for the night." Anca set her bag down. "We have a good sight line down the hallway here. There's some shelter from the rain and this passage works as a chimney for a fire."

Craita shook her head and eyed a climbing path up the shaft.

"We're wasting time."

"We're both hungry and tired. We wouldn't be able to handle an ill-tempered deer in our state. Goodness, imagine if the Beast found us."

With a resigned sigh, Craita let go of the vines. She knelt and untied her flimsy bed roll from her pack.

"Fine. We both could use some rest, the hike out of this forest is not going to be easy. Assuming the others haven't already killed the damn thing and left us for dead."

"We'll leave at first light, promise."

Chapter Twenty-Two

Eugen sat on the wall, sword in one hand and a Queen's Company hunter bandaging the other. His skin burned with the traces of acid and pinching bites. The squirming things nearly ripped all of the flesh from his left arm by the time they escaped. It wasn't his choice to leave Anca behind.

After the initial retreat, he tried to break through the wriggling horrors again. The nest must have been nearby because they never ceased coming. Eugen reaped a bloody toll, his own skin and flesh melting with every kill. The pain they inflicted was nothing compared to the desperate fear that tried to burst from his ribs.

She wasn't safe. She was isolated.

Anca could handle herself, but that didn't stop the worry from burrowing into his guts like a hungry rat. Eventually, it became clear that staying in the forest was risking the accompanying Sulia hunters more than himself. Remembering Anca's promise to protect them, he relented and left the forest. He was a gruesome sight as they staggered out of the tree line, more of a corpse than a man. Not that it mattered. The hissing wounds were healed into painful, pale pink skin by the time they reached the fort. Only the Flame kept him alive.

The rest of the hunters trickled back three hours ago. Bleeding, exhausted, and terrified, none of them had successfully tracked the Beast or even seen it. There had been signs, of course. Its tracks circled around the forest, but always led them into the mouth of some other nightmare. The Beast was toying with them.

All of this did not bother him as much as who was

still out there. There was still one team that had not returned. She was out there, but she was still alive. He felt it in his bones. It wasn't in her nature to fall prey to some random twist of fate.

However, Nobil Varcop had. So many of their hunters had. Why not her?

A spark of anger fizzled in between his eyes. The veins in his right arm bulged against his skin, his breathing growing heavy. He told her to run. It seemed the right thing to do at the moment, but now he wished that he kept her within eyesight.

The hunt is over. She is dead.

That's not right, he told himself. The Flame was growing. Every moment he looked at the increasingly dim forest line, his despair deepened.

"Does that hurt?" the hunter asked as they tightened a bandage.

"Just get it over with. I like my quietude when on guard duty."

"Lord Eugen, you must be exhausted. I've barely put you back together and you're already itching to keep watching out for—"

"I said finish your mending and leave me."

Eugen sat at the top of the camp's wall that looked out to the northwest. He set his forehead against the top of the wall, hoping it might drain the terror in his skull. When he closed his eyes, he felt that he could still see the northern tree line. Every detail of the shrubs and trees was committed to memory by now. The hairs on his neck prickled, a shaky panic trembling into his hands. When he couldn't see the tree line, maybe that would be the moment she decided to emerge from the gloom.

She found the Beast. That was the only explanation

for what could have delayed her. Eugen listened to the stories the survivors told. It was a bestiary of snapping jaws and stalking claws. None of that was enough to stop a Nobil. There was only one thing that could.

A nervous thought crossed his mind. There is that *other* thing.

He had pressed it out of his mind since they set a path for the Lost Lands. Seeing Zahrea again was bad enough, but it could be avoided. What were the odds of Anca finding that quiet, overgrown tomb? Not a tomb, as Eugen once thought it had been. It was a prison. Kept there despite his demands until Astasia found a good excuse to release it.

He had shadowed Anca through the forest, tracking her heartbeat as distantly as he could. The trail was lost a few times, but eventually he found her. Eugen planned to waylay her if they moved in the right direction. Even though it might be where the Beast was lurking, she couldn't be allowed to know. She was too smart. Sharp like the hunter's needle that stitched a gash on his arm back together. Anca would not miss the connection to him.

It was bad enough when the consequences were arrest and execution. He would lose her forever. Anca would never forgive him. Eugen barely understood what she meant to him yet, but it still shook the Executioner to his core. Why did he ever believe this could work? Anca and him never had a chance, but not because of the Nobils. Eugen knew that he never deserved her in the first place.

He could tell her that he tried to kill the damned thing, but that wasn't enough. The chance for redemption was lost when he agreed to shut up about the whole matter. Astasia ignored his request to exterminate that botched project and now they would both hang for it.

The Households would be crueler than anything Astasia could imagine. Only one Nobil broke that rule. She was somewhere beyond the darkened tree line. The sun marched lower in the sky, as they prepared to shut the door entirely.

"That's the last of it for now," the hunter at his side said. He stood to leave and secured the bag of medicine over his shoulder. "Get some rest. Please."

Eugen said nothing until the hunter left his sight. He itched to grab the blade, leap over the wall, and plunge into the coming night. It was a rash impulse, but goodness needed to be protected. There was far too much bad in the world to let the worthwhile ones twist in the wind. His fingers wrapped around the handle of his sword. The idea was far too tempting. Surely, the camp would be fine under Marin's watch.

The thought settled in his stomach like a sour egg. Was he so crazy that he would trust that curmudgeon?

"Hey, ass wipe!"

Eugen groaned and lifted his head from the wall. He looked across the tree line. It calmed his nerves for only a moment before the dread set in again. It was just as empty as the last time he looked.

Marin pushed a Queen's Company hunter out of the way as he crossed the camping ground. His ax was not drawn, but the Doia's glare looked sharp enough to kill. Trailing three paces behind him were two Sulia hunters with matching scowls.

"You sleeping while our Nobil is out there hunting?"

Eugen idly grabbed the handle of his sword. It was

a reflex to take it with him, but he recognized the foul urge in it like an acrid smell. The snarling Flame in his chest spoiled for a fight. The taste of violence earlier had whetted its appetite.

"I want to see her safely returned as much as you. Just resting my eyes for a moment, it's been a long day."

No need to antagonize, he thought. He's as scared for her as I am.

"Ha! Rest. Good to know you'll admit to being useless. A real Nobil wouldn't have let her go off alone."

"A Nobil did go into the field," Eugen said. "I fought to get to her until I was nearly bone and cloth. Now I need to babysit a grumpy, old man while the moon is up."

Marin stopped at the foot of the wall. His shouting had drawn the attention of the handful that remained behind. Initially as brave as their Doia, the Sulia hunters grew aware of a handful of Queen's Company that emerged from their tents. None of them were armed, but Eugen could trace their pulse.

Each one was gearing up to scrap. Muscles flexed and hearts raced. Their pupils dilated. Hands balled into fists. The two companies had been waiting for an excuse since the debacle at Moura.

The Blood Flame leaned against his neck like a confidant, whispering violent words of encouragement. The Doia had a stiff left shoulder and mild arthritis in his left elbow. His hearing was worse to his right and the setting sun would make an ideal environment to fight. In the harsh orange glow, the old man wouldn't be able to see well. With his Othersight, Eugen could have done it with his eyes closed.

Marin kicked the ladder on the wall.

"Get down here. I've got a bone to pick with you."

"I don't think you want me to."

The words slipped from his mouth effortlessly. Marin's nostrils flared, his red hair making him appear as though he had his own Blood Flame. The Doia did not reach for his weapon, but his fingers wriggled toward it.

"Maybe Vali had the right idea. Just wasn't the proper Sulia to fight."

It was too much. Caving to this rage was accustomed, but he remembered how he felt around Anca. Closing his eyes would have given Marin an opening, so Eugen stared into the space just beyond the angry Doia.

Peace, assurance, safety. She reminded him of what he could be. Whatever the Nobils said about him did not matter. He could stand on his own two legs and control himself. Should the hunt succeed, should Anca return, everyone would know that they were wrong about him.

"I don't want to fight with you, Marin." He forced the words out like stones caught in his throat. There were a dozen foul, profanity-laced tirades he would have preferred.

"Afraid you'll lose? Damn it. She's out there because you blew our best chance back at Moura. This is your fault!"

"It was her decision. This is her hunt. You're not the only one who wants to find her."

Marin rolled his eyes. It made Eugen want to spear him through and drink the blood that came out of his heart. No, these were not his thoughts. The Flame put ideas in his head.

"You're not welcome," Eugen growled at the thought.

You cannot deny me, it rumbled in his head. Marin's voice pulled him back to the moment.

"Oh, just run out and get yourself killed. That would be smart. At least we'd all be rid of you."

One of his hunters stepped forward. She snarled, shoulder bunching and fingers curling. Eugen saw the intent before she set a foot within striking distance.

"Stop!" Eugen bellowed across the camp and the hunter froze in her tracks. They were trained to fear him. They would never act against his wishes, at least in his presence.

Scratchy sheets, the lavender smell in her hair, the warm fire in his chest.

He thought of these things as he let go of his sword. It settled against the wall above. The writhing din of the Blood Flame felt like thorns catching on the skin of his back. Each movement was a conscious effort to walk away from the dreadful thing. Eugen jumped down then stretched back to standing as quick as he could, uncertain how Marin would react.

The Doia's eyes lingered on the sword left on the battlement before trailing back to Eugen. His fists were raised up to his hips, ready to swing if he needed to. The pulsing green in Marin's neck betrayed his fear. He stank of it. That was bravery though, wasn't it? Fighting like a feral dog even when you wanted to run.

"Put your fists down," Eugen said.

"Do you think she'd ever accept your help? I don't know what's come over her, but she knows the truth about you. This is all a play. She told me as much."

No, she wouldn't do that. Maybe at first. After all, he once despised her. Hated that way she talked and walked. For her, it was double that back at him. Times had changed.

Marin shook his head. The old bastard wanted him to fight. He felt it as the Flame crept closer once again. If he was itching for a fight, wouldn't it be justice to give it to him?

"You're angry. I know what that's like."

"What you have isn't anger. Anger can be righteous. I can be angry when a bastard leads someone I love down a bad path. No, you don't have anger. You have a disease. You get mad the way a chicken clucks. There's no meaning behind it. Like the rest of you. You're a feral son of a bitch who should have burned with his family."

Something was off. Marin was angry, but the venom that poured from him felt diluted. Eugen had been around the Doia long enough to know he was crass and protective. Never vindictive though. Marin wanted Eugen to fight him, but he didn't want to throw the first punch. This didn't stop the Blood Flame from pounding in his ears. On the wall above, Eugen's sword flaked with cinder. The orange gem in the hilt burned like a furnace.

"I bleed just like you."

"Then I'll make you bleed, you bastard. You're making me feel plenty of pain. The pain when your only family marches to its own oblivion."

"I don't know what it's like to lose family?"

Eugen stepped closer to Marin. Sweat dripped down his neck, tension tingling his palms. His back hunched like a wolf ready to leap. The Doia found the perfect place to hit him.

"I don't know what it's like to watch my family burn? Sweltering, blistering, surrounded by flames and penned in to roast like kindling? I watched, gagged and bound, while they were murdered by people exactly like you."

Marin shrank back. Eugen knew he was losing it. As he vented his rage, his new credo rang in his mind: Be better. His palms opened, stretching his fingers as wide as he could. The effort made his limbs shake. The blade above him spouted a torrent of cinders.

"I would bet you had a hand in it. You must have been there that night. Which of my family did you drag to the bonfire? Which of my friends did you douse in oil? You have wounded me in ways that I should kill for."

Light began to gather in his veins. The Flame would grow too strong soon, he had to turn back. He closed his eyes and bowed his head. As long as the Flame saw a foe in front of him, it would ache for blood.

"Why do you want to fight me?" Eugen asked.

"Because someone should suffer for this. By the stars, it's going to be you."

Marin's shoulders sagged as he tried to catch his breath. The Doia's piss-and-vinegar attitude deflated in the space of a moment.

"I can't let her die alone in the dark. Not her, not after everything she's worked for. If I don't get a chance to say goodbye to the closest thing I've had to a daughter, I swear I'll end you."

Tears gathered in Marin's eyes, but he wiped them away as soon as he realized they were there. The Doia needed a shoulder to lean on, even when everyone was supposed to hold onto him. Marin would never accept Eugen's help. He could try though.

"She's still alive," Eugen said.

"You don't know that. All of that magic in your veins doesn't give you foresight."

"Call it a hunch." Eugen tried to speak low and even,

a difficult task. "She survived the Beast before. She survived me. Everything out there will be lucky to stay out of her way."

The barest hint of a grin crossed Marin's face before he banished it. The Doia stood a little straighter. Eugen looked over to the gates, locked and set for the evening. The sun was almost gone, just the barest hint of light left in the sky. Purple and black swallowed their world.

I know you can make it, he thought. Just survive the night.

An idea crossed Eugen's mind. No, it was too bold. It might start a fight if he tried. Or it could take down the first wall between them. Once this was all over, it wouldn't be just Anca he would have to make peace with.

"How about this, Doia Marin."

Ah shit, here we go, Eugen thought.

He set his hand onto Marin's shoulder. The old man's eyes widened, spine pulling rigid. It reminded Eugen of when a cat was dropped into a tub of water. A moment of indecision before complete panic. Eugen released his breath. Marin waited for him to speak, jaw chewing with thought

"Come first light, we'll ride out together."

Marin looked at the hand resting on his shoulder and then back at Eugen. His features never shifted from frigid surprise. He nodded then slowly pushed Eugen's hand off of him.

"Aye." His voice was low and cautious.

Marin stepped away from him and ran his fingers through his hair. Only once he was a few paces away did his fists unwind. Marin shrugged. "At least, I could use you as bait. Might make up for some of this."

Eugen smirked.

"You won't even have to tie me up."

Marin stormed back toward his side of camp, a wary eye checking to make sure the whole exchange was not a fever dream. The Sulia hunters followed him out. This marked three times he had pulled himself from the brink. His fingers toyed with the sack of calming herbs on his hip, still unsure if it was time to do away with them.

A few Queen's Company still milled about.

"Back to your tents. Get some rest. This hunt isn't over."

Not by a long shot. Eugen was not going to let this fall apart at the last moment. They were so close. Even after this disastrous night, there had to be a way forward. As long as they had some measure of strength, a Nobil could never be defeated.

The only thing that could stop all of this was if his worst fears were real. Those dead secrets he thought were long gone. She was not back yet, which meant one of two things had happened. Either she was dead or she had discovered the truth. Anca might know everything now.

The legacy of a monster would be his headstone. He would be brought back in a cage. Worst of all, she would hate him. It sent tendrils of panic up his back, droplets of sweat flitting back down along his spine. The thought made him want to climb the wall and vanish into the lightless wild around them.

He ripped the bag of calming herbs from his hip and pressed it to his nose. Floral, slightly minty. His vision swam and the embers of Blood Flame calmed. As he climbed back up the ladder to retrieve his sword, and then on the walk back to his tent, Eugen clutched the herbs to his face. It felt as though it was the only thing rooting his feet to the ground.

Chapter Twenty-Three

Their makeshift camp was cramped. Without tents or even real bed rolls, their packs would have to do for bedding. They sat across from each other and chewed on old bread and a bit of salted meat. The small fire was just warm enough to defy the cold. Down from the passage above, echoes of the night came to them. Grunts, roars, and heart-shaking shrieks of prey in their last moments.

Their situation could be worse, but that did not mean Anca felt grateful. Even with the bell traps behind them and the sizable drop above, the ferocity of this forest surprised them all. Maybe she just did not want to think about everything they had gone through. She suspected worse things were to come and this might be the last peaceful night for a long time. Anca was glad to share it with someone who might need a quiet night as badly as she did.

Craita remained sullen. She picked at her food, staring past the fire and on to some deeper rumination.

"To Matei." Anca raised her waterskin.

There was no recognition in Craita's eyes at first, but it came quickly. "To Doru. Neither of them deserved that. No one does."

They took a small drink, conserving what they had left.

"They both met the Fated Death. I'm not sure that makes it any less painful," Craita added. She drew into herself again, fiddling with the knife between her hands. Anca straightened up and tried to catch Craita's distracted eye.

"Did you know Matei well? I think you said he was your friend."

A moment passed before she answered. Anca thought she might have closed up for good. Craita grimaced and tapped the flat edge of the blade on her finger.

"He was a mentor. Like I said, I never knew my family and the company was the closest thing I had. He showed me the ropes and taught me how things are done."

Anca thought of Marin. Some of her first lessons were with his surly, gruff demeanor. Time eventually drew the wit out of him and she could not put the stopper back on it. He would be safe behind the walls of their fort, she hoped. That didn't exclude the chance for danger. Stuck in the same place as Eugen without Anca accounted for by nightfall, she had reason to worry.

"We all have that person. We get all the glory and food we could ask for, but people can crack. Being hunted. Killing. It wears on you. Not sure I would have made it without people of my own." It was Anca's turn to find her hidden memories in the fire. The licking tongue of flame danced as if they fought to listen to her speak.

"Everyone knows the danger of what we do," she continued. "I guess we just didn't appreciate what we were walking into. I thought we were ready. So confident that I could stroll in and put this thing down. Now, I'm not sure the Beast is the biggest threat out there."

Anca had lost quite a bit since she departed, but only

some of them were physical things. She had lost people, supplies, and sleep. Her patience for this world was already fraying and now it was almost entirely gone.

She had lost hope that anyone in a position of power gave a damn about those underneath them. There were now questions about Eugen's role in this. All of these coincidences piled on top of one another in a fragile stack. She came here thinking that the throne could be worked with. Now she did not know what sort of resolution she desired beyond conflagration.

"That's why I'm scared," Craita said in a small voice.

She cradled the knife in between her hands, her eyes set on the small fire between them. So close, Anca pushed just a little more.

"Scared of what?" she whispered.

"They're family to me. I don't have anything if I don't have the company. You've got your legacy. All of that power and wealth is quite a leg to stand on."

Anca hissed a cynical breath through her teeth. From the outside, it must look like a dream. If only she knew about the Nobils, about jilted fiancés, and the horrible loneliness of power.

"There's less than you'd think. No one is truly content."

"I shouldn't be surprised. Eugen suffered more than either of us."

His name made Anca squirm. He was so vehement about changing things. Was it just a ploy? How much of it was his game?

"He's been a man for a long time. Eugen's in charge of himself. His bad decisions are his alone." Anca swallowed. "Just like myself."

"Those compliance orders were from the throne. You can't blame yourself."

"Can't I? The Households have enough force to challenge the throne and enough authority to run their own lands. The only cost would be their wealth and privilege. That's too much for most."

Her fingers ran over the fine studded leather on her arms. It was dyed deep blue and the snaps were refined iron. She traced the clothing to her shoulder and dug her nails into the neat stitching. It was commissioned upon her ascendance to this title. She had not paid a single royal talon.

"I'll never shirk from this mantle. But in a way, I'm no better than the rest of them. That's why this must work. If there is anything I don't know, you need to tell me now. Everything is going to change once we get out of this ruin."

Anca set her palms on her knees and caught Craita's gaze. Doubt had shaken her, but she was made of stern stuff that would never truly break.

The mage was ready to talk.

"I don't know everything. There's just rumors about the senior members of Queen's Company. My hands aren't clean, I've done my share of things I won't ever admit to. However, I'm kept out of some things between Eugen and the senior hunters."

"So he's twisting the whole thing?"

Craita's eyes lit up as if she saw an error growing in front of her.

Concern twisted her brows as she said, "It was never his idea. We are the Queen's Company. Astasia's commands matter above all else. I was lying earlier. It's an open secret that Eugen came and went between the

Lost Lands a couple of years ago. Matei was in charge of everything while he was gone."

"What was Eugen doing?"

Anca's heart throbbed, each one more painful than the last. It did not matter how much it would hurt, because she would pay it back to him once the weight of his lies was measured.

"No one knows, but he seemed weakened afterward. He was bruised and scarred. It was like he had been in a fight every single time. It's a long journey out here and back, but it was more than that. He always seemed optimistic. For someone as dour as Eugen, I figured he would be angry about getting his ass beat that often."

Craita's reluctance fell away. Anca listened, her mind beginning to stray to what she would do when she got back to camp. It was not clear if Eugen could die, but he could feel pain. House Sulia was the cleaning crew and Eugen was the handler. It had only been pure coincidence they stumbled upon this place. Sheer dumb luck that Anca happened to have a mage who could help her. The ruse almost worked.

"It all stopped two years ago. He assured us the trips were over and we got back to business as usual. Eugen did not want anyone to even acknowledge it after that. He was so crestfallen after it was over. It was like he lost something. He was quiet. The Blood Flame didn't even emerge properly. It took months for him to get back to his old self."

"Like remorse?"

The question pushed through Anca's anger. A small part of her wished that Eugen was somehow innocent. Anca did not need him to topple the throne. He was still a victim.

"Maybe? Even if I could get a word out of him, he wasn't in the talking mood."

"And how many of you know this?" Anca asked.

"Not sure. The rumors had some traction, but a lot of us thought it was just gossip."

Anca's fists curled tight, her thoughts somewhere between strangling Eugen as soon as possible and practicing the calm mindset she would need before she did. Killing him was not foremost in her mind. Something still hoped they would find their way back after this.

"You can't kill him." Craita's eyes traced Anca's face.

Perhaps she was not as controlled as she thought so.

"You're so certain?"

"I've seen people try. You saw what Vali did to him and he shrugged it off like a papercut. The magic in his blood won't let him die."

There it was again. That damned magic won't let him die, only suffer. Eugen wasn't just a man. He was two spirits in one body. One was ferocious, bloodthirsty, and cruel. Anca learned firsthand what it was capable of. The other held her so tenderly, his gaze so vulnerable and fierce. That other part of him would have died for her.

Separating the two was out of her hands. The only way to do it would be to shatter his sword, the Focus through which the Flame flowed. That would be difficult in ideal conditions. Only Eugen could make that decision. If he did, he would lose everything. All of the talents and gifts of his Nobil bloodline would leave along with the cursed magic.

"Besides, that's not what I meant." Craita kicked at a pebble.

Anca squinted at her across the fire, an innocent eyebrow raised.

The mage's features relaxed a little and a knowing smile pulled at the corner of her mouth. Anca had been certain they were quiet. All of their interactions were bluster and annoyance. Anything that betrayed how she felt about Eugen was left on the scratchy sheets of her bed.

"What did you mean then?"

Craita shook her head, but spoke anyway.

"I don't think anyone else knows. I mean, I don't even really know, but the way you two look at each other."

"We hate each other," Anca lied.

Craita clicked her tongue and looked away from Anca.

"I guess it's because I'm closer to both of you, one of the few who sees you both. You're saying all of the right things, but your eyes tell a different story. He hasn't said anything directly, but I've heard how he talks about you. And I've seen how you look at him."

Anca was the one to look away this time. The fire felt too warm on her face, the armor suffocating her skin as a nervous sweat rose on her back. It was inevitable that someone should notice, but Anca's lies to herself sounded too foolproof.

"We didn't mean to—I mean—we still don't know what it was."

Craita's eyes widened and she leaned forward. "Woah! Something happened? When? Where?"

Anca winced. Perhaps there was a dark alcove in the fortress she could hide in.

"It was impulsive. I think you're the only one who

knows. Shit, I thought we hid it so well."

Anca cursed as she wrapped her arms around her knees, but there was a lightness to admitting it. She would have talked to Craita for hours in another circumstance. Any goodness from their fling was marred by the truth.

"I was just spitballing. I'm pretty good at reading people and it was just some weird looks and the way his voice would soften whenever you came up."

"Fuck. Listen, you can't tell anyone. After what you've just told me…" Her gaze fell to the crackling fire between them. It was how she felt. He had lied to her and that was enough to crumble any desire that still smoldered inside of her.

"Oh stars, after what I've told you. I'm sorry, Anca."

The Nobil raised a hand to silence her.

"It's fine. I'm glad you told me. It doesn't matter what I felt for him. There are bigger things at work here."

Their conversation died. Only the crackling of the fire punctuated the thoughts that played across their faces. After a minute of silence, Craita glanced over the Nobil's icon pinned to her shoulder.

"What are you going to do?"

She wanted to burn it all down.

"I'm not sure yet. Go to sleep." Anca set her plate down and took a comfortable seat against one of the walls. "I'll get the first watch and wake you later."

Craita lied on her bed roll and gave a last warning glare before she rolled over. "Don't you dare leave without me. This is my fight as much as it is yours."

Anca's thoughts lingered on the Executioner. Not the man, but the idea. Her family had marched with two companies of royal regulars and two other Households,

Keller and Maciter. Every hunter of House Furloc carried that Flame in their blood. Each one was a berserker who could not die. When tasked with how to stop the tidal wave of blood, they had to ditch their normal tactics.

So they burned them to the ground. They razed the countryside and put every single Furloc to the torch. It was barbaric. A hideous way to die that her family had sunk to in a moment of desperation.

The same urge to succeed at any cost beat in her veins. Anca was afraid of failure, same as her parents had been. A bloodsucking fiend awaited her if she did not succeed, sitting on its throne with all the splendor of the land. Not only would it devour her, but it would grow stronger. It was the thing that had pushed her parents to barbaric acts. Now she considered if it was her turn to follow.

Shrieks and roars in the forest above faded with time, the blitz of killing after sunset finally ended. By the time swapping watches came, Anca had an idea how they could end this for good.

The nightmares were strong that night, but a new monster was added to the cast. It was a hulking thing made from rage and fire. Even as she evaded it, she couldn't escape a sense of sorrow. Even though she still saw something of a friend in its warped features, it could not live as it was.

****

Morning came. They finished their meager breakfast: some cheese that smelled too much like smoke and the last of their gorge berries. The campfire was doused, beds rolled up. The passageway above had thankfully not changed overnight. Long vines and cracked stone made for decent climbing.

"You start. You're lighter than me," Anca said.

"What about the bell traps?"

"I'll get them. Go ahead. I won't be far behind."

Craita gripped a vine, gave it a tug, and climbed to the larger mesh of vines and rock above their heads. Anca headed toward the hallway. Before she could round the corner, one of the chimes rang in the darkness.

Craita stopped her climb and looked down.

"What was that?"

Anca listened closely. The bell rang again and a rattling growl echoed toward them. That noise, the vibrating drawl that leaped around their camp during the fire. The Beast that had killed so many.

Their quarry had found them.

Anca reached for her weapon, but left it in the scabbard. She still had a flare, but her back was against a wall. No support, tired as a rented mule, and nowhere to retreat to, these were bad odds. She cursed under her breath. Running was the only option.

"Climb faster."

Craita climbed and Anca followed up after her. The first vine she grabbed snapped and she leaped onto another one. The stone crumbled under her boots, sending her scrambling for another foothold.

As she moved upward, the growl came again. This time it was directly below.

The vines around her shook as something farther down began to climb. It yowled with hunger. Dry vines crumbled in her fingers and stone chipped away as she grabbed at them. She was moving faster than most, but it was still too slow.

Doru and Matei came to mind, ripped to pieces far

from home, away from anyone they loved. Their bodies would never be found.

Enough of that. Climb, she thought.

Craita clambered over the top. She looked down, her eyes widening.

"Climb faster, Anca!"

A howling shriek bellowed up from behind and she felt the thump of its paws beating into the stone below. Vines thrashed and shook. Looking back up, Craita was not at the top of the hole anymore.

"Craita! I'm almost there."

The small purrs of the Beast echoed off the walls. The sunlight ahead was so close, a violet curtain just out of reach.

Craita appeared again, Focus glowing an amber as brilliant as a sun rise. Her hand was raised with fingers spread wide. The ground rumbled and a pile of small boulders rolled beside her. It craned upward like a snake and peered into the chasm below. Small pebbles rolled over the edge and bounced off of Anca's shoulders.

Anca's stomach pulled tight, throat clenching as she considered being buried alive. Craita's face was unreadable as she gauged the distance between Anca and the Beast. She swore she felt a hot breath at her ankles.

She could not breathe.

Anca was only a few feet from the top of the tunnel. Its panting grew louder as it snapped its teeth together in anticipation. Craita reared back, cupping an imaginary orb in her hand, then thrust her open palm downward.

The pillar of rocks followed.

Anca hugged the edge of the cave wall and closed her eyes. Warm summers on the plains. Marin. Her father's warm voice when he called her Little Knife.

Eugen's laugh. His eyes. She saw everything she would lose and held to it. Pebbles bounced off of her head and she braced for the annihilating blow.

Boulders passed right over her, dust and grit coating her neck, and traveled down. The Beast squealed as the weight crushed down on it.

The pitch-black monster, coated in the smoky weave of pure Shadow, tumbled down and caught a vine two dozen feet below. The rocks shattered on the ground with an ear-splitting clap. Gripping the wall dozens of feet below now, it looked up and screeched.

The last, frenzied stretch of climbing hardly registered in her mind. Anca clambered up the side and took Craita's hand at the top. The mage pulled her over the edge, her own fingers manically scratching at the dirt. They were on the far end of the large, grassy mound that the fallen bastion had created.

"Did you seriously think I was going to—"

"Only for a second," Anca said, unable to fight the relieved grin on her face.

The Beast lingered near the bottom of the chasm. It paced in a circle and then darted back into the unlit ruins below.

"Thank you. I'd be dead if you didn't."

Craita slapped her shoulder and jerked her head toward the tree line.

"Thank me later. We still have to get out of this forest. We're going back to camp, right?"

There was a specific way it had to go. As she tried to push the near-death experience out of her head, she focused on the bigger picture that would require a far more delicate effort.

"I need you to be loyal and honest, for now."

"To Eugen? Even after what we think he did?"

Anca nodded. It burned her to encourage it. "You're going to tell him that I know everything. Not when we get back though. Here's what we do."

Anca and Craita spoke in hushed tones as they moved across the barren, forest floor. Before she stuck a knife in Eugen's back, she had to give his better half a chance.

Chapter Twenty-Four

When the inky blue of morning twisted into purple, Eugen decided it was time. He was uncertain if he slept or just closed his eyes and waited. Minutes felt like hours, hours like agonizing days. No crook of his cot was comfortable enough to soothe his worries. Every sound that echoed from the forest sent his heart thudding. It was right to wait, no matter how badly it sat in his chest.

He scooped some cold water into his face and brushed his teeth as quickly as he could. He left his acid-damaged pauldron behind. The lighter the better today. There was no need to notify anyone else. Anyone who came back yesterday was too tired to go back out. The remainder needed to stay put. It would be Marin and himself.

The risk crossed his mind. He didn't think Marin would try anything funny, not in the middle of these woods. They were the most talented hunters left. If Marin did murder Eugen, and Anca did not survive the night, they had no chance of survival. Marin did not even know the lay of the land.

Eugen would have to play stupid as well. Even though he had traipsed through these woods months ago, it would be easy to act clueless.

It was this or leave Anca unsupported for another day. She was smart enough to know when to hide. He doubted she would try to fight her way free in the middle of the night. He might have done that. A dumb, brash move that was all guts and no brain.

Near the gate, Marin dumped a pail of feed into a trough for their horses. His usual, smarmy tenor was clear over the dim chatter of songbirds. Marin cooed as he introduced himself to Eugen's mount.

"You don't seem so bad for being his horse. That's a pretty mane you've got. Oh, there we go."

Eugen chuckled as the horse leaned into Marin's hand, enjoying the stroke along his neck. He stopped a dozen paces from the Doia.

"Whatever I think about your rider, I'll make sure you stay safe like my own horse. Does that sound good to you? 'Cause one of you is gonna have to carry two riders once we find her."

Eugen cleared his throat and Marin dropped his hand from the horse's mane like it had bitten him. His eyes looked just far enough to recognize Eugen before adjusting his own armor with needless tidying.

"It's a fine horse. Can't deny that."

"Same to yours. I've heard good things about your stables."

Marin adjusted the bridle on his horse. "Oh yeah? Who told you that?"

Anca had, but that might have pissed Marin off. Eugen kept quiet as he crossed over to his own horse. He didn't get any further than hitching his sword to the side of the animal before a voice shouted from the high wall.

"It's her!"

Eugen's heart nearly seized. Breath caught in his throat. He would not be able to move on if the guard was mistaken. He imagined himself breaking the gates down and sprinting to her. He would do it if he allowed himself one more breath. If he let himself react, it might tip everyone off that something was amiss between them. No, he had to be certain.

"What?" Marin shouted back to the guard on the wall.

"Two of them, but one looks like Nobil Sulia."

The racket roused nearby hunters. Cheers rose from the House Sulia tents, but Eugen was not ready to celebrate yet. A handful of strides and he was at the doors. He kicked away the smaller blocks under the gate and pressed his shoulder under the crossbar. Marin lifted the other side and they discarded it as quickly as they could manage.

Eugen pulled one of the heavy gates open and gawked across the dark green sea of grass that extended to the shadow haunted woods. Barely noticeable in the faint light, two heads bobbed above the weed covered field. Their pulse was slightly heightened. Not desperate, but relieved. At least one of them was.

The other was too calm to be panicked or scared. Perhaps nervous, their heartbeat slightly growing as they approached. The patter of her pulse was unmistakable. He clenched his fists and hoped to Flame and Shadow and whatever else that he was wrong.

There was still a chance his secret was safe. As they pushed through the tall grass, his heart sank when he saw her face. Her lip was twisted into a grim scowl. A wrinkled brow made no effort to hide the turbulence beneath, and those green eyes, hard as steel.

His stomach clenched. For the first time in years, there was not a drop of anger that the Blood Flame could call on. The nervous pulse was Anca's.

Marin was the first out the door to meet them, Eugen

freezing in the gateway as the worst outcomes coursed through his mind. With a bellow, the Doia crossed the ground and wrapped his arms around her.

"Oh, you scared me. Scared me so bad! But by the Triad: Flame, Life, and Water, I'll not turn away a little good luck. I swear it to you, all three of you bastards." He jabbed a finger at the sky. "Just like I promised, I'll never say another bad thing about a mage."

Marin pulled Craita over and wrapped them both in his arms, the mage's face caught between pleasant surprise and vast discomfort. Anca peeked over his shoulder, green eyes tracing over the interior of the camp and the slowly gathering crowd of hunters. They stopped on Eugen.

For a breath, it was like she had dropped dead. No emotion. No thought. Just a cold recognition that held more scorn than the first time she looked at him. It was a hunter's glare. His skin itched at the heat under his collar. It felt as though the ground turned to water under his feet.

Craita escaped Marin's arms and was met by a group of Queen's Company. Many of them clapped for Anca's arrival as well. The mage gave Eugen a heavy bow.

"Lord Furloc, I'm glad to see you."

There was a hesitancy in her voice as well. What had they found? What had they seen? Craita was as loyal as they came. She was more like Eugen than any of them. He put on his bravest smile and gave her a stiff nod.

"Happy to see you survived. I was worried."

Craita raised her head, but he could see the same look in her eyes that Anca had.

"I'm guessing the others did not make it?" he asked.

"They didn't. Matei is dead. Doru too," Anca said.

She spoke over the chatter, her gaze fixed on Eugen.

The aloof professionalism they tried out last time was long gone. This was crisp anger. Just like when they had first met.

Marin closed his eyes. The last week weighed heavily on the Doia and this was the first crack in his armor. The vulnerability that bubbled under the surface last night almost broke through. Almost.

"I feel like I knew it. Just a sense of it when you didn't come back after. If you had not come back—" Marin started.

"How many did we lose?" Anca cut him off, but Marin seemed glad to have his train of thought interrupted.

"Six, counting Doru and Matei. We barely have the numbers to hunt this thing down properly."

She patted Marin on the shoulder and steered him around to the camp. The gates slid shut. Eugen kept his promise of distance, but the temptation to let her know how much this past night had challenged him burned in his throat. This other flame, the clarifying light that she filled him with, was barely held back. Eugen flexed his fingers and swallowed it again.

There was something wrong here. Something had changed and his suspicions terrified him. Caught between the joy of her survival and the dread of what came next, he felt like it would pull him in half.

"Nobil Sulia, I thought the forest had bested you," he said.

She smiled, the fakest one he had seen in days.

"Not yet. You won't get to bury a Nobil."

"I am sorry to hear about Doru."

"That's very kind of you. If you will excuse me, I need a moment to compose myself. Marin, follow me."

She took a step away, but he was not done. This was far too vague and there was too much left unanswered. The Blood Flame pounded behind his eyeballs. It almost drove his steps forward by itself.

"What did you find? Did you run across the Beast?"

Her pace was quick, but groggy. Eugen guessed that they had not slept well. Anca did not look at him, instead she glanced across the common ground to Craita. The mage watched the two Nobils, lips drawn tight despite the questions that the other hunters pressed on to her.

"We took shelter in a cave overnight and the Beast found us close to dawn. I didn't want to try fighting it with just the two of us."

The words chilled him, but the bubbling anxiety stampeded over it. There were no caves around here. It was flat as parchment. There was only one thing that could be mistaken for a cave.

Not mistaken, he realized. She's covering her tracks.

"Cave?" He forced out a chuckle.

"It might have been a depression or something, Shadow has done strange things to this place. However, I have a few ideas. We might be able to finish this hunt tonight."

"Really?" Marin scoffed.

"How much lantern oil do we have?" she asked.

"Three weeks worth if we ration it. Close to twelve days if we keep burning them bright."

"Could we spare half?"

Eugen's eyebrows furrowed. "The Trigvan didn't ask for oil."

"What's the plan?" Marin hitched his thumbs to his belt.

"I will need the rest of our flares and close to half of

284

our oil. We can't hunt it like some dumb animal. We'll have to lure it into a trap."

"And burning down half the forest is your idea?" Marin asked.

"Not all of it. I need to get some rest, but can you put oil in as many flasks and waterskins as we have free? Anything that can travel."

She turned on her heel without another word and headed toward her tent. Eugen did not follow straight away. Anca had a bead on something. Those words, like some dumb animal. You don't hunt with fire like that, at least if you cared at all about the forest. She expressed too much concern over the Trigvan. They weren't combatants yet and she wouldn't be so reckless to burn down their homes without provocation.

There was one other foe that was hunted with fire. Anca's family penned it in, their allies helping trap them all in one place so they could be cleansed. Only their bones and ashes remained.

Eugen paused again outside of the closed flap. Inside, he heard her wince in pain as buckles were undone. She slept in her armor. A deeply uncomfortable experience, he could not imagine doing so in the deepest, darkest forest around.

He needed clarity. Not knowing the truth would drive him mad. He reached for the flap and his other fears reared to life. Of course she knew. It would be better to head her off. If he gathered his hunters now, they could take the Nobil hostage before she told the others. The Flame pushed the ideas into his head.

He didn't want that. Eugen could never hurt her again.

What if she was playing cool as they planned? He

wondered how much of this was a creation of his own. Eugen was the one acting strange. Thoughts of that night crossed his mind. Fingers entwined, her hair in his face, her legs wrapped around him as he thrust.

Do not trust her, the Blood Flame told him.

Minutes before, he hated being caught between past and future. Now the present seemed the only safe place. Behind lay mistakes he could not change. Ahead of him, a vast uncertainty that seemed darker than ever before. He had to know, even if it might destroy everything he hoped to achieve.

Eugen quietly opened the flap and stepped inside.

Chapter Twenty-Five

She was exhausted, but a night of sleep was not an option. At sunrise tomorrow morning, the Trigvan might have a warband on their doorstep. They were out of time and she was out of patience. And all of this had to be sorted away before the task beyond it: confronting Eugen and then the queen.

Her tent was as she left it. The bed was unmade, sheet tossed to the side and pillows still bent into the shape of his shoulders. Her mind went back to how different things had been one day ago. She ran a hand over her arm, remembering his rough palms on her skin. As if she had fallen back into that lust-fueled night, his voice filled the tent.

"It's a good plan."

Eugen stepped under the eve of the tent. Her breath caught as she realized it was the present and not just a memory. He crossed his arms, keeping his distance.

"I can't help notice the similarity to another instance of arson."

Whether she expected him to recognize the inspiration so quickly, it did not change what had to happen. If he caught wind of any suspicion on her part, this entire thing could fall apart.

"I'm sorry if you're hurt. I thought of the last time the Households beat something that defied expectations. This has been a disaster from the start. Nothing has worked. We need to think outside the box."

"I'm not offended. As before, whatever happened between your family and mine is history. There's only what's before us and needs to be done." He paused "Unless things have changed."

Anca did not like the way his fingers pulled tight, as if bracing himself. As much as she wanted to pry the truth out of him, this wasn't the place. Craita needed time to plant the story. Anca had to get him out of her tent now, before either of them did something stupid.

"What do you need?" She cocked a hand to her hip and rubbed the bridge of her nose. "I would like some rest before I head out this evening."

"Just you?" he asked.

"Queen's Company are our escorts. Isn't that clear to you?"

"After everything that's happened? We're both hunters, Anca. If we work together, I have no doubt we can do this before sunrise."

Annoyance flared between her eyes. Eugen had no friends or family. She played with him fairly and gave him a chance to prove himself. It was a lie this entire time. The only thing missing was why he did it.

"It is my kill to claim. You'd know that if you were a hunter as you say you are."

Eugen's emotions usually vacillated between fury and aloof disdain. It was odd to see him confused. Pain flashed behind his eyes. It hurt her to be so cold. The bond they forged was authentic, even if she didn't have a label for it yet. She had to hurt him to keep the distance she needed.

"I thought that we understood each other. We have the back and forth out there, but I know you see me better than anyone else here." His eyes searched her face.

She still could. Anca saw him with as much clarity as anyone ever had. He was a fellow victim of the throne, a friend, and a lover. There was something else though. It was a shame so awful that he buried it below his rage and guilt. The Blood Flame ruined his life and he still wouldn't let it go.

"All I need to do is kill this Beast and bring it back. I need you to watch our backs while I do that."

Eugen snorted. "What? To sit and wait for the Trigvan?"

"We are exposed and undermanned. I wouldn't leave anyone else to protect this place. You did your best to keep us safe. Now it's my time to hunt."

Eugen stepped closer and she took a step back. Anca didn't understand the emotion that fluttered in her chest. The pain on his face yanked on something in between her ribs.

"What is this? I thought we would plunge in after this thing together. When the killing stroke fell, it would be the both of us that did it."

"I can't trust you, Eugen. I forgave you for your slip at the camp, but it got away because of you. We almost had it. If you could control yourself, Doru and Matei and so many others would still be alive."

He shook his head, sucking in deep, confused breaths. Eugen shifted his weight from foot to foot.

"It won't happen again, I promise. What happened out there? Why are you even bringing this up?"

Her defenses finally failed. Anca's body snapped to action and she pushed him away, stumbling into the corner of the tent. Tears boiled in her eyes, held back only by the white-hot anger shooting through her. She snarled at him as she spoke.

"Let it go, damn it!"

Eugen rubbed his chest. His features twisted in disbelief as he put it together. "What?"

"You keep telling me that I can trust you, but I can't ever do that if you aren't in control of yourself. I know you didn't try to kill me back at Moura." She pointed at his chest. "*It* did. You are choosing it over us every time you take up that sword."

"The Blood Flame?" he spluttered. "Let it go?"

She nodded.

"You can't be serious."

"Do I look like I'm fucking joking?"

Eugen rose up over her, his lips twisting into a jagged line.

"I'd lose everything, Anca. Every part of me that the queen finds useful is bound to it. I only survived yesterday because of it. When your hunter tried to kill me, I survived because of it." He stabbed a finger toward the ground. "I am the man you know because of it. It's been a part of me for so long. You'd ask me to throw that all away?"

How could he be so blind, she thought. She stepped closer, nearly shouting into his face.

"It almost killed Marin. You nearly murdered Vali. You are a puppet who enjoys his strings. Don't you see that? Dozens are dead because you let it get to you. There's no room for mistakes. There never was, but now it's our necks on the line. The legacies we want fixed, the changes we want to make, it doesn't happen if you can't pull yourself together. Every time I try to let you in, it twists things. You've got a hair trigger. I have no use for a faulty tool."

His lips pulled back to bark a response, but he flinched. Her words cut deep. Doubt was a rare emotion for such a headstrong killer. Eugen's sword was not on him, but he looked into the distance. She was certain it was calling to him right now. It wouldn't accept this sort of dressing down from her.

"I can hear it in my head, Anca."

His voice cracked. The flash of anger in his eyes wheeled back and the vulnerability behind it made her weak. She saw the man who spoke so softly to her, the one who loved her so tenderly in his muscled arms. The wounded beast in front of her nearly doused the anger in her heart.

"It's talking to me. It pollutes my feelings. The Flame is happy when I let myself go. It boils my blood and feeds on my emotions in turn. It's raw power."

"It's a curse. This is all your fault."

She fought the urge to grab his hands. Her resolve wasn't strong enough to suck the softness from her voice. "Just please, Eugen, try to let it go. You're out of control."

Those wounded eyes looked deep into hers. His lips parted, an admission of some sort behind them. She sensed his surrender to the pain. Eugen hated this. Somewhere deep down she knew that. This last step had to be of his own choosing.

Eugen's eyes snapped shut and a low growl rose in his throat. He straightened his back and balled his hands into fists. His chin snapped back and forth. When his eyes opened, a hazy anger clouded them. He flexed his broad shoulders, hissing with a low breath. Eugen was still in control, but she saw the flicker of Flame in his brown eyes. The Flame stared back at her, smothering the man deep behind a veil of emotion.

It twisted like a knife in her gut to see him like this. She had seen the man inside, the one who had his own flaws and mistakes. Eugen would need to make up for those, but there would never be a first step as long as that evil controlled him.

"You're wrong," he snapped. "I'm in control. It doesn't rule me."

"Please."

Their voices grew louder as they lost their sense of where they were.

"I can have both! You should have seen me when you were gone. I damn near ran headlong after you. I was terrified, Anca. I sat up and waited. It nearly tore me in two, but I pushed through it!"

"You shouldn't have to fight like that to not lose it. That isn't normal."

He flicked his head to the side dismissively.

"Come on, we aren't normal. Whatever this is between us is extraordinary and different and I have loved every second of it."

"Don't you dare say that." She nearly clapped her hand over his mouth. Inches from him, she glanced outside of the tent. Thankfully, no one was near enough to hear.

Her heart might have wilted. It would have been so easy to look past it. Only Craita knew so far. If they kept it that way, they could kill the Beast, go home, and claim a new fate together. She could have everything she wanted, even a new partner who truly understood her. All of it was right there to take.

It just required her to forget Doru. To forget Vali, Matei, and the dozens of others who met their Fated

Death because of Eugen and the queen. There was no way around it.

Swallowing this coal would burn her alive.

"What happened between us that night was a mistake," she whispered to him. "Do not come back to my tent or I will throw you out. Do you understand? This is bigger than whatever we might feel."

She fed him lies. The crackling energy between them still lingered in the space between their lips as it did the night before. That would never go away as long as they lived. Until things were made right, Anca had to ignore it.

Eugen's mouth parted with a half-formed question. She felt what he would say. It was an admission of guilt. He would spill it all right here and grovel as he had before. The fear of losing her might have broken this beast's resolve. She wanted him to walk out of the tent before he admitted everything to her.

Please, she thought. Please don't make me kill you.

It never came. A veil of light orange filled his pupils and the nervous, weak sparkle in his eyes disappeared. Eugen nodded, his fingers tracing along the edge of her arm before the Executioner stooped out of the tent.

She watched him go, standing on the other side of the tent flap as his steps faded into the din of the camp. Anca took a shaky breath and wiped her eyes clear even as more threatened to come. The Flame did not fully take him, even if he suspected that the secret was out.

She feared that everything would come apart right there. The fight would spill from the tent and burn up the last vestiges of trust in the camp. Alternatively, she could have come back to a camp full of dead Sulia hunters and Marin hung from a flagpole.

She could not give up on him yet. Eugen was ready to change. He just wasn't ready to consider the cost. She needed to know why he did this, but only when the time was right for it. Only then would he be able to decide for himself. He was strong enough to remove the Flame from his essence, Anca knew it. She laid down in her bed and tried to ignore the smell of him that still lingered on her pillow.

It did not take long for Anca to doze off. Every second of it was tortured by memories from the forest. Shadow beasts from her past mingled with newer nightmares. She was alone. The tall trees stretched too high, even the branches were beyond the veil of shadow around her. Only in this dream, the monsters were hiding from her.

Marin shook her awake four hours later. Preparations were made under his watch and the remains of House Sulia would be ready to leave in less than an hour.

She went for the navy-blue cloth of her Household. Slipping shiny chainmail over her head, she grabbed the necklace of teeth she had worn at the convening. Stealth would not matter. She decided to give House Sulia one last ride before it all came down on their heads. One last Night Bane flare hooked to her belt, bow and quiver, and the shining scimitar on her hip, she left the cramped, inglorious tent.

There were only fourteen hunters left. Nearly an even split, Queen's Company outnumbered them with eight to their six. If she counted Craita as an ally, that made them even. Anca was shocked to see the tensions in camp had eased. Queen's Company hunters bundled supplies for Sulia hunters. Her own hunters double checked the wall's defenses before they left. Grief had a strange way of uniting people.

Craita grieved for Doru as much as Matei, a move that inspired more compassion from her fellows. When the time came to reveal Eugen's treachery, she hoped it would be enough sympathy. Queen's Company were sent to the walls, coilguns loaded. Marin and her six hunters waited for her on the parade ground. Their horses were ready to ride, but she waved them off.

"We won't need those. We're going on foot."

"Seems risky," Eugen growled.

He crossed from their side of the camp to oversee the final preparations. His unconcerned grimace had returned, head tilted to the side. The sword gleamed with a dull light on his back. She imagined the Flame pulling on his spine, making him dance to its tune.

"They will give us speed, but make us easy targets. Horses are too loud. They will be easy pickings as well. No horses."

Several of her hunters took the horses back to the makeshift stables.

"How far are we going?" Marin asked.

"Through the tree line, but not too far. I've got a feeling it's been following me since last night. We'll give it some bait it can't resist."

"Bait? Well, it won't be my ass. I'll have you know that," Marin grumbled.

"I'll be the bait." She turned to Eugen, curious if a wrinkle of emotion would break his scowl.

As she hoped, his expression cracked with a streak of worry. The Flame was not so dominant that he was completely gone. Anca continued and tried to keep her own composure.

"This thing got me thinking about what we might have been missing before. You're right that the fortifications at Moura were off. It kept us safe, but we didn't have a good enough lure."

"You're going to bleed yourself?" Eugen asked.

"It won't be able to resist. No walls, no fires, just me. Or at least that is what it will think."

"Perhaps we should have a signal if you need support."

Eugen's hands trembled. He gave an irritated groan as the light of his sword grew. The Blood Flame would push him to keep her here. She was glad that some sort resistance remained. Whatever warmth she had breathed into him was not going quietly.

Keep fighting, she thought.

"No." His lips fidgeted as he chose his words. "Stay here and keep the camp safe." Without any other way to keep her at bay, he discarded subtlety. "What happened out there?"

"I told you. Doru and Matei died. Craita and I found shelter and overnight the Beast almost killed us."

"No, no." Eugen paced closer to her, his finger raised as if to point out her lie. "What did you find?"

Anca shook her head, eyes lighting with the same dangerous glint she used on so many people before. "Not here."

He was not fazed by her snarl, but leaned back and clasped his hands behind him casually. The other hunters turned to their conversation.

"Whatever it is, we've got business to settle when you return. I'll be here, thinking."

She motioned for her hunters to fall in behind her as the main gate opened. Anca gave Eugen a brief nod before leaving, but he did not return it. He glowered like a wounded beast.

Chapter Twenty-Six

They arrived at the killing ground right on time. The sun's golden rays pushed back the dismal murk of the forest for the time being. It bought them the time they needed. Anca heard smaller Shadow beasts lurking out of sight. Luckily, the fanged things were intimidated by the busy hunters.

There were no spare hands today and Anca dove into the work alongside her own hunters. Marin loudly complained about his knees. They dug small burrows for themselves and masked them with foliage and fallen branches. She rubbed a pungent game scent on her neck and arms. It was easier to call it game scent rather than bear piss.

Anyone not digging was tasked with the many containers of oil they brought. They emptied flasks and lamps onto the dark grass, forming a series of circles. At the center of these lines, eight Night Bane flares were set into the ground. A quick fuse was tied between them to make a complete loop.

"The digging wouldn't be so bad if we didn't smell like a toilet," Marin said.

"It's not that bad. Maybe you just smell."

They were almost finished. Just one or two more hours and they would be ready.

"You remember the last time we had to work like this? Not just let the others handle it?" she asked.

Marin set his shovel in the ground and stretched his back. "Two years ago, I think? With that beast that was burying its eggs?"

It took two days to track the monster to its lair. The creature was somewhere between an eagle and a wasp. It preferred to take livestock, but resorted to absconding with people. Like any wasp, its young needed a fleshy incubator before they could hatch. They dug up whatever was left of its victims from their shallow graves. Maybe Marin chose not to focus on that part.

"We can get back to that now, eh?" He grunted as he flung a shovel of dirt aside. "Real hunting like we should be. No more needless banquets. No more Nobils luxuriating at the cost of others."

She buried her shovel into the ground. Another hard conversation. Another opportunity to do the easy thing instead of the hard thing.

"We need to talk about that Marin." She climbed out of the burrow. "I need to talk to everyone about that actually."

"Not getting cold feet, are we?" Marin laughed, but sobered when she did not join in.

"The plan's still on. There's just one detail that you all need to know."

Orange light bled through the trees as Anca called the few remaining hunters together. They followed her out here under a promise: they would make this world a better place. The spirit of that was still true. She considered what might come in between now and the day they claimed victory. Bloodshed was not guaranteed to follow, but she knew better than hope for the best outcome.

"I discovered something yesterday while I was

isolated with Craita. What I told you all was true: we took shelter overnight and barely escaped the Beast of Moura. We found a cave of sorts. It was an old bastion that was not marked down on any map. It was the birthplace of the Beast. We found where it came from."

"It didn't lay eggs, did it? Any pups?" Marin asked.

"It was not born of Shadow alone. Craita helped me piece it together with what she knew about Queen's Company."

Anca took a deep breath before she plunged them all into the madness to come.

"The throne made it. Astasia has known from the beginning that this creature is her own creation. Eugen appears to have a hand in it as well, but I'm less certain to what extent. It's a creature infused with Shadow on purpose. A weapon built to bring the Households in line and crush any other resistance."

Her hunters did not laugh or disagree. They clenched their jaws tight and squinted all the harder through their thoughts. They believed her.

"I know what you're all thinking. This is intolerable. All of their lies and vileness were somehow barely the beginning of it. They sent us out here to clean up their mess. We can't let this be forgotten. I intend to expose them all. Once the Beast is dead, our next goal will be to arrest Queen Astasia."

"About time," one of her hunters mumbled.

"What about Eugen? Are we circling back to hit them when they're not aware?" Marin asked.

"We need someone to guard our backs. The Trigvan might come at the stroke of midnight or they may give us a few hours. Additionally, I'm not convinced that Eugen is ready to throw in his lot with the queen."

Marin pushed an aggravated sound out of his throat, one hand pulling on his hair.

"How can you even consider that? His hands are bloody. If this is true, he might as well have helped massacre dozens of people. It's abominable! We're supposed to kill monsters, not make more. What could there possibly be left to debate?"

She was furious with Eugen, but the urge to protect him leaped up before she could pull it back.

"It's the Blood Flame inside of him. If you listened to anything I said, you'd know that his thoughts are not his own. Eugen will answer for what he's done, but can you imagine a better witness? If I can convince him to give it up, no one will question his testimony."

Marin scowled at her, but the other hunters did not match his displeasure. They watched the two spar like they were on the mat. Their opinions were in the balance. If she overcame Marin's final resistance, it would bring the rest of the hunters with her.

"You're assuming he will just go along with your plan. Why would he give up something that literally makes him unkillable? He's not surrendering just because you asked."

"I can convince him. I'm not just some Nobil that he hates."

She loved Marin, but his bitterness would undo their best chance to knock the queen off her throne. Only the truth could convince him. Curling her fingers together, she felt like she was sixteen again and explaining to her mother why she took the Nobil's best bow out hunting.

"I've come to know him better than anyone else in our company. All of that anger is just armor. Armor that he's cultivated because of our grudges, by the way. He and I are closer than you think."

Marin's eyebrow raised with panicked suspicion.

"C-closer?"

Anca's hands trembled. A trail of sweat ran down her back, fighting the urge to let it go. As much as she wanted to force Marin into line, he had to choose to do so.

It felt as if she peeled off all her protection. Vulnerable amid these horrible woods, the truth was overdue. She had avoided it intensely for days. It felt like fresh morning air to say it out loud.

"I care for him, Marin. I don't know what to call it, but it's more than friendship."

"More than friendship?" he repeated.

"We've both been on a road we didn't want. He's the best hunter out there besides myself. Eugen thinks like we do. If you got your head out of your ass, you'd see that. I did my best to hide it to you all, but I can convince him."

"You don't mean—" The words choked in his throat.

Marin waited for her to banish his fears. They were used to this routine. Whenever Marin thought it was as bad as it could be, she found a way to pull him back. Not this time. She shrugged her shoulders and nodded.

"Yes."

Marin stumbled back as if she struck him. Anca spoke before his overreaction came.

"There is a decent man underneath that rage. It's the anger inside that makes the monster. Without it, I think he can be an ally and more than that. But it has to be his decision to let it go. That's why I haven't moved against him. Yet."

Her Doia was stuck on this revelation. Marin mumbled to himself, eyes tracing over the trees behind her. "Him? When? How did I miss this?"

"If we can keep Eugen on our side, it's another voice in our—"

"But why? To what end, Anca?"

Anca tried to draw her head out of the singing heat that swallowed her. Just make it clear to him, she thought. She proceeded with the facts as Marin deafened himself to reason.

"Should that fail, we can do this without him. Craita is willing to help. The sheer suggestion that Nobil Varcop is dead because of Astasia—"

Marin's scowl hardened. "There's an entire kingdom of hunters and nobles and merchants who would be better suitors than him. Did you have to jump in bed with the worst bastard possible?"

It boiled her blood to see him fixate on this. Her instinct was to explain the boon. She was comfortable with the politics, but Marin's raw emotion drew the truth out of her. Anca's voice rose.

"Because for the first time in, I don't know how long, I feel something! It's not just an alliance or a negotiation between wealthy landowners. This isn't something I've been told to feel. It's stuck in my heart like a dagger and it might kill me to pull it out. I'm alive when I'm around him. I feel seen and heard, not perceived by my title alone. Whatever this is, it's more genuine than anything I've felt before."

Marin's scowl dimmed. His arms rose as if he might throw them around her, but he clenched his fists and swallowed.

"And he feels the same about you?"

Her heart jumped to answer, but she paused. Anca didn't know anymore. There was a part of him that still did, but the Flame might be in control the next time she saw him. Eugen was scared and alone. She was certain that he would run back to the Flame. It was more important than ever that she convinced Eugen to give it up.

"I believe so."

His shoulders fell.

"I was afraid of that."

Marin walked back toward her with his eyes on the ground. When he looked up, the fear was replaced by something that might have been acceptance. His face was twisted in consternation, but she recognized the warmth in his blue eyes.

"While you were gone, we had a…confrontation."

"What?"

"We didn't fight. Though I wanted him to. With you gone, I was in a bad place. Eugen would have been right to draw against me. I wanted to hurt him. The bastard was right on the edge, but he didn't do it."

Anca's mouth drifted open as she listened.

"I haven't seen him hold himself back like that since the night of the fire. He did it because he had faith in you. I don't know what it is, but you've done something to him. If anyone can get him to let go of that curse, it's you."

If Eugen kept himself together, even with Marin breathing down his neck, then he deserved a chance to turn it away. Her heart beat harder against her chest. A part of her regretted how she spoke to him. She wanted to pull him around her and tell him that he could set himself free. She wished she had the power to do it, but knew that excusing him would do nothing.

If he couldn't let go of the darkness inside of himself, then she would leave his bones in this forest along with her heart.

****

It was the darkest night she had seen in weeks. The moon was smothered by clouds. Stillness. Silence. Only her breath and the beat of her heart interrupted the inky dark of the woods. Anca heard distant movement as things rooted through weeds and grass.

Her hand throbbed from the cut on her arm. Nobil blood, infused with Life magic, dripped onto the dry ground. She shook away another shot of pain from the wound. Anca scolded herself for the lapse of focus. The creatures of the woods could not resist the tantalizing smell.

Did they sense her purpose? It almost looked like a trap: trap: a lone woman standing in the forest without a bit of light around her. She breathed in, the smell of soil and pine almost choking her.

A twig snapped. Close to her now, whispering rose in her ears as something approached. Shadow babbled as it turned its antediluvian gaze toward her. She drew her sword, the curved blade of Sulia, and waited for the next sound. Motes of green light melded with the vague glow of everything else. Only when it sprung to kill did she see it.

Anca shifted her footing. A shriek broke the night as claws pounded the earth. Pincers snapped with hunger. It was almost on top of her.

She struck a swift slice through the joint between its neck and shoulder. She bent her knees and its momentum skewered itself on her weapon. Arteries ripped and blood soaked the ground beneath her. It took one last vicious swipe with whatever life was left in it. Too weak to move, it fell next to the growing pile of other creatures who came before.

She reaped a tally on the forest. One for Doru, one for Matei, one for the hunters they had lost, another for Moura. The list went on. They had two legs, four legs, scuttling claws, and knotted knuckles. Biting fangs and grinding molars. It made no difference.

The whispering did not quiet. It spoke louder, words forming from the wriggling ether around her. It touched her hair and pressed against her boots. Anca tried to push the voice out of her mind. The babble made it nearly impossible to listen.

She knew why it was so active. The Beast was nearby. She focused on sounds beyond the whispering. Her eyes went up to the canopy, remembering how the Beast snuck up on her before. She doubted enough time had passed for its wing to heal.

The hair on her neck stood on end. Something stalked her quietly amid the numerous shadows around her. She could not see it yet, but the nagging instinct wouldn't leave her. The dead creature at her feet took its last breath and she was left alone with the babbling voice of Shadow.

Breathe and listen. Focus on your instincts, she thought.

A noise rang through the forest. It was metallic. A snapping, popping sound that echoed between the trees. She knew what predation sounded like, when predator found prey, and that was not it. That was the sound of a coilgun.

Before she could tell the others, a spot of darkness

stood up on its hind legs.

The Beast sailed through the air with its claws extended forward. She barely ducked out of the way as it shredded the armor on her shoulder. It rolled back onto its legs, lupine snout pulled back to reveal dripping, jet black fangs. It squatted back onto its haunches and readied to lunge again.

"Now!"

Hunters in hidden bunkers lit the fuses in front of them. Lights burst from the ground and flaming circles sealed Anca and the Beast in with each other. Sparks lit the buried Night Bane flares. Each one exploded with a flash of purifying light and the Beast roared. Its skin cooked and the weave of Shadow boiled off.

It felt like an oven. Her overworked body wanted to collapse under the heat, but she could not allow her quarry to escape. She breathed in smoke and coughed. The flares would only last for a minute more. If the fight took too long, the fire would suffocate her and the Beast would escape.

Its veil of Shadow wafted aside like a cloud in the wind. Hairy, scarred skin rippled with unnatural strength and it clamped its long, clawed fingers over its eyes. Anca stepped forward and stabbed. Her sword plunged into the Beast's shoulder and it leaped away from her. It nearly fell into the wall of flames and staggered back toward her.

"Just you and me. No tricks."

Its red eyes snapped to Anca, aware that there was only one way out of this. The Beast leaped overhead. It whipped its tail at Anca, but she brought her small buckler up to meet it. She lashed out and cut through the tip. Blood sprayed overhead and it swung with its claws.

Its weight pressed her against the ground, one claw whipping to her sword arm. The killing points cracked her shield and a stray claw stabbed her exposed shoulder.

She flung soil into its face. The creature stumbled off her and tried to clear its eyes. Anca circled around and drove her sword into its side. It roared in pain and swung its bloody tail at Anca. She dodged and drew away.

She coughed as a plume of smoke swallowed the burning arena. The flares dimmed: only seconds left. After that, it might risk the flame to escape. She dove in with her sword, but retreated as claws and teeth snapped after her. There was no safe way to land a vital hit. Anca landed a cut along its leg and kicked at its knee. It drew backwards, but gave her no opening. A moment of hesitation was all she needed.

The plan came to her in a flash. Years of hunting experience taught her that a hunter risks their life and limb to get what they want. Anca was used to pain. With blood pumping in her veins, she did not have time to consider how much it might hurt. All she saw was her chance to end this.

She dropped her shield and slipped her bow along her left arm. She leaped at the creature with her sword raised. It came to meet her with open jaws. Her left arm lifted toward its mouth and jammed the middle of her bow into its teeth. Its mouth snapped closed and her bow splintered, but did not break. Anca winced at the feeling of her arm held in between its jaws. Its fangs punctured through her flesh, but her weight carried the beast down.

Before it could draw back for a second bite, her sword punched through its neck. A vicious scream ripped from her throat, pain shooting along her arm as she drove down with the killing urge. She twisted the blade and ripped to the side. Bones broke and flesh tore from its shoulders, only a patch of skin and muscle kept the head attached to the body.

Anca pulled her arm back, the bow still lodged in the creature's fangs. Its red eyes widened and a final wheeze left the shredded remains of its throat. The flares dimmed as the Beast of Moura quietly died.

The smell of fresh blood washed over her. Fire tore along her arm. She guessed that the bones were fractured. She kneeled there, dripping with black blood, and threw her head back. A shout burst from her and carried through the forest.

It was finally done. In her voice, she vented all of the loss she kept buried inside. She screamed for the enemies who waited beyond that night.

"Sulia!" Marin screamed with a full-throated roar. He stomped his feet and clanged his sword on his shoulder. The burrow hatches were pushed aside and hunting guards climbed out.

They all joined in her yell and filled the forest with their victorious shouts. They kicked dirt onto the burning rings of oil and opened a path to her. She flicked her sword and severed the last bits of skin holding the head to its body. Anca gripped it by the scalp and held it high for everyone to see.

Beyond the hunter's torches, she caught the glimmer of steel. She had been too occupied with the Beast to hear them arrive. Her stomach turned. Icy fear smothering the victorious fire in her chest. They were already in position.

Anca recognized the black leather armor and silver chainmail. Stubby coilguns aimed at them from several feet away. Behind them, Eugen's Focus glimmered in the cold night.

Chapter Twenty-Seven

Eugen's chest heaved, tormented by the emotions that whirled within. Craita confirmed it to him: she knew the truth. If Anca lived, she would spread the story far and wide. They would take him to the gallows. No, he would burn like his predecessors. These bastards loved their theatrics.

Yet, she had not said anything. There was time to reveal him before everyone. Anca could have doubled back and attacked the fort during a change in the guard. He waited for it until he couldn't take it anymore. Everything he expected her to do failed to materialize. Eugen decided he would not wait for judgment to find him.

He rallied his hunters to put an end to this.

The thought made him squirm. She was wounded. He could smell the blood on her. As she reached for her bow, a wince shook her entire frame. The shattered weapon dropped from her fingertips. This wasn't right. She needed help. The pang of sympathy would not go away, no matter how loudly the Blood Flame tried to persuade him otherwise.

"Nobil Sulia," he called out. "Congratulations are in order."

Her hunters wheeled around and readied their weapons. Some strung their bows, but the click-slap of coilguns gave them pause. His hunters positioned themselves in such a way that only Anca would be able to see them in the dark. Their practice against armed rebellion gave them an advantage. Only the dim glow of the Executioner's weapon gave them away.

"Why are you out here, Eugen? I thought I told you to guard the camp."

Her voice wavered with pain. She was playing coy even as she bled. Eugen rolled his neck and let the annoyance weigh down his words.

"I told you I was thinking. Why suddenly I was your enemy again? Craita enlightened me after you left. She told me everything, Nobil Sulia."

Eugen reached over to his mage and patted her shoulder. Craita held a coilgun as well, her Focus dangling from her neck. When she told him the truth, the Flame nearly burst from his veins. Only the herbs kept him stable, huffing from the bag as though it was life itself. The Flame dictated his thoughts and actions for the last few hours. Without friends, without warmth, it was a familiar crutch.

"I can't let you tell them. This secret stays here. I'm not going to let the royal brat's penchant for power games bring me down."

"Typical. I should have guessed as much." Marin spit on the ground. "She told us everything about you. The Beast, your own little pet. Why don't you lower those fancy weapons of yours and settle this like hunters."

"I barely knew of the thing before I told her to kill it. I'm ashamed that I helped create it, but that isn't how the game works. I've been silent too long. I'm beyond forgiveness."

Anca stepped toward the gun line and raised an

empty hand. A wiggle of that sun-like warmth filled him, but the Blood Flame was quick to lunge upon it. It didn't want him pulling magic from anywhere but a place of hate.

"Then make me understand. Why help her make monsters?"

Eugen shook his head. Was he insane? How would spelling it out make it any better? She was part of the Households. Even if she understood, she was still one of them.

She understood before, he thought. He looked at the pulsing in her neck, the dripping blood from her arm. Eugen refused to look into her eyes. If he did, there was no telling what he might say.

"It doesn't matter. You're just like the rest of them."

"Eugen."

He shivered at her voice. She spoke the way she did in their lonesome moments by campfires and darkened hilltops. It pulled his eyes to her and something inside quieted. The raging of the Blood Flame was a distant, noisy rattle in his sword. The orange Focus seated in it still flaked. The Flame roared in his body, but his mind was trapped in her emerald eyes.

The soft gleam made him weak. All of his strength could melt away and sink him into the ground as he remembered how warm she felt against his chest. The raging of the Flame made him tremble. Words pushed into his head, but he forced them out so that he could speak.

"It's telling me to kill you, Anca. It's always told me to kill. I hate it worse than Keller. Worse than the queen. You all burned my family up, but this Flame set the fuel under their feet."

Shut up, it said. You need me. You only have me.

Anca nodded. Her mouth pulled tight as her fingers drifted toward her sword. It was her off hand, but he had no doubt she could still fight him to a standstill.

"Keep going."

Eugen's own hunters threw side glances at their master. This was hardly the implacable juggernaut they knew. Would they turn on him? The Flame was quick to put that worry in his head.

"Astasia told me it was a cure. I struggled to control the Flame and she offered me a way out. Her mages found some way to snuff the Blood Flame without cutting me off of magic entirely. I could keep the Othersight, all the gifts of my Nobil bloodline. I could still be useful and free of this monster inside."

Eugen's shoulders fell. He dragged the tip of his blade through the dirt as he walked closer. The scared man handcuffed to the rabid dog could finally talk. His sword rattled in his fingers as it tried to fill his veins with power. Eugen gritted his teeth, an incisor catching his lip. He was coming apart at the seams. If he gave in, the Flame would take over in moments.

"They prodded me. Drew blood by the liter. Her ghouls sliced me open just to find out if I could regrow organs. But I did it. Anything for a cure. They needed to understand how the Flame worked inside of me. It's the strangest thing about my bloodline. The Flame would kill anyone else, but we are kith and kin to it. That's all they ever wanted. They just wanted to know how the elements can inhabit a physical body. If Flame could create such a formidable creature, what could the others do?"

He was within a few steps of her now. If he reached

out, if he felt her touch on his skin, Eugen would collapse. The Blood Flame squirmed under his skin, a vein in his neck pulsing like an earthworm. The world took on shades of orange. He didn't have long.

Anca's eyes widened as the picture fell into place.

"The Beast. It's half Shadow."

Eugen tried to nod, but nearly fell over.

"A beast, half made of Shadow. A man, half made of Flame. I was their last chance to figure it out, with the rest of my family dead. They wanted a House Furloc they could control. Something that would cut right through any army that challenged them. Especially the Households."

"Shade and smoke," Marin muttered.

"My legacy wouldn't just damn me. It would only deepen the darkness. My new bloodline would be an army of Shadow beasts. Roving nightmares that would kill generations more. The only reason they stopped was they thought I was desperate enough to kill Astasia."

A hush of voices passed through the hunters around them. Eugen tried to talk, but his throat dried up. He leaned his weight onto his sword and backed away from Anca.

"She's poisoned him," a Queen's Company guard said.

"Enough of this!" another bellowed.

Coilguns aimed at Anca, but they never had time to pull the trigger. The earth trembled below them.

Craita tumbled across their firing line and swept her hand back toward them. Her Focus lit up and the ground listened without hesitation. The ground collapsed, every Queen's Company hunter stumbling and tripping backward. The sinkhole swallowed them up, too deep to climb out of.

"We're on the same side, all of us. We're all fighting each other when the queen deserves our anger." Craita lowered her weapon and spoke over the two Nobils. House Sulia watched the mage, their crossbows pointed straight at her heart.

Eugen choked and groaned as he stuffed down the Flame inside. He tried to tell them to spare her, but it came out as a rasping wheeze. Craita had no hand in his crimes, but the Flame wanted bloodshed. It didn't matter whose. After a long moment, Marin lowered his weapon, released the tension from the string, and let it fall onto the ground.

"Put them away," he muttered to the others.

Eugen gasped for air. He turned to Anca and found her inches from him. She reached out and he pulled back with a shudder. The Flame twisted his fingers with a killing urge. It filled his head with images of his fingers around her neck.

"Don't! It hates you. I can't say what will happen if it is provoked."

He saw red, but her green eyes stood out amid the building heat. He reached for the calming herbs at his belt and untied the string. It could buy him time, the time he needed to make sense of this.

As he brought it toward his face, his arm flinched. Pain coursed down his muscles and the tendons spasmed. The Flame jerked his arm back and then toward the woods. The herbs disappeared into the veil of night.

"No!"

It came out of his throat like a scream, Flame's chortle in his ears. He took one step to chase it down, but his knees refused. His prey wasn't over there, it was right here. The Flame would make him kill.

Let me in, it said.

"Let it go, Eugen. Please. You've made mistakes, but without it clouding your eyes, maybe we wouldn't even be here."

He leaned on his sword. She was within his reach. Close enough to cleave in two.

"What then? I get to drink from a water dish provided by the Households?"

His Focus grew brighter. Dull orange light built in his veins.

"There's always a second chance, even if you can't see it. We can still fix this, Eugen. Come with me."

She reached out her hand, not touching him.

"You're bleeding. You need medicine," he managed to say.

"It doesn't matter if you are going to kill me."

Those emerald eyes glittered with warmth. He cared for her more than anything else. They both were fighting for a better future. His future had to have her in it.

"They'll kill me. The Households will never forget."

"Let it go. Without that fire in you, there's nothing to fear. I've seen that."

Eugen shook his head. When it dawned on him, he felt the Flame wriggle inside. It had not been some thoughtless request when she told him to let his magic go. She meant it.

It was insane, but had he ever truly considered it? Destroying his Focus would cut him off from the elements. There were stories about the torture it would inflict. He would have nothing but his own will. His thoughts wouldn't be haunted by that heat.

You would never. I'm all you have, it said.

"What would I be? Without this strength, I don't even know if I'd survive."

"You wouldn't have to listen to that voice. Your decisions would be yours to make. You wouldn't be a monster anymore."

It would mean killing the most familiar part of himself. Without it, he would step out into the world alone and cold. His eyes rolled to the reptilian details of the sword. It was forged to instill fear in his enemies, but all he could see now was the monster within the blade.

"This ends now, Anca."

Eugen heaved the sword from the dirt and raised it upward. She did not break eye contact with him.

"Do it then."

Kill. End her.

The Blood Flame poured into him. His veins blazed with light, and sweat gathered on his neck. He twisted the sword in his hands. It was the same pose he took for hundreds of executions prior to this night.

Come on in, he thought. I will need every ounce of you to do this.

Anca didn't budge. Looking into her eyes, she understood what was coming.

With a flip of his wrist, he spun the blade downward and plunged the tip into the earth. Lodged into the ground, Eugen pressed his foot against the flat of the blade. He roared as he leaned his weight into it.

The Blood Flame panicked. It felt as though his heart might overwork itself as it pounded harder than before. Darkness crept into the edges of his vision. His lungs gasped for breath and came up short.

"Do it Eugen!"

Don't do this. You need me!

It pried at his fingers. That hateful, second heart tried to pull him away. The sword slowly cracked. Shards of brilliant light traveled down the blade and littered cinders around him. The gemmed pommel flickered. It felt like his own body was splintering. He screamed against the impulse to relent.

"Never a monster. I don't need you. I never will again!"

With a final push, he yanked the handle in one direction and pushed in the other with his foot. Light bloomed in the forest and sent the whispering shadows scattering back into the trees. His Focus shattered with a roar of flame and a spout of cinder. Smoke bellowed from his mouth and ears. The world twisted around him, unsure which way was up. It felt like his guts might evaporate from within as lightning bolts of pain shot up his spine.

Eugen collapsed. His face planted into the moss as he writhed. His stomach clenched and heaved, but nothing came up to relieve him. The towering Executioner twisted on the ground, pouring smoke from his mouth. He thought it might last forever. His existence was nothing but pain.

A pair of hands ran down his back and a voice spoke in his ear. Everything beyond the pounding agony in his head was faint as a moth's wings. It did not last forever though. The pain lessened as the smoke from his mouth wisped to nothing.

All the lights were gone. The orange glow of his sword was extinguished. The green pulse of Life vanished as well. Eugen laid in complete darkness.

"I'm cold." His voice was a hoarse whisper.

He felt weaker than a baby. Weaker than the dead.

Sleep was the only thing for him now. Eugen was unsure that he would ever wake up. He knew he might die on this forest floor. A soft hand caressed his cheek, the last thing he felt before darkness took him.

Somewhere in the ache, Eugen knew he was free.

Chapter Twenty-Eight

Four Weeks Later

"To House Sulia!" Queen Astasia toasted Anca from across the feasting table.

"To Nobil Sulia." Nobil Keller sounded as if he had just drunk vinegar.

Up and down the long tables, Nobils raised glasses next to hunters and townspeople. The cheers rose from around the room, some genuine and many playing for the queen's new, favorite Nobil. Maciter pounded the table with his brawny fist and bellowed like a bear. Anca drank deep from her cup of wine and took in the exultations that echoed down the great hall. It was the celebration of her victory. Tonight, Anca was the star of the show.

Tonight was special. It was the first step on the road to justice.

Decorated with blue banners for Sulia and royal green banners, the Sulia Feasting Hall was filled with everyone she despised. Keller moped behind his bounty of food, firmly in her shadow. Paegra and the other Nobils pasted on their fake smiles. Everyone in the room knew which way the wind was blowing. She had not invoked a vote for Elder Nobil, but they believed it was inevitable.

Astasia sat across from Anca. Dressed in a blood red gown that trailed behind her like a carpet, she was a vision of excess. Handlers were nearby to ensure no one trod upon it. The high waisted dress swirled from blood red to snow white when it reached her shoulders. A few loose weaves bound it to delicate shoulders. Her gold jewelry glittered under the bright lights overhead.

Anca mimicked the queen's style: a strapless navy-blue dress and a ribbon around her neck. Her hair was bound in a single, twisting braid that laid over her shoulder. Small bones were knit into it. A crown of bones sat on her head. Smaller than Astasia's tiaras, it was a gruesome thing compared to the queen's jewelry. Anca looked like spoiled royalty. The queen fell for the new look instantly.

"It's so good to see you here Anca, dressed so properly. First, I was gifted a ceasefire on our southern border. Now, my favorite hunter. My beautiful Anca. You're blooming, darling."

Astasia smiled wide and reached her fingers across the table liner toward her. She cooed like a nanny despite being so young. Anca did not forget the words they shared before. She was certain the queen had not either, but appearances were more important. If Anca would lead the order soon, Astasia had to be on her good side.

"Where is that delicious fiancé of yours? I figured he would be drinking all this in. He is such a delight."

Anca returned the smile and patted the queen's hand. Victor was long gone by the time she returned. The story of his flight was related to her soon after she arrived. He gathered his things and returned to his parent's lands with a sizable payoff from her personal fortune. It was enough to sting, but not enough to go after him.

"I think I brought a cold back with me. Sick in bed

on the big day. He is remiss to not say hello, but cannot imagine the idea of sickening the queen herself."

Astasia pouted.

"How disappointing. It's not the only grim news of the night. I am sad to hear about Eugen's fate." Astasia's face twisted in well-practiced sorrow and clicked her tongue. "I thought the line of Furloc could not die?"

Anca thought over what happened that night. He finally did it. Eugen proved himself more than a monster. Cradling his head in her lap, she never saw him so peaceful as he drifted off. The shattered shards of his sword glittered under their torches, the last light that would ever meet the horrid thing.

"He finally met his match then. He fought valiantly, but it ripped him limb from limb. He died with honor." The words almost caught in Anca's throat. "There was no body to bring back. It was so mangled."

"Ah, ta tat ta! I do not want to hear the gory details, thank you," the queen tittered and took another drink of wine.

Keller stared at her with his one good eye, goblet pressed against his lips. He wore a simple eye patch. She didn't need the other eye to see the suspicion in his face.

"Dead. Just like that?" he asked.

"Well, not so sudden as a match strike. He nearly had the creature. His rage clouded his judgment. For all of his strength, he lacked the precision to survive."

At the other end of the hall, mixed in with her own hunters, a hooded woman turned her ear toward the discussion. Craita's face was barely discernible under the deep cloak, but Anca saw the conflict in her angry pout. Eugen had been a beast, but he was her family. The mage chewed on her lip, but did not move from her post. She patiently waited for Anca's signal.

Maciter laughed and slapped the table. Silverware jumped from his plate and a glass of wine threatened to tip over.

"That's the dog. From his ears to his ass. Don't you remember how he frothed at the mouth? He was unhinged. Such a hateful creature could not survive forever."

"And his entire company was destroyed. Do you believe that? Such a loss for the kingdom, but we will endure. Oh, that reminds me." Astasia rolled her eyes as her frown twisted into a bright smile within a heartbeat.

She leaned across the table, the music and conversation masking her voice to everyone beyond Anca and Maciter. "Without Queen's Company, we will be hard pressed to keep the worser rebels in hand. The former territories of Bire and Stancu are growing fractious. They struggle to keep up with perfectly reasonable quotas. I thought the poor would work harder if they were so hungry. In any case, we might be forced to step in soon."

Anca's stomach turned. It was the sick pull that came whenever a new compliance order came in. This might be something worse. Usually, they were delivered by messengers and letters. She could stew and gnash her teeth all she liked away from royal eyes. On this occasion, she would have to accept it with a smile.

"I want House Sulia to assimilate the property of House Bire. Maciter, we will be splitting Varcop and Stancu between Paegra and yourself."

Maciter gave Anca a careful glance before stitching a smile onto his face. She followed suit and played with her braid like a bored child.

"Whatever you need, your majesty," he said with a grin.

"I've been looking forward to this since I had to clean up Bire's mess," Anca scoffed.

The queen clapped her hands together.

"Excellent. You'll both have your hands full. There's talk of communes. They would dare to question their tithes. We should damn well know what they can live with. We need to eat too. They need a reminder that negotiation isn't an option. I won't let us look weak with this grand victory still so fresh in mind."

Astasia popped a grape into her mouth and gestured to her servants. "Hold my train, I want to speak with the other Nobils."

This shallow, uncaring act was agony. Pasting smiles and cruelty onto her face felt like shaving with a rusty razor. In front of the world, she was a newly empowered Nobil. One of the youngest to have such sway over the order.

Her coup had passed without notice. With the official vote to oust Keller expected to come, all of the Nobils turned to the business of placating Anca. There was still a game to play with this newfound power. Their trust needed to be earned, and the queen's affection had to be fostered.

For the time being, they still listened to Keller above all. That last bit of resistance was her problem. There were no illusions that Keller's wounded pride would poison the rest of them against her. She hated it, but Anca needed the old man on her side.

Craita raised her eyebrow to Anca. She nodded back and rose from her seat. Keller had finished most of his food, but still picked at a thick crust of sourdough bread.

Craita crossed the hall and lingered nearby.

"Nobil Keller." Anca gave him a small bow. "Could I speak with you privately? There is something that I need your advice on."

"It's bad form to gloat after you've won." The old man rolled his eye.

"I promise it isn't that," Craita said. "Hear her out, will you?"

Keller grimaced and looked over the new arrival. "And who are you supposed to be?"

She ignored his question.

"This might involve us working together for a change," Anca said.

Keller looked away from Craita and swirled his wine. "I thought you didn't need anyone else. You've got the urchin on your side now. What can I do that she cannot?"

"Come now, Keller. We both know that twit in a gown doesn't know everything. We're both Nobils. I promise it won't take long."

Keller lips screwed up in thought. He glanced at Craita before blowing a raspberry and standing. Anca caught his arm as he wobbled off his chair.

"Fine, show me the way."

Anca led him out of the hall and down a set of winding stairs. Craita followed closely behind. The lavish festivities above were just loud enough to mask their exit.

The sounds of the party faded as they descended into the lower levels of the bastion. The windowless halls were lit by amber light bulbs. They buzzed like noisy crickets as Anca led them through a side door and into a lightless chamber beyond.

"Finally going to kill me then?" Keller asked, only a small note of humor on his voice.

"Not yet." Anca lit a candlestick and set it on the table. Craita closed and locked the door behind them.

"There's the Anca I know. You've been so prim and nice. Especially to our liege," Keller said.

The small room only had a single table and chair. A bucket of water and a sponge sat in the corner. A rack of parchment scrolls lined the far wall. Anca walked to the far side, looking for a particular shelf.

"I can look good without being a sycophant for the queen. It's useful to make her think I'm ready to crush our people under her heel."

"Are you killing me or not?" Keller lazily drew a knife. "It might have been wise to disarm me."

"Put that away." Craita grabbed Keller's shoulder and made him sit in the chair. "Just listen."

The old man did not fight it, perhaps a little too tipsy and sad to resist.

This was it. Everything she set in motion began tonight. Keller was a stubborn bastard. Selfish and stingy. She made sure to rub her ascension in his face all she could before tonight. Now that he was at his lowest moment, he might consider her offer.

"The Beast of Moura was created by the throne. It was an experiment with Shadow magic gone wrong and I was sent to clean it up. Eugen helped create it, but was unaware of his role. They told him that they could cure his Blood Flame. In truth, they needed to know how to infuse a living creature with elemental magic. Once he protested, they told him that they destroyed their little project. A lie, as always."

Keller giggled and looked at Craita, hoping it

sounded as ridiculous to this stranger as it did to himself. "This is quite the story."

"They were going to use it against us. Imagine an army of Furlocs, but with Shadow instead of Flame. If the queen pushed the Nobils out of the picture and held the northern border with these things, she could turn her full force to the south," Anca explained.

"They just sued for peace."

"Because their plan never worked. They successfully made a hybrid of Shadow and flesh, but it couldn't be controlled. It must have escaped. Once they figured that out, they sent us after it."

Keller rapped his fingers on the table. He seemed entertained, but paid too much attention to what she said.

"All of those deaths. We lost a Nobil for the first time in decades because of that thing. She knew about it all?" he asked.

"She is not going to make this right. So we're going to."

"By doing what, exactly?"

"We'll tell them all." Craita leaned around Keller's shoulder. "Starting tonight. Her majesty is right up there. Ready for a pair of manacles."

Keller twitched. "That's insurrection. All of those loyalists in Thronetown won't take this lying down."

Anca leaned against the wall. "Ever dream of a chance to knock Astasia down a few pegs? I know you've always thought she was a problem, just for different reasons than me. This is our chance."

She waited for Keller to speak. The amusement in his features drained away entirely. He bit his lip and rapped his fingers on the table once more.

"Even if I believe you, you have no evidence."

"I have the eight surviving members of Queen's Company. They saw what happened and heard the rumors." She nodded to Craita. "This is Mage Craita of Queen's Company. She's been my confidant for some time. Her access to the Royal Archives has offered up enough parchment to point us in the right direction."

Keller forced a hard breath out of his nose and waved a hand at her. "Risky to pin your testimony on a mage. You know how people might react."

Anca couldn't resist the pull at the corner of her mouth.

"And there's one more."

She pushed the hidden switch under several rolls of parchment. A loud hiss came from the wall and one of the shelves swung open. Behind was a small, windowless room. Though it had the trappings of a jail cell, a simple straw mattress and soft sheets were laid on the floor. A pile of books sat next to it, one of the thinner ones left open to a page. A shape moved within and a man stepped into the light.

"Stars above."

Keller stood from his chair, his fingers trembling around the puny knife in his hands.

Chapter Twenty-Nine

Eugen leaned back against the sliding shelf and fixed a hand to his hip. He flashed a wolfish smile at the Nobil. She imagined he enjoyed seeing Keller like this. Though he appeared every bit the intimidating man he was before, something was missing. That sizzling air that made the hair stand up on her neck was gone. Keller was too scared to pick up on its absence.

"Sounds like a lovely party up there. Thought I might join you all," he said.

Keller gasped. He stumbled over a fistful of questions before choking something out.

"You're supposed to be dead."

Anca stepped between the two men, her gaze leveled straight at the quivering old man.

"He can attest to every dirty thing the queen ever ordered him to do. When they invariably question my story, we'll have him and a few of his remaining hunters for proof."

The old man struggled to tear his eyes away from the former Executioner.

"Is this all true, Furloc?"

Eugen nodded. "It is."

The elder Nobil wrinkled his face, unable to fully put the pieces together. His mouth opened and closed like a fish as he paced back and forth. It was not the start that Anca was hoping for.

"But, he's a Furloc. Are you saying you trust him?"

"He's not the creature you remember," Craita said.

"Of course he is. As long as the Blood Flame courses through him, nothing has changed."

Anca and Eugen shared a look. His eyes always flashed with tension before, but they had taken on an easy calm. The impulsive monster was long gone. All that remained was just Eugen.

"And what if it was gone?" His deep voice sent shivers down her spine.

Keller laughed and continued pacing. He stopped after no one tried to convince him otherwise. He looked between Anca and Craita before turning back to Eugen.

"You're joking?"

"Do I look like I'm laughing?"

Anca had lied to them all when she returned. They got everything they wanted: the mad dog finally lost his mind. Without his royal handlers, Anca did what was necessary. Eugen Furloc died the same night as the Beast of Moura. Fitting that two beasts should perish in the same hunt. All of the Nobils ate it up. Whatever respect she earned from killing the Beast, putting Eugen down counted double.

"I didn't lie when I said the Executioner died that night," Anca said. "The detail I've left out was that Eugen survived. He's severed his connection to the elements. That includes his Othersight, our gifts, and the Blood Flame."

Eugen stared at the floor with a distant, vacant look. She worried that it was too much to let go of. Refusing her gifts was unimaginable. It was such a large part of her identity that losing it made her question what she would even do. That Eugen was now in that exact position made her nervous. Guilt burrowed into her stomach.

She would help him through this. Without his testimony, it was unlikely that Keller would agree to this. Without him, she wasn't sure her heart would make it either.

"That must have hurt," Keller said.

"You have no idea. I've felt pain before, but I nearly died that night."

Nobil Keller crossed his arms and pushed his tongue into his cheek. He finally looked away from the Executioner as he chewed over an idea.

"So, you can't do anything anymore? You're just normal. You're as weak as any of them?"

Eugen's lips twisted into a scowl, but he was quick to plaster it over with a mean grin.

"Weak as any of your hunters? Probably not. But I can't track your pulse anymore. I can't see in the dark. My thoughts are my own and your petty insults won't make me foam at the mouth."

"Is that so, you dog? Bastard pig, son of a whore and a wretch?"

Keller visibly braced as he spat the insult out. Craita giggled, but Anca kept her eyes on Eugen. She hadn't pushed him far since that night in the forest. She was pleased to see him slowly blink at Keller.

"I've been called worse."

His face clouded with some brooding thought. Pain perhaps. His brown eyes traced the bricks of the floor as his mouth drifted open. Eugen took a slow breath.

"What is it?" she muttered.

A light came to his eyes as he took her in, the shadow banished from his features. Anca didn't miss how the pain lingered deep in his eyes though. Something was wrong.

"I'm fine."

Anca fought the urge to hold him close. It was enough to tell Keller that Eugen was on their side. That she was fucking him could wait for another day. There was a long road ahead, but he was content right now. Eugen was free for the first time since he was a child. If none of this worked, at least she could say she saved one person.

"Eugen isn't totally getting off free," Craita said. "We understand that not everyone will forgive him so quickly."

Keller scoffed and bulged his eyes.

"No shit. Paegra told me that he isn't satisfied that Anca got to do the deed. He will want him tried and executed. Preferably with his own sword. I'm guessing you have another proposal for me?"

"Eugen will serve in House Sulia as a hunter," Anca said. "He will carry no rank and never be able to rise to the position of Nobil again. He will not be allowed to hunt outside of Sulia territory. He won't be your problem."

"Too worried that he might fall back into his old habits outside of your care?"

She could have punched him. The bastard still thought that Eugen was some wild animal.

"I'm worried that the other Nobils won't be able to control their hunters. Or themselves. Even without the Flame, he's got a target on his back."

Keller nodded and sat back down in the chair. He rubbed his palms across the table before balling his hands together.

"So why me?" Keller asked.

There it was. The request that could kickstart this entire rebellion. It was rumored that one day the Households would finally do it. The crown fought tooth and nail to repress it and keep them in line. Anca never imagined she would be the one to light the match.

"We have an understanding. You might not like me, but you've always accepted me as part of the order. I can't say the same for the others. The other's acceptance was contingent on the queen's favor. There's no telling what they might do if the choice is me or Astasia."

"So, you want me to bring them onto your side?"

Anca put her hands on the table and loomed over Keller. She kept her features as neutral as she could. If he felt that he was threatened, he wouldn't accept. If she came across as pliant, he'd walk all over her.

"This is happening with or without you. The only question is do you want to be on our side or face a tribunal when we win?"

Keller ran a hand through his beard. These old bastards were so hard to read and harder to work with.

"What will you do when you're done, Nobil Sulia? Assuming you win?"

"I haven't thought that far ahead yet."

That was not entirely true. Once the queen was in a prison cell and her supporters pacified, she suspected that the Nobils would have it out. Nobil Paegra seemed to be agitating for his time in the sun. He would have to be dealt with. Whether Keller got a seat at the table or his own cell depended on what happened in the coming months.

Keller drummed his fingers one last time and stood up.

"You've swayed me. I know we have not been kind leaders. The order fails as we get old and wealthy. Perhaps myself as well. I will do my best to get the remainder of the Nobils on our side. But when we win," he pointed at Eugen, "I don't ever want to see him again."

"That makes two of us," Eugen answered.

She fought her smile. It would have been the vengeful kind that waited too long for succor. For the briefest moment, she understood the surging vitality that Eugen had fought his entire life. Every second that it took them to go back into the hall and lock up the queen was intolerably long. Anca eased off the table and extended her hand to Keller.

"I find those terms acceptable."

He hesitated before shaking her hand. It was quick and over within a moment. In that small span of movement, their world was sent onto a frightening path that she hoped was the right one. If it meant no more compliance orders, no more conscriptions, and no more Executioners, Anca was certain it was the right way.

Craita slipped her Focus from her pocket and opened the door, a small grin on her features.

"Very well. Shall we commit treason together?"

Keller stepped aside and gestured toward the hallway beyond.

"Ladies first."

****

Astasia floated over to a collection of other Nobils. Toward the main gates, her royal guards stood by with bored expressions. At least fifty people were between them and their monarch. Marin lingered near the stairway as Anca emerged back into the party. He did not ask any questions. When both Keller and Eugen came up behind her, he nodded and set a hand on the pommel of his sword.

"Give me a minute. We'll be ready."

Marin set off and snapped his fingers at a trio of hunting guards. Anca waited for Eugen at the top of the stairs. She still worried about how much he could take. There was a difference between cruel insults and confronting the person he wanted revenge on worse than anyone.

"Are sure you can do this?" she asked.

A resolute grimace settled on his face. Eugen flexed his hands as though he might beat the queen to death himself. After a moment, he looked back at Anca and cracked a small grin.

"Me? I'm not the one who's arresting her."

She wrapped her fingers around his. This day was the only thing she thought about for the last few weeks. Everything that would come after boiled in her brain. The worries were swept aside at Eugen's touch. Anca wasn't doing this for herself. It was for everyone who had suffered under the crown. This was for Eugen, her parents, the people of Moura, Pese, and every other citizen of the throne. This was the right choice.

Anca let go of his hand and crossed to the front of the room.

"Queen Astasia Stratra!"

The hall fell quiet. Everyone turned to face her. She hated this damn feeling. Through the sea of leering eyes, she found the pair she cared about. Astasia tore herself from a conversation with Nobil Margest. Her fake, friendly face still held together with delight.

The queen looked between the other three figures

near Anca and all of that prepared properness deflated. Her smile collapsed into an ugly sneer and those crystal blue eyes filled with fear. Anca heard her heartbeat from across the hall. Astasia was scared.

"Nobils! We've all been lied to. During my hunt for the Beast of Moura, certain facts came to my attention. We all assumed it was just another creation of Shadow. We've never questioned where they come from, why would we now?"

Astasia pointed at Eugen and took several delicate steps toward the exit.

"He's supposed to be dead," she said in a voice that lacked even a drop of cheer.

The Nobils nearest to the queen reached for their weapons, squinting across the hall with complete shock. A murmur grew into exclamations of fear and outrage. Anca felt the situation spiraling. She had to say something to shock them out of it. If there was even a little bit of a mad dash for Eugen, Astasia would slip away in the chaos.

"Queen Astasia made the Beast of Moura as a weapon. She is the reason why Nobil Varcop is dead."

The Nobils who had crossed between their monarch and Eugen froze. Paegra shook his head, sword still raised. Margest and Maciter lowered their weapons, not quite ready to accept the truth.

"That's insanity," Paegra said.

"Keller, you're with her?" Maciter asked.

Keller stepped forward and the agitation amongst the crowd dried up. He gestured to Eugen and Anca.

"She's been true of heart. You all know that, even though some of us never agreed with her on much of anything. What's more, Eugen is no longer bound by the

Heretical Flame. Still a condemnable bastard. However, he is free of that wild magic we've always feared. House Furloc is truly dead."

Anca gave Keller a grateful nod before continuing. "She would have built an army of those things if they knew how to control it. Eugen thought he was being cured. Really, he was the blueprint. When he found out what they used him for, he demanded its destruction. They lied to him, just like she's lied to all of us."

Anca looked deep into Astasia's hateful eyes. She saw the corroding, toxic, mean creature behind her leering beauty. Her perfect teeth shone under the lights as her lips snarled. It was strange to see her face reflect what was truly inside.

"Moura is gutted because of her. Nobil Varcop is dead because of her. She knew it was there for years and did nothing. While we were protecting others, she was busy making monsters."

The queen reached for a tray of food as Nobil Maciter turned to her.

"Is this true?"

Astasia smashed the silver tray into his face. He reeled back into Paegra and Margest. At the end of the hall, her guards surged to life. They barreled forward with their halberds raised. Three steps into their sprint, Marin stepped into their path and raised a coilgun. Cocking a shot into position, ten more Sulia hunting guards emerged from the crowd. All of them armed with Queen's Company coilguns.

"I've not used this much, but I know which way kills people," Marin said.

Astasia slid to a halt as two hunting guards drew swords against her. Eugen reached into his pouch and pulled out a set of manacles. He jingled them and stepped forward.

"I believe crime and punishment was my specialty."

Anca, Eugen, and Craita crossed down the center of the grand hall. Nobils Grotor, Carlut, and Paegra stood to the side, a dazed look on their faces. Zidre and Margest drank down their wine with increased ferocity and munched on peanuts.

Maciter grabbed Astasia by the arms and pulled her closer to them, her beautiful flats digging into the polished floor. She writhed in his grasp like a snake held by the back of its neck.

"You fucking idiots! You have no idea what you're doing. I'll give you all the money you could ever desire. What about all the food you want? I'll make you kings! We could have been more. We could have been so much more if you helped me."

"Shut your mouth."

Maciter roughly tossed her at Anca's feet. The queen looked up at Anca through the messy curls of her golden hair. She planted her foot and pulled a shiny blade from below her dress. Astasia lunged forward with the slim dagger in hand.

Anca moved before she even recognized what the queen had. She sidestepped the blow and wrapped her hand around the queen's arm. Anca pressed the heel of her other palm into her throat and bent the royal elbow in a way that it shouldn't go. Not enough to break it, but certainly enough to hurt. Astasia screamed and dropped the knife from her hand.

There was no need for what Anca did next. However, she couldn't resist. She dreamed about it often enough that it felt like she had been practicing for this.

Anca clenched her hand into a fist and punched as hard as she could. Her knuckles crashed into the queen's nose, a snapping noise echoing across the hall as Astasia fell to the ground. Anca shook her hand loose. Her knuckles would hurt quite a bit, but that was worth it.

Eugen kicked the silver dagger away from the queen and grabbed her arm. Hoisting her up, he brought her hands behind her back. The manacles clamped around her dainty wrists.

"Be glad you're Anca's prisoner and not mine. My executing days might be over, but I would make an exception for you," he said.

"You stain. What do you think they'll do with you after they're done with me?"

Eugen pushed the back of her knees and made the captive kneel.

"You want to charge her?" Eugen asked.

Anca straightened herself and said the words she had practiced for days.

"You are hereby under detention of House Sulia for crimes against the people of our land as well as conspiracy against the Households."

Astasia spit blood onto the ground and cackled. Her voice was wet as the crimson river leaked from her nose. "Those aren't crimes! I'm the fucking queen. What authority do you think you have without me?"

Anca gestured around the hall. It was packed with guests. Most of them House Sulia, but hunters from every single Household watched. The royal guards, still held hostage near the doors, observed with the ferocity of an irritated snail.

"You see this? I broke your royal nose and not even one of these people gives a damn. You kept them wealthy, but you were not loved. I don't need your authority to do what's right. Your rule is at an end, Astasia."

She gagged on the visceral, nearly black fluid dripping from her face and spat out more. Her eyes never left Anca, bright with mania like the Blood Flame. Astasia shook her head and a nasty, clogged laugh came from her chest. As it rose higher, she descended into a wet cough.

"Oh, Anca. You think you're smart? Like this move hasn't been on the board for years? I saw you coming. Not tonight, admittedly. Skullduggery? Deception? This stuff is in my blood. You think this is going to slow me down even a little bit?"

Astasia craned her head closer to Anca like a friend confiding a bit of gossip.

"When my grandfather died, my grandmother fought to deny my dad's ascension. It was her time, she said. My dad warned me before he died. Said to worry about my mom. He said that she couldn't be trusted not to kill me. She was afraid that I'd take the throne early. When my mom was dying, she said to worry about my uncles. They had a claim because I was so young. I was fifteen after all. She had a point. I had them taken care of, didn't I, Eugen?"

He shifted uncomfortably on his feet, the line of his mouth pulling tight.

"I've always got a plan, Anca. But go ahead if it makes you feel like you're in charge. I'll be your prisoner for now. It will be more fun when I get to kill each and every one of you."

Anca repressed a shudder and nodded to Eugen.

"Take this thing to the dungeons. I want her watched

341

at all times."

Eugen at his worst was nothing compared to the nightmarish creatures she hunted. Despite this, there was something about Astasia that made Anca's skin crawl. The look in this young woman's eyes was uglier than any Shadow beast. It was pure malice. She was full of the sort of depravity that only humanity was capable of. She considered if it were better to kill her here than let this maniac keep breathing.

Anca would not take the role of Executioner. If they had any hope of making this right, Astasia needed a trial. Anca would not risk making her a martyr.

Chapter Thirty

As the guests filtered out under the cloudy night sky, a pall of trepidation hung over them all. The celebration ground to a halt after Astasia was arrested. Keller and Maciter lingered behind to ensure the queen was secure. Nobils Zidre, Carlut, and Grotor left without more than a polite bow to their host.

Margest clapped her arm. His other hand held a small basket of sweets and rolls from dinner. He was with her. She was happy to have the support, but knew Margest was a frontier Household. Far from the seat of power, Sulia and Keller would take the hit before his Household felt any pain.

The only one missing was Nobil Paegra, the greasy haired, avian-decorated, expert tracker of the Households. She had seen him only once before the scene descended into chaos. His face had gone pale, even more than his usual pallor. There was no doubt that he feared a future where Anca held more power than merely Elder Nobil. It would be a while before she forgot the flags of Death he left out for her. Derisive, boastful, her worries about him grew. Would he take Astasia's side if he got a better deal with the loyalists?

Anca gave the order to fortify their borders. There were no walls for them to man, only a series of outposts and watchtowers that kept an eye on the roads leading to Bastion Nilor. There would be some time before the royal administrators realized anything was amiss. Their foundling rebellion would need every minute of it.

Nobil Keller was the last to leave. The armored, clockwork convoy he came with was eager to get out of Sulia lands and back home. Surely, they wanted to see that their loved ones were safe. He climbed onto his horse and looked out to the horizon.

"There's still a chance they won't fight," Keller said.

"You know them better than I do. Are there enough cowards among them to consider suing for peace and letting the queen rot?"

Keller shook his head. "Don't let that young girl fool you. Just because she is in a prison cell doesn't mean she can't reach people. There are more assassins in the throne's pocket than just Eugen."

Fear could make desperate people do unthinkable things for their own survival. Even starting a war to save a monarch they hated.

"What is our next step?" he asked.

Anca cocked her head to the side. She never knew him to ask for anyone's thoughts or directions. Even in his dealings with Astasia, he was loath to agree to whatever the ex-regent wanted.

"You're asking me? Nobil Keller, finally taking someone else's advice?"

"It's your rebellion, Nobil Sulia. You are plunging us into strife and struggle, but it is the right thing to do. I will concede that my intentions have not always been just. You are too naïve. It will get you killed someday." He shifted on his horse. "Maybe my old age is making me sentimental, but we've lost enough young hunters. We can't afford to give up anymore."

Keller's lip was slightly upturned, his chin lifted in a challenge. It wasn't in his nature to give kind words freely. She couldn't deny the satisfaction of finally being seen for her talent. Recognized by the oldest of the order, no less. Anca bowed to him.

"Thank you, Nobil Keller."

"Call me Gregor. Expect a messenger raven at dawn."

He whipped the reins of his horse and the metal convoy hissed to life as pistons snapped to action. She watched them until the stone gates closed. When the iron cross bars drew into place, Anca allowed herself a deep breath.

There was so much to do, but she already moved the stars above to get where she was. Her legs begged for a chance to sit. This ridiculous gown felt strange to march about in. It sparkled like a gem among the harsh architecture of her fortress. She realized how much she looked like royalty.

A nervous flush rose from her stomach and made her skin crawl. She personally deposed the queen. Would people assume she would take Astasia's place? If she went about in elegant clothing like this, they might think so. She was afraid that they would expect it from her. This land had only known iron-handed monarchs from its inception until tonight.

Would they ask her to rule in that brat's stead? Could she even bear to carry such a mantle, knowing the prior owner had spilled buckets of blood in the quest for absolute power? Anca rubbed the faint brands on the back of her hands. She was already marked by the throne. Marked for rebellion. Or usurpation? Good intentions did not always lead down the expected path.

Anca shook away the thought. It was ridiculous to worry about such things right now. She was exhausted. Sleep would calm her nerves.

Bastion Sulia was quiet. It was as though the entire Household held its breath. Rumors spread into the town beyond it. The guards and servants whispered until she came near. They greeted her with warmth and some even congratulated her for locking the queen down below. However, everyone had the same question in their eyes: what comes next?

Anca wished she could tell them.

She reached the door to her chambers and found it ajar. Night air whistled under it and the sound of fire crackled within. There was a heartbeat inside. Steady, deep, and evenly timed like a clock. She knew it better than anyone else's.

Eugen had lit the hearth and stoked it with a few logs. The dinner table was empty besides a small platter of old bread. Across the room, Eugen's armor was thrown on top of a nearby chair where it dangled in the breeze.

He wore a loose, tan undershirt, baggy at the elbows. Anca let her eyes roam over the smooth muscles of his forearms. His black trousers clung tightly to him. The belt laid discarded at his feet. Eugen leaned against the window frame and stared out across the darkness. He did not turn his head as she entered.

At ease. Free of the Blood Flame. No reason to hide from anyone ever again. She drank in the sight of him a moment longer. For the last few weeks, she kept thinking about what they were. It wasn't a new struggle. Foes at first, they were certainly lovers now. By the heat in her blood, she knew that she wanted him tonight. Sleep wasn't the only thing that would mute her worries.

Beyond the heat in her loins, the joy in her chest threatened to pour out of her. They did not need to hide. She didn't need to chase him down or worry if he would descend into apoplectic fury. He was hers and she was his. When he eventually turned to see her, it would not be with a worry over their next banquet or how she was perceived. Eugen would want to know how she felt.

This was hardly a fling. She incited a rebellion partially to keep him alive. Anca intended to keep him nearby in the ranks of House Sulia. Not just in her bed, but at her council. The right words finally came to her.

She wanted to share a life with him.

It was a grand thing to say about someone she barely knew. Besides the time together, all she knew of his life was a collection of horror stories and whispered rumors. Anca was certain that he wasn't innocent, but he wasn't all bad either. In fact, she thought he was a better man than most these days. There might be a war at their doorstep, but she was determined to learn more.

Anca pushed the door closed, the click of the lock loud enough for him to hear. He turned on his heel with a frightened look in his eyes. It faded once he saw her, but the tension in his shoulders did not go away.

"I'll close the window. I didn't mean to suck all the heat out of the room, but I just couldn't resist the view."

"That makes two of us then."

Anca made a point to eye-fuck him as plainly as she could. Eugen looked back out the window before putting it together. His eyes followed the curve of her blue dress, from her ankles to her hips to her cleavage. He licked his lips and took a deep, hot breath.

"You look fantastic in that dress."

She felt like she would combust if this dress stayed on her another minute. The way he looked at her made her want to fall asleep in his arms. Anca wanted to press her ear to that broad chest and listen to a heart that beat free of the Flame.

"I hate this dress."

"Really?"

"I need you to rip it off of me."

He gave a small grin and adjusted his shirt before turning to the window. Anca walked closer as he closed it and slid the lock into place. When he turned back, she was only a few steps away. He gave a small shout, his fists clenching. Eugen managed a weak smile, but his wild eyes rechecked the room.

"What's wrong? Eugen, it's just me."

She cupped his face, caressing him even as he looked away from her. Anca frowned and tried to catch his eye. It was clear that he did not want to look at her. He was ready to toss her into bed just a moment ago and now it was like he had seen the Beast again.

"It's not you. It's—I've never known what it's like without our gifts. I'm still getting used to it." He gave the room another pass before his deep brown eyes settled on her. It broke her heart to see the pain lingering in their warm depths. "It's so quiet. I feel like I've got wool over my ears."

It was not just the Flame that was gone. Their sharp hearing, enhanced scent, reflexes, all of it. Whenever she wondered how she could exist without those talents, she compared it to some faceless person. Normal people could not miss what they did not know. Moreover, she decided that it would be similar to death if she had to give it all up.

Eugen knew exactly what he lost. His freedom had taken his ears. At least, the ears he had grown up with. It took everything that made him exceptional to the rest of the world. Though he had been given a chance by the Households, he wasn't in control anymore. Her stomach wilted as she realized that his fate was now inextricably linked to hers.

His face scrunched against tears, eyes reddening with a glimmer. He leaned against Anca's hands as though he might fall over without her. Eugen wrapped his hands around her forearms, fingers tracing over her skin.

"I can't guess what is outside that door by the sound. Anyone could be coming down that hallway and I wouldn't know it. Everything is softer. The whole damn world is just an echo. I keep telling myself the food tastes the same, but it doesn't. Imagine losing your sense of smell. Imagine losing your fingers, your hands, your feet."

She stroked his neck. He was free from the Flame, but there was always going to be a price. More than the insults he would have to bear, she hated knowing that she was the cause of this pain. Anca wanted to press her lips to his face if that could somehow drown out his agony.

"I can't hear your heartbeat anymore." His voice cracked as the words slipped from his lips.

She almost wept. Partly for what he lost, but also for what she had found in the creature once called Executioner. The man standing before her was so unlike the monster she first met, but still had the same scars. Knowing that he still loved her barely soothed the blister on her heart.

"Eugen," she whispered.

Anca turned his chin to the side and rested his head against her breast. Her heartbeat quickened with his skin against hers, the smell of him swallowing her whole. The smoky aroma was fading, allowing the smell of pine and citrus to bloom. The stain of the Blood Flame would eventually leave him entirely.

Eugen's breathing slowed. He drew his broad arms around her, his fingers caressing the nape of her neck. She could feel his hot breath on her breasts. All she could think of was how she wanted his mouth on them. If it would soothe him, if it could make things a little better, she would ravage him every night to drown his anguish.

"I knew it wouldn't be easy, but it keeps catching me." He rested his forehead against hers. His eyes were red, but Eugen grinned through it.

"It was my idea." She looked down at his chest, unable to face him as she spoke. "I know your pain is my responsibility. You gave up so much for me and I promise you. I promise—"

He shook his head and pressed a finger against her lips.

"No, Anca. You don't own any of it. I should have done it a long time ago. I knew what I was, but that suited this world. No one worried about one more monster as long as it was on a leash. I wanted to give it up. You are worth losing everything for."

Eugen glanced at her lips. Licking his own, his arms tightened around her as she pressed her body against his. She pushed her hips forward and it drew a low moan from his lungs. They drew closer as though they were one creature. Their breath quickened, hearts almost in sync. As she tried to pull him toward the bed, he hesitated.

"I should go. I am still a guest here."

His fingers slipped, but she grabbed the back of his neck and pulled their lips together. It made her essence crackle like it always did. That tingle that ran from her mouth, down her neck, and along her spine. Her tongue slipped against his and tasted him.

She did not lie to him when they first made love. Anca wanted his pain and his power. Now with nothing but his pain left, she would soothe it.

Eugen's hands swept down her waist before squeezing her thighs, his fingers pulling at the hem of her dress. The fabric drew up her leg to reveal her bare thigh. She wrapped her leg around him.

"Stay," she said between kisses.

"I shouldn't." He squeezed her ass and roamed up her back.

"Stay."

The dam opened. Now, Eugen and Anca's future wove together at her bedside, her heart beating out of her chest with joy. Hesitation had kept them apart while Eugen's body recovered from the trauma of that night. He stayed in the dungeons of Bastion Sulia, the majority of its occupants unaware of what lay in its foundations.

Anca pulled her dress over her head, and he was on her as soon as the soft blue fabric hit the floor. Eugen lifted her from the ground, her legs wrapping around his waist, and he pressed her against the burgundy bed.

A sharp pop cracked from the hearth.

She kissed his neck, but his hips froze in place. Eugen's fingers left her waist and he gasped. It was as if he'd been shot. He turned toward the fire, eyes locked on the hearth across the room like it was a predator.

"Eugen, look at me." She kept her voice soft.

The lust was gone from his face. His cheeks drained of color, the happiness that she stoked gone in a flash. Anca's heart nearly broke to pieces as he pressed himself against the headboard. She traced the panicked flow of blood in his veins. Shallow breaths passed through the tight line of his mouth. She moved to his side and ran her hands down his chest.

"What's wrong?"

She damn well knew what was wrong, but prayed she was mistaken.

"I want you more than the sunrise tomorrow, Anca. I want you. But there's something in me that won't calm. It isn't rage. I don't know what it is. I don't even really know who I am anymore. If I change, if I'm not who you thought I was—"

She shushed him. His fingers traced up and down her arm, but the desire had left him. They wouldn't be able to ignore that wound inside of him. If he wanted sex, she'd give it to him. If he needed to sob, she'd hold him. If he needed to scream, she would bear it. Her sense of responsibility did not allow for anything else. Despite what he said, her guilt was inescapable. Imagined or not.

"It's been on my mind too," she said. "Whether you would resent me for losing everything you used to be. Whether it's smart to pursue this on the precipice of what's going to happen. We barely know each other, but this feels real to me. When I'm around you, it's like I'm breathing again. All of these years and I've been choking behind this prestige. I was hardly alive. It was suffocating."

She slid her hand up his shirt and let it rest over his heart.

"There is so much uncertainty ahead that it might

drown us if we were alone. But we're not. As long as I'm with you, and you're with me, we can keep each other above the water. Whenever those doubts fill your mind, think of me. Think about us. Because my heart has not wavered, and it will beat steady for you. Even if you are not near enough to hear it."

A warmth filled his eyes so great that she thought that it might have swallowed his ache for a time. His lips parted to speak, but after searching her face he instead kissed her. It was slight and delicate. Meant to be savored as a final touch rather than an opening shot of lust. His fingers traced the hollow of her neck. She felt as though he said the words they had not yet broached.

I love you, she heard in his pulse. Even as she hoped he would pin her to the bed and help her forget the world beyond, just for a bit, he pressed his forehead to hers.

"I don't think I can. Not tonight." He pulled her closer and laid his head on her chest. "I need you though. Please."

Anca wrapped her arms around him and leaned back against the pillows. She blinked away the sting in her eyes. If he needed a place to sulk, she would be that for him too.

His breath eased. Some time passed and he seemed to forget the burning hearth. Sleep took him and his eyes drifted closed. She ran her fingers through his hair, unable to shake the seething pang of guilt inside of her.

Eugen would improve with time. She knew that much about him. He was a survivor and losing the Blood Flame had not changed that. One day, whether by morning or in a year, he would stride tall and brave again. This man had not fought through the inferno of his childhood, chained himself to a despot, and shattered his bonds to magic just to cave to his own weakness. He was wounded, not broken.

Yet, he was wounded because of her. She could scarcely hold the thought between her ears: would they ever be the same? Would he ever open up to her as he had or would he think of her as another scar on his essence? The three trials of Eugen Furloc, she thought: The death of his family, Astasia, and Anca.

After sitting with him for an hour, she decided that the thoughts would eat her alive if she lingered. Of course he would still love her. They had not said it, but she felt the sounds boiling behind his lips. She had fought the urge to say it herself. Anca steeled herself against the worry nibbling at her bones.

She slipped out from the bed and eased his head against the pillow. She worried that he would wake up, but Eugen only grunted as he settled onto her bed. A pulse moving about the room would have tweaked that once killer instinct inside of him and he would have shot awake. Except that was not Eugen anymore.

She pulled on a nightgown and fixed a patterned wrap around her shoulders. Winter was almost fully upon them. The battlements would be chilly. Anca stepped out of her room and gave one long glance to the man in her bed. When he woke, it would be back into a quiet world. Every breath was a reminder of what he gave up.

Anca feared that she wouldn't be enough.

The halls of Bastion Sulia were silent as a grave. Usually taciturn and void of late night revels, she felt her own anxiety reflected in it. The cold stone felt like a mirror, her bones made of the same stuff as the floor under her feet. Her blood trickled in the oil lanterns above her. It was her home and she worried for it as much as she did for Eugen.

War was coming. She had no illusions about the loyalists she hoped would cower. They would fight. At the very least, they would fight to ensure they still had their fortunes at the end. The few guards on night watch gave her a curt nod as she stepped onto the frosty walls around the fortress. When asked if she needed a coat, she shook her head. They must have felt her desire to be left alone. They did not trouble her after that.

The wide plains of Margecei spread out ahead of her, clutched in frigid darkness. Shadow whispered in her ear. Maybe it felt the fear in her heart. Perhaps it knew how Bastion Nilor would respond and it merely waited for the hammer to fall. If it knew whether they would lose or win, she did not listen. Their fate would be decided by their actions, not by the whims of the elements. Not Shadow. Not Flame.

A squawk rose through the night and Anca picked out the green pulse of a bird in the sky. It was a raven by the call. The creature flew from the east, from Bastion Keller. The Nobil had told her to expect a messenger raven by the morning, not in the middle of the night. She whistled after the raven's call and it dove toward her. It knew the signal that their ravens were trained by. That was a Nobil's raven.

The bird landed on the battlement and offered its leg. Anca scratched its neck with a finger and undid the binding. The message was tied with another small wrap of twine. This was her choice. Her decision. Anca's fear threatened to indulge the whispered threats of the living night. She closed her eyes and remembered who this was for.

This was for everyone who ever died believing they were safe under the Nobil's watch. This was for Nobil Varcop. This was for her mother and father. This was for Doru and any hunter who met the Hunter's Death, cold and alone. This was for Eugen. This was for herself. After decades of facing the destiny laid out in front of her, Anca was finally in control of her fate.

She opened the note and readied herself for the war nearing her doorstep.

Acknowledgments

This is a deeply personal story for myself. It started out as a fun story about hunting monsters and devious court politics. I didn't expect to pour so much of my soul into it.

Growing up around anger, and learning to be angry as a result, it was very difficult to recognize the effect it had on others. Admitting that was just the start. I've had years of therapy, practice, mantras, and mindfulness and I still feel it bubbling under the surface at times. I'm much better now, but not perfect. That never-ending battle to contain the roiling heat inside, to see it as poison and not power, inspired the heart of this story.

To my wife, your love and support has carried me through so much. This story exists because you challenged me. There would be no Anca and Eugen without you. Now and forever, you are my greatest adventure.

I have to thank C.M. Leyva, Gillian Campbell, Kate Duarte, and Kevin Loughrin. They all had a profound effect on this story. This story has changed so much since draft 1 and nothing has changed more than the ferocious romance between Anca and Eugen (#LetThemPine). This story has had four different endings and they have read three of them at this point.

I want to thank my editor, Morena Stamm, and the rest of the TWRP staff. I am consistently blown away by the lengths they will go to help their authors. Morena has such a sharp editorial vision and I am thrilled to work with her as I kick off my first of many romantasy novels.

Lastly, I want to thank you. Whether you've followed my books for a while or you have no idea of who I am, I am so glad to share this story with you. If you are like me, and don't want to be angry anymore, I hope you too can let it go.

A word about the author...

J. Von Tobel began writing cheesy horror stories in high school when not playing Dungeons & Dragons. A member of the Chicago Writers Association and Chicago North Romance Writers, he lives in Chicago with his wife and two overly-excitable dogs.

www.ingramcontent.com/pod-product-compliance
Lightning Source LLC
Chambersburg PA
CBHW072310020726
47501CB00002B/462